IF I could TURN BACK TIME

By Nicola Doherty and available from Headline Review:

The Out of Office Girl
If I Could Turn Back Time

NICOLA DOHERTY

IF I could TURN BACK TIME

headline
review

First published in 2013 by HEADLINE REVIEW
An imprint of HEADLINE PUBLISHING GROUP

1

Cataloguing in Publication Data is available from the British Library

ISBN 978 1 4722 0995 5

Typeset in Giovanni-Book by Palimpsest Book Production Limited,
Falkirk, Stirlingshire

Printed and bound in Great Britain by
Clays Ltd, St Ives plc

HEADLINE PUBLISHING GROUP
An Hachette UK Company
338 Euston Road
London NW1 3BH

www.headline.co.uk
www.hachette.co.uk

To Alex
(my hero)

PROLOGUE

Oops. I did it again.

It was meant to be a quiet Christmas drink – single, not plural – with Rachel. And instead . . . I cover my eyes and roll over, trying to make sense of what happened. Did that bouncer actually come with us to the other nightclub, or am I imagining that? And did we really get a rickshaw? I have a blurry memory of Kira singing 'Jingle Bells' and the driver pretending to be a reindeer. But worst of all, I was going on about David. I promised myself after last time: no more getting drunk and talking about David.

Weirdly, though, I feel sort of OK. I cautiously test for my hangover but I'm whole and hearty. I don't even have a headache. For once it seems I actually remembered to drink that pint of water before I went to sleep last night.

God, it's like the Sahara in here, though. I must have left the heating on. I can already picture the texts I'll get from Deborah today: 'Zoë, please can you not leave the heating on all night as it's very expensive.' 'PS is that cup on the sideboard yours? If so, I advise you to wash it.'

Yawning, I stumble out of bed to turn off the radiator. That's strange: it's not on. I decide to open the window: a blast of cold, icy air will revive me. I draw back the curtains – and instead of a snow-covered front garden, icing-sugar hedge and slushy path, before me is a blinding blue sky, a sunlit street and green trees.

I shake my head and rub my eyes. Is it possible that all the snow could have melted in the night? But what about the trees and the sun? A girl is walking by wearing – I peer closer to the window to look – a short, red summer dress. With bare legs. I gasp aloud and grab the curtain to steady myself.

Then I realise that's not the only thing that's wrong.

I'm not in my own bedroom.

Instead, I'm in another one – that I never, ever thought I'd see again. I take in the familiar scene: a large double wardrobe with a built-in bureau, bare except for a comb, a bottle of sunscreen and a pair of sunglasses. A double bed under dark blue sheets with white piping. A Babolat tennis racket and a tall stack of back issues of the *British Medical Journal*. I'm in David's bedroom! Heart pounding, I sit down on the bed and clutch the sheets in my hand. They're real; I'm not dreaming. Was I so drunk last night that I came to David's apartment? Is it possible that we had some kind of reconciliation, and I've blanked it out? Or – sweet baby Jesus – did I just *break in*?

But what about the weather? It's meant to be Christmas, and from here it looks an awful lot like midsummer. And where the hell is all my Christmas shopping?

I've never been so frightened in all my life. Either I'm having a really bad hangover or else something *seriously* freaky is going on.

ONE

12 hours earlier
23 December, 7.15 p.m.
'What about this one?' he asks me, pointing out yet another ring. This one is emerald cut, not big but flawless, with a platinum band. It's gorgeous. I smile at him and start to put it on, but he stops me.

'Allow me,' he says, in a self-conscious gentlemanly tone, clearing his throat. He picks the ring up and slips it carefully on to my finger. 'I want to make sure I can do this properly when it comes to the big day,' he adds in his normal voice, loosening his tie. He looks so nervous.

'It's lovely,' I say, turning my hand so that it catches the light. 'A real classic. I think this is the one, you know.'

'Really?' he asks, looking worried. 'I don't know. I think I could see her more with the round one. Would you mind trying it again?'

'Of course.' I patiently slip the ring off and put the brilliant cut diamond back on, holding out my hand so that he can see. He stares at it in concentration as if there are secret messages emanating from it that will help him make the right decision. I've explained to him that I don't normally work on this counter and he might prefer to wait for one of our jewellery experts, but he says he's already done all his research; now he just wants to see the rings in action, as it were. I'm glad I did my nails yesterday. Essie Ballet Slippers is the least these rings deserve.

As I look down at his bald head poised over the ring, I allow

3

myself to drift into a fantasy that it's David who's just slipped the ring on my finger. I've come home from work to find him waiting on my doorstep in the snow. He's flown over from New York with the ring in his pocket. Or, no – he's taken me to New York, to spend Christmas with him there. We've spent the afternoon in Tiffany's trying on rings, before finding the perfect one. Now we're back in his apartment on the Upper East Side near Mount Sinai hospital, opening a bottle of champagne and calling our families and a couple of friends. I start itemising the friends and their reactions, but then decide not to bother: I want to focus on David. Later we'll curl up and watch the snow falling outside, with Christmas carols playing softly in the background. 'This is the best Christmas present I could ever have,' David says, gazing into my eyes.

'Me too,' I say, gazing back.

'This is tricky,' my customer is saying. 'I thought it would be easy when I saw them on but I still can't picture which one she'll prefer.'

My eyes flick discreetly to the huge Art Deco clock on the wall behind him. Twenty past seven. We close at nine, and I need to make a few more sales; there's someone waiting already. I can feel Karen, my boss, watching me from the other end of the counter.

'Do you have a photo of her?' I ask. I'm probably not supposed to do this, but it will give me an idea of her style.

He takes out his phone and shows me a picture of a dark-haired girl, laughing into the camera. Black biker jacket, red skull-printed Alexander McQueen scarf.

'The emerald cut,' I say. 'Definitely the emerald cut.'

Five minutes later, he's happily on his way, ring in hand. I watch him go, thinking of his girlfriend opening the hot-pink velvet box on Christmas morning. Now I feel even worse after letting myself have that daydream about David proposing, because it's not going to happen. Mainly because we broke up three months and nineteen days ago.

'Zoë, can you tidy up this counter, please? Quickly.' Karen is right beside me now, practically breathing down my neck. She's extra picky today because so many people from head office come to the store to help out at Christmas, and naturally she wants to impress them. Across the way Julia, the head of womenswear buying, is on scarves and gloves, and even Mr Marley, our mysterious MD, is rumoured to be working on the chocolate counter.

'Are you doing anything nice for Christmas, Karen?' I ask, as I tidy up and get a new supply of boxes and wrapping tissue ready under the till.

'Just the usual,' she says shortly. After a minute she adds, 'How are *you* getting on, darling? Oh my goodness, it's manic, isn't it?' I'm surprised by this sudden affection, but then I see she's not talking to me; it's Louis the head menswear buyer, who's passing by our counter. They start chatting about something, and then Karen glances at me, and they lower their voices and start whispering. I used to get paranoid when this happened, that they were talking about me – but now I know they're just gossiping in general.

As they whisper, I take a second's breathing space and slip my foot out of my shoe, to do a quick calf stretch on one side and then the other. Even though I wear flats every day now (something I never thought I'd do), I've developed a tiny blue line on the back of my calf since working here, and I'm terrified it might develop into a varicose vein.

The shop is full of people, all rushing around doing their last-minute bits, with parcels and bags on every arm. There's an atmosphere of good-humoured panic; people are smiling and chatting, comparing notes on their purchases. It's as if we're all backstage getting ready to put on a big play together. 'Have Yourself a Merry Little Christmas' is playing and there's a delicious scent from the miniature tree on the counter, which is decorated with tiny clove oranges.

I love Christmas. Everything about it: seeing my family, curling up and watching old black-and-white films on TV, going to Midnight Mass at the Pro-Cathedral in Dublin, drinking Baileys at four in the afternoon and eating whatever I want. I love the general sense that normal life is suspended and something

5

wonderful could happen at any minute. This Christmas, of course, I won't be seeing my family. They need me to work on Christmas Eve and St Stephen's Day – Boxing Day, as it's called here. My parents are upset ('What kind of a job doesn't let you come home for Christmas?') and I feel guilty. But as I told them, twenty-eight is plenty old enough to have Christmas away from home.

'Hi, Zoë,' says a voice beside me. 'How's it going?' It's Harriet, my fellow womenswear assistant: very young and very sweet and easily the nicest person at work.

'Hey! Are you on here now? I thought you were on stationery?'

'No, Karen told me to swap with her. She just left.'

'One of the buyers is on stationery, isn't she?'

'Yes,' says Harriet, looking puzzled. 'But what difference does that make?'

'Well, Karen likes to network.'

'Aaah,' says Harriet, comprehension slowly dawning on her round, pretty face. I know Harriet is a bright girl – she's studying for an English degree at Leeds university – but she doesn't always pick up on store politics. She's as well off.

Suddenly I spot, browsing at the opposite counter, one of my nemeses from secondary school: Kerry-Jane Murphy. Oh, God. She must have come over to do her Christmas shopping. She's wearing a sleeveless puffa jacket over a cashmere polo neck, and sheepskin earmuffs around her neck. Little bags from Jo Malone, Petit Bateau and Liberty's dangle from her leather-gloved fingers. Her hair is even blonder than usual, she's coated in Saint Tropez, and I think she might have had Baby Botox. I turn away, desperate for another customer, but for literally the first time today, there's a lull. I frown at the cash register, pretending to be doing something that requires great concentration, and pray she'll go by without spotting me.

'Zoë *Kennedy*?'

At the sound of her unmistakable South County Dublin voice, I look up and pretend to be thrilled and amazed. 'Kerry-Jane! Hi!'

'Oh my God!' she says, except in her strangulated accent it comes out as 'Ew moi Gawd!'. 'Do you . . . *work* here?'

'I do indeed,' I say brightly. 'I normally work in womenswear but I'm helping out down here because it's so busy.'

'But . . . what *happened*? I thought you were working for Accenture.' She makes it sound as if I'm begging on the street.

'PWC. I was, but I left in January—'

'Ohhh.' She nods. 'Were you . . .' She mimes slitting her throat, which I presume means 'made redundant'.

'No, I resigned. I really wanted to work in fashion, so . . .'

She recoils. 'And you ended up *here*? Like, on the shop floor?'

I have a picture of myself splayed on the polished marble floor like fashion road-kill. 'Sure. I'm hoping to move on to—'

'I mean, it's a beaudiful store, don't get me wrong. I always come here the week before Christmas. I just never thought I'd see you doing *this*, you know? You were always so ambitious.' She cackles. 'Hey. You know Sinead Devlin has her own accessories label? People are going mad for her stuff. They're stocking it in Harvey Nicks and she was in *Vogue*. She was at the ten-year reunion. Why didn't you come?'

To avoid people like you? If I had a pound for all the people who've told me about Sinead Devlin's success, I'd be – well, I'd have a lot of pounds. In fact I did try to contact Sinead but I never heard back from her.

'Oh, I was busy. How are you, anyway? Were you looking for anything in particular?'

'I'm grand! Not a bother. Still working in PR, doing luxury brands mainly. You probably heard; Ronan put a ring on it.' She pulls off one of the gloves to show me a gaudy pavé-encrusted rock. 'The wedding's next July, near Avignon. That's in the South of France. Here. Why don't you come, for the afters? The flights are cheap enough. You might meet someone . . . or are you seeing anyone at the moment?' Her beady brown eyes light up with eager anticipation; she knows I'm going to say no.

'Um, no. I was seeing someone but it didn't work out.' Why am I telling her this?

'Aaaaah,' she says with false sympathy. 'I'd say it's hard enough

7

to meet guys while you're working here, is it? Listen, I'd love to chat more but I'd better head off. I've still gotta hit L'Occitane and get something for Ronan's mom. But *mind* yourself, will you? Hope it all works out for you.' With that, she reaches over to pat – actually *pat* – me on the head, and swishes off in a cloud of Chanel. I'm still reeling from this, when she pops back a second later for a parting shot.

'Sorry, Zoë, which way is the Hermes concession? Ronan needs another tie.'

Smiling sweetly, I wave a hand and point her in the wrong direction.

What a wagon! The whole point of moving to London was to get away from people like her and have my career change in peace, and then move back home two years later in a blaze of glory, as a head buyer for a top department store or with my own boutique. Now she's going to be telling the world and his wife about how Zoë Kennedy is working on the till at Marley's. Well, so what? I was lucky to get this job, and there are loads of prospects for promotion here, even if they haven't quite worked out yet. How is she able to still hop over on shopping trips, anyway? I thought everyone was broke back home. Hermes ties, how are you. She's probably just pricing key rings.

I haven't seen Kerry-Jane for about five years and I've just realised she now reminds me of someone. Someone I really, really dislike . . . who is it? Oh. Of course: Jenny. That's one of my biggest regrets. I should never have been so jealous of David's female best friend.

'Excuse me! Excuse me!'

With a guilty start, I see the lady standing in front of me waiting to be served; she's so tiny I almost overlooked her. She's maybe in her eighties, with a slightly faded brown raincoat, blue-rinsed hair and huge square glasses, and she's carrying a cane.

'I'm sorry to keep you waiting. How can I help?'

'Ooh, thank you. I would like some cufflinks for my godson,' she says in a quavering voice. It takes her quite a long time to finish her sentence and I wonder if she might have had a stroke at some point.

'Of course. What sort of thing have you in mind?'

It takes a little while to find out her budget, and choose the right thing, but eventually we settle on a lovely pair of square silver cufflinks, which I gift-wrap for her. She pays in cash, taking the notes carefully out of a worn little purse embroidered with flowers. It's so teeny-tiny it kind of breaks my heart. Her knotted hands shake a little as she puts the package in her plastic-laminated shopper. My hands twitch to help her, but I manage to stop myself – she might not like it. When she's finished, she looks up and gives me an unexpectedly sweet smile.

'Thank you, dear,' she says. 'Merry Christmas.'

'Happy Christmas to you, too,' I say, feeling a happy-customer-warm-glow that makes me forget all about Kerry-Jane. I don't care what people say about shopping not making you happy; I know that the right purchase does make people happy. As I tidy the other cufflinks away, I notice the little embroidered purse, abandoned on the counter.

'Oh no!'

'What is it?' asks Harriet.

'My customer left her purse. I'm going to run after her, OK?'

'OK,' says Harriet, trustingly. She's obviously forgotten we're not supposed to leave the counter, let alone the store, unless the building's on fire or something – and even then we'd probably need Karen's permission. But I'll be quick.

'I'll be back in ten minutes.' I grab the purse and rush out, past make-up and accessories, past bags and scarves, past the lobby with its uniformed doorman and the big flower display, and look left and right.

I can't see her. It's dark, of course, and Regent Street is thronged with people pouring in and out of shops, looking in all the lighted windows or just ambling along gawping up at the Christmas lights that are strung all down the street like illuminated necklaces. There's snow on the ground, and I'm wearing a thin angora sweater with short sleeves (black, as per Marley rules, but with a keyhole detail at the back, from Whistles). It is *perishing*. But I'm not giving up; she can't have gone far. I'm guessing she's headed towards the Piccadilly line rather than Oxford Circus. I push past someone in a Santa suit, to get a better look, and I see her little figure making its way painfully slowly along the pavement. I sprint after her, dodging the crowds.

'Excuse me,' I pant to people, finally catching up with her. 'Excuse me?' She can't hear me, so I have to dodge in front of her. 'Hello! You left your purse . . .'

'Oh, my goodness. How silly of me. Thank you very, very much. I would have been lost without this.' She takes the purse and carefully drops it into her shopper, while I frantically rub my arms to keep them from seizing up. We're standing in the middle of a crowd of shoppers, right by a roast chestnut stall. The smell makes my mouth water; I barely had time to grab half a sandwich at lunchtime.

'I'm not surprised to have such good service from Marley's. It's a very special place,' she says. 'The windows particularly. People used to say . . .'

No. Really? Is she really going to stand here reminiscing? Does she not feel the cold? After the heat of running, I feel like I'm being attacked with icy knives. A charity mugger looks as if he's about to approach us but then changes his mind.

'. . . and if you stand in front of the windows in the week before Christmas, and make a wish, you'll get your heart's desire.'

'Isn't that lovely,' I say, not really taking it in. The crowd surges towards us, and a woman with tons of bags pushes past, almost knocking my new friend off balance. I reach out to steady her.

'All these crowds are quite frightening,' she says, looking shaken.

'Would you like me to get you a taxi?'

'Oh, I couldn't put you to the trouble.'

'It's no trouble.' By the time I manage to hail a black cab, my teeth are actually starting to chatter. I help her inside, and repeat her directions to the driver.

'Happy Christmas!' I wave at her through the window.

'Happy Christmas. And don't forget to make a wish,' she says, lifting a shaky finger.

I hurry back to Marley's, hoping I haven't been gone too long. One of the perfume girls, not seeing my name badge, darts forward and sprays me with something floral before I can stop her.

As I approach my counter, I run straight into Karen.

'So you decided to get some fresh air, Zoë? Give yourself a little break?' She's wearing a fixed smile so that any passing customer will think we're having a nice chat, but I know better.

'I'm sorry.'

'You know you're not supposed to leave the counter ever. Under any circumstances. And did you forget that you're wearing several thousand pounds' worth of store property?' My hand goes to the diamond-and-emerald pendant hanging from my neck. I *had* forgotten, in fact.

'I would have thought', says Karen, 'that someone who used to have a very fancy job as a *management consultant* could be a bit more professional and not decide to wander off . . .' I nod, trying to look suitably apologetic, and just stand there and wait for it to be over. I wish she wouldn't do this in the middle of the shop floor; despite her manic grin I think it must look really odd to customers.

When Karen finally lets me go back to the counter, poor Harriet looks apologetic.

'I'm so sorry, Zoë,' she says. 'I tried to cover for you but it didn't work. Was she super angry?'

I shrug. 'Yeah, she gave me the hairdryer. But don't worry, it wasn't your fault.'

'What hairdryer?' Harriet looks puzzled.

'It's just an expression; it means she gave out to me.'

'Gave out what?'

As I try and explain that 'giving out' means 'scolding', I think: Karen was right. I *was* really impulsive and stupid. Just like I was with David . . . but before I can start obsessing again, I throw myself back into work, determined to make my target by the time we close.

As I leave the building, I pause for a minute to look at the windows. Although I pass them every day they still hold a real magic for me. Each one is a fabulous cornucopia, piled high with beautiful, mismatched things: shoes and glasses and plates and watches, gloves and scarves, gold baubles and silver bells. On the Regent Street side of the building are the Fairy Tale windows. My favourite is the Snow White window, with the witch in full-length black Armani and the huntsman in a Prince of Wales check suit. On the shorter side, the one that leads into Soho, we have the Four Seasons.

My favourite window is Summer. It shows a man and a woman: he's wearing a white polo shirt and faded jeans (both Ralph Lauren) and carrying a picnic basket piled with treats from our food hall, and she's wearing a long white dress from Theyskens' Theory and a huge, shady dark blue hat. They're standing on a green lawn with a gorgeous painted backdrop: green trees, a deep green lake and a perfect blue sky with just a few clouds overhead. They're both beautiful; it's the perfect summer's day; the park looks like heaven.

I'm fully aware that it's crazy, but the male mannequin reminds me of David. He has the same confident stance, and he's looking down at the female one the way he used to look at me. I feel my eyes welling up, and blink them quickly to stop myself crying.

I wonder what David's doing right now. It's 4 p.m. in New York – he's probably at the hospital, operating or doing ward rounds or clinics. Manhattan must be so Christmassy. I can picture him walking down Fifth Avenue with his arm full of packages, or outside Macy's, handing a dollar to the Salvation Army Santa . . . then turning back to the willowy model/nurse beside him and sharing a Christmas kiss.

To distract myself, I think of my parents taking me to see the windows of Brown Thomas in Grafton Street, when I was six or seven. I was utterly enchanted by it all: the toys and the decorations and especially the moving figures.

'Does Santa make all that stuff?' I asked my dad.

He explained to me that while Santa's elves made some of it, a lot of these presents were made by ordinary Irish people.

'Like your dad's dolls' houses, and the playground stuff his company makes,' said my mum.

'But if you ask Santa you can have anything in this window you want,' said Dad, ignoring Mum who no doubt gave out to him later, for putting such an idea in my head.

This reminds me of what the old lady said, about making a wish and getting your heart's desire. Obviously it's nonsense, but on an impulse I close my eyes briefly, and murmur under my breath, 'I wish I could have David back.'

I open my eyes again and roll them at my reflection in the window. What a nutter. I start walking briskly down Beak Street, feeling very glad that no one saw me.

TWO

I'm meeting Rachel just off Old Compton Street, in a strange little bar we stumbled on a few weeks ago. White fairy lights dangle from the ceiling, all the lamps and the fireplaces are decorated with tinsel, and Nat King Cole is singing 'Chestnuts Roasting on an Open Fire'. Even the waiters wear Santa uniforms and antlers; it's like a Santa grotto gone mad, or the bedsit of a particularly keen Christmas elf.

The place is packed with Christmas shoppers and office workers, but I eventually find Rachel standing in a corner. A group of guys nearby are checking out her long legs and slim figure in her polo neck and black pencil skirt, but she doesn't see them; her smooth, dark head is bent over her BlackBerry, thumbs ablur. Seeing two women leaving, I throw myself into their seats, and wave frantically at Rachel until she comes over.

'Good woman yourself,' she says, giving me a hug and sitting down. 'Trust you to find a seat when it's needed.'

'It's great to get the weight off the legs,' I say with a sigh, stretching out and shrugging myself out of my damp suede coat.

'You sound like my mammy,' says Rachel, grinning.

'I know. Ooh, nice top.'

'Thanks. I bought it in Gap on my way into work this morning. I haven't had a chance to do any laundry for about two weeks, thanks to my lovely employers.'

She rolls her eyes to heaven. I smile, thinking that Rachel

doesn't fool me: she might complain about selling her soul to a corporate law firm, but I know she loves her job. I reach over to feel her sleeve. 'May I? Mm, nice. Merino and cashmere mix?' I feel a little buzz of satisfaction as Rachel nods, and think: I am learning from my job. I wouldn't have known that a year ago.

'So, any news on your case?' The case doesn't sound very riveting stuff – it's a dispute over who owns a lot of oil tankers – but it's a big deal for Rachel.

'Well . . . we just heard today . . . we won!'

'Oh my God! Congratulations! Here – let me get you a drink to celebrate!'

'No need. This is called a White Christmas,' Rachel says, pouring me a very dangerous but delicious-looking creamy drink from a steel pitcher. 'God knows what's in it but it's good stuff.'

'Thanks. Cheers! So what does this mean for you?'

'Well, it mainly means that I have this partner on my side now. I think. Which is good news for making senior associate some day.' She's grinning all over, and I'm thrilled for her, and a little envious. Rachel really has made smart decisions with her career – unlike me. She wanted to be a lawyer; she studied law. Whereas I wanted to work in fashion, but studied Business and French because it seemed more secure, and then ended up in a job I hated before finally deciding on a career change at the tender age of twenty-seven. And now I'm twenty-eight, nearly thirty, and I'm still wearing a name badge. Aargh. I sip some more of my cocktail.

'Are you looking forward to your Christmas with Kira?'

I nod. Rachel knows that I am a spoiled only child so this is new for me, to be away from my parents at Christmas. But I'm lucky I have somewhere to go: I'm spending Christmas with my Australian friend, Kira, and her six flatmates, who share a massive house near Westbourne Grove. Kira's making a big roast, and we're going to play Twister and drinking games.

'Kira's had flu, so I hope she's better now.'

15

'Flu wouldn't stop her gallop. She is the most unstoppable person I've ever met – bar you,' says Rachel.

'I don't feel all that unstoppable these days.' I tell Rachel about running into Kerry-Jane at work. 'She was asking me why I didn't go to the ten-year reunion.'

'My ten-year reunion was very weird,' says Rachel. 'Everyone was married with three kids. I felt like a freak. One girl has four, can you imagine?'

'Not even.' I can barely look after myself, let alone some baby. The song 'Last Christmas' comes on. I've never really noticed it before, but this year it is on literally all the time, and every time I hear it, I think of David. I try and snap out of it and pay attention to what Rachel's saying.

'So did I tell you I'm going to be working on a case in Manchester in the new year? Big insurance fraud case. It's actually a pretty interesting one because—' She stops and frowns, looking at me. 'Why do you look so sad?'

'Do I? I didn't realise. It's just –'

'What?'

'David . . .'

'Oh, God. What about David? Have you heard from him?'

'No. It's just – David trained in Manchester.' All of a sudden my face is crumpling up and I'm swallowing tears. 'I'm sorry.' I feel so pathetic; I promised myself I wouldn't bring David up tonight, let alone start crying when we've barely had two drinks.

'Zoë, you have to stop torturing yourself over David. It's done. You have to let it go.'

'I know. I just can't help thinking, if I'd only done things differently I could be in New York with David right now.'

'But . . . OK. Let's be a bit practical here for a second. You wouldn't have been able to work there without a visa. It would have been a big sacrifice for someone you'd known for less than a year. And anyway, didn't you always say you're only staying in London for two years, and then you're moving back to Dublin? Where does New York fit in with all that? What would your parents have said?'

16

'I would have worked something out. I would have pounded on the door of every single boutique and store in New York till I got a job, legal or illegal. And David's fellowship is only for a year, and he's talked before about moving back to Ireland. It could have been so perfect –' I choke up again and put my head in my hands.

Rachel pats my shoulder. 'I know it's hard. Believe me, I know. But that's life, you know the way?' she says gently. 'These things happen and you just have to accept it.'

I look up. 'But I don't believe that. I've *never* believed that. I think life's what you make it.'

'I know you do, but there are limits. Sure, look at me and Jay,' she says. 'It's not easy seeing him at work every day. I wish I'd never been involved with him. It was the worst decision I made all year. But it happened and I can't change it.'

'Oh. Really?' Rachel was furious when it turned out that Jay had a secret girlfriend – understandably. I didn't realise that she'd been that devastated, though. 'Was it really your worst decision all year?'

She nods. 'Either that or signing up for that fitness boot camp. I paid for eight sessions and went once.'

I feel bad; I probably wasn't much use to her when the whole Jay thing imploded in September. Rachel is so sorted and confident in every other way – she even owns her own studio flat, which seems like a miracle to me. And she always attracts real high-flyers: always bankers or lawyers, all really good-looking, with something really glitzy about them: they'll have a pilot's licence, or live in Hong Kong half the year, or be half-Russian and half-Swedish, or something. But none of her relationships ever seem to work out. I don't get it.

'Have you been in touch with Jay at all?' I ask curiously.

'Well . . . promise you won't laugh?'

'I'll do my best.'

'I sponsored his moustache for Movember.' She looks at me, and we both start laughing. 'I know, I know. I was feeling weak.' She groans, putting her head in her hands.

'What did he say?'

'I got an autoreply. "Jay and the Bandit Moustaches are grateful for your donation of £20!" It was a wake-up call.'

'You know, I'm still Facebook friends with Oliver. He really liked you.' Oliver is a surgeon, a really lovely guy and a friend of David's. He and Rachel kissed once on a drunken night out, but it didn't lead to anything, much to his disappointment.

Rachel makes a face. 'He was too nice.'

'What do you mean, too nice? The two of you were always arguing.' Every time they met, Rachel and Oliver managed to get into some heated debate about something, like politics, or fox-hunting, or whether or not women should change their names when they get married.

Rachel shrugs. 'He's just not my type. And he's so tall . . . Not to be mean, but it's kind of freakish how tall he is. And his ears stick out.'

'But he can't help that. He's so lovely, and he was so into you. Would you not just give him a chance?'

'OK. Let's make a pact. New year's resolutions: you will get over David. And if I ever see him again, I will give Oliver a chance. Deal?'

'Deal. Now let me get you some champagne to celebrate!'

Waving away Rachel's protests, I go to the bar and order two glasses of champagne. I probably shouldn't be drinking these on top of the cocktails, but to hell with it: we need to celebrate Cachel's rase. I mean, Rachel's case. I am a bit drunk. I take the champagne and carry it back carefully to our table.

'All right, ladies!' says a voice behind us. I turn around; it's Kira, muffled up to her ears in a full-length black puffa coat and white scarf, her short blond hair peeking out from under a pink beanie cap. Her pretty face is pale and peaky; she looks terrible, in fact.

'Kira!' I say, giving her a hug. 'How are you feeling?'

'I'm feeling human again, sort of,' she says, sitting down and emerging from her coat like a caterpillar coming out of a cocoon.

'Sorry to crash your drinks . . . I just had to get out of the house.' She gives a racking cough. 'It's the winters,' she adds plaintively. 'I still haven't built up resistance.'

'You're a tropical plant,' says Rachel. 'Should you be out this evening?'

'Probably not, but honestly, if I have to see *Cash in the Attic* one more time, I'm going to puke. I was even starting to find the guy in it hot.'

Kira works as a fitness instructor in my local gym; I take her Zumba and Body Pump classes, and we've become friends. She was amazing when David dumped me – dragging me off the sofa and taking me out on fun nights against my will.

'Hey, where's your Mini-Me? She not coming out tonight?' asks Kira.

Rachel starts laughing, while I frown at Kira. 'Harriet is not my Mini-Me. Don't be mean.'

'I'm just kidding! She's a sweet girl. Does she still copy all your outfits?'

'No . . . I asked her not to.' I still feel bad about that, actually; I had words with Harriet one day, after she'd bought the same green snakeskin pumps as me, and she was crushed.

'So where's the party?' says Kira, rubbing her hands together. 'What's the plan?'

They both look at me. Even though I've only lived here a year, and they've been here much longer, I've somehow become the party, bar and club advisor. Which I don't really mind. Part of me just wants to go home and eat Quality Street in bed, but it's the last time I'll see Rachel before she flies home to Kildare for Christmas. I'll stay out for one.

Four hours later, I fall out of my taxi, drunk as a skunk. Ouch. How did that all happen? We were having a quiet drink, and then we got chatting to those guys . . . and then Kira started kissing one of them, and then we all went somewhere else. As the taxi chugs away, I look up at the sky, cold and remote and full of stars.

It makes me think of that cartoon with mice, where they sang 'Somewhere Out There'. David is somewhere out there. I stumble up the steps, which are covered in snow, and bang the front door loudly by mistake. That will wake up Deborah, my flatmate, but that's tough. I crawl into my bed, and fall into a drunken sleep, dreaming that David and I are mice in New York.

And then I wake up in David's bedroom.

THREE

Looking around, I drink in every familiar detail: the abstract art prints, the tasteful, pale carpet and white walls. David's prized tennis racket is there. So he must still live here. Is it possible? I have a mad vision of him having *pretended* to move to New York, while secretly being here, hiding out in Maida Vale, just to get away from me.

I have to see David – if he's here – and figure out what the hell is going on. My hand is shaking so much it takes me a few goes before I can open the door. I walk upstairs towards the kitchen. There's nobody there, but there's a smell of coffee lingering in the air and an empty cup in the sink. He must still be here.

But he can't be. David doesn't live here any more.

What if I've been drugged, or kidnapped? What if the person who now rents David's apartment saw a photo of me or something – I skip over the details – and decided to track me down and drug me and bring me back here?

Instinctively, I pick up a big knife from the draining board and clutch it for reassurance. I'm standing at the top of the stairs, rotating around with the knife out, when I hear a noise from behind me. I turn around to find a strange man, with wet brown hair and sleepy brown eyes, who's just walked out of the bathroom completely stark staring naked.

'Waaaaaaaaaaaaaaaah!' I scream. 'Aaah!' I brandish the knife at him.

'Woah! Wait! It's OK!' he says. He holds out his hands to placate me, which makes me scream even more. He suddenly seems to realise he's naked and runs back into the bathroom, then re-emerges with a towel wrapped around his waist. He's very tall, and slim: his stomach is practically concave above the towel.

'Don't come any closer!' I yell. 'I've already called the police!' I don't know where that came from but I'm pleased at my presence of mind. 'If you come near me, I'll scream the building down and I'll chop your balls off!' I hold up the knife threateningly.

'Zoë! Stop!'

I stop, open-mouthed.

'I'm Max! David's friend. We've met before. Don't you remember?'

I lower the knife and stare at him. Tall, with a mop of thick dark hair, and brown eyes under thick, straight dark brows. I do remember, very vaguely. Some night in a pub. He's a doctor – no, a scientist. Some friend of David's from university or something. But obviously he had clothes on that time.

'Didn't he tell you I crashed on the sofa last night?' He ties the towel more securely around his waist, and holds out his hands again. 'I'm sorry I scared you. I thought you'd already left. Hence the, ah, nakedness.'

'Where is David?' I say hoarsely.

Max looks blank. 'He left for work a while ago.'

This is all too much. 'He was here? And he left? But why? Is he coming back? What's going on?'

Max is looking at me very strangely. 'Zoë,' he says, 'don't worry. Everything is going to be OK. Why don't you come here and sit on the sofa for a second and take a few deep breaths? Then once you're feeling more yourself, I'll make some tea and we can call David. I think I must have given you a shock.' He

22

reaches out slowly and takes the knife from me, gently but firmly. I let him guide me towards the sofa, and I sit down heavily. My breath is coming and going really quickly and shallowly.

'Did you have a good time at the theatre?' he asks.

'I wasn't at the theatre! I met up with Rachel and Kira.' Didn't I? What the hell is happening?

'Oh, really?' Max says. 'Well, I am pretty sure David is here in London. I thought you and he went to see *Hamlet* last night, but of course I could be wrong. I had quite a few drinks myself last night, so I'm probably not the most reliable of witnesses.' He starts telling me all about his night out, which involved three pubs, a 'rancid nightclub', and then an after-party with a bottle of champagne in someone's fridge left over from Christmas 2007.

'We had some trouble opening it, so we had to smash it, and then we were worried about shards so we sieved it through my friend's scarf,' he's saying.

I'm thinking. I did see *Hamlet* with David. But it was months ago. In the summer.

Outside, I can see the sky is blue, and there are green leaves on the tree. It's a warm, sunny day: a summer day. Max has a tan.

'What day is it?' I ask slowly.

'Thursday,' Max says, giving me a strange look.

'But Thursday the what?'

'The, um . . . twenty-second of July.'

I shake my head. 'It can't be. It can't be! Oh my God, oh my God, oh my God!' My breath is totally out of control now, and I'm flapping my hands and hyperventilating. Max scrabbles around, and finds a paper bag. I breathe into it quickly, before I have to wave my hands some more.

'This is a trick, isn't it?' I gasp. 'You've put something on the windows. Like a filter, or a – a screen.'

He shakes his head. 'No trick.'

I decide to pinch myself, to see if that helps. It doesn't really, it just hurts. And then – I don't know what makes me do this – I reach out to pinch him, just to see what happens. He roars indignantly and swats me away. So he's real, at least.

'Hey! Stop it.' He grabs my shoulders and looks at me. 'Calm down. Breathe. Look, you've had a shock. Maybe some memory loss or something, I don't know. But I promise you, it will be fine. OK? Look at me. Everything is going to be fine.'

I gaze into his steady brown eyes, and I realise he's right: I have to try and calm down, or at least pretend to. I take a few deep breaths, and he slowly releases my shoulders.

'Sorry,' I say. 'I'm not a nutter. I'm fine, honestly. I just – is there a newspaper or something? Can I see today's date? It's 2010, right?'

Max raises his eyebrows. 'Well, I don't have a newspaper, but . . .' He takes an ancient mobile phone with a cracked screen from the coffee table, and shows it to me. Thursday 22 July. He gets up, and puts on the kettle, while I stare at the phone in disbelief.

'Will you be OK if I go and put on some clothes, while this boils?' he asks. 'I'll be five minutes.'

'Yes. Yes, I will.'

Max disappears and I take a few deep breaths. I can feel myself getting panicky again – what if I blink and I'm in, I don't know, Viking Dublin? Or ancient Egypt? How long is this going to stay like this? Am I back for good? I try to think of who to ring, or ask for help. I suppose I could ring NHS Direct. 'Hi, I think I've travelled back in time. No, nothing major, just six months. What would you recommend?'

'Do you take milk or sugar?' Max has reappeared. He's wearing hideous baggy jeans and a faded purple T-shirt with 'Man . . . Or Astro-man?' on it. Because he's David's friend, I'd expected him to dress a bit more like David – smart, slightly preppy – but he's scruffy. Not in a hipster way: in an 'I get dressed in the dark' way.

24

He's towelled his hair, and his massive brown mop is completely vertical.

'Just milk. Thanks.'

I watch Max rummaging in the cupboards and fridge. His arms and legs are very long – he barely has to stretch in order to reach the highest shelf. I wonder if Harriet would like him; she likes tall men. Then I laugh aloud. I've time-travelled – either that, or I've lost my mind – and I'm still finding the time to do some matchmaking.

'Something funny?' he asks.

'Uh – sort of.' I shake myself. If this is really happening – and it seems like it is – I'd better start acting more normal. 'I was just wondering why I didn't see you last night.'

'Here you go,' Max says, handing me a mug of tea. 'Well, I got in late myself.' He sits down opposite me, holding his own mug. I stare at mine. Plain white china from Heal's, with a thin lip, because David hates drinking from mugs with a fat lip. I've drunk from this mug so many times.

'I'm in the process of moving to London – slowly. I've been living in California for the past four years, in Berkeley,' Max continues.

'Oh.' The mention of America instantly makes me think of David's post in New York. 'Are you a doctor too?'

'No. I'm a neuroscientist.'

I think this is coming back to me now – I do remember David mentioning how his friend Max spent a few nights on his sofa, but I didn't see him while he was at the flat. His T-shirt has an ink stain on one shoulder and I look at it, thinking: how did he manage to get an ink stain on his shoulder?

'I'm living in Oxford at the moment,' Max continues, 'with some friends, but I'm working in London, at UCL. So I'll need to find an apartment here at some point.' He sips his tea. 'How about you? I think David said you live near here?'

'Yes, yes I do. I mean—' Do I even have my keys with me, or

clothes? Do I still live in my flat? I have no idea what to expect.
I can feel the panic returning.

'Are you OK?' Max asks.

'I don't know where my handbag is. It wasn't in David's
room.'

Max stands up and walks over to the kitchen breakfast bar,
and pulls out one of the chairs. 'Is this it?' he asks, lifting my
bag up.

'Yes! It is.' My lovely, lovely Mulberry Alexa bag. I rifle through
it quickly and it seems to have everything: purse, Oyster card,
keys, mobile – my old one, not my new one – diary, three lip
balms, make-up bag, perfume. As I cradle it in my arms I feel
reassured.

'I have to ask you,' says Max, 'did you take something last night?
I mean, something that could have made you black out?'

I look up from cuddling my bag. 'Oh. God. No, I mean, I
can see why you might think that but honestly . . .' I pause and
look into Max's concerned dark eyes. He obviously thinks I've
been ingesting some weird drug cooked up in some Dutch lab,
which has caused me to flip out. But, honestly, what am I going
to tell him? 'I think I've travelled back in time but it's OK
because now I can persuade David that I'm not a psycho'? Best
not.

'I'm fine,' I tell him. 'I think I was really hung over and
disoriented and – I just wasn't expecting to find David gone
and you here. That's all.' I smile at him. I shouldn't really be
sitting around in my nightie chatting away to David's random
house guests. I need to get myself together and try and find
out what else is going on – get in touch with David, get to
work and everything.

Work. Holy crap, work!

'Shit.' I stand up. 'What time is it? I must be really late for
work.'

'It's, ah, eight thirty-five.'

'Oh, shit. I'd better go! Listen, thanks, Max – thanks for the

26

tea and everything. It was nice to meet you.' I grab my bag and start charging down the stairs.

'Hey, wait,' says Max. 'Are you sure you're OK to go in? Do you want me to call David?' He follows me to the top of the stairs.

'No, no, thanks,' I call out. I open David's wardrobe, crossing my fingers. Please don't let me have to be naked like Eric Bana in *The Time Traveller's Wife*. But there it is: my navy Zara dress – a Mouret lookalike – sleeveless with a racing back and a green trim, and my nude patent leather wedge heels. It's like seeing old friends again. I reach out and touch the dress, feeling the fabric under my fingers. I can feel the floorboards under my bare feet. When I move, they creak and I can smell the faint remnants of David's aftershave. I know that it's not an illusion; I'm here, now, back in time.

How on earth has this happened? I try and think back to last night – or what I thought was last night. I was out with the girls . . . and before that I was at work . . . I got into trouble with Karen . . .

Wait a second.

The old lady. She told me about making a wish, and I wished to have David back.

And now it's July, and we're still together. Which means . . . is it possible? That the wish I made outside Marley's has *actually come true*? I feel an actual shiver course down my spine. Unbelievable though it seems, it's the only explanation. Another wave of weirdness whooshes over me and I have to sit down, clasping my hands to my head.

Forcing myself to stay calm, I flip through my diary, trying to reorient myself. If today's the 22nd, I saw David just last night – and I'm meeting him again tomorrow. It's written in black and white: 'D, 8 p.m., Warwick Avenue tube.' I remember now. This was the night that we had the huge row about Jenny, when everything started to go wrong. But it hasn't happened yet!

27

'Thank you, God,' I murmur under my breath. I don't know how long this is going to last or what's going to happen, but for now – either I've died and gone to heaven, or else I am back with David. And I'm hoping that this time around, I'm back for good.

FOUR

As I let myself out of David's flat and pass by the Prince Alfred pub on the way to the tube station, I think back to the first time I met him in that very pub in June. It was a pretty dramatic introduction, and not just because I was on a date with another guy at the time.

I'd met Matt the week before at a very raucous party at Kira's house. My vague memory from the party was that he was fun and cute: short and dark with snappy brown eyes and a great physique. Tonight, it was clear that the amazing body came at a price. After half an hour listening to him drone on and on about his triathlon training schedule, I was shocked at my poor judgement. I gazed at his half-full pint glass, willing it to be empty (my own glass had been empty for quite a while). The second he finished it, I was out of there. *Please, please drink up*, I thought. It was twenty-five to nine; if he would only get a move on, I could still make it home in time to see *The Apprentice*.

'Of course the Big Daddy is Ironman Hawaii,' Matt was saying, shovelling another handful of Nobby's Nuts into his mouth. He'd nixed my suggestion of ordering food – which I was now really glad about – but instead was on his third bag of these. 'That's top of my list. But first –' he held up a finger to stop me getting too excited – 'you do a series of qualifying events. They're Ironmen too – well, Ironmans, of course. Ironmans is the plural of the event and Ironmen is the men, well, theoretically people but obviously mainly men, who've completed it. First I'm going to do the one in Bolton. Then there's the one in Tenby, in Wales.' He shovelled in more nuts. 'Then—' He coughed, and patted himself on the chest.

'Are you all right?' I asked, offering him my glass of water.

He shook his head, started to gasp and then to choke. Now his face was changing colour, from pink to dark red. People were falling quiet and turning around to look. I jumped out of my seat, and started bashing him on the back as hard as I could, desperately trying to remember how you did the Heimlich manoeuvre. Then I felt myself being pushed firmly aside, and a man – a young man, wearing white, with dark blond hair – thumped Matt once, firmly, between his shoulder blades, then half lifted him out of his chair, and was clasping his torso from behind, and squeezing him abruptly – once, twice, three times. Oh, so that was how you did the Heimlich manoeuvre.

'Bloody – hell!' gasped Matt, finally coughing and breathing again.

'I'll get you some water,' said his rescuer.

'Here,' I said, handing mine to Matt, and trying not to stare at the man who had just – well, saved his life. It was hard, because he was *gorgeous*. Short, damp hair suggested he'd just had a shower, his skin was fair and clean-shaven and his light eyes were direct, with dark circles under them. His strong shoulders and arms made me think of tennis and swimming, rather than hours pumping weights. He was well-built but not too tall, and wore jeans and a polo shirt: preppy, and hot. Clean-cut was the word that sprang to mind; but there was something else – a kind of calm confidence that was pretty attractive. Very attractive, in fact. My mouth was slightly open, so I quickly closed it.

'Thank you very much, mate,' Matt was saying, holding out a hand. 'Don't know how that happened.'

'No bother,' said the man, shaking his hand and glancing at the empty packets of nuts. 'You should be grand now. Take a few sips of water.' I did another double-take. He was Irish! In fact, I

30

was pretty sure he was from the same part of Dublin as me. I was opening my mouth to ask him, when Matt said, 'Let me buy you a drink. Least I can do.'

I could've sworn the guy glanced at my empty glass before saying, 'Thanks, but I'm on call.' Then, when Matt thanked him again, he said, 'Don't mention it, my pleasure.' And he gave me a quick glance, and a half-smile, before leaving. It was just a brief flash, enough for me to notice their army-green colour, but it left me feeling strange, almost jolted. I watched him walk back to his friend – an extremely tall guy with glasses and sticky-out ears – before reluctantly tearing my eyes away.

'Well, that was all a bit odd,' Matt was saying. He shook his head slowly, his eyes full of the mysteries of life and death. 'Phew! I would've hated to go before the Bolton Ironman.'

'I'd understand if, you know, maybe you'd like to go home and take it easy?' I asked hopefully.

'I think I need a drink first.'

'Of course.' After a second it became clear that this round was on me, so I got up and went reluctantly to the bar, thinking that it was hard to walk out on a date with someone who'd just escaped death. As I went back to Matt with another pint for him – no more nuts, I'd decided – and a stiff G&T for me, I couldn't help stealing a look at the guy in the white polo shirt. He was looking at me. When our eyes met, we both smiled before I looked away.

Matt, incredibly, seemed to recover within minutes and was soon chatting away about his new training gizmo, called a garment or a gremlin or something. I was still pretty shocked myself, and very relieved that he was OK. If that guy hadn't appeared from nowhere— I decided to stop thinking about handsome strangers and focus on poor old death-surviving Matt. And to try not to think that I preferred it when he was quiet, even if I wouldn't have wished a choking death on him. But soon I could *feel* someone watching me from across the room, and I couldn't resist looking over. He was smiling at me. I smiled back and then lowered my eyes quickly. This was getting ridiculous, not to mention really rude. But Matt didn't appear to notice a thing.

'Just going to the little boy's room,' he said.

I smiled and nodded, thinking how I loathed that expression. Then, with a start, I saw that the guy in the white polo shirt had stood up at the exact same second as Matt, and was walking over to me. I assumed he must be going to the bar – but then he stopped right in front of me.

'Hi again,' he said, holding out a hand. 'I'm David Fitzgerald.'

'Zoë Kennedy,' I said, thrilled and terrified at the same time. Surely Matt would come back at any second? My heart was thumping already, and when I felt his warm, strong hand in mine it went even faster.

He raised his eyebrows, and I could tell he was clocking the fact that I was Irish, but he didn't comment on it. 'So my friend Oliver and I have just been discussing a question of medical ethics,' he said.

'Oh?' I said, trying to sound nonchalant. I glanced over at the friend, who was pretending to be absorbed in his phone. 'Which is?'

'We were wondering whether your . . . boyfriend?'

'Not boyfriend! First date.' I hesitated, then added, 'Last date, to be honest.'

'Oh. That bad?'

I leaned forward. 'He can only talk about one thing: triathlons.'

'That's three things, surely,' said David. I laughed. Seeming encouraged, he put his hands in his pockets and leaned back on his heels. 'We were wondering whether he could be considered to be my patient. I'm a doctor, you see,' he added. 'And if he were my patient . . . it would be extremely unethical for me to ask you for your phone number.'

'Right,' I said, feeling a flutter. As if this guy wasn't already attractive enough! Ever since I could remember, I'd had a thing about doctors; I loved *House*, and *Grey's Anatomy*. 'And what did you decide?' I looked nervously at the back of the room: Matt was bound to reappear at any minute.

32

David rubbed his eye with an index finger before saying, 'We don't think basic first aid is in the same category as an ongoing patient–doctor relationship. So if you were willing to give me your number, I'd like to buy you a drink some time.' I detected a flicker of uncertainty in his eyes that made him even more attractive. I smiled at him and said, 'Sure.'

And then something strange happened. The whole pub, the background chatter and clinking of glasses: everything seemed to fade into the background, and it was just me and David. I noticed that there was a faint scar on his chin, and shards of yellow in the green of his eyes. It could only have been for a few seconds, but it seemed to last for ever.

As I began to give him my number, I was dismayed to see Matt emerge from behind the toilet door. He was getting closer with every digit and I sped up – but not too much; I wanted David to get it right.

'. . . Seven eight three six,' I muttered, just as Matt reappeared behind David.

'Great.' Smiling at me again, he put away his phone, gave Matt a friendly nod and carried on in leisurely fashion to the bar. I looked nervously at Matt – but he seemed to have missed the entire thing. He didn't even seem to have noticed David putting away his phone: he was too busy checking his own phone as he sat down.

'What did he want?' he asked, half looking at me and half typing out a text.

'He was just checking I was OK. Because of the shock, and everything.'

'Ah. Nice one.' Matt nodded over at David, and gave him a thumbs-up.

Three days later, David rang me and asked me out. Partly out of nerves, I started suggesting pubs near me.

'Of course it all depends on where you work,' I added. 'Where do you work? If you're central, then there's quite a nice pub called the—'

'Actually, I'd like to take you for dinner at the Oxo Tower. Next Wednesday at eight?'

'Oh. OK. Great.' With most of my dates, I was the one who took care of logistics, but clearly that wasn't how David rolled.

I was even more impressed when I got to the Oxo Tower. Our table was on a terrace with an incredible panoramic view over the Thames. There was a gorgeous streaky violet sunset – just like one of the printed Etro scarves we'd just got in store – and the shimmering lights of the city were emerging like stars. You could see as far as the London Eye and Canary Wharf. It was one of those experiences I'd dreamed of when I moved to London but hadn't actually had, until now.

Over dinner, I found out that David was twenty-nine, and was working as a registrar in cardiothoracic surgery at St Mary's in Paddington.

'I'm sure you hear this all the time but I could never be a doctor – I hate the sight of blood.'

'You get used to it. Do you see this scar?' He pointed to the faint, V-shaped scar on the side of his chin. 'I got that when I was a junior doctor, assisting on my first ever coronary procedure. We'd been working for a couple of hours, and it got too much and I fainted. Slammed my chin on the floor and had to have seven stitches. But I forced myself to go back, because I knew that was what I wanted to do.'

'Why?'

'It's the pinnacle of surgery. You can botch up a person's leg, and they'll live, but the heart is life or death.' He poured me another glass of wine. 'What about you, what do you do?'

I told him I'd moved to London to find a job in fashion, preferably as a buyer, but I was currently working as a sales assistant at Marley's. I was worried that he would look down on my lowly job, but he just said, 'I'm sure you will be a buyer, if that's what you want. You're clearly a girl who does what she sets out to do.'

We chatted for a while about work, and then he set down his drink and looked at me intently. 'So, Zoë. I think it's about time

I asked you.' I stared at him, my heart racing. 'What part of Dublin are you from?'

I laughed. 'Blackrock. You?'

'Donnybrook. Will we get the whole where-did-you-go-to-school and do-you-know-my-cousin-Joe over with?'

So often I'd met Irish people in London who were obsessed with this kind of conversation. I liked that David had a sense of humour about it. When David said he went to Belvedere, I nodded in approval. I liked Belvedere boys; they weren't as arrogant as some of the other rugby-playing schools like Blackrock.

'So whereabouts in Donnybrook do your folks live?' I asked him.

'Oh, just near the Merrion centre.'

'Oh, so more towards Sandymount? Which road?' I was curious now: I had my suspicions about why he was being so reticent.

'Shrewsbury,' David said, proving me right. Shrewsbury Road was the most expensive road in the whole of Dublin, full of huge Victorian mansions; at the height of the boom, a house sold there for 58 million euro. His family was obviously loaded, but I liked the fact that David was low-key about it.

'That's a long way from Belvedere, though, isn't it? How come you didn't go to Gonzaga?'

'My dad went to Belvedere. And yes, he is Dermot Fitzgerald from the Mater Hospital.' He grinned. 'I know you didn't ask that. But everyone in Dublin does. That's why I came to study here, at Imperial, instead of the Royal College of Surgeons in Dublin where all the Fitzgeralds have gone since the Ice Age. My dad still hasn't forgiven me.' I detected a hint of tension beneath the joke, which somehow made him even more attractive – if that was possible.

'Well, fair play to you for getting out of town. I know what you mean about Dublin. It's such a goldfish bowl.'

'Exactly,' said David. He gestured outside at the glittering lights of London, spread out beneath us: the Houses of Parliament, the London Eye, the Gherkin, the half-built Shard. 'Whereas London's a cold, cruel metropolis, where nobody cares where you went to school or who your old lad is.' He raised his glass to me. 'You're going to love it.'

I smiled, but felt uneasy. I only planned to stay in London for a year or two, max – just enough time to kick-start my career. Then I would go home. But David sounded settled enough in London. Of course, it was only our first date and *way* too early to be thinking about anything like that, but . . .

'Would you ever see yourself moving back to Dublin?' I asked casually.

'Sure,' he said. 'Especially now that my dad's retired. How about you?'

I nodded, thrilled. What were the odds that I'd come all the way to London to meet the perfect Irish guy?

From then on, we saw each other as often as possible. With all of my previous boyfriends, I was the one who made plans and scoured listings guides for interesting things to do. But David made decisions and took me places – even when he was exhausted. We went to Shakespeare's Globe; to the River Café for dinner; for Martinis at Duke's Hotel. He even took me to Wimbledon to see Federer (his favourite player) decimate Arnaud Clément. Sitting there in the blazing sunshine, watching the players racing back and forwards, two white blurs against the green grass, and seeing David's handsome profile beside me, I had to pinch myself.

David was also the first guy I'd ever been out with who would say no to me. I first noticed this when we went to the cinema together, about two weeks after our first date. I was convinced that the person behind me was kicking my seat. David told him to stop, and he did for a while but it soon started again. We moved, only for the person beside me to start rustling her sweets. But when I wanted to move a second time, David refused.

'People are always annoying at the cinema, Zoë,' he said. 'You just have to ignore it.'

This actually made the rustling stop. And it made me realise that I couldn't order David around the way I had my previous boyfriends – like my ex, Paul, who still periodically contacted me on the lamest of excuses. I knew David really liked me; but I also knew I could never take him for granted. For the first time in my life, at the age of twenty-seven, I was in love. And then . . .

And then it all started to go wrong – or rather, I ruined it. But I'm not going to think about that now. As the train reaches Oxford Circus, I step out, feeling full of gratitude for my second chance.

FIVE

'Rachel,' I hiss down the phone. 'Rachel, can you hear me?'

'Yes,' she hisses back. 'Why are we whispering?'

'Because something amazing has happened. And I wanted to tell you in person, but I can't wait so I had to phone you.'

I can hear her intake of breath. 'Are you and David engaged?'

'Oh – no, that's not it.' I feel momentarily deflated, before I remember: that could still happen! 'No, I just – oh God. Look, I know this is going to sound crazy, but . . .' I hunch down even lower so nobody can hear me. Which is difficult, because I'm on the street, on my morning break. 'I've turned back time.'

'You what?' Rachel says. 'What do you mean, you've turned back time? Have you bought a new moisturiser or something?'

'No. I mean –' I hesitate. Rachel doesn't even believe in star signs. Can I really tell her I've experienced time-travel?

'It's hard to explain. It would be easier if we met up. Are you free this evening?'

'No, I'm having dinner with Jay. He's taking me to the Coq d'Argent.' She sounds really excited about it. 'We were meant to go last weekend, but he was sick.'

I'm about to ask what the hell she's doing seeing him – but then I remember: of course. *She's still going out with him.*

'Rachel –' It's on the tip of my tongue to tell her about Jay and his carrying-on, and that his mystery illness last weekend will soon be diagnosed as 'secret girlfriend-itis.'

But there's no way I can tell Rachel what's happened. She would think I was nuts. I'll just have to try and warn her another way.

After I've talked to Rachel, I call my mum. I tend to ring after a long journey, and time-travel must surely qualify.

'Are you OK?' I ask her, suddenly full of anxiety. 'And Dad?'

'He's grand, Zoë,' she says, sounding bewildered. 'He's down at the factory.'

Dad is meant to have retired from his business, building and outfitting children's playgrounds, but last summer – I mean, this summer – he got antsy about the guy he'd left in charge and started hanging around the place again. Mum and I chat for a while, and then she says, in the warm tone she uses when talking about David, 'And how's your young man?'

'Well . . . he's grand! We went to the theatre last night.' I'm so happy I don't have to disappoint her with bad news. Mum *loves* the sound of David and I really can't blame her.

'Isn't he wonderful the way he does all that, while he's working all the hours God sends.'

'He is indeed.' I smile happily at the thought that David is still in the present tense.

'I forgot to tell you,' she adds. 'That poor old Paul dropped by the other day.'

My relationship with Paul was one of those things that really should have only lasted a month or two, but because we worked together, had lots of the same friends and lived near each other, it turned into two years. His parents live in Blackrock, near mine – they've even become friends, which hasn't exactly helped Paul move on.

'Did he? What was he wanting?' I remember this well, but I pretend to act surprised.

'He'd a story about some shoes of yours. Said he found them when he was moving house. They look years old, Zoë. I don't know will you want them at all, and they don't fit me.' Mum used to be a huge Paul fan, but since David's arrived on the scene, she's dropped him like a hot coal.

'Oh, no, Mum. Just give them to the St Vincent de Paul Society, if you don't mind.'

If David is the one that got away, Paul is the one that won't go away. I used to feel guilty about him, but now I know that by the end of the year, he'll meet a lovely girl, a dental nurse, and the calls and texts will finally stop.

We hang up, and I exhale happily. It's a gorgeous, bright summer morning in Soho. All the young hopefuls are out: fashion interns dropping clothes back to designers, media interns hand-delivering tapes and CDs with the next big thing on them, models on their way to castings, actors preparing for auditions. I stare at a girl wearing what looks like an original 1950s blue circle skirt, with a shrunken denim waistcoat and a red printed headscarf. I remember her! I saw her six months ago! I grab on to the side of the building: it's still solid and hot to the touch. But time travel or not, my break is nearly up, so I hurry back inside.

Six months ago – or yesterday – it was freezing outside the store and really warm inside; now it's the opposite. The blast of air conditioning hits me as I walk inside, deliciously cold after the heat of the streets. When I get back to the till Karen is waiting for me, looking at her watch. I've been gone for less than my allocated ten minutes, but she always looks at her watch whenever I return from a break, and when I arrive in the morning, and when I leave in the evening.

'There you are,' she says. 'I'd like you to take over on the till, please.'

'Of course.' I wonder what she would say if I told her I was actually six months early, rather than two minutes. In fact, could this even be considered overtime?

Karen is in her early thirties, and quite attractive if a little plump, with an oval face and a small, pursed mouth. Her dark hair is always twisted up in a neat updo, and she wears the same make-up every day: a hard smokey eye with lots of blue eyeshadow.

She's also pretty suspicious of me, seeming to think that I think the job is beneath me. In my first week, when I asked her if it was OK to give a credit note if a customer was a day past the month's return limit, she said, 'I would have thought a *management consultant* could work that out.'

'She's threatened by you,' Rachel diagnosed instantly when I told her about it. 'It's textbook. She sees you've all this glitzy experience and it intimidates her, so she's trying to put you down.'

'What glitzy experience? I've no glitzy experience! I was a junior analyst. I just did spreadsheets all day.'

'But you went to Trinity and you worked for PWC. She probably thinks you're after her job – and that you could do it better than her.'

In fact, I'm after another job – I want to be a buyer – but I know that won't endear me to Karen either, so I've decided to just smile and develop a thick skin where she's concerned.

'I've got a meeting with the guy from Hugo Boss,' she says. I stare after her as she goes, remembering her saying this before. This *all already happened*. I don't know if I will ever get used to it.

'Just this, please.' A fiftysomething customer with a helmet of blow-dried auburn hair is placing a feathery pink Philip Treacy hat on the counter. I stare at her and at the hat. I remember her; she's going to return it next week, saying she didn't think it went with her hair.

'Are you sure?' I ask her, on a mad impulse.

'I beg your pardon?'

'Sorry, I just wondered if you wanted anything else.' I reach under the counter to get a hat box, packing it in carefully with tissue paper.

'No thank you,' she says, taking her bag without looking at me.

'You're welcome,' I say, but she's already gone. It's amazing how many customers can get through a whole transaction without once looking you in the eye.

It's one of our quiet days. It's not nice to think I'm going to have to go through all this again, as well as the good stuff – the slow hours when you're on the till, you've done all the restocking, and there's nothing to do but stare into space and occasionally give people directions to the loo, or descend on one customer like a vulture to ask them if they're all right. I much prefer being busy.

It's so weird to think that the July sales – which I remember vividly – haven't even happened yet. I feel a swoosh of weirdness, like a rush to the head. I suppose it's possible that I might be hallucinating. I'm fully prepared to blink any minute and find that all of this has vanished and it's December again.

A flash of blond hair out of the corner of my eye tells me that Julia, the womenswear head buyer, is going by on one of her floor walks. Most of the buyers for other departments work in the head office which is in Paddington, but the womenswear buyers all work in the building. I always feel so envious when I see them coming in – striding past holding their cappuccinos, or clutching lookbooks or samples, chatting to each other about the show they've just been to or their last trip to Milan. It's my dream.

The buyers all work on the sixth floor. You can't even go up there in the regular lift; they have a special lift that you need a pass to use. I've only been in it twice; once, when I went up to the sixth floor, all psyched up to have my interview for the job of Assistant Buyer, and again when I went down, knowing I'd made a hames of it.

'It's not that we don't think you have potential, Zoë,' Julia, the head buyer, told me. 'But you have so little experience still. You're just not there yet.'

She suggested doing an evening diploma in fashion. It's a great idea but I can't really afford it. Mum and Dad have offered to pay for it, but I don't want to let them do that; I want to make it happen myself. And also, a diploma would take a year, and I can't face waiting that long.

But wait a second. Walking along, beside Julia, is the old assistant buyer, Hannah. The one who's about to leave. Which means the interview *hasn't happened yet*. I have a second chance!

I watch in excitement as Julia and Hannah walk around, stopping to examine different racks and displays. It's not their normal day for a floor walk; I think they're finalising the sale mark-downs. Julia picks up a geometric print shift dress, and I blink as I remember her doing exactly this, six months ago. 'These aren't performing too well, are they?' she asks Hannah. 'What's the feedback?'

Hannah seems stumped. Julia looks at her expectantly, and then drifts away, towards the Marlene Birger rack. I know what's going to happen next; Hannah will come over and ask me.

'Hi, Zoë,' she says, glancing at my name badge and looking a bit flustered. 'Can you give me any customer feedback on these shift dresses?'

Hannah is tall and willowy and has a mane of blond hair that she often flicks from side to side. I know that she's dating some photographer who is apparently very well-connected, and that she's about to leave to take a new job in fashion PR.

'Well, they're very gappy, apparently. You can fit your whole hand in between the buttons.' It's the exact same answer I gave her last time. But this time I add, 'I'll tell you what is selling really well, though: the maxi dresses. I think all the sizes sold out in a few days. Black is huge, but customers have been wanting them in different colours too.'

Julia's come up to join us now. Her hair is also long and blond – except while Hannah's is shorter and straighter, Julia's is curly, and trails almost to her waist. I look hopefully at her, wondering if she heard my little contribution – or if Hannah will at least acknowledge it. But, just as she did last time, Hannah turns her back on me, literally blocking me from Julia's view, and says, 'If you ask me, the cut on the shifts isn't great. We have had good feedback on the maxi dresses, though. I think we should look at ordering some more colourways.'

'OK, we'll look at the figures,' says Julia.

I don't believe it. When this happened first time around, I just thought Hannah didn't want to look clueless in front of her boss, which was annoying but at least made sense. But now I know she's about to leave. Would it kill her to give me a crumb of credit?

'What about all these Ikat prints?' Julia has moved away, and is holding up a different, sleeveless shift dress. I can barely contain myself: I remember these! We marked them down, and then Keira Knightley was seen wearing one, and it was featured in *Grazia*; we sold out within a day, and they were marked down, and we could have sold loads more. I open my mouth, trying to think of what to say or how to put it, but I'm interrupted by a customer.

'Excuse me. Which way is the ladies'?'

I give her directions, still feeling dazed from everything that's happening. Julia and Hannah have already left without so much as a backward glance. I can't believe that I'm so dense, and that this is only just dawning on me.

I know all this stuff.

I know what's going to sell – and what isn't. I know that they're going to mark those boyfriend jackets down, thinking they're over, but we could have sold more at full price. I know that the midi dress is going to stay full price when it should have been in the sale. I know that the reorders of the maxi dresses are going to come in too late, and we're going to miss the boat with them. I rack my brains, trying to think what else I could tell them.

But tell who?

As soon as Karen reappears, I decide to take a risk and just ask her.

'Karen – you know the sale next week?'

'Yes, what about it? It's too late to change the rota, I'm afraid.'

'No, no. It's just that if I had some ideas for what should go in it – who could I tell?'

Karen looks at me as if I'm speaking Martian. 'Ideas for what should go in the sale? What are you talking about?'

'Just suggestions about things that are going to sell well, or not.'

Karen just stares at me blankly for a minute and then says, 'Oh. Of course! Why don't you just go up to the sixth floor and ask to have a chat with the head buyers, or even the MD? I'm sure they'd love to hear your tips. Meanwhile, I'd like you to go to the stockroom. There are some clothes that need steaming.'

Our store is upmarket, but it isn't particularly trendy like Harvey Nichols or Selfridges. Our biggest-selling brands are Jaeger, Gucci and Louis Vuitton. But we're also making the effort to attract increasing numbers of younger shoppers, with labels like McQueen and Temperley and Marc Jacobs – though I think we could afford to have more. I sometimes gather, from things I hear Karen saying, that there's exciting stuff happening at a strategy level and I wish I knew more about it.

The stockroom is in the basement. It's huge, with racks of products and shelving units going up so high that you need ladders to access some of them. Harriet is there, steaming away. I seem to remember that we had some kind of falling-out during this steaming session, but I can't think over what.

'Oh, hi, Zoë,' she says, adding, exactly as before, 'I'm halfway through this rack, so if you could start on the other one? If that's OK, of course.' She says it quickly, as if not wanting to give me orders.

Harriet is a student, working here during her summer break from studying English at Leeds University. She's very dreamy and romantic; she told me that she wanted to study there so that she could walk on the moors like Cathy in *Wuthering Heights*, which I think says it all. I can sort of see why Kira called her my Mini-Me. We're both petite with dark hair, pale skin and blue eyes, except that Harriet's hair is lovely and wavy and mine is poker straight, fine and flat. I would love to have big, bouncy hair, but it's never going to happen. I take up my position beside Harriet and get the steamer out. I love steaming; it's very soothing to see the creases disappear like magic, and somehow much more satisfying than ironing.

'By the way, I got those green snakeskin flats! I really hope you don't mind,' Harriet says, holding out an apologetic toe to show me. 'I just couldn't resist them, and there was only one left pair in my size.'

Of course! Today was when we had our falling-out about Harriet 'channelling' my style. It was probably because we had the same 40 per cent employee discount, but I couldn't help noticing that she kept buying the same things as me. I tried not to be childish about it, and I said nothing when she got the grey chiffon midi skirt from Ghost, or the white lace Jaeger top, but these Marc Jacobs flats were the last straw.

'The shoes too?' I said. 'Harriet, come on. You're turning into my clone.' She was crushed, and I'd felt bad for weeks afterwards.

But this time I can handle it all differently.

'Of course I don't mind,' I say nicely. 'They look great on you.'

She beams, and I think: this is *incredible*. Not only can I get David back – I hope – I can also be a better friend, and avoid all sorts of mistakes. I'm definitely not buying that neon yellow tank top, or those leather trousers. I'm not going to go to that salon where I had that disastrous eyebrow dye that left me looking as if I had two caterpillars on my face.

'How is your flatmate hunting going?' asks Harriet.

'What?'

'Aren't you interviewing flatmates this week?'

'So I am. Um, fine.' Great! I'm not even going to have to waste my time doing this: I'll just pick Deborah, the same as before. She is a bit dreary and bossy, but she's fine.

I wish I could think of what to do about work, though. I have all these predictions but how can I put them into practice?

46

'Harriet, what would you do if you really believed in a product – or you knew something was going to bomb – and you wanted to tell people? I mean the management?'

She looks at me with round eyes. 'I don't know,' she says, looking confused. 'Probably nothing?'

I nod, thinking this is quite sensible. This is just a holiday job for Harriet, so there wouldn't be much point in her sticking her little head over the parapet. I imagine what would happen if I followed Karen's sarcastic suggestion of going upstairs to tell the senior buyers my ideas – maybe adding that I've come from the future. I'd say it would take about thirty seconds before security came and hauled me away. But a lot of them will be helping out on the floor next week, during the sale. Maybe I'll have the chance to give Julia, or someone, some insights at least.

'So what did you do last night?' Harriet asks me.

'Um –' Harriet is the one person who probably would believe me if I told her I'd turned back time, but it's not worth the risk. 'David and I went to see *Hamlet* at the Globe.' This reminds me of Max, and I wonder if he's going to say anything to David about the state I was in this morning. I really hope not.

Harriet puts down her steamer and clasps a long-sleeved T-shirt to herself, oblivious to the fact that she's just creased it all over again. 'That's so romantic. You're so lucky!'

'I *am* lucky,' I agree fervently, thinking that she doesn't know the half of it. 'What about you, what did you do?'

'I met up with some school friends I haven't seen in ages. We went to Hyde Park and had a picnic. It was really fun.'

I stare at her. Old school friends! 'That's it!' I tell her.

'What's it?' she asks, looking even more confused.

I make some reply, thinking: I have to contact Sinead Devlin as soon as humanly possible. If I'm lucky, she won't have signed with Harvey Nichols yet. I can show the buyers here her designs, and I'm positive they'll see her potential. And I'll impress them during the sales, and I won't mess up the job application for Assistant Buyer. I steam away energetically, feeling the excitement mount. I am going to *make* this happen.

SIX

It's five to eight on Friday and I'm about to meet up with David. I'm so excited and nervous that I feel sick, and my fingers are shaking; I can barely fasten my necklace around my neck. I stand back and review my appearance, double-checking my fake tan from top to toe. It's one of the down sides of being a pale Irish person. Even though my hair is nearly black, there is literally no melanin in my skin whatsoever. So not only do I have to slather on the Factor 50, but I also wear fake tan every day from May to September. It is a hassle but it improves everything about me: hides flaws, makes me look healthier, more toned, even happier.

I've decided not to wear the same dress I wore last time we had this date. It was very pretty – white lace, knee length with short sleeves, very Dolce and Gabbana via Topshop – but it's tainted now by association. Instead I'm in a white silk T-shirt from Alexander Wang (70 per cent off at The Outnet) and pink shorts with high black espadrilles.

Before I leave, I sit down and take a few deep breaths, and flip through my new purchase: a copy of *The Rules*. Some of the advice is a bit cringey ('Put lipstick on when you go jogging!') but the main message seems to be to always look great, play hard to get, and to keep things light and upbeat instead of moaning or picking fights. Which is exactly what I'm going to do.

*　*　*

I've avoided coming down towards Warwick Avenue, where David lives, because it made me so sad (I also listened to 'Warwick Avenue' by Duffy on repeat, until my flatmate Deborah begged me to stop). When I catch sight of him waiting outside the exit, wearing a light blue shirt with the sleeves rolled up and jeans, I have to stop walking and take another deep breath.

'Zoë.' He steps towards me. 'You look nice.'

He kisses me, and I respond passionately. It's like our first kiss all over again. It *is* our first kiss all over again. For the first time in months, I breathe in the faint scent of aftershave on his skin, feeling weak at the knees.

'Hey, you,' he murmurs in my ear, sounding just a little surprised at the warmth of my welcome. David's voice is one of the things I love most about him. It's a normal voice, not especially deep or light or anything. It's just kind of mellow and a little bit hoarse in a way that drives me wild.

I step back and look at him properly: his green eyes, his tanned skin – now a bit paler from working indoors – right here, in front of me. I just can't believe it. David. Here, voluntarily with me.

'Are you all right, Zoë?' he asks, frowning.

'Oh yeah – I'm grand!' I want to turn cartwheels, but obviously I can't; I have to act normal. Normal, but better.

'I've booked us a table nearby,' he says, as we start walking together away from the tube. He turns to grin at me. 'I tried to find a pop-up for you but I don't think I'm hip enough to know where they are.'

'Sorry?'

'We were talking about pop-ups the other night – remember?'

'Oh yes! So we were.'

I'd forgotten that conversation. And I'd forgotten this is one of David's jokes; that I have my finger on the pulse and that he's really uncool. It's true that David doesn't have his finger on the pulse (except at work, of course). His music collection is a couple of dusty REM and U2 CDs, and he's more likely to go to an art exhibition than some underground gig in Dalston. But I love that

50

about him; I much prefer it to those hipster boys who judge you by your choice of music.

'But I suppose it depends how you define it,' David continues. 'If you and I got a bottle of cider and drank it in the park, would that be a pop-up?'

I laugh. I'm about to suggest that we should actually go for a picnic in Hyde Park, if the weather stays nice, but then I stop myself. I'm not going to babble away nervously, or suggest things for us to do; I'm going to let him do all the chasing, all the time.

David glances at me, seeming a little surprised that I'm being so quiet. 'So . . . had a good day? How was work?'

The last time he asked me this, I remember complaining about Karen being mean to me. But now I decide to be more upbeat. As *The Rules* suggest, I'm going to radiate confidence and act light, happy and a little bit mysterious.

'It was great. I've an idea for a brilliant new designer I'm going to suggest to work. We were in school together.' I'm about to tell him about how I tracked down Sinead Devlin's number and left her a message, but there's no need to go into all that detail. 'How was your day?' I ask.

'Fine. Long. Nobody stole the students or nurses so we had lots of backup, which meant I got lots of cutting time, but you don't want to hear about that. So this is the place,' he says, as we turn the corner. 'It's such a nice evening, I thought we should sit outside.'

I remember it well: the Summerhouse. This is the scene of the crime. This where David told me that his parents were coming over, and mentioned that 'we' – he and his best friend Jenny – always went to tea at the Connaught with them. And I felt so hurt and left out that I was completely unreasonable and threw a massive hissy fit. Of all the mental things I did with David, this was one of the ones I've regretted most.

But I'm prepared. I have my second chance now. And I'm going to get it right.

'Zoë? Is everything OK?' David's looking at me strangely,

because I've come to a dead halt, like a racehorse in front of a gate it's tripped on before. 'Don't you like it?'

'What? Yes! It's lovely,' I say, remembering just in time that I haven't been here before.

A waitress shows us to our table. It is lovely: all striped table-cloths and wooden furniture. The whole place is set on the canal, which is reflecting the golden sunshine, so it's like being on a boat. There are little bunches of sweet peas on all the tables, and it's intimate without feeling cramped. We're right next to the tableful of banker-types in red jeans that I remember from last time. With the view over the water, and the sun-drenched atmosphere, the whole effect is very beachy-Americana-chic.

'This place is gorgeous. It reminds me of the Hamptons,' I say as we sit down.

'In the States? Have you been there?' David asks, sounding surprised again.

'No. But I've seen it on TV,' I admit.

David laughs, and I feel a glow of pleasure: he still laughs at my jokes. At the beginning, David loved my sense of humour, and smiled at my little mistakes. He thought it was hilarious when he referred to his scrubs and I thought he meant beauty products. I loved making him laugh, and played up to it, but then I overdid it and it began to get on his nerves. But not this time.

David orders two glasses of champagne, and I smile as I remember how he loves champagne and will order it at any excuse.

'Are we celebrating?' I ask, thinking, *I certainly am.*

'Yes. We're celebrating the fact that it's Friday . . . and I have the whole weekend off. And I'm seeing you.'

Wow. The whole evening was so tainted in retrospect by Jenny-gate, I had completely forgotten this nice moment of David ordering champagne.

'Cheers,' David says. 'So you're all right, are you? Max said you were acting a bit strange yesterday morning.'

Damn him – so he did say something.

52

'No, honestly. I was just a little hung over. And I wasn't expecting him – I got a fright.'

'Sorry about that. I gave him my keys a few days ago but I wasn't sure when he was going to rock up – it all depended on this experiment he's been doing. Ever the unpredictable Max,' he adds, sounding amused.

'He's a scientist, is that right?'

'He does cognitive neuroscience. He's a bright guy. I think he could really do some good work, if he applied himself a bit more.'

'Is he a friend of yours from Imperial?'

David shakes his head. 'We were both at Imperial. But we were neighbours when we were small, in Putney, before we moved back to Ireland.'

Of course. The lovely little street in Putney where David lived until he was twelve, next door to Jenny, making mud pies and doing finger painting together.

'Are you ready to order?' asks the waiter.

Here's an important opportunity to do something different. Last time, I ordered linguine with pesto, and when I was brushing my teeth that evening, I noticed a dot of green on one of my front teeth. It might not have been there all evening, of course, but the idea that I'd had pesto in my teeth *while I was yelling at David about Jenny* was so unbearably awful that I wanted to die.

'I'll have the chicken please,' I say.

David orders steak – he's addicted to red meat – and we start to chat. I have to pinch myself: I'm *here*, with him. I've missed it so much, I don't even mind if I remember some of his stories from last time.

'So what's the gossip at St Mary's?'

'Well, my boss threw the anaesthetist's mobile phone across the room when it started ringing during surgery. And you remember Andrew, whose girlfriend is always complaining about his hours?'

'Yes! I do!'

'They've broken up.'

Last time, I didn't think too much of it, but now I see it's a perfect chance to show how laid-back and non-clingy I am.

'That's so unreasonable! He can't help his hours.'

'No, he can't.'

'I really don't understand girls who need their boyfriends with them twenty-four-seven. I *love* my alone time.' I run my fingers through my hair and lean back in a carefree and independent way.

I wonder if maybe I've overdone it, but David is looking at me in admiration.

'I'm really glad you see it that way. It is difficult, but I think if the relationship's strong enough it should be possible.'

Yes! Thank you, God, I say silently. *Thanks, mystery old lady.*

'But I'm lucky these days with my schedule,' he continues. 'In fact, I was thinking we should go away for a weekend. Maybe the weekend of the thirty-first and first?'

'Oh, that would be lovely!' I can barely contain my excitement. 'Except, isn't that the weekend your parents are coming over?'

David frowns. 'God, so it is. How did you know about that?'

Oops. That's a very good question.

'Oh, I . . . well, I thought you said the first weekend in August. The other day, on the phone,' I improvise.

'Really? I don't remember telling you.'

Oh, no. What if he thinks I've been peeking in his diary? Or worse, what if I give the game away completely some day, by knowing something about the future that I'm not supposed to know?

'Well, my memory's obviously going,' David says. 'They are coming that weekend, you're right. But we could go another weekend, maybe.'

Thank God he seems to believe me. If David found out about the whole time travel thing he would think I was mental and break up with me. And who could blame him? I'm relieved that the waiter has arrived, causing a distraction.

'Any desserts, teas or coffees for you?' he asks.

David shakes his head and looks at me enquiringly. He has a very sweet tooth, but he also has iron discipline and never orders dessert. Last time, I ordered a double espresso plus coffee cake, and I was so wired from it that I'm positive that it contributed to our argument. In fact, I think of it now as the coffee that ruined our relationship.

'Just a mint tea for me, please,' I say.

I'm tempted to refer again to the topic of our weekend away, but I force myself not to. Let David bring it up if he wants. Instead, I'm going to bring up Jenny-gate and show how cool I am about it.

'So, what are you planning on doing with your parents when they come?'

'I'm not sure. We always go to tea at the Connaught with them . . .'

When I hear him say it again, it's such an innocent statement that I can't believe I went so ballistic over it last time.

'Oh, you mean you and Jenny?' My tone is genuinely unconcerned. He looks up and I can see the surprise, and relief, on his face.

'Yeah. My parents are big into traditions,' he says. 'A drink at the Shelbourne on Christmas Eve and Mass at the Pro-Cathedral, two weeks in Wexford in August – end of August, because you get a nicer crowd then – and tea at the Connaught in London. How about your parents?'

I think he might be trying to change the subject, but I need to emphasise the fact that I'm fine with the whole Jenny thing.

'I'd say it's also nice for them to see Jenny,' I say easily. 'My parents always like to see my school friends, or Rachel, whenever she's in Dublin.'

He nods, looking relieved. 'Tell me about it. My old man remembers the names of all the guys who were on the Senior Cup Rugby Team with me. And their dads' names.' He pauses. 'The thing is with Jen, though, they were very close to her parents. So I think Mum and Dad always like to keep in touch with her even more for that reason, you know?'

55

'Of course.' Now I feel *really* bad. I knew Jenny's parents were dead, but I never made the connection: no wonder David's parents like to see her.

'I'm glad you understand,' he says. 'Hey. Speaking of Jenny . . . are you still looking for a flatmate?'

What? He couldn't want me to move in with her. Could he?

'Yeah. Sonia's moving out. Why, does Jenny . . .?' I trail off, thinking frantically of excuses.

'No, sorry, just talking about Jenny reminded me of Max. He's looking for a place.'

'Oh.' This is new. 'I don't know. I'm sure he's very nice, but I've never lived with a guy before. And he seems a bit . . . I don't know. Didn't you say he was unpredictable?'

'Well, you might have to put up with his weird schedule and some eccentric habits. But I'm sure he'd be fine to live with. You don't have to, of course,' he adds. 'I just thought it would save you the hassle of looking for someone.'

I'm about to tell David no, because I have someone in mind. But then it occurs to me: by doing Max a favour, I can show David what a reasonable, accommodating girlfriend I am.

'Well, I could show him the flat. Would you like that?'

'I would actually,' David says. 'He could keep an eye on you. In case you get any more of these strange hangovers.'

I smile at him, feeling a warm glow. I suppose I only have to *show* Max the place. I can always say no later.

'I'll text him your number,' David says, pulling out his phone. Then he looks around for the waiter impatiently.

'Why are they never here when you want them?' he mutters. I look at him affectionately, remembering how he always gets really antsy when he can't get hold of a waiter the second he wants one.

'We're not in a hurry, are we?'

He raises his eyebrows and gives me a look that makes me blush. 'I am.'

When the bill arrives, David looks at it quickly and gives the waiter his card.

'Let me go halves,' I say, but he just shakes his head. 'Your money's no good here,' he says.

David hardly ever lets me pay for things. I know I should feel guilty about this, but I just don't. David is very generous, plus he earns a lot of money and I don't. Anyway, according to *The Rules* I must not pay, ever. I can cook him dinner or (if I remember correctly) buy him a baseball cap, but that's it. To be honest, on my salary, that's not a hard rule to follow.

David reaches out and strokes the side of my hand with the tip of his finger – all the way from the wrist to my fingertip. He's barely touching me, but it sends shock waves up and down my entire system.

'Let's go home,' he says.

SEVEN

Drifting slowly out of sleep, I remember, with a blissful feeling, that I'm here with David. Last night is played back to me in slow motion; walking home together full of anticipation, and then that spine-tingling first proper kiss of the evening, as he made the nightcaps we didn't bother to finish . . . and then the way he undressed me on the way to the bedroom, removing my clothes bit by bit as we went down the stairs. We got delayed on the stairs for a while. Then finally being close to him again; the smell of his skin, the feel of his lips and fingers . . . hearing him whisper in my ear 'You're so gorgeous, Zoë . . .'

Or did he? Suddenly I'm afraid to open my eyes, in case I find myself alone again, with the December snow falling outside. But then I hear a familiar quiet snore. Thank God!

I peek over cautiously: David's asleep. I cringe as I think of what I did when I stayed over last time, after our fight about Jenny. I had woken David up, for a start, by snuggling in to him. Then I'd suggested going out to brunch. David didn't want to, so we stayed in and had cereal at the flat instead.

'Do you want to go to the cinema, or something?' I asked. 'Or we could rent a DVD?'

'No thanks. I have a squash game at two, and I need a quick warm-up first.'

'Oh. OK,' I said, feeling uneasy. Did he really have a squash game or did he just want to get rid of me? I left, with a new and unpleasant feeling of impending doom.

David stirs in his sleep, and turns over so he's facing me. 'Morning,' he murmurs, then turns over again, pulling most of the duvet with him.

I slip out of bed, and go quickly to the bathroom where I brush my teeth – with only a small amount of toothpaste, so it's not obvious – and put on some moisturiser, comb my hair, groom my eyebrows, and put on a very tiny amount of cream blusher. It's so lovely to see this immaculate bathroom again, with all David's familiar products: good quality, but not too metrosexual. I reach reverently for his aftershave – Davidoff Cool Water for men – and take a whiff of it. When I was very down, after we broke up, I used to treat myself to a sniff of the sample bottle at the men's aftershave counter at Marley's. But now I can smell the real thing any time!

I put the aftershave back carefully, making sure he can't see I've moved it. Then I slip outside where I put on my underwear, and the T-shirt I brought along for the morning after. I start doing some gentle stretches; reaching up in the air and down to my toes. Then I go through a full sun salute.

David has opened his eyes now. 'Hey, Cirque du Soleil,' he says sleepily. 'What's the deal?'

'Oh, just some yoga.' This is actually a manoeuvre recommended by *The Rules*. They don't really recommend staying over with a boyfriend, but if you do, then in the morning, rather than staying in bed and clinging to them, you should get up and do stretches as part of the whole leaving-them-wanting-more routine. It seems to be working; David is watching me attentively.

'Yoga's dangerous,' he says, without taking his eyes off me. 'Get Oliver to talk to you about yoga-related injuries.'

I just ignore him, and after a final, graceful forward bend, I straighten up. 'I think I'd better get going.'

'What – already?' he says, sounding really surprised.

59

I nod. 'I've got a yoga class booked for ten,' I say, seeing the time on his alarm clock. It's nine-fifteen so that's plausible.

David throws off the covers, and jumps out of bed. 'Oh, no you don't.' He grabs me around the waist, pulling me back towards the bed and covering me with kisses, while I shriek and hit him, laughing.

'Don't go to yoga,' he says. 'Stay here. We can do some other moves.'

Wow! This is really working!

'I'd love to,' I say. 'But I've already paid for it, so . . .'

'Well, if you have a death wish, who am I to stop you? Go and get bendy.' He kisses me, and I melt into it. How lovely it would be to spend the whole day here, maybe have breakfast in bed, and spend the day in bed together, only getting up in the evening to make some dinner, but I am determined to have demand for me exceed the supply.

He wraps his arms around me, and we both look at each other reflected in the mirror on his wardrobe. 'You are hot stuff,' he murmurs, bending to kiss me again. Then he frowns at his reflection, leans forward and presses his fingers to his hairline.

'What?' I ask, though I know what he's looking at.

'Just the ravages of time.' He flings himself back into bed. 'I don't mind being short, but I'm not prepared to be short and bald.'

'You're not short!' David is five feet nine, which I think is average – I'm short, anyway, so I don't mind. 'And your hair's not receding. Not even close.' I think it's so cute that he thinks that: he has great hair. But he does worry about it; he even owns hair-thickening shampoo.

David smiles, shrugs and closes his eyes. 'Keep saying that,' he murmurs. I reach for my bag, to dig out the leggings and sandals I've brought to walk home in. It would be very handy to keep a few things like this at David's so I don't have to carry everything around with me. But I can only imagine what *The Rules* would say to that.

60

'So what are you doing for the rest of the weekend?' I ask casually.

'Absolutely nothing,' he says, 'if I can help it. Playing squash and writing a paper for a conference. Oh, I'm seeing Jen tonight, but that's it.'

I take a second or two to compose my face into a normal expression – rather than an angry-witch one. Bloody Jenny, seeing him on a Saturday night. Doesn't she have her own fecking friends to bore? And also . . . he doesn't seem to mind that I'm leaving so early. Does he actually *want* me to leave? And why hasn't he mentioned that weekend away again? But then I stop myself. Don't get mental again, Zoë, I tell myself. Just don't.

David yawns. 'So do you want to join me and her for the cinema tonight? She wants to see some French film . . . we might go for a crêpe afterwards. You in?'

I'm meant to be meeting Kira and her flatmates tonight. I could ditch them and join him and Jenny. The old Zoë would have done it in a heartbeat. But, with a massive, massive effort, greater than putting away a packet of Jaffa Cakes after having only one, or getting up off the sofa when *America's Next Top Model* is starting, I decide not to. Be strong, I tell myself. Don't just drop your plans and accept crumbs – or crêpes.

'Actually, I have plans.'

'Oh,' David says. 'Who with?'

'Just a girls' night out,' I say absently, pretending to be absorbed in my reflection and fluffing up my hair. 'Nothing too crazy.'

In actual fact, we're all broke so our plan is to stay in and watch *Legally Blonde II* and drink wine and eat pizza. But David doesn't need to know that. I glance over at him. He's lying back on his pillow, looking at me speculatively. I've got his full attention now, I can tell. He's picturing me out and about, all glammed up, being chatted up – brilliant! Let him have a snooze-fest evening with Jenny the Wonder Bore, and think about what he's missing.

Picking up my bag, I pause to pat my Burts Bees lip balm on, and blow him a kiss. 'Catch you later,' I say, turning to walk out the door.

'Hey,' he calls. 'Kennedy.'

I turn around. 'Yes?'

He looks so cute with his sleepy face, dark circles under his eyes, his gorgeous chest and shoulders half-covered by a sheet.

'If some guy tries to chat you up, text me and I'll come and sort him out.'

'I'll do my best.' And, giving him another little wave, I walk out of the bedroom.

EIGHT

I'm totally euphoric. I did it! I was elusive and alluring, and kept him wanting more. I would have loved to have spent more time with David, but the whole reason he was so keen for me to stay was because I was playing it cool. I need to keep it up. Not for ever; just for a little while, until I'm more sure of him.

It's another lovely, hot morning full of the promise of summer. I can't get over how great the weather is – surely it wasn't this good last time around? Being able to step outside with just a T-shirt and leggings is absolute bliss. I look down at my feet in their Havaianas with my dark mauve pedicure: Essie Demure Vixen, and sigh happily again. Passing the deli on Formosa Gardens, I see couples having breakfast together outside, reading the papers or laughing companionably. I decide: that will happen for me and David. It will just take a little time.

I'm just walking down Castellain Road, when an unknown number starts calling me.

'Hello?'

'Hi, Zoë, it's Max.'

'Max?'

'David's friend?'

'Hi! Sorry. I wasn't expecting to hear from you so soon,' I say distractedly, hurrying across Sutherland Road before I get squashed by a Chelsea tractor. 'Are you calling about the room?'

'Yeah, I am. I'm actually in Maida Vale right now, so I was

wondering . . . well, if maybe I could see it today. If that suits you, I mean.'

'Oh . . .' Today seems awfully short notice, but I can't actually think of an excuse aside from the fact that I'd rather be in the park. 'Sure. I'm not home yet, but if you come over at ten?' I give him the address. 'You're not coming from David's, are you?' I really hope he wasn't on the sofa last night – God knows what he would have seen and heard.

'No, no, I'm somewhere else. Thanks, see you soon.'

As soon as I hang up, I remember: after telling David I'm going to yoga at ten, I've told Max he can come over then. What if he mentions it to David?

OK, so that in itself doesn't matter. I can always say I changed my mind. But it makes me realise the potential danger if he moves in. What if he tells David how my hair clogs up the shower drain, or that I sometimes (well, often) don't wash up immediately after myself, or that I love to watch brainless DVDs and slob out eating pizza on a Friday night? Or seeing my home wax strips or my fake tan, or the mess my room can get into? Not that any of those things would be deal-breakers in themselves, but still: I don't think I should let David's friend backstage.

By the time I'm home, I'm regretting ever having told him he can see the flat. I decide that I'm going to give him a quick tour, just to be polite, and then make up some excuse. I'm whisking around doing some last-minute tidying – though actually the place is pretty clean – when there's a buzz at the door.

'Hi, come on in.' I buzz him through, hoping that was Max I just buzzed in, and not some random axe-murdering stranger.

It is Max. He has a black nylon backpack on his shoulders, and is wearing an ancient-looking brown T-shirt and those terrible, baggy American jeans again. Never mind a new home: he needs a re-style, stat.

'Come on in! Welcome to my humble abode.'

'Thanks.' He looks a little less confident than he did the other day, when he was talking me down from a ledge. I'm surprised that our initial naked encounter hasn't put him off wanting to come and see the flat – shouldn't he be mortified? But seeing him come up to the top of the stairs, looking around and taking in every detail of the sitting room – the windows overlooking Elgin Avenue, the white walls (I painted them myself in May) and brown couch opposite the TV, the Wayne Thiebaud print above the fireplace (mine), the bookshelf and the black IKEA table – I can tell he just really wants somewhere to live.

'So do you want to see the room first?'

'Yeah, that would be great,' says Max.

Sonia's room is frighteningly tidy, as ever, even though she's in the middle of moving all her stuff out. A small double bed, made up with super-neat corners (she prefers blankets to duvets – that says it all); a built-in wardrobe and desk with IKEA lamp, magnolia walls, one poster of a flower, also from IKEA. Loads of pink glittery pens lined up for her studies. A suitcase. And that's pretty much it. I always think she must have a cupboard some-where, like Monica's in *Friends*, full of all the rubbish and junk that normal people have, and some day I'll open it and be buried under an avalanche.

'Wow,' says Max. 'She's a real slob, isn't she?' He takes a step forward into the room. 'It's a good size.'

'Full disclosure: mine is smaller so I pay forty pounds less a month.'

He nods, and goes to peer out of the window, which overlooks the back of the building. 'Can we use the garden?'

'I'm afraid not. It belongs to the man in the basement flat.'

'The Selfish Giant,' he says. 'So is there any outside space? A balcony or anything?'

'Nope,' I say cheerfully. 'Sure, you'd never find a place in this area with outside space, at this price.'

Max follows me obediently while I show him the rest of the flat. This always strikes me as a weirdly embarrassing ritual. It's like doing a striptease for someone, except instead of whistling and throwing money at you, they just nod politely and say how lovely it is. Or maybe it's strange because you're showing them your little world and they have to ooh and aah even if they're thinking, 'What a dump.' The truth is, the flat is a bit of a dump, but that's why it's affordable.

I'm not going to bother with the hard sell: he can take it as he finds it. 'This is the kitchen – all the original fittings circa 1975. Washing machine, but no dryer, and a microwave. Without which I would starve. Oh. I forgot the bathroom . . .' It's reasonably clean. All of my posh L'Occitane toiletries are really for display; my Palmolive shower gels and old loofahs live in a toiletry bag. I notice him clocking my line of shampoos. I have six different brands that I rotate, and they're all lined up in order of use.

'Do you get enough hot water?' he asks.

'Sure,' I say, surprised. 'And this is my room – sorry, it's a little messy.'

This is a lie: I've just tidied it. There is a lot of stuff lying around still, but the one thing that is in perfect condition is my wardrobe. All of my winter stuff has been put away in vacuum-packed bags, my summer clothes are all arranged by style and type of garment, and all of my shoes are in their original boxes with Polaroids outside (taken for me by Paul, my ex, so that all the more recent boxes have crappy digital print-outs).

Max puts his head inside, obviously not wanting to tread in my domain.

'It has a little more character than your room-mate's.'

I think we've spent enough time in my bedroom, so I lead him back out of the room. Hearing a noise, I turn around: he's managed to knock over a little vase that was sitting on top of my bookshelf, and the rose has fallen out of it, along with the water. It's not broken, though. He picks it up and looks anxiously, first at it, then at me.

'Sorry,' he says, handing it back to me.

'It's OK,' I say, putting it back on the shelf. 'Everything's all crammed in there.' As we come back down the corridor, I'm thinking: I'm definitely not giving him the room. He'd have the place destroyed.

'And . . . this is obviously the sitting room. Take a seat. Oh – don't sit there, that's the broken part. Try the other bit . . .'

'So what's the landlord like?' Max asks, shifting obediently.

'Well – he's very lazy, to be honest. He will fix things if it's a dire emergency but he tends to neglect us a bit otherwise. He's undercharging us so I don't push it,' I add. 'Most two-bedrooms in this area go for about twice what we pay. Just so you know.' I might as well be honest, since I'm not going to let him move in.

'That sounds perfect. Our landlady in San Francisco was obsessed with feng shui and she was always coming over to check we weren't putting the trash in the relationship corner.'

'Oh, dear. So who were you living with?'

'I lived with a couple of other friends from Berkeley. Computational neuroscientists.' He grins at me. 'You can picture the scene: three scientists, all eating pizza and watching TV together and having incredibly geeky conversations. People said it was like the Big Bang Theory.'

I nod, thinking: so he's probably not house-trained.

'Would you like some tea?' I may not be planning to offer him the room, but he is David's friend.

'Yeah, that would be great. Do you want a hand?'

I decline, giving him mental brownie points for asking, and head into the kitchen where I put the kettle on to boil and reach down for our two most respectable mugs, a sugar bowl, and a milk jug. Max won't be telling David that I served him milk from a carton. I add a couple of Kimberley biscuits which my mum posted me recently.

'Here you go,' I say, bringing in the tea tray. I take a seat on the other sofa, at right angles to him, wondering briefly if I should offer to swap so that he doesn't have to sit on the broken one, but then deciding not to bother.

'A tea tray,' he says. 'Cool. Now I know I'm back in London.'

'More importantly, you're in an Irish person's flat,' I say, putting the tea down beside him. I check the tea is brewed enough, and pour it out. Max adds milk to his, and then dips his spoon in the sugar bowl and takes exactly half a teaspoon. Then he shakes a little out so that he has exactly a quarter teaspoon – and then finally puts it in his tea. I look away just in time so he doesn't see me staring at him.

'So where's your room-mate?' he asks. 'How come she's leaving?'

'I think she's probably at the gym. Her company was previously based at Paddington but it's being transferred to Watford Junction. She's happy because she can live in Watford at a cheaper rent.'

He nods. I think that's all he needs to know about Sonia, the world's most boring flatmate, and her habits.

'So . . . you know David from living in London, is that right? But you're younger than he is?'

'Yes. His family lived on the same street as mine, in Putney, before he moved to Ireland – and we moved to Bristol. But my parents live in Wales now.'

'So do you know Jenny as well?' I can't help asking.

'Oh yeah, I know her,' Max replies. I can instantly tell he doesn't like her, and give him another mental brownie point.

Max picks up a Kimberley and examines it for a second from several angles.

'This is an interesting biscuit. What is it?'

'Kimberley – it's Irish. My mum sends them over,' I say, amused at his analytical approach. 'So have you seen many places?'

'I've seen eight. I really want to find somewhere soon. I'm trying to set up an experiment here, but I've also agreed to help out on a project in a lab in Oxford, so between working and flatmate interviews, I'm all over the place. It would be good to have a base.' I can see he does look very tired; he's quite pale under his tan and freckles, and his hair is sticking up everywhere. I wonder why he hasn't managed to find anywhere yet. He's reasonably person-able, though maybe a bit eccentric.

'I've never had to do the whole flatmate interview thing,' I remark. 'Sonia and I were just lumped in here by the landlord. What do they ask you about? Is it what time you get up, and stuff?'

'No, it's more like: what are your strengths and weaknesses, what can you contribute to the flat, where do you see yourself in five years' time, what are your best and worst habits . . .'

'Oh, my God. You're kidding! Really?'

He nods. 'One house I went to see during the week made me hold up a piece of paper with my name written on it, so they could photograph me for their records.' I start laughing at this, and he smiles.

'I mean it's fine, I get it, they want to pick the right person. But also, they want to get the perfect person, which isn't possible.'

I don't agree with that. Of course you can find the perfect person – isn't that what flatmate-hunting, and dating, are all about?

Max shakes his head abruptly, as if he hadn't meant to get into that. 'Anyway, I don't really want to live with a whole houseful of other people. I did that in Berkeley, and it was fun, but I'm sort of over it now.'

'So what did you tell the people who asked you that?' I ask curiously. 'About your worst habit.'

'That I was a chronic sleep-walker and I had a habit of turning on the oven while I was asleep.'

'That's not true, is it?' I ask, doubtfully.

'No. But I knew neither of us was interested, so it didn't make any difference. But if you want the complete, honest truth . . .'

'I do.'

'Well, one vice I have is that I love to take really long baths. I mean, disgustingly long.'

'How long is disgustingly long?'

'Um . . . two hours?'

'Two hours?!'

'Ideally. But I would always check first to see if anyone else needed the bathroom. Or else I'd wait till everyone else was out. I didn't have a tub in California – but with the London weather I think I'm really going to need baths.'

Hm. If he's going to be wallowing in the bath every night while

I want to do my fake tan, I can rule him out with a clear conscience. 'What's your routine like?'

'I keep odd hours. Sometimes I can work pretty solidly, and I'll even sleep at the lab, so you'll barely see me for days on end. Which is more of a plus, I suppose. But then once that eases off, I tend to go out a lot. Or I could easily spend two or three nights in a row at home, watching TV.'

'What kind of TV?' I ask suspiciously. It had better not be endless football.

'Preferably rolling news, or *The Simpsons*.'

'Do you watch football?'

'No. I don't like competitive sports. Though I do like swimming – and rock climbing. And surfing, so I might be away the odd weekend doing that.'

Good. I look at him speculatively, and for the first time I think – maybe I could live with him. I suppose he'd be a lot less fussy than Deborah.

'So, David said you work in fashion?' Max asks.

'Well, sort of. I'm a sales assistant in the womenswear department at Marley's.'

He looks at me enquiringly. I look at his T-shirt and add, 'It's a big department store. How about you? I mean, I know you're a scientist but what exactly are you researching?'

'Well, I'm basically studying memory. How memory works, and what different parts of the brain are involved in remembering different stuff. Broadly speaking.'

My head snaps up. 'Are you serious?'

'Ah . . . yeah. Why?'

Because maybe you could help me find out if I've gone crazy or if my memory is playing tricks on me, or if I've really travelled back in time.

'Oh – no reason. It sounds interesting.'

'It is. And I'm hopeful about my latest idea. I really just want to be able to concentrate on it.' He picks up another Kimberley – his third! – and starts crunching it. 'That's my big focus right now.'

'What's it about?'

He immediately launches into an explanation of something I don't understand at all – something about the frontal lobe or cortex or something and scanning people's brains. I gather it's got some sort of relevance to Alzheimer's. As I watch him wave his arm around to demonstrate things, dropping crumbs all over the carpet, I think: this guy is not going to be telling David anything about finding hairs in the bath. He's not going to notice. And he's not going to make me sign up to a housework rota, or complain if I make noise after 8 p.m., like Deborah did. Will do.

'So what do you think of the flat?'

'It's perfect,' he says immediately. 'The room, the location – it's great.'

After all the cross-questioning from the other potential flat-mates, it's very nice to hear that. Even Deborah, who ended up taking the room, never described it as perfect – she just looked around and said: 'Yeah, it's fine'. He's much less demanding. In fact, this could be ideal. A laid-back male flatmate, who will let me do whatever I want. Why have I never thought of this before?

'So do you have any deal breakers as regards flatmate behaviour? Anything that really annoys you?'

He frowns. 'Not really. As long as people don't steal my stuff, I'm pretty happy.'

We discuss the rent and bills, and I tell Max it's a year lease, with a break clause.

'Ah,' he says, 'that reminds me. I should tell you that there is one thing . . .'

Oh, here we go. He has a pet snake? He's dating twins? He needs a whole room for his china doll collection?

'There's a small possibility that I might have to leave London in six months. I hope not,' he adds quickly. 'But my current funding is only going to last for another six months. And there's a possibility that I might have to try and get funding elsewhere, maybe

71

in Germany or the States. I don't want to – I really want to stay in the UK – but I just thought I should mention it.'

'Oh,' I say. Well, that's a bummer. I don't want to be flatmate-hunting all over again in six months' time, assuming I'm still in this dimension.

'Sorry. I should have told you earlier. I mean, it might not happen, but I wouldn't want to spring it on you either.'

So that's why he hasn't got any of the rooms he's looked at previously. He's been too honest. Most people just wouldn't say anything; they'd sign up and then leave if they had to.

He gets to his feet. 'I should get going. Thank you for the tea, and everything.' He brushes down his T-shirt, and then seems surprised that the crumbs have gone on the floor. 'Sorry.'

'It's OK. I'm afraid it does seem a bit short, six months.' I stand up too. 'Like you say, it might not happen, but—'

'Don't mention it. I'm still looking around, anyway, checking out some short lets . . .'

I manage to stop myself from blurting out, 'But short lets cost a fortune in London.' Poor guy – it is miserable having to flat-hunt. He looks resigned, but I can tell he's disappointed. As he bends to sling his bag on his back, I notice that my address is written on the back of his right hand – he must be left-handed. For some reason, the scribble strikes me as a bit poignant. I'm not sure if it's feeling sorry for him, or wanting to do David a favour, or thinking that I'd like to have a laid-back male flatmate for a change instead of Deborah with all her rules – but I make a sudden decision.

'Listen, Max,' I say. 'If you want the room you can have it. It doesn't matter if it ends up being a bit short. As long as you help me find someone new if you do have to move out.'

'Really?' He looks delighted. 'Hey, that's great. You're sure? Thanks, Zoë. This is really great.'

I make sure I have his number and we make arrangements about deposits and keys. After he's left, I go to the window and watch him stroll across Elgin Avenue with what looks like a spring in his step. Well, it's nice to do a good deed. I've taken in the homeless. And also, he's an expert on memory! If anyone can help me find out what's happened to me, it will be him.

That evening, as planned, I meet up with Kira and some of her housemates, in their huge house in Westbourne Grove. I almost fall over when she answers the door. Last time I saw her, she was pale, miserable and coughing in her winter coat; now she's tanned a perfect caramel colour, wearing tiny turquoise printed shorts and a little white racing-back tank top. It's as if she's come back from the dead.

'Have I got something on my teeth?' she asks.

'No! Nothing.'

It's really weird watching the same DVD and having the same conversations – about Kira's work (her boss has refused to let her go away over Christmas, and she's furious, but I'm happy because it means I'll have somewhere to go), and about Kate Middleton and Prince William (I have to bite my tongue from saying that they'll get engaged in November). She also makes a remark that I'd dismissed at the time – she has some pretty cynical views about men and relationships – but which now gives me food for thought.

'It's easy to get any guy to fall for you,' she says. 'Just find out what his ultimate sexual fantasy is, and give it to him as often as possible.'

'Hmm,' I say. I've never actually asked David what his ultimate sexual fantasies are, and I don't think I'd have the nerve to – not yet, anyway. But now that I think of it, I remember us getting very frisky one evening, sometime in August, when we were on his roof terrace. I was paranoid that the neighbours would see us so we went inside, but he seemed disappointed. And the same thing happened another time, coming back from a concert on Hampstead Heath late at night. He wanted us to linger a bit but I was having none of it.

But if that really is what does it for him . . . It would be really

73

embarrassing but I suppose I could give it a go. I'll think about it, anyway.

'Earth to Zoë,' says Kira. 'Have another drink.'

Now that I've had a few drinks, I'm dying to text David. I've any number of reasons – I could tell him that I saw Max about the room, or ask him how the film was, or just say hi, but I remember *The Rules*, and I stop myself. I am not contacting him; I'm going to reply, but that's it. A watched phone never rings, so I put mine away to avoid temptation.

NINE

I'm fizzing with anticipation as I arrive at work on Monday. I managed to track Sinead Devlin, and visited her yesterday in her warehouse/flat in Hackney. It's funny; I thought she was ignoring my emails because she was a fabulous successful designer, but she's actually just very scatty. She was thrilled when I said I wanted to show her designs to the buyers here, and I have her lookbook right here with me.

'Morning, Zoë,' Bruce the sleazy security guard says, glancing at me with very little interest. Good. Last time he leered at me because my skirt was too short; today's black pencil skirt is obviously a much safer bet. I'm also wearing a gorgeous scarf Sinead gave me, looped around my neck; I hope it brings me luck.

At around 11 a.m., Julia and I are on the fitting rooms together, just like last time. I forgot how hectic it was; getting them in and out efficiently, taking huge armfuls of clothing in and out, putting them on rails and sorting them, cleaning up all the incredible debris people leave on the floors; one particularly glamorous woman leaves five empty packets of soya nuts. I'm just wondering if maybe I should wait until the end of the day before telling her about Sinead, when Julia turns to me.

'That's a great scarf,' she says. 'Where's it from?'

I turn to her, delighted. 'Oh! It's by a friend of mine, a young Irish designer. She's hoping to get into a showroom soon, and launch at London Fashion Week.'

'May I take a closer look?'

'Of course!' I hand it to her. She examines it carefully. It is really cool; from a distance it looks like a floral pattern, but when you look at it closely they're actually fossils and stones, in different shades of blue, on a taupe background.

'These are silk, but her winter collection is in a model cashmere—'

'Have you got this in a size ten?' asks a voice beside me. As I deal with the customer, I'm on tenterhooks – is Julia interested or not? But as soon as there's a breathing space she returns to the topic.

'It's gorgeous. Have you seen any other samples?'

'Yes – in fact, I have her lookbook, if you'd like to see it.'

'That's handy. Why don't you show me at lunch? I'll be going up to my desk to check my emails at twelve-thirty. Bring it to me then.'

'Oh, great! I'll just—' I'm so institutionalised that I'm about to explain that I don't normally get lunch until one, but we're swamped by another wave of customers and there's no more time for talking. Just as well; she doesn't need to know the times of my lunch break. I didn't even have to bring it up or pitch it to her! She spotted the scarf herself! Now I just need to figure out how to get upstairs for twelve-thirty.

Around eleven forty-five Julia leaves to go elsewhere and Harriet comes to take her place. She's excited about a guy she's just met through friends. He's texted her and said they should hang out soon and she's replied to say she'd like to, but now she's worried that wasn't enough.

'Maybe I should have suggested a time and a place?' she says.

'Absolutely not. Let him do the running,' I reply.

I don't add that this guy is going to continue sending texts saying they should meet up, and that they never will. She asks me for loads of advice as it is; if I started predicting the future for her it would be a disaster.

'What time are you on lunch, Harriet?' I ask her.

'Twelve fifteen to twelve forty-five. Why?'

'Will you swap with me? I go at one.' As soon as I explain why, Harriet is thrilled for me. 'That's so amazing!' she says. 'You're brilliant, Zoë – good luck.'

I notice that as well as the green snakeskin sandals, she's now bought my exact navy sleeveless blouse, but in black. Well, never mind: I owe her.

As soon as I'm on my break, I race over to the till where I left the lookbook, hidden carefully in a drawer under some catalogues. I'm horrified to see Karen is flipping through it curiously.

She looks up as I approach. 'Zoë! Why are you away from the fitting rooms?'

'I'm on my lunch break. I swapped with Harriet.'

'How come?'

'Um – I was hungry?' Oh dear. That was the wrong answer.

'Well, that's your look-out. You're assigned those breaks and you're not supposed to swap them around.'

'I understand. Could you make an exception just this once, though?' I ask.

Her eyes narrow even further. 'Do you think you're an exception to the rules, Zoë?'

'No,' I say meekly.

There's an agonising pause, and then she says, 'Fine. But just this once.'

'Thank you. Um . . . Julia asked me to bring that lookbook upstairs to her.'

'Oh. I thought one of the buyers must have left it behind.' She snaps it shut. 'I'll bring it up to her.'

Damn. Now I'm going to have to come clean. 'Actually, it belongs to me. I know the designer.'

'Ooh.' She makes an exaggerated 'how fancy' noise and opens the book again and takes another look. 'You know the designer, do you? Well, of course you do.' She flicks through a few more pages.

77

She's clearly dying to find some way to object, but she can't, so she hands it over, saying, 'Make sure you're back here on time, and don't make a habit of swapping your lunches.'

'I won't,' I reply, and hurry over to the lift. I don't have a pass so I just wait and within a few minutes, someone comes along. I've seen him before; he's Asian, tall and handsome, with a penchant for gentlemanly clothes like three-piece suits. Today he's resplendent in a beautiful blue linen jacket, white shirt and knee-length shorts with sockless moccasins. I think he's Head of something, but I don't know what.

'Going up, girlfriend?' he asks, in a terrible approximation of an American accent. He smiles at me and I notice his blue contact lenses. Clocking the lookbook under my arm, he gives me a swift up-and-down look that I know is taking in every detail of my outfit.

'I hope so,' I say.

The sixth floor is just as I remember it; a glossy monochrome open-plan, lit by beautiful little green reading-lamps like ones in a library. It's much cooler than the rest of the building. I stride along, trying not to gawp at everything: racks of clothes here and there, mood boards on the walls, a girl dressed in skinny jeans and Converse trainers loping along holding a huge camera. Passing by the glass-fronted room where my interview was, I shudder as I remember what a mess it was. Will be. Hopefully won't be – a mess, that is.

Julia's office is at the end of the floor. She's gulping down some sushi, drinking a Yoga Bunny Detox and looking at her huge Mac computer. Her hair is in a French plait that goes all the way down her back.

'Oh, hi!' She looks blankly at me for a minute but then seems to remember and waves me inside.

'Here's the lookbook,' I say, advancing confidently. 'Let me know if you want to know anything else. Her contact details are inside, or I can just return it to her if you decide against it.'

'OK. Have a seat, why don't you? Just move those things off the chair – I'll take them.'

I lift a pile of For All Mankind jeans and silk tops off the chair and hand them to her. The room is small and messy, with piles of magazines and other lookbooks, swatches of fabric and portfolios strewn across her desk and on the floor. I notice a silver-framed picture with two small children on her desk. They're very young; no wonder she always looks so knackered.

'So this girl is a friend of yours?' she says, opening the book.

'Yes, I was in school with her. She graduated from the NCAD – that's in Dublin – a few years ago, and she's been working full-time for a knitwear designer ever since.'

'These are super,' she says. 'I love the colours. And you say she doesn't have a showroom, or an agent?'

'No, she's working out of her flat, in Hackney.'

'Great. Well, I'll definitely get in touch with her. Thanks, Zoë.'

'No problem.'

She closes the lookbook and smiles at me. It seems to be time to go, so I stand up and turn around. But when I see the glossy, buzzing office, full of people doing the job I want to do, I can't bear to walk around, so I turn back.

'Actually I had a few other ideas I wanted to mention.'

'OK,' Julia says, looking puzzled.

'I just . . . you know the brown Ikat dress that you were looking at the other day?'

She raises her eyebrows. 'Yes, I do. What about it?'

'Well, Keira Knightley's got one, and she's planning to wear it. And . . . those boyfriend jackets are really popular. I don't think they should be marked down, because I think we could sell a lot more of them. Also all maxi dresses – I think we could sell a lot more of those, particularly if we get them quickly, and in more colours. I mean colourways.'

Julia is looking at me, chopsticks in hand, half bemused and half amused.

'Run the Keira Knightley thing by me again?'

'Just that she's go – got one.' I was about to say 'going to wear one' but that would make me sound like a stalker. 'And we're the only place that stock them besides Harrods, so ours will definitely sell out, so we shouldn't put them in the sale.'

'How do you know she's got one?'

'Um – she's a friend of mine.' Oh, God almighty, did I really just say that? I did. I have no idea why. I just couldn't think of anything else.

'Really? How do you know her?'

'We, um, through mutual friends. I have a friend who runs a café. In Primrose Hill. And Keira's a regular there.' Where is all this coming from? I've never even been to Primrose Hill.

'I see.' Julia looks at me in mild surprise, obviously reassessing me. 'And you're backing the boyfriend jackets and maxis. Anything else?'

'No – except maybe that we might have a few too many bootleg jeans in. And I think the midi dresses are going to be hard to shift.'

She frowns. 'But they've only just dropped. Is this based on previous sales, or is it just a prediction?'

'Well, just a prediction really.'

I'm a bit hesitant to say this because I don't want to sound as if I'm criticising her choices, but she just nods and hooks a piece of sashimi up.

'Fair enough. It's always good to get feedback from the sales floor.' She points at the lookbook. 'Tell your friend I'll be in touch with her. The designer, that is – not Keira.' She smiles.

'Thanks. OK, great. Thanks, Julia! Bye!'

I hurry back out, catching sight of the big Swiss-style clock on the wall; it's exactly a quarter to one. How am I going to get back down in the lift? Luckily, a very tall girl lopes along towards the lift, accompanied by the camera-wielding girl I saw earlier.

'Bye, Agneta, take care,' she says, flashing her pass at the lift and waving us both inside.

I glance discreetly as we go down, noting her elongated frame and sky-high cheekbones, and think: this time last time, I was on the shop floor folding T-shirts. And now I'm in a lift with a real, live model! All I have to do now is wait, and pray, for my predictions to come true and I might have my own pass to this lift before long.

I've done my best to avoid checking my phone, but I'm very relieved to see that evening that I have a text from David. Not getting in touch with him is definitely working; he's making all the running now. The only drawback is what it says. 'Pub quiz tomorrow. Are you there? x.'

TEN

The pub quiz was such a nightmare that I really don't want to go through it again – but on the other hand, it is something I want to do differently.

Even first time around, I was dreading the whole thing for three reasons. First, it was a waste of a beautiful July evening, even if the Auld Shillelagh was quite a nice pub, with a high ceiling and big doors that opened on to the street. Second, I hate quizzes, and I was terrified of looking stupid in front of David's friends. Third, I would be seeing Jenny for the first time after my meltdown with David. But David loved his weekly pub quiz and I was so relieved that we were back on track after our row that I went along willingly.

When I arrived, I wasn't surprised to see that Jenny was already installed and sitting beside David.

'Hi, Zoë,' she said with a thin, quick smile.

'Hi, Jenny, it's lovely to see you,' I said, in equally fake fashion, wondering for a second if David had said anything about our fight and really hoping not.

David went to get me a gin and tonic, and as soon as he sat down again, she turned away from me and resumed the never-ending story about what her consultant, Roger, had said and done that day. We heard a lot about Roger, who apparently was the top vascular surgeon in the entire world and who, incidentally, thought Jenny was pretty great as well, much as she hated to admit it.

'He's just constantly stealing me for surgery. It's so embarrassing . . .'

As Rachel put it, Jenny gave a very good account of herself. I couldn't decide if she was attractive or not. I didn't think she had a pretty face, and her blue eyes were cold, but I did envy her thick, bouncy blond hair and her tanned skin – she was one of those people who went golden brown after half an hour in the sun, damn her. She also had a great figure from all her aggressive and expensive sports – riding, sailing, skiing and, of course, tennis, which she played with David almost every weekend. She often rocked blue shirts with the collar turned up, pearl earrings and deck shoes, but tonight for some reason she was in a knee-length black wrap dress. I felt a bit slutty in my low-cut peasant top and short shorts, not to mention totally excluded from the conversation.

'Did you hear about the Fergusons?' she was asking David now. 'They've just bought a house in Chelsea. Four mil. I was well jell when I heard.'

'They were neighbours of ours when we were younger,' David explained to me.

'I've seen a picture of it, it's amazeballs,' said Jenny.

Jenny was addicted to that kind of slang, like 'bez' for 'best mate' and 'appaz' for 'apparently'. And she never lost an opportunity to show me how well she knew David, how close she was to his family, and how much they had in common. Including this quiz, which Jenny went to every week with him, even though it was a long way from Putney, where she lived.

'We pretty much win almost every time, don't we, David? We've never come lower than top three. Don't worry, though, Zoë, you won't have to answer too many questions. Oliver's pretty good too. Oh, there he is.'

Oliver was heading towards us, unwinding himself from all his high-visibility cycling gear and juggling a pint of beer, a helmet and his bike's saddle. He was basketball-tall at six foot six, and already had a bit of a stoop from bending over the operating table all day.

'Don't worry, the cavalry's here,' he said, clapping David on the back and sitting down beside me.

'How was work?' I asked him, relieved that someone nice had arrived.

'Oh, just a few fractures. Nothing you couldn't have fixed yourself with a bit of training, Zoë.' He pushed his glasses up on his nose, and ran his hands through his dark hair. 'Now, let's kick some trivia butt.'

I liked Oliver. He wasn't gorgeous – his ears were a definite drawback – but he was funny and self-deprecating, always making cracks about orthopaedic surgery basically just being carpentry. *And* he'd spent a year in Nairobi, volunteering for Médecins Sans Frontières. Despite these great qualities, though, his crush on Rachel was still unreturned.

The questions were all impossible: even David and Oliver, who obviously prided themselves on their trivia skills, were flummoxed at times. There was a round on football (David was good at that) and a round on identifying flags (Oliver was very good on those) and lots of questions about obscure bands which none of us could get. I knew David hated losing anything, whether it was an opportunity at work, or a squash game or a quiz, and I really wished I could do something to contribute, instead of sitting there like an airhead.

By the time we had a break before the final round, I hadn't been able to answer a single question. Jenny, on the other hand, had answered loads. She sat back, looking smug, and yawned ostentatiously. 'Sorry. Bit of a ke-nackering weekend.' She took a slug of Diet Coke; she was permanently attached to a can of the stuff. 'I worked twenty hours straight, after a week of nights. Sometimes I wish I had a fun job like you, Zoë. Just to go somewhere nine to five, and not have to think – it must be brilliant.'

I opened my mouth to retaliate, but Oliver, who always tried to keep the peace, interrupted.

'The fact that we're all awake is a bit of a miracle,' he said.

'I'm not just tired: I'm NHS tired,' said David, who didn't seem to have picked up on Jenny's dig.

The guys then started talking about something else, but Jenny turned to me with a sly look.

'You know,' she said, 'I'm dreading David's parents coming over. I just know that after tea, they're going to drag us out for dinner, and drinks . . . it'll take me a week to recover.'

I couldn't believe she was rubbing my nose in it like this. I took a deep breath in an effort not to throttle her. 'That's nice,' I said, through gritted teeth.

'I have to see them every time they come over,' she went on. 'There's no escape. They're great, though, so friendly and warm . . .'

'That's lovely. You and David are like brother and sister, aren't you?' I said, thinking this would put a stop to her gallop.

'Not at all,' she said instantly. 'We actually lost touch after David moved back to Ireland, when he was twelve, but then we reconnected five years ago through Facebook. I knew that he'd gone into medicine too but then we discovered that we lived near each other in London, and we knew people in common, and were both about to start at the same hospital. Isn't that just amazeballs?' she finished triumphantly.

'Amazeballs,' I agreed faintly.

Oliver glanced at me, and I had a feeling that he was picking up on the tension.

'You're looking very smart tonight,' he said to Jenny, and I thought how nice it was of him to try and change the subject, because there was no other reason to compliment her. She was wearing a totally ordinary black wrap dress, probably polyester mix. If I held a match up, it would probably catch on fire, I thought longingly.

'Thanks,' Jenny said. 'I never bother with dresses usually but it was hilarious wearing it this evening! I got wolf-whistled at on the street when I left my flat . . . and then a man gave up his seat on the tube for me. Ridonkulous. Men are such idiots.' She smiled at David, who rolled his eyes at her in a friendly, teasing way that stabbed at my heart. Then she pushed him in a playful, possessive way, and he – I couldn't believe it – pushed her back.

I couldn't stand it any longer. An evil impulse took hold of me.

'That's so stupid!' I said, sympathetically. 'That dress is really flattering. You don't – oh, sorry. Sorry. Ignore me.' I pretended to be embarrassed.

'What are you talking about? He didn't think I looked pregnant, if that's what you mean,' Jenny snapped.

'Oh, I see. You mean he thought you looked attractive. Well, that's great.'

'Zoë –' David said, sounding reproachful.

The final round had a 1980s theme. To my relief I was able to answer two questions – Who sang 'Land Down Under' and what was George Michael's real name? – and felt so relieved that I wasn't being a total dimwit.

'Question nine,' said the compere. 'Which well-known Irish figure was kidnapped in 1986?'

'Brian Keenan,' said David.

'Yep. Brian Keenan,' said Jenny, patting David on the arm in approval. 'Put that down, Oliver.'

'No, no, it's a trick question! It was Shergar,' I said suddenly. I was reluctant to contradict David but I was positive.

'Are you sure?' said David, frowning.

'Positive. My dad is really into racing and I remember him talking about it –'

'So when was Brian Keenan kidnapped?' asked Oliver.

I didn't know.

'I thought it was 1986,' David said.

'Well, I was only born in eighty-five, so I can't say,' said Jenny. 'I didn't realise you were that old, Zoë.'

'Stop it, Jen. OK, we'll put down Shergar,' said David. 'Shh, next question.'

'And question ten, our final question this evening. Prince Charles and Diana, Princess of Wales were married in 1982 in Westminster Abbey. Who designed Diana's wedding dress?'

Everyone looked at me expectantly. Oh, God. The one fashion question of the evening, and I couldn't answer it. I could picture the dress – the original meringue – but I could not remember who designed it. Was it Caroline Charles? Or Amanda Wakeley? I knew it was something very English-sounding.

'Well?' Jenny asked me, with the patronising look that made me want to punch her.

'It was a woman, wasn't it?' said Oliver, surprisingly enough. 'My mum is a big Diana fan,' he added, in explanation.

'I think it was Caroline Charles,' I said uncertainly. Oliver obediently wrote it down.

'Oh, I really hope we got those last few questions right,' Jenny said, as we handed in our papers. 'It would be totes cringe if we didn't . . . Do you know who I saw today?' she asked David. 'The lovely Hilary.' She turned to me. 'One of David's exes. She's a nurse. He's dated quite a few nurses, haven't you, David?'

David rolled his eyes at her and said to me, 'Don't listen to her.'

'Shush, kids, they're reading out the answers. Hey, we're not doing too badly,' Oliver said, making notes on the back of a beer mat.

'Hopefully we'll make the top three,' David said.

When the 1980s answers were read out, I started biting my nails.

'Men at Work . . . Kenneth Clark . . . yes . . . yes!' said Oliver. 'We're doing well, team!'

'Question eight. Whose kidnapping caused waves in 1986? The answer is . . . Brian Keenan.'

There were the usual cheers and groans from all over the room. I was so mortified I couldn't look anyone in the eye.

'The Randy Registrars said Shergar – nice try, horse lovers.'

'I thought we put Brian Keenan, didn't we?' said Jenny. 'That was what you said, David.'

'No, we put Shergar,' David said. He smiled at me, as if to say, 'It doesn't matter,' but I was so embarrassed I couldn't meet his eye.

'And question ten: Who designed Princess Diana's wedding dress?'

Please let it be Caroline Charles. Please, please, please . . .

'The answer was Elizabeth Emanuel. An extra point if you mention her husband and collaborator: David and Elizabeth Emanuel.'

'Oh-oh,' said Jenny. 'Hashtag fail.'

At the end of the night, when the scores were all read out, we were hovering around the middle. We missed being in the top five by two points. In other words, thanks to me. I heard Jenny say quietly to Oliver, 'Well, we know who the weakest link is.'

'Don't be silly, Jen. We did fine. But we won't let those bastards beat us next time!' said Oliver, throwing a biro at the team beside us, which contained people he knew. She just shrugged, while I thought: how could David be friends with this bitch from hell?

Afterwards, when David and I were walking home, I couldn't let it rest.

'I'm sorry about the wrong answers.'

'Don't worry about it,' he said absently.

'I know, but I know you wanted to do well . . .'

'It's fine.'

This wasn't exactly the response I'd hoped for. We walked on in silence for a few minutes.

'And I'm sorry I was a bit rude to Jenny. It's just . . . I think she goes overboard sometimes on the humble brags. Don't you?'

'What's a humble brag?' David asked. I could tell I was on a bad track but went right ahead.

'It's when you're pretending that you're joking or complaining, but you're actually showing off. Like boasting about drinking too much with someone's parents, or about men giving you their seat on the tube.'

'She didn't mean it that way,' David said shortly. 'And why did you tell her she looked pregnant?'

'I didn't! I just misunderstood what she meant about the guy giving her his seat!' I felt entitled to a white lie.

David rubbed his hand over his face, looking exhausted.

'Look, I'm really tired. Can we agree to disagree? And can you be a bit more polite to her?'

I stopped dead. 'I *am* polite to her. She's the one who's a bitch to me! All the time, and you just ignore it!'

'Zoë, I was in theatre for ten hours today. I don't have time for this,' said David.

'Sorry,' I said in a small voice.

We went home together, and made up, but it was the second nail in the coffin.

None of that happens second time around. Jenny's face falls further and further as I give correct answer after correct answer – as many as I can remember, but not so many as to appear suspicious.

'Kenickie. Winston Churchill. Um, 1949.' Oliver is writing down the answers as fast as I can give them, and David is looking at me with incredulous delight.

'I never knew you were so up on your history, Zoë,' he says.

Jenny, meanwhile, is looking at me in disbelief.

At first, she makes an even bigger effort than last time, in order to outdo me, and gets very opinionated in the sports round. 'Germany. Definitely Germany. Spain won the year before.' But halfway through, she decides to act, instead, as if the quiz is beneath her. By the time we've got to the break before the 1980s round, she's completely tuned out, and is talking to David about consultants. 'Try and avoid him if you can. I heard he plays the Carpenters at top volume in theatre. For realsies.' She yawns ostentatiously, and swigs her Diet Coke. 'Sorry. Bit of a ke-nack-ering weekend. I worked twenty hours straight, after a week of nights. Sometimes I wish I had a fun job like you, Zoë. Just to go somewhere nine to five, and not have to think – it must be brilliant.'

'You'd love it,' I agree, giving her a warm smile. She looks confused; it seems to take her a second to work out that this was an insult. *The Rules* don't have any tips for dealing with horrible female friends, but the general mantra is to act carefree and confident. So I'm treating myself to one dig at her, and then I'm being super, super nice.

'The fact that we're all awake is a miracle,' says Oliver.

'I'm not just tired: I'm NHS tired,' says David.

'You know,' Jenny says to me, 'I'm dreading David's parents coming over. I just know that after tea, they're going to drag us out for dinner, and drinks . . . it'll take me a week to recover.'

'That's Irish parents for you,' I say cheerfully. 'You'll just have to get in training for it.'

'Uh – yeah, we will,' Jenny says, deflated. I smile at her serenely.

Oliver glances at Jenny, and then at me.

'You're looking very smart tonight,' he says to her.

'Thanks,' Jenny says. 'I got wolf-whistled at when I left work, and then a man gave up his seat on the tube for me. Ridonkulous. Men are such idiots.' She rolls her eyes, but she doesn't look quite as cocky as she did last time.

'They sure are. But who can blame them? Black really suits you,' I say, feeling like Mother Teresa.

It's very satisfying to see the disconcerted look on Jenny's face as she weighs up the possible value of the compliment against the pain of having to thank me. But it's even more satisfying to see the smile on David's face as he sees me being nice to his friend.

'Hey,' David says to Jenny. 'Guess who Zoë's new flatmate is?'

I see the look of horror on her face and read her mind: she thinks we're moving in together. As soon as David says, 'Max', though, she recovers.

'Max Taylor? Make sure he doesn't set your flat on fire. Remember the time he tried to melt sand to make glass, and all those little pieces of stone exploded?'

'Come on . . . he was eight.'

'Their kitchen ceiling was all black for weeks. How long's he staying with you for?'

'I don't know. It's a year's lease.'

'Probably the biggest commitment he's ever made in his life. You must admit he's pretty flaky,' she says to David.

'Well, is he going to pay the rent?' I ask, alarmed.

'Yes! He's not flaky. He's a bit too laid-back for his own good, but he'll be a perfectly good flatmate – don't worry, Zoë.'

I nod, unconvinced.

'Hey,' David asks me, 'how did it go with the designer that you were showing to work?'

'Oh – the buyer really liked the lookbook, thanks. She's going to get in touch with Sinead.' I'm so touched that he remembered.

'That's fantastic,' says David. He leans forward to give me a sideways hug, and kisses my cheek; Jenny looks away. 'That's going to raise your profile at work, isn't it?'

'I hope so,' I say. 'Of course it all depends, they might not—'

'OK, shush everyone. It's time for the final round,' says Jenny.

I'm on a total high as the questions are read out. I can't resist answering every single question I can remember, which is all of them.

'Question nine. Which well-known Irish figure was kidnapped in 1986?'

'Brian Keenan,' I whisper; David nods at me in approval.

'And question ten, our final question this evening. Prince Charles and Diana, Princess of Wales were married in 1982 in Westminster Abbey. Who—'

'Elizabeth Emanuel!' I'm so excited that I don't realise that I've actually whispered the answer before he's even finished asking the question.

Nobody seems to have noticed, but Jenny looks at me suspiciously.

'Hey!' she says. 'How did you know—'

Shit. I decide to ignore her and quickly say to Oliver, 'Actually, put David and Elizabeth Emanuel. That's her husband's name.'

'I'm impressed,' says Oliver, writing it down happily.

'She's cheating!' says Jenny.

'What?' The other two stare at her.

Jenny stands up, knocking her chair over. 'This girl is CHEATING!' she yells at the top of her voice, pointing at me. The whole pub goes quiet, except for Robbie Williams playing in the background.

'I am not!' I say indignantly. Although she does sort of have a point. The whole pub is gazing at us, thrilled at the prospect of some drama. David and Oliver are staring at Jenny, and at me. 'What are you talking about, Jen?' David asks.

'Catfight!' calls someone hopefully at the other end of the room.

'Well, this is a first,' says the compere, a short, no-nonsense older man. 'Talk amongst yourselves, folks.' He turns off the microphone and comes over to us.

'I *knew* there was no way she could know all those answers,' Jenny says to him, and turns back to us. She's bright red and so furious she can barely talk. 'She – she answered that last question *before* you'd finished reading it out. She's seen the questions before, or else she's been looking the answers up on her phone. I'm positive.'

'Hold on, hold on,' says Oliver. 'There must be—' But Jenny's already made a grab for my bag and is rifling through it.

'Jenny, stop it!' says David.

'Hey! Are you out of your mind? Give that back to me!' I start to pull it away, but she empties it out on the table, to reveal Hubba Bubba chewing gum, three different kinds of lip balm, my Oyster card and keys, wallet, notebook, Mac powder compact, some stray receipts, hairpins, a straw from Starbucks that came with a frappucino, my work ID and a flyer for a sample sale. My hairbrush and two lipsticks go whizzing along the floor. Oliver, bless him, gets to his feet and starts retrieving them for me. David is still looking at me and Jenny in shock.

'I don't even have my phone with me,' I tell her. 'I left it at home by mistake.' I hold up my hands. 'You can frisk me if you like, but I don't have any notes concealed anywhere. There's nowhere to hide them anyway, is there?' I'm wearing a fairly skimpy, tight, striped maxi dress from Splendid. David and Oliver's eyes run up and down me a second longer than necessary before they nod in agreement.

'Actually, I changed that question at the last minute. I was going to ask where they went on their honeymoon but I decided that was too obscure,' says the compere.

'But she answered it before you had finished! How is that possible?'

'I don't know, but that question was never written down, so—'

'It was just luck,' I protest, but Jenny's running her hands under the table as if checking for secret compartments. 'And how could she have known all that stuff about the Second World War? She works in a *shop*, for God's sake!'

'OK, that's enough,' says David sharply. 'You need to calm right down, and apologise to Zoë. We'll handle this,' he says to the compere, who shrugs and returns to the bar.

'Soz,' Jenny says, sounding like a sulky teenager.

I did not appreciate the shop girl comment, but I'm going to be the bigger person here.

'Don't worry about it,' I say graciously. 'It was just a misunderstanding. Why don't I get us all a drink?'

'You don't need to do that, Zoë. Sit down. I'll get a round in.' David goes to the bar, patting me on the shoulder.

'Right. Well, we've had a bit of a family handbag over there, but it's all sorted now,' says the guy on the microphone. 'Are we ready to hear the answers now?'

There's a bit of a tense silence at our table as we all drink our drinks and concentrate on listening to the answers and marking the other team's score. Jenny still has a very sour face and won't look at me. I almost feel sorry for her – but not quite.

'We are doing pretty well,' murmurs Oliver. David squeezes my knee under the table, and smiles at me with a strange expression in his eyes. It's almost as if he's seeing me for the very first time.

'And the results. In third place, We Live in Kilburn but Like To Pretend We Live in Maida Vale. In second place . . . The Teaminators. And in first place . . . the Randy Registrars! Terrible name, and you need to work on your esprit de corps, that's French for team spirit, folks, but you've won by a whopping ten points.'

Everyone starts shrieking. I put my hand over my mouth in genuine shock. I didn't realise I'd remembered quite so many correct answers.

'Excellent! Go team!' says Oliver, thumping me on the back.

'Congratulations to all,' says the compere. 'Up you come for your cash prizes.'

'Go ahead, Zoë,' David says. 'Collect it. You deserve it.'

I decide I may as well milk this moment for all it's worth, and I stride up with my head held high, feeling like Angelina Jolie collecting an Oscar. I return to our table and divvy out our winnings – £40 each!

'You're coming next week, right?' says Oliver. 'We have to make this a regular thing.'

'Yes, we should,' says Jenny, looking at me through narrowed eyes. 'Since you have such a gift for it.'

Everyone looks at me expectantly. Oh God. How do I get out of this?

'Um, OK, sure. I'd love to!'

Jenny opens her mouth to say something else, but David gives her a look and she shuts it again quickly.

'I'm really sorry about Jen tonight,' David says, as we walk home slowly together through the quiet side streets that lead to his flat.

It's a really hot night, and although it's nearly eleven, he's still in a T-shirt and I'm just in my maxi dress. 'She was being a total nutjob.'

I'm about to say something like, 'As per usual,' but I remember *The Rules* and decide to be gracious about it.

'It's not a big deal,' I say magnanimously. 'Maybe she's under stress at work, or something.'

'Of course she is! We all are. I was in theatre for ten hours today; I was not in the mood for her hysterics. I just don't know what got into her. But you were really cool about it. Thank you.' He slings an arm around my shoulders.

We're coming up towards the communal gardens near David's flat – one of those locked squares where only residents have the key. I'm so thrilled with how this evening's gone, I'm wondering if it might be time to implement another plan.

'Hey, we should go into those gardens some time,' I say casually. 'For a . . . picnic or something?'

'Yeah, sure.'

Hm. Maybe 'picnic' wasn't a clear enough euphemism.

'Have you got the keys on you?' I ask in a husky, seductive voice. 'Maybe we could go in and . . . take a stroll.'

The Rules aren't big on initiating sex, but they do say you can occasionally make a playful overture. Except David doesn't seem to realise that's what I'm doing.

'What, right now? Isn't it a bit late?'

I stop, and lean against the railings in a sexy, abandoned way. 'It's so hot.' I fan myself with my hand and add, taking the huskiness up a notch, 'Why don't we just go in and . . . lie on the grass?'

Oh, God. If he doesn't get the hint – or worse, if he does but doesn't want to do it – I am going to be so humiliated.

He frowns, and for a second I think he's going to ask me if I'm feeling OK, or something. But then a slow smile spreads across his face.

'Sure,' he says, looking delighted. 'Let's, ah, get those keys . . .' He starts rummaging eagerly in his pocket.

95

The garden's empty and dark – thank God. I scan the surroundings as thoroughly as any undercover bodyguard, and conclude that we probably can't be seen. We start strolling along the gravel path, and then on to the grass. David takes my hand. I shoot him a flirty, seductive look, but at the same time I'm looking up at the buildings and wondering if anyone happens to be into stargazing and have their telescope out. Or what if there are those security lights that flick on in reaction to motion? But then I try to put those thoughts out of my mind. *Relax, Zoë*, I think. *Think adventurous, seductive, uninhibited*.

'This is a . . . nice chestnut,' I say in my seduction voice, leaning against a huge, spreading tree. Then I kick myself: nice chestnut? He's going to think I have some kind of tree fetish.

But David doesn't seem to care. He pushes me up against it, pinning me to it with his body. He leans forward as if to kiss my mouth, but at the last minute, he starts kissing my throat slowly. Meanwhile his hand is trailing down from my shoulder to my back, and my hip, and then behind . . . It all feels so great that, to my total surprise, I'm getting quite into it. Just as long as nobody comes along.

Now he's reaching down and slipping his hand under the hem of my maxi dress, and sliding his hand slowly up my leg. I'm glad I wore a thong. Though obviously a shorter skirt would have been easier. But – do I really want to be someone who deliberately wears short skirts in order to have sex in bushes? Suddenly there's a rustle from behind us that makes me jump out of my skin.

'Oh my God! What was that?' I whisper urgently.

'Nothing. A cat or something.' David continues to kiss me.

I peer anxiously, but I can't see anything. Whatever it was, it put the heart across me, as my mum would say. Oh God! I can't believe I just thought about my mum. I'm not sure if I can do this.

'David, what if someone sees us?' I whisper.

'Oh, wow,' he groans. 'Say that again.'

Gosh. I might be mortified, but this is obviously really working for him. I take a deep breath and force myself to go with it. I repeat, injecting a lot more girly apprehension into it, 'What if someone *sees* us?'

This gets quite the reaction from him, and soon we're at the stage where, if someone saw us, it would be pretty catastrophic. And my dress is probably getting terrible tree-bark stains. But by now, I'm getting really into it too. I'm just praying we can escape without anyone seeing us. Not praying, obviously; I wouldn't ask God about something like this. Oh, for feck's sake. First my mother, now God?

'Are you OK like this?' he murmurs hoarsely. 'Or do you want to lie down? You can go on top.'

'No, this is good. This is great.'

It's a bit of a fiddle at first, but then we get the right angle. David is so incredibly strong; I can't believe that he can sustain this position, especially after working a fourteen-hour day. He's so turned on that it only takes a few minutes, which is just as well, because strong and all as he is, and though I'm fairly supple, you couldn't keep that position up all night.

David disentangles himself gently from me, and we both slide down and collapse on the grass. Wow. Maybe it was the hot summer night, maybe it was the naughtiness of being out of doors, maybe it's relief that nobody saw us – but now that it's over I decide: that was pretty darn hot. Even if Kira would probably think it was incredibly tame and vanilla, I'm proud of myself. And David is looking as if all his Christmases have come at once.

'That was unbelievable,' he says faintly, rolling over to face me. 'How did you know I've always wanted to do that?' He's grinning but looking really intrigued.

'Oh, have you?' I say innocently. I'm relieved, though: it doesn't sound as if he's done it loads of times before. For some reason, I've always been worried that his nurse ex-girlfriend was much more adventurous that me.

'Well, if anyone finds out, I'm straight off the garden committee, I'll tell you that.' He kisses my ear. 'You are hot stuff, Zoë Kennedy.'

'I'm glad you think so,' I say demurely.

ELEVEN

'That's so great that you're meeting David's parents,' says Rachel. 'When did he ask you?'

'Just last night. After we, um, went to a pub quiz.'

We're in Jigsaw in St Christopher's Place behind Oxford Street, having a quick look in the shops before going for dinner. Rachel needs a dress for, in her words, 'another fecking wedding' next weekend, and I am seeking the perfect dress to meet David's parents in. I can't believe he asked me . . . in fact, I still can't believe any of this is happening. Every day I expect to wake up and find myself alone in December, but it's still July, and I'm still with David. I stroke a pair of leather shorts, sighing happily to myself.

The other piece of wonderful news – which I'm saving until we have dinner – is that Julia loves Sinead's designs, and they're going to stock them in the store. What with meeting David's parents, and work success . . . travelling back in time is just the *best*!

'OK, I think that's me done in here. How about you?' says Rachel.

I shake my head, and we leave. 'Did you want to look in here?' I ask as we pass a shop that specialises in wedding-guest outfits.

'The bride has banned it.'

'What?' I had totally forgotten about this, but Rachel takes out her BlackBerry to show me the bride's stipulations for her guests' dress wear: hats, feathers or fascinators, and nothing from this particular shop.

'Jay thought it was the funniest thing ever. He said I should turn up with no hat, wearing their stuff from head-to-to.'

My heart sinks. This thing with Jay has been eating away at me. I wish I could warn Rachel that he's seeing someone else, but I have no way of proving it.

'So, he's going to the wedding, is he?' I know he's not, and I have to admit I'm asking out of pure divilment – or rather, I'm hoping that Rachel will see for herself that he's selfish and unreliable and break up with him, and save me from getting involved.

'No. It's such a pain. There's nothing worse than going to a wedding alone when you're actually with someone. You still feel like a spare tool and it's not as if you can take the opportunity to meet other guys . . .'

'How come he can't make it?' I ask as casually as possible.

'He has to work,' Rachel says quickly, sounding a bit defensive. 'He would if he could but I told him not to worry about it. It's all the way over in Kildare, so . . . anyway, will we try in here?'

'Sure.' I already know that Rachel's going to get a dress in this shop – a black cocktail dress – although I tried to persuade her into a pink one.

It's hard to switch off the work side of my brain completely when I'm shopping. As soon as we walk in I'm watching the sales assistants, wondering how long they've been on for and whether they get commission, looking at the range and the layout of the shop and wondering where they'd fit in in our store if we had a concession. Last time around, I just watched while Rachel tried things on. But I think meeting David's parents calls for an investment dress, bought without my employee discount.

'Oh, guess what else?' I say to Rachel, as I pull out a silk blouse to take a closer look. 'David's friend Max is going to take the room in the flat.'

'Oh, really? What's he like?'

'He seems nice. I've only met him once. Well, twice.'

'What does he do?'

'He's a neuroscientist.'

'Gosh. Is he geeky?'

'I'm not sure if geeky is the right word. He's maybe more eccentric than geeky.'

'Eccentric how?'

'Well – he just comes out with unexpected things. Like, when I interviewed him for the flat, he told me he likes to take really long baths.'

'Really long baths?' Rachel's eyebrows shoot up. 'What kind of a pervert tells you that in a flat interview? I bet he was trying to get into your pants.'

'Rachel, don't! I've got to live with the guy, and you're going to start freaking me out.' But I'm laughing.

'I can just see him now: you're home from a hard day's work and he's pouring out the bubble bath . . . lighting the candles and beckoning you in . . . putting on the Barry White . . . champagne's chillin' . . .'

'Rachel! Stop it!' We're both laughing like lunatics, and it takes us a few minutes before we can calm down and go into our cubicles to try our dresses on.

'Here, what do you think of this?'

I look out of my cubicle to see Rachel standing in front of the mirror in a knee-length black shift dress with a white trim. It does look good on her – a paper bag would look good on her – but it's the most boring dress I've ever seen in my life.

'Mm. I don't know. You look great, but what would your Bridezilla say to you wearing black to her wedding?'

'It's black and white. OK, I'll try on the pink one for you.'

She reappears a second later in the pink dress. It is even prettier than I remembered it: a really simple shift shape, with a fitted waist and an unusual pleated, sculpted neckline. It shows off her knockout figure, and the colour really flatters her complexion and pops against her dark hair. 'I love it,' I say immediately. 'It's perfect. You should get it.'

She looks dubious. 'I don't know if I'm really a pink person. And the neckline is a bit weird . . . How's your one?'

'It's pretty cute . . .' I step out, modelling a simple navy mini-tunic, very form-fitting.

'With what underneath?' Rachel asks.

'What do you mean? Shoes! It's a dress.'

She has a point, though. I decide to look for the most appropriate one I can find and settle on a wrap-over sleeveless coffee-coloured silk dress with a polka-dot print.

'Oh, that's only gorgeous on you,' Rachel says. 'Very neat and simple. And you could wear it again for weddings and christenings . . .'

I'm not so sure. Looking in the mirror, I feel like a forty-year-old version of myself.

'It reminds me of the dress Julia Roberts wears to the polo match in *Pretty Woman*,' Rachel continues.

'Where are you going with that comparison?' I ask, disappearing back into the cubicle.

'What about some court shoes with it?'

'I don't own any court shoes,' I admit. She's right, though. No point doing things by halves. I find a pair of nude patent heels – very Kate Middleton. When I try them on, the outfit is very smart, but somehow not really me, and the shoes are way too expensive. But then I remember David saying his parents were quite conservative. David himself is pretty formal – well, most of the time – so if he said his parents are conservative they're probably like something out of a Victorian novel.

Looking at the dress again, I decide it will work. I can picture it now: the four of us laughing together over our tea, me looking elegant with my hair in a neat chignon, David's parents exchanging approving glances . . .

'Are you getting the black dress?' I ask Rachel, hoping the answer will be no.

'I'm not sure. What do you think?'

'I loved the fuchsia-pink one. Honestly, it looked amazing on you.' I look at her, and focus all my powers of persuasion on her, going the extra mile that I didn't last time. 'You *have* to get it. I'm telling you.'

'Really?' Rachel holds out the black dress to examine it again. 'I suppose I already do have a black dress.'

'You've about ten of them.'

'OK, you're right. I'll get it.' I'm thrilled that I've persuaded her.

After we've paid, Rachel pauses to send a text. 'Who're you texting?' I ask idly.

'Just sending a picture of me in the dress to Jay. Showing him what he's missing this weekend.'

This is awful: I have to tell her. We head outside, and immediately put our sunglasses back on because, joy of joys, it's still sunny. We walk up Oxford Street, dodging the inevitable crowds, and take a left turn up towards St Christopher's Place. I love St Christopher's Place: it's like a little Mediterranean square full of shops and restaurants with a big sculpture in the middle, tucked behind Bond Street tube station. This evening it's packed with people sitting outside restaurants, wearing sunglasses. The roar of voices and laughter is rising up into the evening air, and altogether it feels like a Friday night even though it's only Wednesday. Carluccio's is hectic, but we manage to get seated outside after a short wait.

'London's a completely different place in the sun, isn't it? It's as if we're all permanently on holiday,' Rachel says, as we sit down, stowing our shopping bags under our table.

I look at her happy face and decide maybe I won't tell her. Not tonight.

'You know, I'm really glad you got the pink dress. It looks absolutely gorgeous on you.'

'Thanks,' Rachel says. 'That coffee dress is gorgeous on you too.' She picks up her menu and takes a look. 'Oh no . . .'

'What?'

'They don't seem to have the – oh, no, they do. Phew. I thought they didn't have the penne giardiniera.'

I've actually never known Rachel to have anything else when

103

we come here: she really is a creature of habit. When the cute Italian waiter comes to take our order, Rachel orders her penne and a half-bottle of wine. We're trying not to drink entire bottles between us these days, so sometimes we end up ordering two half-bottles instead, which somehow doesn't seem as bad. I decide to have the two-course menu but first I check that I can have a salad with my Chicken Milanese instead of potatoes. He says yes to that, but no to me having a free side dish of courgettes instead of a first course.

'Zoë, you're hilarious,' Rachel says, shaking her head. 'Only you could try and customise a two-course menu and get away with it.'

I shrug. 'I like things how I like them.'

The waiter arrives with our white wine; Rachel tastes it and he pours us both a glass. As I watch the golden liquid swirl into our glasses, I find myself wishing that my first encounter with David's parents involved alcohol. Does that mean I'm an alcoholic?

'Zoë?' I look up. 'Cheers!' Rachel says.

I decide to stop thinking about the forthcoming meeting with David's parents, and the dread of having to tell Rachel about Jay, and just enjoy the feeling of sitting down for a nice evening with my best friend.

'Oh, Rachel. Guess what. You know I told you about that girl who was in my school? The fashion designer?'

'Oh yeah. What's the story?'

'Well, they love her designs, and they're going to stock her stuff! It's all confirmed! I just heard today.'

'This is brilliant, Zoë! I'd say you've really caught their eye. Will this get you on the buying track?'

'There's an assistant buyer job coming up soon, so . . .' I hold up a pair of crossed fingers. Rachel holds them up, back.

'And things are obviously going great with David, too,' she says. 'Meeting the parents. Where is it all happening, do you know?'

'I think the plan is to have tea at the Connaught.'

'The Connaught? Oh, my God! He's like something out of the

nineteen-fifties. Sorry, Zoë, I didn't mean that in a bad way . . .
I meant in a kind of Don Draper way.'

Rachel looks sincere, but I feel a bit miffed; although she
approves of David as husband material, I sometimes get the
impression that she thinks he's a bit stuffy or uptight.

'Well, as a matter of fact—' I stop abruptly, wondering if I really
want to share this.

'What?'

'OK, you have to promise you won't tell anyone. But . . .' And
I lower my voice and fill her in about what happened the previous
night.

'No!' she shrieks. A couple of people look around at us, and
she lowers her voice. 'You wild things. Well, that's pinned my ears
back. Are you sure he's Irish?'

'Yes, I'm sure.' I feel myself blushing hotly. 'But promise you
won't tell anyone.'

'No? You don't think the Trinity alumni magazine would be
interested – or your mum?'

'Rachel, if you dare . . .'

'I'm only messing with you. Not a word. Though I must say
I'm impressed. He's obviously mad about you.' She forks up a
piece of penne, and asks, 'How often do you and David see each
other?'

'About once a week – sometimes twice. It's not much, but with
his hours and everything . . . I think it's pretty good going. Why
do you ask?'

'Oh, no reason. I just wondered.'

I decide to change the subject; I feel bad talking about how
well things are going with David – and at work – when I'm planning to break it to her about Jay. We spend a while chatting about
this and that, including news of mutual friends and family.

'How are Roisín and Ríona getting on?' I ask.

'Grand. Roisín's just been promoted to captain and Ríona's
working on a big story for the *Sindo*.'

Rachel has two older sisters: one is a journalist and one is in the army, and they're pretty competitive. They're both married and Rachel gets a lot of grilling over her boyfriends from them.

'And how's work?'

'Fine . . . busy. I've been thrown into the middle of a new case because another associate has just left, and I've no idea where all the paperwork is and can't ask anyone – especially not the partner, because he doesn't respond to emails, or the spoken word.'

'What a nightmare. What's the case about?'

'Oh, it's about who owns these oil tankers . . .'

'Oh!' This is the one she ended up winning! I just wish I could tell her, but I have to settle for saying, 'You'll be fine. I absolutely know it.'

'Thanks. Jay says I should use the senior associate more, which is good advice, so I'm going to.'

My heart sinks as she describes all the advice Jay's given her over this work thing. The thing is, he's not a slimeball all the time. If he was, it would be much easier.

'What is it, Zoë? You look really worried.'

'Nothing.' But I'm struggling with my conscience. This is one of the things Rachel was most annoyed about in retrospect; that he made an excuse to get out of this wedding in order to attend another wedding, with his girlfriend. Which had loads of work people at it. This was how Rachel found out about it; she was looking at photos of the wedding, much later, and saw Jay there with the other girl. She felt really stupid about it.

'Don't tell me. David's asked you to have a threesome?' She starts to laugh, but then trails off when she sees my face.

I start slowly, hoping to bring it up in a roundabout way.

'No, it's about Jay. I just . . . have you ever wondered if he might be, well, up to something?'

'What do you mean, up to something?'

'Well, that he might be seeing someone else?'

The waiter – a gorgeous, curly-haired Italian guy – chooses this moment to reappear and clear away our plates.

'Any coffees or desserts for you, ladies?'

'No, just give us a minute please,' says Rachel. 'Zoë – what are you talking about?'

'Just the fact that he's often sick for whatever reason. And he's often not free on the weekend. And your colleagues don't know you're seeing each other . . .'

She's instantly on the defensive. 'But he *was* really sick! I was just over-reacting when I couldn't reach him that time. And just because we're being discreet at work . . .' She breaks off abruptly, as if she's just thought of something. But then she goes on, sounding more and more upset, 'Just because things are going perfectly with David and you're off winning pub quizzes and meeting his parents and having sex in bushes, doesn't mean everyone else's relationship is a disaster!'

'Rachel! Shhh!'

The elderly couple at the next table are giving us a scandalised look: I'm bright red. The curly-haired waiter has just reappeared and also clearly heard. He gives me a wink, as if to say, 'Sex in bushes? Nothing wrong with that.'

'Can we have the bill, please?' I ask, giving him a look.

We're not the kind of people who storm out of restaurants – well, I might, but Rachel definitely wouldn't – but I can tell that she wants to storm. Instead, we sit in awkward silence while we wait for the bill, and then each pay by card. And then there's a problem with the card machine, and we have to wait a further five minutes, not looking at each other, while they bring out another one. As we leave the restaurant, I expect us to walk towards Oxford Circus station together, as we normally do, but Rachel says, 'I'm going to get on at Bond Street station. I'll talk to you later.' And she walks off, leaving me in the middle of the packed, laughing, bustling summer evening crowd with my dress in my bag.

It's the most awful fight we've ever had. And Rachel and I never fight.

It's so hot, I decide to walk some of the way home, to try and clear my head. As I walk along the side streets towards Edgware

Road, I keep wondering if I did the right thing. Now I've upset Rachel, and she still doesn't believe me. Why couldn't I have made up a better story? I could have said that Harriet got talking to a customer who dropped a hint, I could have added that she was buying Spanx, or something, and was really unattractive . . .

And then I remember something else. Harriet's house is going to be burgled. But when? I think it was just after my disastrous shot at the assistant buyer interview, which was on Thursday 5 August. Her grandmother's jewellery was all taken, and Harriet was upset for days afterwards.

I'll have to think of some way to warn her. I make a note of it in my diary, reflecting that this time travel business is getting more complicated than I could ever have – hah – predicted.

TWELVE

It's Saturday afternoon and I'm running around frantically, trying to get ready to meet David's parents, when my phone rings. I rush to answer it, hoping it might be Rachel, but it's my mum. I put the phone on speaker and continue to do my make-up as we talk.

'I won't keep you,' she says. 'Is it today you're meeting David's mother and father?'

'Yes, Mum, it is.' She knows well that today is the day, but she's trying not to make a big deal of it, and I love her for that. 'I'm pretty nervous, but I'm sure it'll be fine.'

'Don't be nervous! Sure, why would you be nervous?' she says. 'Just be yourself, and they will absolutely love you. What are you wearing again?'

'Why don't you Skype me in five minutes and you can see?' I throw the dress on, power up my computer and sign into Skype. Once Mum's called me, I put the laptop on my bedside table and step back to let her see. I trust Mum's judgement on clothes – she has great taste – and I'm relieved when she says, 'That's beautiful, Zoë. I love that colour on you. Was it expensive?'

'Um . . . no, not really,' I say automatically, crossing my fingers behind my back.

'And are you wearing stockings?'

'No, Mum! It's roasting outside. Why would I wear tights?'

'No need to snap at me, Zoë Kennedy. It might get cooler later

109

on. Anyway, I can tell you're busy getting ready so I'll say goodbye for now. Just be yourself and they'll love you.' She pauses and says, 'I'm so glad you've met a nice Irish man. Wouldn't it be lovely if some day . . .'

I know what she means: 'Wouldn't it be lovely if you and David ended up moving back to Dublin together?'

'Mum, we've only been going out for three months . . .' But at the same time I'm thinking, I hope some day, we will. After all, it's now 31 July – just over a month to 'break-up day', 4 September – and things are going really well.

I say goodbye to Mum, and continue putting on my make-up with slightly shaking hands. David's told me a fair amount about his parents. I know his parents are both from Dublin and his father was a heart surgeon, now retired. And his mother was the Dublin Rose in the Rose of Tralee beauty competition in 1974. It all sounds totally normal, but I'm so nervous. I just really, really want them to like me.

But it's more than that. I've branched into a new path now – there's no 'last time' to learn from and I'm on my own. I really, really hope I don't screw it up. *The Rules* are silent on the whole meeting-the-parents thing. The only relevant advice seems to be the bit where they tell you to walk tall and be a 'creature unlike any other'. I'll do my best.

I stand back, check myself over one more time, and add a vintage brown leather clutch bag that used to belong to my mum. I eased up on the fake tan – I don't want David's parents to think I'm a 'painted hoor' as my dad would say – but now I'm worried I look too pale. I have a moment of doubt: am I lamb dressed as mutton? But then I tell myself I'm just channelling Kate Middleton – and look what happened to her!

The closest tube station to the Connaught Hotel is Bond Street, though it's still a good fifteen minutes' walk. I suppose most people don't arrive there by tube. I've cut it a bit fine and I have to hurry through the huge squares with their green gardens and white houses at a slightly brisker clip than my shoes are really fit for. Though they seemed so sensible when I tried them on in the shop, now they feel very uncomfortable, rubbing madly against my left heel. As I walk up the steps of the Connaught, I'm trying not to limp.

It's one of the most beautiful and genuinely swanky hotels I've ever been in: all dark red velvet, polished marble, brass, dark wood and softly mellow chandeliers.

'Can I help you?' says someone, coming forward.

'I'm meeting some people for tea. Their name is Fitzgerald.'

'This way.' He leads me through what seems like acres of dark-pannelled, hushed, beautiful rooms. The carpet is beautifully soft on my aching feet, but the whole thing is strangely intimidating. It's not that I'm not used to fancy hotels – I've been to the bar at the Savoy, and to the Shelbourne in Dublin loads of times, and I've stayed in some nice places with my parents. But I'm very nervous, and wishing I was meeting the parents in a slightly more informal setting.

We enter a lovely room that overlooks the green square outside. At the end of the room, I see David with two older people, who I take a wild guess are his parents. They're almost engulfed in huge armchairs, and there are tea things in front of them – they must have arrived and ordered early, which doesn't exactly put me at ease. It seems to take months to get from one side to the other, and I feel smaller and smaller as I approach the table. But I remind myself of *The Rules* advice to hold my head high, and try and look as if I've just flown in from Paris (I presume they don't mean dishevelled and travel-weary).

I arrive at the table. 'Hello. I'm sorry I'm a little late.'

'Don't worry,' says David. He looks very handsome in a navy jacket over a light blue shirt and tie and chinos. I've never actually seen him in a suit or jacket before and I immediately decide this is his most knee-trembling look. Getting to his feet, he kisses me on the cheek, squeezing me discreetly on the elbow. 'Mum, Dad – this is Zoë. Zoë, my parents.'

111

I shake David's mother's hand, noticing that she is absolutely stunning, with David's green eyes and perfect bone structure. I can see where David gets his looks from.

'It's lovely to meet you, Chloë,' she says.

'Zoë,' David corrects her.

'Zoë, of course!' she says, laughing in a way that gives me a fleeting inkling that she might not be the brightest tool in the box.

'Dermot Fitzgerald,' his father says, in a commanding voice, shaking my hand with a bone-crushing grip. He's tall and thin, with a hard, tanned face and short, iron-grey hair. He's wearing a jacket and tie too and looks every inch the celebrated surgeon, accustomed to bossing fleets of doctors around and having nurses and patients fawn over him.

'Hi, Zoë,' says a fourth voice. A familiar voice.

I turn to my right, where concealed in one of the huge chairs – like a Bond villain or Dr Evil in *Austin Powers* – is Jenny. I'm surprised she's not stroking a white cat, or saying, 'Miss Kennedy, we've been expecting you.' I look at David, barely able to conceal my shock and bewilderment.

'I didn't know we'd be seeing you here today,' Jenny says.

How *dare* she? Before I can stop myself, I say, 'I didn't think I'd be seeing you either.'

'Oh, we always see Jenny when we're in London,' David's mother – Irene – says complacently. I stare at David, but I can't tell from his expression whether he knew about this or not.

'Sit down, Zoë,' David's father says to me.

I'd love to, but there isn't actually anywhere to sit.

'Take my seat. I'll get another,' David says, and goes off, leaving me sitting with my three new friends. I take my seat gracefully, being extra careful not even to cross my legs, but to lean both knees to the side as the nuns taught us.

'So anyway,' Jenny says, 'there I was, first day on the job, the consultant scrubbed out halfway through, and I had to finish it, never having done one by myself before!' She slaps her thigh with mirth.

112

'No better way to learn,' says Dermot. 'See one, do one, teach one.'

They continue on with the medical chat while I sit by, dumbly. I'm still in shock. How could David have brought her along to such an important occasion? Especially after what happened at the pub quiz? David's mother doesn't contribute either, but looks on, smiling placidly. She's very perfectly put together, from her little navy linen shirt and tan linen skirt, and her flat driving shoes that look more expensive than my entire outfit. She looks completely self-contained and is showing no interest in me whatsoever.

David rejoins us with a waiter carrying a chair for him, and sits down.

'I'm not sure there's enough tea for Zoë,' Jenny says, glancing at me sympathetically. 'We got through this pot so quickly. Will you order some more, David?' she asks him in a cosy, couply way.

She's wearing a striped shirt, pearl earrings, a pair of chino-type trousers and brown leather loafers. She's also lounging back, with her legs crossed. With my silk crêpe dress and court shoes, I look completely overdressed and not half as smart. Jenny and Irene's outfits say: I belong here. Mine says: I'm all dressed up for a big occasion. It doesn't say much for my fashion smarts.

'So, Zoë,' Dermot says, turning to me. 'Which hospital are you at these days? What department?'

'Um . . . I don't work at a hospital.'

'But you're a nurse, are you not?'

'No, Dad. Zoë works in fashion,' David says.

'But you come from a medical family, surely?' asks Dermot.

'I think you're thinking of David's last girlfriend,' Jenny says wickedly.

'Ah!' Dermot laughs heartily. 'Can't keep up with them.' Jenny cackles. I look sideways at David, but he's very busy pouring the tea.

Irene has obviously just caught up with the conversation and heard the word 'fashion'.

'What job is it you do?' she asks me, turning her head towards me slowly.

For a wild minute I'm almost tempted to say 'I'm a shop girl' but I don't.

'I work in womenswear, in a department store,' I explain. 'Marley's.'

Silence descends, while Jenny smirks madly.

'Really,' says Irene, looking at me in polite bewilderment. 'Do you work . . . on the till?'

'Well, sometimes.'

'Zoë used to work as a management consultant,' says David. 'But she's had a career change recently and she's aiming to become a fashion buyer. Which is really great.' He takes my hand and squeezes it, smiling at me. I look back at him gratefully.

'I wish I had a fun job like that,' says Jenny. 'Much more glamorous than being covered in scrubs all day – and all night.' She glances at Dermot, who beams his approval. I decide that if she refers to my job as a 'fun job' one more time I'll slap her around the head, parents or no parents.

'Ah, you young ones don't know you're born,' says Dermot. 'When I started back in the day, we had to do one on, one off – every second night was a night shift. And we had to do everything that came our way, from an ingrown toenail to a brain tumour. There was no ultrasound – you had to be able to diagnose someone from the end of the bed.'

I turn to look at David, but to my dismay he and Jenny are exchanging conspirators' looks. His says, 'God, listen to my old man bang on again.' Hers says, 'David, he was great in his day, just like you are.' Nobody catches my eye, so I look at the ceiling.

'Well, you work so hard,' Irene says. 'You're both great men for the work and for the books. David has always been a hard worker too, and very bright. Chloë, did you know that David got six hundred and twenty points in his Leaving?'

Wow – that is basically genius level. David mutters, 'Mum, we don't need to hear about my Leaving results again.' It's actually quite cute to see him act like a sulky teenager.

'And he played for Belvedere in the Leinster Senior Cup final.'

'Semi-final,' Dermot says, meanly.

David just grins and says, 'We were robbed.'

Jenny has obviously been thinking of the best way to add to this love-in and bring herself back into the spotlight.

'I think it's certainly true that doctors in your day, Dermot, worked even longer hours than we do. But on the other hand, for us, jobs are much harder to come by. Especially in a specialism like cardiothoracic surgery. I mean only 50 per cent of registrars like David will get permanent jobs as consultants.'

I didn't realise this. But I can tell Jenny knows what she's talking about, God damn her.

'Well, you'll just have to make sure you're one of them,' Dermot says to David.

'I will be,' says David in the calm, confident tone I love so much.

'When is this ARCP you're doing?' Dermot asks abruptly. 'Next week, is it?'

'Next Thursday. The fifth.'

'Do you know who's on the board?'

'No.'

'Austin might know, I'll ask him. Are you prepared? Do you know what you're going to say about fellowships and the rest?'

'Yes, Dad, I'm prepared,' David says, keeping his voice level with an effort.

'This is a yearly review registrars have to do,' Jenny tells me patronisingly. 'David is sure to do brilliantly, Dermot,' she adds. 'He's so talented. And his consultant really rates him.'

'But you're changing consultants this week, are you not?' says Dermot.

'Yes, I'm going to be working with a guy called Mark Kinney.'

David's father stops frowning and claps him on the shoulder.

'You'll be grand. Sure, he was born holding up his hands for gloves,' he says to Jenny.

'Oh, absolutely,' Jenny says. 'Some things are just meant to be.'

She looks at me with a smile as she says this, and I smile back, wishing I could smother her in her chair's fat cushions. What does she mean, anyway? Does she think she and David are meant to be?

'Well he didn't lick it up off a rock. But that doesn't explain his brother,' says Dermot gruffly.

'Oh, how is Conor?' asks Jenny, referring to David's younger brother, who I gather is a bit of a slacker dude.

'He's wonderful,' says Irene.

'Wasting his life away,' says Dermot.

'He has just finished studying Arts at UCD, where he got a two one degree,' Irene says impressively, 'and now he is doing work experience at RTE and is thinking of applying for a master's.'

'Work experience, how are you,' says Dermot. 'He's in bed half the day and in the pub every night, spending his father's money.'

I'm beginning to feel a real kinship with Conor. I bet he and I would get along great.

'I will never forget Conor at Christmas in the flat in Putney,' says Jenny. 'Watching out the window for Santa's reindeer. It was the cutest thing.'

'Oh, yes,' says Irene. 'That was a wonderful time, living in Putney, with Dermot working in Westminster Hospital, as it was then. Do you remember I used to take you children to Kensington Gardens after school?'

'Of course I do! That was so much fun!' Jenny coos. 'Do you remember the Round Pond, and all the little boats? David, do you remember that time . . .' She launches into some supposedly hilarious story about David trying to steal a motorised boat off another little boy. Dermot and Irene are loving it; he's practically in tears with laughter. I try to smile.

David turns to me. 'How was your week, Zoë?' he asks. 'Zoë's just discovered a new designer for her store,' he tells the others.

116

Irene immediately stops talking, as does Jenny, so that I find myself the focus of attention. I tell them about Sinead and the scarves, but somehow it doesn't sound as impressive as it should. I desperately try to think what to add. 'And we had a preview of some of the Christmas collections the other day. Lots of capes.'

They all look at me blankly.

'I got a beautiful sweater the last time I was in London,' Irene says. 'I just can't remember where.'

'Was that the chocolate brown one from MaxMara?' asks Jenny eagerly. 'It was just beautiful!'

'You've a great memory, Jenny,' Irene says, shaking her head. 'I never remember a thing.'

I look at her, thinking: is this an act? Or is David's mother actually quite dense?

'Speaking of good memories,' says Dermot. 'Did I tell you I bumped into Maurice O'Connell there in the Shelbourne?' And there follows a lot of reminiscences about someone who was a friend of Dermot's and Jenny's father or something.

I don't understand what's happening. How is this going so wrong? I normally get on great with people's parents. If only I could catch David's eye, it would be OK, but he's listening to the story of Maurice O'Connell. I'm feeling more and more invisible. I watch the waitress at the next table clearing up, wishing I could go out the back and hang out with everyone in the kitchen. I wonder if anyone would even notice if I left. I'm feeling so inadequate and beaten-down that I can barely be indignant at the fact that Jenny is here.

The medical talk is going on and on, about so-and-so who's retired and so-and-so who was struck off and someone's daughter who's just been made a registrar. Then, for a change, we talk about the Fitzgeralds' house in France, and their place in Wexford, and whether or not they should buy a flat in London.

'Would you rent it out?' I ask, just for the sake of saying something.

'Oh, no,' says Dermot. 'It would just be handy to have somewhere to stay, the odd time we come over, for the rugby or whatever it is.'

'Sure, you wouldn't know who you'd be renting to, in London,' says Irene.

Wow. They're talking about buying a flat in London, and not even living in it. It's a whole other world.

'So you're from Dublin, Chloë?' Irene says.

'It's Zoë,' David says again, under his breath.

'Yes,' I say quickly, grateful for the flicker of interest. 'From Blackrock.'

'Where did you go to school?'

I name my school, which gets a semi-nod from them. Obviously they know it, but I can tell it wouldn't be their first choice.

'And what does your father do?' asks Dermot.

The impertinence of the question knocks me sideways.

'He's retired,' I reply calmly. I'm about to leave it at that but it would be really rude, so I add, 'He was in construction.'

They nod and I see that satisfies them, because building means money. I feel sort of dirty having played their game – I should have said nothing – but it's too late now.

'We should have some of these sandwiches and cakes, shouldn't we?' Irene says. 'Or we'll hurt the kitchen's feelings.'

'Oh, I'd love some!' Jenny exclaims, sounding as if she's offered her an all-expenses paid trip to Hawaii. Calm down, I think. You got the gig. You're the first choice for daughter-in-law.

'Jenny, my dear, why don't you start the ball rolling.'

Jenny selects the tiniest possible cucumber sandwich.

'Nothing more?' says Irene. 'You certainly don't need to watch your figure. You work such long hours and then there's your tennis. Have you and David had a chance to play recently?'

'No, but we're thinking of training for the marathon together next year,' says Jenny.

If she uses the word 'we' in relation to her and David again once more . . . well, I probably won't do anything. I wonder how

Rachel is getting on at her wedding. I wish I could escape from the table of hell and call her, but I can't and anyway, she won't want to hear from me.

'That's a very fancy dress, Zoë. Are you going on somewhere after this?' Jenny asks innocently.

'No.'

I think a simple response shows her rudeness up more, and I'm pleased to see she does look slightly abashed. But when I glance at David, he's talking to his father about rugby and I don't think he heard a thing.

'Now my dear, you're low on tea, will you have some more?'

I look up, unsure if Irene is addressing me or Jenny, and tentatively hold out my cup. But she's pouring tea for Jenny. To cover my mistake, I quickly put the cup down and reach out instead for the mini Victoria sponge on top of the lazy Susan. I don't exactly understand how the next thing happens, but my bracelet, which is quite a loose one, seems to become caught in the lazy Susan. I then do something very stupid: instead of putting down the cake, and taking my bracelet off to untangle it properly, I decide it would be more discreet just to give it a quick tug. Next, I watch in slow-mo horror, as the entire thing, cakes, sandwiches and all, comes down with a crash, my bracelet snaps and the teapot spills all over the tablecloth and over Dermot's lap. As the crash happens, the whole room seems to go quiet, and then everyone starts shrieking at once.

'God almighty, I'm burned alive!' roars Dermot, jumping to his feet and hopping up and down. The front of his suit trousers are completely drenched.

'Oh no! I'm so sorry!' Terrified that he'll have first degree-burns, I lose my head and grab the nearest intact glass of water and hurl it at his lap, without thinking.

'Aaargh! Get away!' he howls.

'Oh no – I was just trying to –' Unable to stop myself, I start swabbing at Dermot's trousers with my napkin before he literally slaps me away.

'What's happening?' Irene is saying in polite bewilderment.

'I think Zoë's bracelet got caught in the cakes,' Jenny tells her soothingly.

I blush scarlet and start dabbing at the dripping table instead, trying not to look at all the drowned cakes.

'Hey, easy, tiger,' David murmurs, helping me mop up. 'Can't take you anywhere.' He gives me a reassuring wink, but I am mortified. The waiter has now arrived and taken over cleaning operations. Everyone stands around in stunned silence.

'Are you –' I ask Dermot tentatively.

'I'll live,' he snaps.

'You see, this is why I don't wear dangly jewellery,' comments Jenny to no one in particular.

The waiter stands up and asks, cautiously, 'Can I move you to a different table?'

'No. We're finished.' Dermot looks at his watch. 'I'll have to change. Irene, did you pack another suit?'

'I'm so sorry,' I say to him, again.

Dermot ignores this. 'We're meeting John Austin at six,' he says to David, blotting at his lap with a napkin. 'You should stay here and say hello. You too, Jenny.'

'David, I'm going to go,' I whisper to him, while his parents are distracted talking to Jenny.

'I'll walk you out,' David says, patting me on the arm.

I break in tentatively to his parents: 'It was so nice to meet you. Thank you for tea. I'm sorry again . . .'

'Not at all,' says Irene. 'Goodbye, dear.' I'm wondering whether we're going to kiss or not, or shake hands, but she turns back to Jenny.

Dermot seems to have recovered his temper somewhat, and he leans in for – a double or a single kiss? I make a quick mental calculation based on Dermot's age and background and decide he'll be a one-cheeker – but no. He goes in for the second just as I'm withdrawing, and then I have to lean back, and it's all just hideously awkward. Jenny's looking on in amusement; I don't even bother saying anything to her. As I turn to walk away with David, I hope I'm not limping too obviously.

As soon as we're in the foyer, I say, 'I'm sorry about the cake stand.'

He shakes his head. 'It's really not a big deal.'

I want to ask how he could invite Jenny, but after making such a fool of myself I don't feel I have the right.

'Are you OK? Is there something wrong with your foot?'

'Oh . . .' I look down. I don't want to admit that I'm wearing new shoes that are too tight. 'I twisted it at yoga this morning.'

'I told you yoga was dangerous.' He leans forward and kisses me on the forehead. 'Do you want me to walk you to the tube?'

I shake my head, not wanting him to see me limping. I decide to pull myself together and not be all miserable in front of him. He's being so good about my debacle.

'No. I'll be fine,' I say brightly. 'Look, you should go back to your folks. You don't want to be late to meet that consultant guy.'

'OK. Look, I'm afraid I'm not sure what our plans for the rest of the weekend are. Can I call you?'

'Of course.' I muster a smile and add a positive press release. 'But I'm out with the girls tonight, just so you know. Now quick, get back to your family!'

We kiss again, and I watch him walk away, seeing how his gorgeous swimmer's shoulders fill out his suit jacket. Then I turn around and start limping towards the tube station. God, what a mess. I tried to be a creature unlike any other: instead, I was just . . . a creature.

I go into Dorothy Perkins to buy a pair of flat shoes before getting on the tube. After the hushed calm of the Connaught, the bright lights, smell of synthetic fabrics and blaring sound of Rihanna is weirdly reassuring. I pick out a few things that catch my eye: a cute pink top with a bird print – bird prints are

121

everywhere these days – and a pair of very high blue suede platforms. As I head to the changing-rooms, I catch a glimpse of myself in the mirror, with my silk spotty dress. I look so ridiculously out-of-place – and it's also a reminder of how much money I spent on that outfit. I decide to forget about doing any shopping. I buy the flats and head home, reflecting that to the £149 for the shoes I can now add £15 for ballet slippers to wear when they hurt.

As I get the tube home, I find myself wishing that David had never even mentioned meeting his parents. And then I laugh. I mean, first I was upset because David wasn't inviting me to meet his parents; now I'm upset because he did. When will I ever be happy?

I dawdle a bit on the way back from the station, stopping to buy *Grazia* and a Frappucino. As I approach our building I see that Max is waiting for me on the doorstep in the sun, wearing a check shirt, jeans and sandals and reading what appears to be a comic book. The entire front yard area is covered in black plastic bin bags, boxes of books, and a wooden crate. I completely forgot he was moving in today, and I'm late to meet him.

'I'm so sorry! I lost track of the time.' I run up the steps to open the door. Max is staring at me, his comic abandoned: either I have something on my face, or I look way overdressed for a sunny Saturday afternoon.

'No worries,' he says quickly. 'I've been enjoying the sun.' He drops the comic into a cardboard box and starts hauling it inside. I attempt to pick up a crate to show willing, but I can't even lift it.

'Don't worry about that,' he says. 'That's wine. You can carry that if you like,' and he nods towards a small backpack.

'You have a lot of stuff.'

'I know. I've been keeping some stuff at my parents' place but they've put their foot down. Feet, I mean. My friend Gareth helped me drive it over, but he had to shoot off.'

'Mm.' I say. As I survey the garden, strewn with leaking black bin bags and battered cardboard boxes, I think: There goes the neighbourhood. I imagine telling Rachel about it and how she would chuckle – but of course, Rachel and I aren't talking. On top of the disaster with David's parents, this is not turning out to be the best week ever. At least I have a night out with Kira and her friends to cheer me up – except that I don't think it will be any different from last time, which takes some of the fun out of it.

'Well, here we are,' I say, dropping my horrible court shoes on the floor as we get inside. 'Welcome. Here are your keys.' I chuck them to him across the room; he reaches quickly and just about catches them. 'I need to get changed now but you know where everything is, don't you?'

'No, that's cool.'

'We can have the full induction later,' I offer. 'You know, like talk about bills, where all the shops are, etc. etc.'

'Sure.' He picks up a box and starts carrying it towards his room. I step to the edge of another box and look inside surreptitiously. It contains a pile of papers, a mug that says Mystery Spot: Santa Cruz, one bowl, one spoon, a half-empty packet of squash balls, an empty Pringles tin and a games console. Plus a DVD box set of *Buffy the Vampire Slayer*. I've never seen this but I hate horror films. Then it hits me: this guy, with all of his mess and noise and unpredictable schedule and guitars and computer games, is moving into my flat and there is nothing I can do about it.

I go into my room, change into tracksuit shorts and a T-shirt, and lie on my bed, flicking through *Grazia* dispiritedly. But I've already read it! Damn. Cheryl Cole is in hospital for malaria, Victoria Beckham is cheering David up after the World Cup . . . tell me something I don't know. Then I turn the page and see Keira Knightley, skipping down the street in Primrose Hill and wearing the Ikat print dress. To make things even better, *Grazia* have very kindly given the number of the supplier – who in turn will be giving our number. I shriek aloud and throw the magazine up in the air.

'You all right?' asks Max, outside.

'I'm fine!' I might have crashed and burned over tea with the parents – but at least there's still hope for my job.

THIRTEEN

'That was such a crazy night,' says Kira. 'I can't believe I thought he was cute. I mean, who wears sunglasses in a nightclub?'

It's around 12.30 p.m. on Sunday, and I'm sitting having coffee with Kira in Lucky Seven. I love Lucky Seven: it's an American-style diner on Westbourne Park Road, with red leather booths and chrome-topped tables and counters. And I love these hungover brunches we have after our nights out. But today . . . I don't know if it's the gloom about meeting David's parents, or the uneasy wondering when I'll hear from him again, but I'm sick of doing the same things all over again.

There is one difference. Last time, I was telling Kira that David's parents were over and that Jenny was meeting them and not me. She just said, 'Don't sweat it. I bet it would've been really boring.' I wonder what she's going to say when I tell her what happened this time.

'Two pancakes?' the waiter asks, balancing two plates. Last time, I ordered huevos rancheros, but then I was jealous of Kira's pancakes, so this time I've ordered them. It's a small victory, but I'll take it. Kira reaches out for them with glee. She's very careful about what she eats in general, but on Sunday she pigs out. It's a hot morning and she's wearing tiny denim shorts and a white racing-back vest, and looks a million dollars.

'I *love* pancakes,' Kira and I both say in unison, and then laugh at each other.

125

'Jinx!' she says, crossing her fingers at me.

'Damn! Do you have jinx in Australia too? I thought it was just an Irish thing.'

'Babe, we have everything in Australia. You'll have to come some time and see for yourself.'

'I would love to.' Australia is on my list of places I want to visit, and Kira's told me she'd love to take me around Brisbane, have me stay with some of her relatives on a cattle farm and generally show me the sights.

'So how did the whole meet-the-parents thing go yesterday?'

'Not great.' I give her a quick recap of everything, except the tea-spilling incident; I'd never hear the end of it.

'Wait a second. Jenny was there? That is way out of order,' says Kira. 'Why would he ask you to meet his parents and then bring another girl along? Is he trying to bring back polygamy or something?'

These are the exact same things I've been thinking – but now I feel I have to defend David.

'Well, she is an old family friend. They'd already invited her and he couldn't un-invite her . . . and her parents are dead, so his parents always look out for her . . .'

'Yeah, yeah, where's my violin,' says Kira. 'She is totally trying to get into his pants, and he doesn't even see it. Men are such idiots.'

I don't say anything, just pour more maple syrup over my pancakes. She might be right, but I don't like her criticising David; I'm the only one who's allowed do that.

'Yeah, well, I wasn't a model tea guest either,' I mutter.

Kira's phone buzzes with a text. She looks at it, frowning. 'It better not be that bitch Emma,' she mutters. Kira is currently having a war with one of her flatmates, which is ostensibly about what time they're all meant to take their shower, but is actually about the fact that Emma doesn't like Kira bringing strange guys home.

'It's Naomi,' Kira says. Naomi is another flatmate, a really nice

126

girl from Tasmania. 'She's asking if we want to take a wander down Portobello after this?'

I remember this outing. We had loads of fun browsing the stalls in the glorious sunshine. Naomi found a lovely cameo ring, and I found some cool antique sunglasses and a beautiful high-necked lace blouse, and then we went to the park and had a bottle of wine beside the lake. It was a really fun day. It totally took my mind off David last time. I just wish I didn't have to have my mind taken off him this time, as well.

'Sure. That sounds great.'

'Excellent,' says Kira. She spreads her arms. 'God, it's good to have Sunday off for once. I can't believe it's August already. All right, London! It's summer!'

She says this really loudly, and in fact she's almost addressing the whole coffee shop. Amazingly, people don't look grumpy: a couple with a kid smile and nod, and one guy lifts his coffee cup to her in a toast. It could be something to do with her skimpy outfit, of course, but I really think the summer's lifting everyone's mood.

'Brunch, shopping and the park. All in all, the perfect Sunday,' I agree happily.

I'm about to suggest that we pay the bill now and leave, when my phone rings. My heart jumps when I see it's David. I was so afraid that he wouldn't call at all this weekend.

'Just excuse me a sec,' I say quickly to Kira. 'Hello? Sorry – I'm just in a café – I'll come outside.' I squeeze out of the booth and stand on the hot pavement outside. The sun is beating down overhead from an achingly blue sky; it's going to be another scorcher.

'Hi,' I say breathlessly, shading my eyes with my hand. 'How are you?'

'I'm fine,' he says. 'Mum and Dad have gone to see some friends in Henley for the day, and I'm in Hyde Park. I wondered if you might like to go on a boat?'

'On a boat? What, on the lake?' I ask, before kicking myself. Where else would a boat be?

'There's a huge queue but if I join it now, I should have something for us by the time you arrive. Can you make it?'

'Ah, let me see . . .' I pretend to think about it. *The Rules* are very strict on saying no to a last-minute date, but I'm sick of *The Rules*. What good did they do me at tea? And I really want to see David.

'Sure. I'm in Westbourne Grove so I'll hop on a bus – see you in half an hour?'

I float back into the diner, beaming all over. 'That was David . . . he wants to take me for a sail in Hyde Park.'

'Aw, really?' Kira pauses midway through pulling on her plaid shirt over her tiny vest. 'But what about Portobello?'

'Another time?'

Kira frowns. 'Ditching the girls for a guy – never good, Zoë,' she says in a mock-stern voice, before adding, 'I'm just kidding. Go, sail and have a good time. And tell him that if he continues to bring Jenny everywhere with him, you'll kick his butt into the middle of next week.'

I try to imagine myself saying that to David, and I can't quite picture it somehow.

'Seriously,' she continues, 'he needs to know that is not acceptable behaviour. Give him hell.'

'I'll do my best,' I say, signalling to the waiter for the bill. 'I wish I had time to get changed though – do you think my outfit's OK?' I pluck anxiously at my ancient blue Penneys T-shirt, white H&M denim shorts and flip-flops, which I literally threw on before I left the house. I thought it was fine at the time but now I feel gross. 'I wish I had time to go home and change into something else – maybe a long floaty skirt, or a little sun-dress . . .'

'You look great! It's a boat, not a fashion shoot.'

'It's also a date,' I point out. 'Well, I suppose I can do my make-up on the bus.'

Kira puts down her coffee cup. 'Zoë, have you ever stopped to think about what David has to see at work all day long? He can probably cope with a fashion faux pas, or a messy bikini line.'

'But that's the point. Because his job is so gruesome, I think that's why he likes nice things so much.'

'If you say so.' The bill arrives, and Kira looks over it carefully, working out our different shares with the calculator on her phone. None of my other friends would be like that over splitting a bill, but I don't really mind it in Kira – it's just the way she is. She's saving madly to start her own personal training business back in Australia.

We pay the bill, and then Kira points me towards the right bus for Hyde Park. The sun's beating down; I'm glad I brought my sun tan lotion and sunglasses, though I could do with a hat. When the bus arrives and the door opens, I'm almost knocked sideways by the heat, and I feel practically glued to the seat as soon as I sit down. As I look out of the window at all the crowds drifting through the streets of Notting Hill, I think about what Kira said. I'm not going to kick David's butt – but I am going to try being a bit more honest with him. I'm going to tell him I felt left out yesterday. Not in a psycho way, but in a calm, rational, adult way. How hard can that be?

After the sweltering hot bus, the park is like heaven: green and gold light filtering through the trees, touching the grass and the tops of people's heads. After a bit of a trek, I arrive at the boat-house and see David waiting near the head of the queue, wearing sunglasses and a white T-shirt and chino shorts. He's the only man I know who can wear shorts without looking even remotely like a little boy.

The lake is full of people rowing or driving pedalos, weaving among the ducks and swans. It looks so incredibly cool and inviting, reflecting all the shade of the green trees. There are only a few tiny puffs of cloud high up in the deep blue sky. With a shock, I realise that this could be the window we had in the store at Christmas – or will have. I have to pinch myself yet again as I think: I'm *here*. With David. It's strange how quickly you can get used to a miracle.

'Hi there,' David says, giving me a quick kiss. 'Are you ready to hop aboard?'

'Yes! Thanks for queuing.'

'That's OK. How are you? Good night with the girls?'

'Yes – we just went out in Portobello.' I want to give the impression I was somewhere glamorous like the Electric; he doesn't need to know we were in a sweaty dive bar with a load of teenagers and alcoholics. But then I catch myself. I am going to be more honest with him. 'Actually, it was a bit of a dive bar with some pretty nutty people in it. We had fun, though.'

'Well, that's the main thing.'

I smile at him, thinking how crazy I've been to censor myself. I don't always have to pretend that I've been having glamorous nights out.

We've reached the head of the queue. We get our tickets and are directed to a little row-boat, bumping its nose against the dock. David jumps in first and holds out a hand. I don't really need it, but I take it anyway because it's romantic. As I sit down, with no mishaps, I think: Why couldn't I have been that un-klutzy yesterday?

'Are you a good rower?' I ask, as we sit down. 'Will I be needing this life jacket?'

'You just lie back and enjoy yourself.'

I lean back and turn my head and watch the green water slip by, sparkling hypnotically in the sun. We pass by two girls who are shrieking and laughing as they try to steer; they're basically going in circles. Then I look back over at David, his strong arms and broad shoulders flexing under his white T-shirt as he pulls the oars smoothly. I'm wearing my sunglasses, so he can't even see me ogling him. He's so cute when he frowns in concentration. And when he leans back, and when he leans forward . . .

'Where did you learn to row?'

'We used to go to Lough Sheelin in Cavan on holiday when we were young,' he replies. 'Me and my little brother would just hop into a boat and take it out among the reeds, and row all the way to the nearest town to buy sweets. Do you remember those marshmallow sweets that came in the shape of dolphins?'

'Oh, my God, yes! They were white. Were they called Flipper or Flippy or something? I haven't seen them in years.'

I smile as I picture a small blond David, rowing along through the reeds. It's such a lovely picture, and such an idyllic moment, that I decide I don't want to spoil it by bringing up Jenny, or the meeting-the-parents fiasco.

'Can I have a go?' I ask.

'Sure. Let's just get out of this busy bit . . . Or, wait. Actually, there's something I want to talk to you about.'

For a second I feel a cold shock; is he going to dump me, because of how badly things went yesterday? But, then I tell myself: Don't be paranoid. If you were going to dump someone, surely the last place you'd do it would be on a boat.

Just as he starts to say something, a pedalo looms into view; the people steering it are clearly not in control, and it's well on course to crash into us.

'Iceberg!' says David, and rowing hard on one oar, swings us around into safety as the pedalo people shriek. 'Land lubbers . . . God, look at those nutters swimming over there. Haven't they heard of Wiel's disease?'

He rows past a few other boats, then lets us drift to a halt under a trailing willow tree, and stows the oars. A few teenage ducks – bigger than ducklings, but still fluffy – float past. David takes off his sunglasses and leans back, looking into the distance.

'So. You know how Jenny was saying, yesterday, about how few consultant jobs there are for us?' he says.

I wish he hadn't begun with the J-word, but I nod.

'Well, it's true. They've trained too many of us, and not everyone is going to make it. Which is part of the reason why we have to put in the hours we do. It's partly the job, of course, but it's also all the extra things like writing papers and going to conferences and all that jazz.' He rubs his eye with his index finger. 'You know I'm starting with that new guy this week, and I'm going to be working flat out for him. He does operations on neonates – newborns. It's going to be extremely intensive.'

I nod. 'I understand.' Which is true.

David looks a little surprised that I haven't kicked up more of a fuss, but he continues, 'But the other thing that I'm going to have to do . . . and this is what I really wanted to talk to you about . . . is go abroad, for a fellowship.'

Wow. I know all about this, of course – but I didn't expect him to tell me about it today.

'I've applied to a couple of places. There's a great cardiac centre in Texas, and one in New York. I've already heard back from a place in Boston, and I didn't get in.'

'Oh. That's disappointing.' I never even knew he'd applied to Boston. And Texas! Since I can see the future I know he's not going to Texas – which is a relief. I'd much prefer New York.

He shrugs. 'I don't know what's going to happen with the other two places, but I'm hopeful. Texas would be fantastic, but so would New York.'

'I'm sure you'll get the one in New York. I mean, I'm sure you'll get one of them,' I correct myself quickly. 'When would it start, and how long would it be for?'

'A year. And it could start any time this autumn – as late as November, or as early as September. I don't know when I'll find out, but it could be very short notice.' He looks at me sincerely. 'But I don't want it to come between us. I mean, there are all sorts of options. I'll have some holidays . . . or you could keep me company for some of it. Or all of it.'

I stare at him, trying to get my head around the contrast between what's happening right now and what happened last time he told me about the fellowship. Last time, we were sitting on his terrace; David had suggested that I come over for coffee. I knew that coffee sounded ominous, but I only realised just how bad it was when he said, with no preamble at all, 'I've been offered a fellowship in New York. It starts in a few weeks' time, and it's for a year.'

I had shaken my head, unable to compute it all. 'What? Just like that, you're going to New York?' I wanted to say, 'But what about us?' but I knew deep down that after all my hysterics, and after barely seeing him for the past few weeks, we were no longer 'us'. And I also knew that he was doing the same thing I'd done to my last boyfriend Paul; presenting the break-up as an unfortunate side-effect of his emigration, rather than something that would be happening anyway, New York or no New York.

'Zoë?' David says now. He reaches out and takes my hand. 'You all right? I know it's a bit of a shock. But I think we can—'

'No, no,' I say, beaming. 'I think it sounds terrific.'

'Do you?' He looks bewildered; he was clearly expecting, if not tears and tantrums, at least a few more worries and questions.

'Of course! I'll be keeping my fingers crossed for you.'

'But would you consider coming with me? For a visit, or for longer?'

I smile at him demurely. 'Of course.'

'Great,' he says. He picks up the oars and starts to manoeuvre us out of our berth. 'Oh, and that consultant I was meeting yesterday – my father's friend – worked in the same place in New York, so that was why I wanted to meet him – though I would have preferred a drink with you.'

David's invitation, and his surprise that I'm not more discombobulated, has given me a boost of confidence. I am going to bring up what happened yesterday.

'It was nice to meet your parents. They seem lovely.' I'm uncomfortably aware that this isn't exactly true. 'I hope they liked me. To be honest, I wasn't sure. I felt . . .'

'What?'

'Well, I wasn't sure if they liked me. I felt a little left out.'

It's the most needy, honest statement I've ever made in my new-Zoë incarnation. I'm glad I'm wearing my sunglasses so he doesn't see how anxiously I'm watching him.

'Well, don't,' David says.

'Don't what?'

'Don't feel left out. Nobody was trying to make you feel left out.'

I can think of various responses, which include: 'It's not that simple' and 'What was bloody Jenny doing there anyway?' but luckily, David sighs, and speaks first.

'Look, I know my parents can be a bit sticky with new people. But it's not you, honestly. My father is . . .' He looks off into the distance towards the lake shore. 'Well, you've met him. He's pretty rigid, and he doesn't really know how to relate to people who aren't patients or other medics. And my mum kind of follows his cue. I wish they weren't so much like that, but they are.'

I really appreciate his honesty, and I've decided I'm going to be honest back.

'I understand. It's just that they get on so well with Jenny, and I can't picture myself having the same rapport with them, ever.'

He frowns. 'They do get on well with Jenny, but that's irrelevant. You were great. And anyway, it's what I think that matters, not them. Even if they disliked you – which they definitely didn't – I wouldn't care.'

'I wasn't great. I spilled tea all over your father.'

'Zoë, he's a surgeon. He's had worse spilled on him than tea, I promise you.'

I'm so relieved. 'Good. I did have a lovely time, and everything – don't get me wrong. But it's been a bit of a strange week. I had an argument with Rachel. Quite a bad one. And I don't know how we're going to resolve it . . .' I hadn't intended to tell David any of this, but it all just came flooding out.

'Yeah? What was the argument about?'

I'm about to tell him, when there's a familiar sound: the ring of his phone. 'Hold that thought,' he says, pulling it out. 'David Fitzgerald. Yes . . . I see. OK. About forty-five minutes – I'll leave right away.'

He looks at me, but I already know what he's going to say. 'It's an emergency. They need me to come in immediately.' He puts away his phone and starts rowing hard towards the boathouse.

'But you're not on call.'

'No, but the consultant doesn't really trust the registrar who is on call, so he wants me. What were you saying about Rachel?' He's rowing so hard now, he's out of breath.

I shake my head. 'It doesn't matter. Would you like me to call you a cab?'

'The tube is quicker. Thanks, though.' He gives me a grateful smile and I swallow my disappointment.

As soon as we reach the little jetty David gives me a quick kiss, vaults out of the boat and starts sprinting at full speed towards the park exit. I knew it was an emergency, but seeing him actually running really drives it home. It is such a pity we're not going to spend tonight together. But it's not as if David's some banker or lawyer; he's running to save someone's life. And looking pretty damn hot while he does it.

A woman at the head of the queue is giving me a strange look. I suppose it must be a bit odd to see a man running away at full speed from a girl, after they've been for a romantic row on the lake together.

'He's a doctor,' I explain. 'It's an emergency.'

'Oh yes, I'm sure,' she says politely.

I don't bother arguing with her; she obviously thinks I'm some deluded woman whose Internet date has just done a runner.

As I walk home across the park, it occurs to me that it would be so much easier in New York. We'd be living together; we'd see each other every morning and every night. I have a vision of myself at the door of our apartment, dressed in a big cashmere sweater over bare legs, waving goodbye to David before heading off to my own job . . . and then I have a vision of the two of us, this Christmas, together in Manhattan.

FOURTEEN

I'm standing by the till on Monday, chatting to Harriet about our weekends, when Julia stops by. 'Zoë. Just the person I wanted to see. Are you free for a chat today? Around twelve-thirty?'

'Oh!' I'm conscious that Karen is watching us. 'I normally have lunch at one – would that do?'

'I've got a meeting at one. I'm sure you could swap with someone else, couldn't she, Karen?' Julia asks her.

Karen is all smiles. 'Of course. No trouble at all. We'll send her up to you then.' As soon as Julia's gone, Karen turns to me and says briefly, 'Swap with Harriet, but this is the last time.' She's obviously dying to rap my knuckles, but she can't, because I'm only complying with Julia's request.

'Sure. Thank you,' I say meekly.

When I get to Julia's office, she's not alone: the nattily dressed Asian guy is with her. This time he's in a bubblegum-pink and green tweed jacket, bubblegum-pink shirt and a shocking-green tie. I don't even see what's going on south of his belt, I'm so dazzled. He's wearing brilliant green contact lenses today, instead of blue.

'Well hello, Zoë!' he says, getting to his feet and kissing me elaborately on both cheeks. I don't think this has ever happened at work before. 'How are you spelling that?'

'Z – O – E. With an accent.'

'Did you ever think of changing it so that it'd stand out more? Like Z – O – O – E – Y?'

Before I can tell him that yes, I did consider it before Rachel talked me out of it, Julia interrupts us. 'Zoë, this is Karandeep Sethi, our Head of Strategy . . .'

'Just call me Seth,' he interjects.

'So Keira wore the dress,' Julia says, beaming. 'And we've sold out in all the sizes, as of this morning.'

'And we love your friend's stuff!' he says. 'Gorgeous cashmere, gorgeous digital prints – and ahem! You forgot to tell us that her flatmate works at *Vogue* and they're going to feature them in the October issue.'

What? I can't believe Sinead never told me that. Though actually, I can. She's so vague, it probably slipped her mind.

'I've been keeping an eye on the styles you mentioned over the past week,' Julia says. 'The boyfriend jackets, and the maxi dresses have been flying out – and the bootleg jeans, and the midis, are sitting there. Exactly as you predicted.'

'Have you got a crystal ball, is what we're wondering,' says Seth.

'Well, not quite,' I say, feeling a little bit of a fraud. 'It was – just a hunch.'

'You obviously have a really good eye,' Julia says warmly. 'And now this dress on Keira Knightley – the footfall and press alone is just brilliant.'

'Friend of the stars,' says Seth. 'How long have you worked here again, darling?'

I'm on the point of saying 'a year' but I remember to say, 'Six months.'

'And what's your background?' Julia asks curiously. 'Where have you worked before?'

'I worked in Brown Thomas in Dublin all through college. In womenswear. And I did a summer at Macy's in New York, stock-taking.' They're nodding encouragingly: so far so good. 'And then I got a graduate job as a management consultant.'

'So what attracted you to that?' Julia asks. 'And why did you leave?'

It's the exact same question as she asked me in the interview. Back then, I made the worst possible reply: a ten-minute speech about how dull I found consulting. The interview ended quite soon after that.

This time, I give the right answer.

'I wanted to gain some really solid business experience, and the job gave me lots of insights into a range of different companies. But my real passion is for fashion, so that's why I'm here. I would really like to get into the buying side of things.'

'You go, girl,' says Seth. 'What did you think about our presentation on the autumn-winter trends?'

Where do I begin?

'I thought it was great! I loved the emphasis on tailoring . . . and the heritage trends, and all the lace. I think that's going to be huge.'

Julia nods. 'Anything you don't like? Or that you don't think will work?'

'Well, to be honest, I don't see maxis continuing into autumn,' I say, trying not to sound impolite. 'And capes – I don't think our customers will actually wear capes, or those long evening gloves. They're just not practical enough.'

'What about the Mad Men trends?'

'Yes, for evening wear, to a degree, but not so much for day wear,' I say, remembering all the piles of big, full skirts and 1950s-style dresses left unsold by Christmas. 'I think fedoras will be huge. And shearling on boots – but not so much on jackets.' I have a vivid memory of marking down a load of sheepskin aviator jackets.

'What will be hot in jackets, then?' asks Seth.

'Oh, down coats. Like, puffa jackets?' I restrain myself from saying that it's going to be a white Christmas. 'And also wax jackets – they're already huge this summer and they'll continue through to the autumn. I also think Kate Middleton is going to be a big style icon,' I add. 'And . . .' I have to tread quite carefully here. If I mention her actual engagement dress, they'll burn me at the

139

stake as a witch when the time comes. 'And she's big into the ladylike, Chelsea look. She wears a lot of LK Bennett, and she also loves Issa, so that's a designer to watch, I think.'

They're both staring at me, fascinated. I know it's partly because my predictions are ringing a bell, but also because I sound so utterly confident. But the next thing, Seth starts laughing out loud. I stare at him in consternation.

'Sorry,' he says, wiping his eyes. 'It's just . . . we're paying a trends agency several thousand pounds a month to tell us what you've just told us in about ten minutes. And quite frankly, I think you're more on the ball.'

Thrilled, I look at Julia, who seems just as impressed, if in a more low-key way.

'I agree – you really have a flair for what's selling,' she says. 'I don't know if you're aware of the changes that are taking place around here. We're trying to refresh our brand and our stock a little.'

'Drag ourselves into the twenty-first century, kicking and screaming,' says Seth.

'And we need people your age, who are in tune with what younger customers want. We're about to advertise for an assistant buyer job, for someone to work directly with me on all aspects of womenswear except footwear – accessories, everything. Would you be interested?' Julia says. She glances at Seth. He's frowning and looks less than convinced. I'm confused – I thought he really liked me?

'Of course I'd be interested,' I say passionately. 'I would love to apply.'

'Fantastic.' Julia gets to her feet. I presume our chat is over, but she says to Seth, 'What do you think?' He nods.

'I'd like us to do a quick floor walk together,' Julia says. 'You have time, don't you? We can explain to Karen if your lunch break goes over.' I'm opening and closing my mouth in shock, but they're already leading me out of her office.

'So, I hope you said thank you to Keira, when you saw her this weekend?' Julia says with a smile, as we go down in the lift.

'What?' I ask, startled.

'I overheard you saying to that other girl, that you went clubbing with Keira and had brunch the next day? Sorry, I didn't mean to eavesdrop.'

'Oh!' I see: she heard me talking about *Kira*. God. They're all looking at me curiously. I know that I should set her straight, but somehow I end up just fudging it instead.

'Yes. We went to . . .' I'm about to say 'nightclub' but then I change it to 'a private members' club.'

'Oh, which one?' asks Seth, looking up from his BlackBerry as we stop on the ground floor and get out. 'I'm in Soho House, and I love it.'

'Um, we didn't – Keira didn't tell us what it was called. It was sort of an unmarked door.'

'Any celebs there? I love a bit of celeb gossip,' says Seth.

'Me too,' says Julia. 'I spend my evenings wresting with sippy cups and reading *The Very Hungry Caterpillar*, so I have to live vicariously.'

They're obviously hoping for a fun story and I don't want to disappoint them.

'Well, Rob Pattinson was there.' I pick him at random, having seen him in *Metro* that morning.

'Ooh! With Kristen or without?' asks Seth.

'Um, without, I think. But Keira really likes him, and she introduced us,' I add randomly.

'Oh, what was he like?' asks Julia.

'Is Keira a good dancer?' asks Seth.

Oh, God. 'Um – he was lovely. Yes, she's great – she's really good at, um, tango.'

'Tango?'

'Yeah, she had to learn how to do it for a film, so she was showing us all. But she was sort of in disguise that evening, so no one knew it was her.' I don't know where all this bullshit is coming from. I really hope they stop asking me about this soon.

Julia says, 'Well, if you can give me an address for her, I think we should send a few more samples her way. Could you do that? You don't think she'd mind?'

'Yes, no problem.' How the hell am I going to find Keira Knightley's address?

'Let's just have a walk around,' says Julia. 'Zoë, what do you think of these Joseph dresses?'

'Um. Well, I think the black will sell really well, but we might be stuck with quite a few of those orange ones?'

I get the game now: we walk around, looking at various garments, while I give predictions, thumbs up or thumbs down. A couple of times I just can't remember, but most of the time, I can tell them pretty accurately what's going to happen over the next week or two.

'It's amazing, isn't it?' I hear Julia ask Seth, who nods.

Meanwhile, Karen has spotted what we're doing and is staring at us, her eyes practically popping out. Julia goes over to her, and Karen quickly puts her helpful face back on.

'So where do you get your ideas from, darling?' Seth asks me.

'Um . . . well, all the usual places,' I say evasively. 'Fashion blogs, just walking around London . . .'

'Well, great,' Seth says. 'Keep it up, darling. Keep walking around London.' He chuckles to himself.

Back at the till, I feel elated. I can't remember the last time people listened to me like that, or took me seriously or thought I had potential. An uncomfortable feeling is nibbling away at me – that I've just tricked them – but I push it away, and instead remember how Julia has actually asked me to apply for the assistant buyer job. I am going to make this happen.

By the time I get home, the adrenaline's worn off and I'm feeling quite shattered, but in a good way. I'm looking forward to sticking a ready meal in the microwave, watching some trashy TV and not talking to anyone.

It turns out I have company, however. The kitchen's been turned into a gigantic catering factory: every pot in the house seems to have been used and all the surfaces are covered in utensils, chopping boards, mysterious-looking dried chillies and packets of herbs. Max is there, taking a giant tray out of the oven. It looks delicious; steaming and golden and covered with cheese, and smells good too. I had almost forgotten about him; I'd half expected to see Deborah standing there, asking me if I'd had some of her milk (I never did, but she was obsessed with this, even to the point of marking levels on the bottle in pen).

'Wow, that looks really good,' I compliment him. I get my ready meal out of its packet, stab it with a fork and put it in the microwave.

'Thanks,' he says. 'I always thought I could make only three things: spaghetti Bolognese, Singapore noodles and Irish coffee. But now I can make enchiladas, too.' He licks his finger. 'I'm addicted to Mexican food and you just can't get it here.'

'Cool.' I stare at my meal rotating, waiting for the ping, my mind running over everything that happened today at work. I really hope all of those predictions will come true. Some of them must, at least. If not – I have wild visions of begging Rachel and Kira to go in and buy up a load of things I said would sell, and me paying them back with the money I earn from my promotion . . . My phone buzzes with a text from David. 'Hope you've had a good day. Are you free on Saturday? I have ticks to War Horse x.' I still get a thrill every time I hear from him, but then I remember: *War Horse* was the night he had to cancel because he'd been up all night operating. I decide not to text him right back yet, but to wait for half an hour, as *The Rules* suggest. They were written pre-texting, of course, but I imagine the same applies.

'Would you like a glass of white wine?' Max asks.

'Oh. I would, actually. Thank you.'

He pours it out carefully and twists it with a flourish – something that surprises me; I would have thought he'd be more into beer.

My meal pings, and after thanking Max again, I carry it into the sitting room along with my wine. What I'd really like to do is watch *Gossip Girl*, but I don't really want Max to tell David about it. In the beginning, David used to tease me about watching trashy TV, but I knew he found it cute. But then he started finding it irritating, until finally he said he didn't want to hear any more about *Gossip Girl, Come Dine With Me* or *Keeping Up with the Kardashians* ever again. I can't wait to tell David about what happened today; I could do with some good PR after my tea debacle.

'Good day?' Max asks, sitting down at the table behind me. I forgot how weird it is when you first share a flat with someone you don't know, and you end up having dinner with them as if it's some kind of bizarre date. I notice he's not using a place mat, and it's on the tip of my tongue to say something, but I restrain myself.

'It was, actually.' I don't really feel like talking, but it's our first night in together and he has given me some wine. 'I've been asked to go for this interview at work, and I'm pretty hopeful about it. How about you?'

'Actually it was great.'

'Oh yeah?' I say, flicking past the news and wondering if I could ever get into *Emmerdale*.

'I'm running the data from that experiment I told you about and it's looking hopeful. I think this is it . . . I think it's going to really come good.' He runs his hands through his hair, making it stick up at odd angles. Tonight he's wearing a T-shirt that says Les Savy Fav; it must be some obscure band. 'That's why I wanted to get a whole load of cooking done. I don't want to have to think about it for the next few weeks.'

'What kind of experiment is it?' I ask, idly curious. 'You're not doing horrible things to mice, are you?'

'No. Though I would, if I had to. There are some areas of research where there's no alternative. I think a cure for Parkinson's or Alzheimer's is a good justification for mouse lives. But I mainly run fMRIs on people . . . sort of brain scans.' He grins. 'You could volunteer yourself, if you wanted. It can be quite interesting.'

It's very tempting, but I need to find out a bit more. 'You can't actually see memories, can you? Like . . . if I had an argument with a friend, you couldn't scan my brain and see that.'

'No, no.' He puts down his fork and leans forward, his dinner forgotten. 'Although, different parts of the brain will be active, depending on the type of memory. There's a famous experiment where they took volunteers and asked them to recall a break-up. When they scanned their brains, the part of the brain that's associated with physical pain had lit up.'

'I can well believe it.' I put down my plate and stare at it, thinking about my break-up with David, and how sad Rachel must feel about Jay. Even if he is a sleazebag, she did really like him.

'So did you really have an argument with a friend?' he asks, forking up more of his enchiladas. 'Or was that a hypothetical example?'

I sigh. He's never going to understand, but I feel like telling someone anyway. He's not David, but at least he's here.

'Well, yes. Basically, she's seeing this guy who's actually cheating on her.' It's strange to be telling him something so personal, but having the TV on makes it easier.

'And you told her that, and she's annoyed?'

I nod, surprised that he's guessed.

'Yeah,' he says thoughtfully. 'It's strange. Nobody really wants to hear that kind of stuff. Even though she probably knows it's true. Want another glass of wine?'

'Yes please,' I say instantly. 'Though I usually don't drink during the week,' I add, untruthfully.

'Really? How do you get through to Friday?' Max asks, pouring me a refill while I ponder what he said about Rachel. I'm wishing more and more that I'd never said anything.

Hearing my phone again, I check it and find a message from Oliver. 'Zoë, pub quiz tomorrow – David can't make it but can you come? We need you!' Aargh. After thinking desperately for a minute, I text him back: 'Sorry! Working!'

'So what—' I close my mouth.

Max looks up from his newspaper. 'What what?'

I was about to ask him what he thought I should do about Rachel, but I stop myself. Why am I talking to my random flatmate about something so personal? And I need to be careful not to confide too much in David's friend.

'What – time is it? I'm going to call my mum.' I stand up, getting my plate and fork together.

'It's a quarter to eight.'

'Thanks. Here, can I give you my parents' number in Dublin? Just in case anything were to happen. I generally do that with my flatmates.'

He nods, and keys it into his phone obediently.

'Do you want to give me your parents' number?' I ask.

He runs his fingers through his hair. 'Um . . . yes,' he says evasively. 'Let me just, um . . . can I get back to you with the right one? They're changing it . . .'

'Oh. Sure. No problem.' This seems very strange, but I don't want to pry. I leave him watching TV and finishing his enchiladas, and go to my room to phone home.

Dad answers the phone, and we have a brief chat. He's had the full low-down from Mum by now, and he's mainly surprised that Dermot made such a fuss over the whole tea-spilling thing.

'And you say he's a surgeon? Should he not be used to a few spills?' Dad says.

'Well, yeah. I'm sure it'll be fine.' I don't want Dad taking agin the Fitzgeralds – he can be a bit overprotective of his little girl – so I gloss over it. Dad hates talking on the phone anyway, so after reassuring me briefly again he puts me on to Mum.

'Hello, my darling,' she says. 'How are you?'

'I'm fine . . . wait till I tell you what happened at work today!'

I fill her in on the floor walk with Julia and Seth. I'm explaining how Julia asked me to apply for the assistant buyer job, when Mum interrupts me.

'That's wonderful,' she says. 'Fingers crossed. Listen, Zoë, I've been thinking. About David's parents. What about sending them a little card to thank them for tea?'

'What?' I'm so discombobulated by the change of topic that it takes me a second to catch up. 'Really? Well . . . I suppose I could. Anyway, then Julia said to me—'

'And you could even quickly apologise again and explain you were nervous.'

'Mum –' I shake my head. 'Are you even listening? I'm trying to tell you something.'

'All right, go on. Tell me. Julie was saying . . .'

'Julia! Not Julie. I don't feel like telling you now.' I know I sound like a brat, but I don't care. 'You obviously don't think it's as important as David.'

'It's not that,' Mum says, which is a total lie. 'It's just that . . .' She sighs. 'I'd love you to come home and settle down with a nice Irish man.'

'Mum – I will. I will come home.'

'When, though?'

'In the next year or two. I've told you that. David wants to move back too . . . eventually.' I don't go into any more detail because, obviously, I'm not 100 per cent sure of David's plans. But Mum obviously sees him as my ticket home.

'I hope so. I was around at Breda's this afternoon,' she says, apropos of nothing. 'She and Aisling were going to the pictures this evening.'

Aisling is my cousin on my mum's side; she's the exact same age as me and got married last year, and lives ten minutes away from my aunt and uncle. I feel a bit guilty every time I hear about her and my aunt doing cosy stuff together, when I've left my parents alone without any other siblings to keep them company. So after Mum's caught me up on their news, I end up agreeing to send David's parents a card.

'Where do they live?' she asks.

'Shrewsbury Road.'

I can tell Mum is startled, but she doesn't comment on the

fancy address. 'Which would be their local church, I wonder? Donnybrook?'

'Mum! Stop it. You're being a total stalker. I forbid you to hunt them down at Mass.' In the background, I can hear my dad telling her much the same thing.

'I wouldn't dream of it,' she says, but she's happy that I'm sending the card so we part on good terms. I'm so worn out from our brief conversation that I don't get round to asking her advice about Rachel; it'll have to wait.

After I hang up the phone, I go to the kitchen to get myself a glass of water. There are ten neat little portions of enchiladas all stacked up on top of each other on the counter. The place is still a bombsite, though: red wine stains on the counter tops, trodden-in cheese on the floor, and he's burned my precious non-stick saucepan. My impulse is to march into the sitting room to ask him to clear up, but I can't: he's David's friend. It goes against my nature not to act right away, but I decide to close my eyes to the chaos, and pray I haven't made a massive mistake by letting him move in.

FIFTEEN

Over the following week, Max begins to drive me spare. He's perfectly pleasant, but he leaves a trail of destruction everywhere he goes. Every time he has a shower he leaves all the towels soaking wet on the floor or on the side of the bath, and worse, stubble in the sink. He eats endless bowls of cereal and leaves them hardening on the counter. I fill them up in water to soak, hoping he'll get the hint and wash them up when he comes in, but they just sit there. One night I'm woken up by what sounds like a massive rainstorm but is actually the shower going. At 3 a.m. Groaning, I turn over and decide to have a quiet word with him about it all, as soon as I've had my interview.

David is still working flat out, and Rachel's still incommunicado, but it means I can spend all my evenings preparing for the assistant buyer interview. I am so glad I can learn from the total disaster I made of it last time.

My first mistake was trying to look professional in my usual interview suit. Of course, Julia was wearing a casual summer dress. The interview kicked off with a few fairly straightforward questions, which I fielded reasonably well, but then it all started to unravel. Julia asked, 'So, Zoë. Can you tell me why we should employ you as assistant buyer, when you don't have any buying experience?'

It was such an obvious question, but I was totally floored by it.

I stammered, 'Well, I work hard and I learn quickly . . . and I really, really want the job?'

Julia looked politely unconvinced. Then she asked me about my background and why I worked for PWC, and I gave a similarly lame answer.

'And . . . which designers do you think we should stock here, that we don't already?'

Another obvious question I hadn't prepared for. Stalling for time, I said, 'Well, I think we should continue to stock a range – from the upper end of the high street, to couture—'

Julia interrupted me. 'We don't sell couture. I think you mean prêt-à-porter?'

'Oh, gosh, sorry. Yes.' I couldn't believe I'd made such a basic error. I knew the difference between couture and ready to wear; what was wrong with me?

'And which prêt-à-porter designers do you think we should stock?' she prompted, slightly less patiently.

I managed to come up with a few names, but I knew that I didn't sound very convincing. To my relief, Julia soon decided to put me out of my misery. 'Thanks for coming up, Zoë. We'll be in touch,' she said, practically bundling me into the lift in her haste to get rid of me.

It was like a guy saying he'll call you, when you absolutely know he's deleting your number. To my surprise, Julia was very nice about it, saying that she thought I had potential but wasn't ready yet. Karen, who knew I had gone for the interview, was over the moon.

As I step out of the sixth-floor lift on the morning of my interview, I think of how sick with nerves I felt last time. Now, I'm starting to feel at home and recognise some faces; the nice girl with the long wavy blond hair and the Converse, who seems to be a photographer; Louis, the menswear buyer, Hannah, the outgoing assistant buyer and, of course, Seth, with his rotating contact lens collection. 'Hi, girlfriend,' he says to me as I pass him, in a pale blue shirt and matching tie, with sharp navy shorts, glued to his BlackBerry as ever.

Julia is wearing the dress she had on last time: cute little gypsy-style smocked summer dress with blue embroidery, and some killer chunky flat tan leather sandals. I remember looking at those sandals in despair after giving a terrible answer, knowing that I'd blown the interview. *But not this time*, I remind myself.

'Hi, Zoë!' Julia says, in her friendly way. 'We're seeing a lot of each other these days, aren't we? Take a seat. Ooh, nice trousers – where are they from?'

'Topshop.' I've paired the coral trousers with my white silk Alexander Wang T-shirt, a chunky, metallic silver necklace, and a pair of black slingbacks from Kurt Geiger. I can't believe I wore a suit last time. For that alone, in fashion terms, I deserved not to get the job.

It's really not a hard interview. Julia kicks off with a few easy questions – who are my favourite designers? How would I describe our typical customer? Then she asks the question that floored me last time.

'You have a great eye, but why should we employ you as assistant buyer, when you don't have any buying experience?'

This time I've prepared a much better answer.

'Well, firstly, because I have shop-floor experience in this very store – I know who our customers are and what they want. I also have a lot of business experience from my five years working as a management consultant. And thirdly, because I will make up for my lack of buying experience with hard work around the clock. If I get this job, I will work so hard for you, I promise.'

I'm not exactly jumping on her sofa, but it's close. She smiles.

'There is a lot of admin in the job – do you realise that?'

I nod violently. 'That's no problem at all.' And I tell her about how I was in charge of the annual 'survey' at PWC, which involved chasing down and collating replies from about three hundred consultants and clients. 'I did it three years in a row.'

'Fantastic. So . . .' She looks down at her notes. 'Which designers do you think we should stock here, that we don't already?'

151

I pretend to take a moment to think, then I reel off my prepared names including Theyskens' Theory and Preen.

Julia blinks at me. 'What a coincidence! We've just been talking to them.'

'Gosh, that is a coincidence,' I murmur. Which it sort of is, right?

'What made you mention those two designers in particular?' she asks. She's leaning forward curiously, and for a horrible moment I feel like a fraud. But I give a fairly reasonable reply, about them representing the best of young British and European talent, and how Theyskens' is the new take on luxe classics while Preen are more experimental, and she nods.

'And now we're adding Irish talent, with your friend's designs. That was a really great spot, Zoë. And everything you said about the collection downstairs . . . It's only been a week but we're already seeing the things you predicted.'

I murmur something non-committal, trying to look modest.

'Why haven't you spoken up about any of this before?'

'Well, I've been . . . learning how the business works.'

'You can say that again.' She gets to her feet and shakes my hand. 'Well, Zoë, we just need to talk amongst ourselves here – but we'll be in touch with you very, very soon.'

I hurry downstairs and go and find Harriet in the quiet end of womenswear. The sale has now ended, and things have resumed their usual dead calm. I notice that she's wearing the same navy Maje midi skirt that I own, but I don't even flicker; I'm too excited about the job.

'What are you doing here on your day off?' she asks. 'Oh, no, wait! I forgot! You had the interview today, didn't you?' She drops her voice conspiratorially. 'How did it go?'

'I think it went well,' I say excitedly. 'She said they'd be in touch . . .'

'Oh, that's so great! Well done!' Her face falls. 'But it won't be the same without you, Zoë. I'll really miss working with you.'

'Hey, wait a second – it hasn't happened yet!'

'I suppose. Well, let me know as soon as you hear. I'm away this weekend with Mum and Dad, but . . .'

'Harriet! So you are!' I was so hepped up about my interview, I forgot about Harriet's burglary. 'Listen . . .'

'What?' Her round eyes are concerned.

'You're going to your uncle and aunt in Gloucestershire, right?'

'Yes! Zoë, how did you know that?'

I forgot that she hadn't told me. I shake my head, not quite sure how to improvise this. 'I just have a feeling . . . a strong feeling . . .'

'Yes?'

'That you might want to be careful locking up this weekend.'

'Really? How come?' Her eyes are like saucers.

I shake my head, deciding I've already said way too much. 'I don't know,' I continue, pretending to sound bemused. 'It just popped into my head. Bizarre. But it might be worth doing, anyway.'

'Yes! Oh my gosh. Now you mention it, the burglar alarm's been broken – I'll phone Mum and make sure we get it fixed,' she says.

I say that sounds like a good idea, and escape off home before I can become any more indiscreet. I really hope I've nailed the interview and got the job; once that's done, then life should become a bit simpler. I hope.

SIXTEEN

It's Saturday the 7th of August. I'm meant to be seeing David tonight, but I know that he's going to cancel around 6 p.m. I'm so ashamed of how I reacted last time; when I think of it I actually cringe.

'Hey, Zoë,' he said, sounding half dead with exhaustion. 'I'm really sorry to cancel at the last minute but I'm not going to be able to make it tonight.'

'Oh, no, David. Really?' I sat down on my bed, and looked at my reflection, all dressed up in my new midi dress with a sequin bodice and chiffon skirt.

'I'm afraid not. I did about ninety hours at work last week, and I had to go in again today and I just can't move. Do you want to see if you can find someone else to use the tickets?' he asked.

In the end I went to see *War Horse* with Kira. I could barely concentrate on all the puppets, I was so busy having angry imaginary conversations with David – and then wondering if I'd ruined things by being so clingy and unreasonable.

This time, when David rings, I'm already home from work and on the sofa, relaxing in a pair of shorts and a T-shirt, doing my toenails.

'Hey, Zoë,' he says, sounding half dead with exhaustion. 'I'm really sorry to cancel at the last minute, but I'm not going to be able to make it tonight.'

'Oh, no. Are you too wrecked?'

'Yeah. I did about ninety hours, and I had to go in again today. I'm lying in bed right now, eating Haribo sweets. That's all I'm fit for.'

'Ouch. You're the one who's going to be needing emergency services.'

'It's like nothing I've ever done before. We operated on a neonate yesterday – a newborn baby, with a heart tumour.'

'How did it go?'

'It was very tough. The parents gave us a bottle of whisky each,' he says quietly. 'Me and my boss. I just wish they'd held off a bit. We're not out of the woods yet, the recovery can be the most dangerous part.'

'Oh, David.' I've never heard him sound this shaken before. I feel awful as I think of the guilt trip I put on him before. 'You sound shattered. Don't worry about tonight, just get some rest.'

'Thanks.' He sounds relieved. 'I would ask you to come over, but I'm not really fit for human company. Also I need to try and get some sleep first, in case something goes wrong with my patient and I have to come back in.'

'The poor little thing. What might go wrong with him?'

'Her. We did a tamponade . . .' I wince as I hear David's explanation of the procedure, which sounds really delicate and dangerous.

'Sorry I didn't let you know earlier. You could have organised something else.'

'Don't worry about it at all,' I say, feeling incredibly virtuous and angelic. 'Why don't you give the tickets to Jenny?' I'm about to add, 'She often seems to be at a loose end on a Saturday night,' but I manage to stop myself for extra brownie points.

'Good idea, I will. How's Max?' he asks, yawning.

'He's fine. I hardly see him, to be honest. He leaves after me and then he's in the lab late most nights, I think. He's out right now, too.' I decide not to mention the fact that Max has been driving me crazy with his mess.

'So, the perfect flatmate,' says David. 'I must meet up with him

155

soon. Get a game of tennis in. Listen, I'd better get some sleep . . . but can we meet during the week?'

The old Zoë would have taken out her diary and said, 'Yes! When?' because she was so anxious to pin him down. But now I just say breezily, 'Of course. Whenever you like.' I don't even add, 'Let me know.'

After he hangs up, I give a sigh of mixed regret and satisfaction. I'm disappointed not to see David, of course, but at least I get to feel like the best girlfriend in existence. I've got a full programme of events for this evening: I'm going to have a bath, do my fake tan and wax, give myself a home facial, and then watch a DVD. I didn't bother doing any of my jobs earlier, since I knew I wouldn't be seeing David.

I've just turned on the water for the bath, when I hear my phone ringing. I dash to answer it, wondering for a crazy second if David might have had a second wind – but it's Rachel.

'Rachel!' I say out loud, before diving on to the phone. 'Hey! How are you?'

Her reply is drowned out by music, but I can hear the word 'over'.

'What?'

'It's *over*,' she says. 'I just confronted him . . . and he admitted it. You were right, Zoë. He has been cheating on me.'

'Really? Rachel, I'm sorry.'

'It's not your fault! And I'm really sorry I haven't returned your call. I should have called you earlier.' She sounds on the verge of tears. 'I should have listened to you.'

'Oh, no, it's OK . . . you didn't know. I mean, I didn't know either,' I add quickly. 'Where are you?'

'In Soho. In Floridita . . . it's where we had our first date.' She gulps. 'I'm sorry to be so pathetic . . .'

'OK. You have two choices. You can come straight here and we can drink vodka and have a fantastic night in. Or I can come and meet you in Soho and we can have a fantastic night out. Which?'

Rachel says something indistinct that sounds like 'boy moy'.

156

She must be out on the street now because I can hear cars and a siren. 'What, Rachel? I can't hear you.'

'I'm going to boil him in oil.'

I suggest to Rachel that she leave Floridita – the scene of the crime – at once.

'Go and wait for me in Bar Italia,' I tell her, pulling on my jeans with one hand. 'Get chatted up by some cute Italians, and you can have a nice prosecco and watch MTV while you wait. I'll be as quick as I can.'

I spend exactly five minutes getting ready: I pull on a tight, white American Apparel T-shirt, my most comfortable wedge heels, a slick of mascara and spritz of perfume, and I'm good to go. There isn't time to wax my legs, or do my fake tan, but it doesn't matter.

As I sit on the tube I find myself thinking about all the times when Rachel's rescued me or given me good advice. She was the one who strongly discouraged me from changing the spelling of my name from Zoë to Zooey. But she also encouraged me to quit my job and move to London, and let me stay on her floor for three whole weeks before I found my flat. When I ran out of money during my J1 summer in New York, and didn't want to tell my parents, she lent me $100 through Western Union. And when David had dumped me, she was at my place within an hour, bearing chocolates, magazines, tissues and a bottle of wine. Now I'm glad to be able to do a favour back. She'll probably just want to have a quiet drink, shed a few tears, and go home, but at least I can give her some moral support.

Bar Italia is full of the usual lively crowd of tourists, Italians, hipsters and randoms. I find Rachel sitting at the bar, knocking back Martini Bianco, talking to a very young but cute Italian guy in a leather jacket, who seems torn between admiration and apprehension. She's wearing her favourite black low-necked top, which is nicknamed the Charlie's Angels for reasons I can't actually remember, and jeans and high heels, and is already very tipsy.

157

'Zoë! Good to see you . . .' she says, hugging me. 'This is – sorry, what was your name again?'

'Gaetano.'

'Gaetano, Gaetano, of course. Gaetano has bought me a lovely Martini Bianco, because he is a gentleman. Unlike some people. People who lie, and cheat and lead double lives –'

'That's very nice,' I interrupt her quickly, beaming at her new friend and wondering what the hell she's been telling him. 'Martini Bianco? I've never tried it –'

'The thing is,' she says, 'as I was just saying to Gaetano, I wasn't even that keen on Jay at the start. I didn't want to get involved with someone at work, and I hated that he did something as dumb and dangerous as boxing. But then he grew on me. The bastard.'

'I know, I know. I'm sorry.' I pat her shoulder.

'I buy you a drink?' says Gaetano to me.

'No, you don't have to . . .' He insists, so I ask for a beer – my standard move when I don't want a guy to have to buy an expensive drink.

'What a sweetheart,' I observe, once he's gone. 'Though you might want to take his number and meet him another time, perhaps?'

'I just can't believe it,' Rachel says. 'I mean, I can't believe I fell for it. But how did you know, Zoë? Tell me honestly – how on earth did you know?'

'I just wondered – with all the absences and everything,' I say uncomfortably. 'But Rachel, remember, you're gorgeous, brilliant, intelligent, you'll meet someone else.'

Luckily Gaetano reappears just then with a Peroni for me.

'I agree,' he says, gazing at Rachel. 'Very beautiful.'

God love him, I think he's barking up the wrong girl this evening.

'The worst of it is,' she tells him, 'we work together. Did I tell you that? Can you imagine having to go into work, and talk to him politely about depositions and where is this file or that file?'

She continues in this vein for a while. Gaetano nods sympathetically, but his eyes are beginning to glaze over a bit. By the time Rachel's said how she *knew* that the girl's deodorant in his bathroom didn't belong to his sister, he's excused himself and gone off back to his friends.

Rachel doesn't even seem to notice. She's staring at the zinc counter and ripping her beer mat fiercely into shreds. The barman comes by, and cautiously picks up her empty glass. He's about to clear away her shreds but she puts a protective hand over them and gives him a glare.

'Men are cowards,' she says darkly.

He scurries off to safety, and I decide it's time to get her out of here.

'Listen. I've got a plan. Let's go somewhere really cool and have a great dance, and forget all about this.'

'Yes! Like where?'

'We could go to Popstarz or Freedom. Or The Edge.'

'Gay bars?'

'Well, it might be safer. Given the mood you're in. It's not that I blame you but you're being a bit scary.'

'Well, excuse me,' she says, sulkily. Then, more sincerely, she adds, 'Sorry, Zoë. You're my friend, my good frien' . . .' She shakes her head violently, and flings an arm around me.

'Rachel, how much have you had to drink?'

'I had a couple of cocktails in Floridita,' she says. 'And now this Martini. I haven't eaten all day. But I'm fine.'

'OK, let's get you some food.'

To my surprise she lets me buy her a pizza slice from behind the bar.

'I feel much better,' she says once she's finished. 'OK. Let's go dancing.'

The streets of Soho are absolutely buzzing with the Saturday night crowd of clubbers, gay men, tourists, hen parties, rickshaws and minicabs weaving slowly past the pedestrians. We pass by bars

159

pumping out music, and catch the eyes of a few cute guys going past. It's such a hot night, just barely beginning to cool down: everyone is wearing T-shirts, or little dresses and skirts with bare legs. The roar of conversation, laughter and music fills the air: it's like a giant street party. On nights like this, I feel a pang at the thought of leaving London – though, of course, that doesn't mean I don't want to go to New York with David. In contrast, Rachel is ominously quiet.

'I can't believe I fell for his lame excuse about that wedding!' she says, as we reach our destination, a funny little club on Wardour Street.

'Well, let's not worry about that now,' I say, guiding her towards the entrance. 'We're going dancing.' Luckily, the guy on the door used to do security at Marley's, and he waves us in with a smile.

'Hi, Zoë!' he says, earning us some dirty looks from the rest of the queue. It's nice to feel like club royalty for thirty seconds.

It's a pretty fun place: one-third gay, one-third touristy, one-third suburbia out for a night out, and overall a reliably good time. They're playing 'Stereo Love' by Edward Maya, which is one of my favourite songs of this summer.

'I love this song!' I yell at Rachel as we descend the stairs towards the downstairs club part. Then I remember the lyrics are all about breaking hearts and I look nervously at her, but she seems fine: she's not shouting or crying, but doing a little dance all by herself though we're not near the dance floor yet.

'What do you want to drink?' she yells at me over the music.

'Vodka and Diet Coke? But not a double . . .' I add, but she's already on her way to the bar.

I dance by myself for a while, then with a group of friendly girls. After two more songs, I realise Rachel's been gone for too long and hurry over to the bar, where I find her nose-to-nose with a scared-looking guy wearing a stripy T-shirt.

'But he knew I would see the wedding photos!' she's saying. 'Why would he take that risk?'

'Come on, Rachel,' I say, grabbing her arm. 'Let's go and dance.'

The music's now changed to 'Maneater', which seems to perk Rachel up.

'Maneater, make you wonk wonk,' she sings tunelessly. 'Becha wisha never metter at all!' A pair of very creepy-looking guys are dancing near her and giving her very appreciative looks. One of them is wearing a tank top and leather trousers and has a handlebar moustache: I can't work out if he's in fancy dress or if this is his usual clubbing gear. She starts dancing with them, doing super-sexy moves which make them completely overjoyed. The moustache guy starts lambadaing with her. His friend tries to do the same with me, but I dance neatly out of reach whenever he lunges at me. 'We're just here to have fun!' I yell in his ear, but he doesn't hear.

Rachel is going crazy now: whirling her arms above her head, shimmying her hips. 'She-Wolf' by Shakira is playing and she's doing the howling and everything: the guys are loving it. 'I'm going to buy *you* a bottle of champagne!' Moustache keeps saying. I'm thrilled to see she looks like she's having a good time. I haven't been clubbing in ages; it's a shame it took a tragedy like tonight to make it happen.

When 'Single Ladies' comes on I can't resist going through the whole routine, which I learned in my dance class the year it came out. Even though I don't do it *quite* like Beyonce, I think I do a pretty good job: I even get a bit of a crowd around me as I do the final crouching down bit, pumping my arms back and forth and flipping my right hand front and back just like Bey.

As I finish the final flip I look for Rachel, but she's not there. I'm worried: what if I lost her? But then I see her weaving around nearby. Her batteries have died, so we go and find a seat. The guys look bereft, and are wandering around looking for her.

'I think your friends miss you,' I say as a joke. Now they're playing Robyn, 'Dancing on my Own'. The lyrics to this one are really sad – it used to remind me of David – so I start talking quickly to cover them up.

Rachel doesn't seem to hear me. Instead she mutters something into her vodka, shaking her head.

'What? I can't hear you,' I yell over the music.

'I've realised something,' Rachel says more loudly.

'What's that?'

'Something very important. Project Rachel', she says with heavy emphasis, 'has been a failure.' To silence my protests, she holds up one finger. 'No. It has. It's been twenty-eight years in development and it's yielded absolutely nothing. Zero!'

'Oh, no, no. That's not true.'

'I'm going to start over,' she says, 'with . . . with Project Roxanne.'

'Are you? What's Project Roxanne all about?' I ask warily.

'Roxanne . . . is much cooler than Rachel. She does kick-boxing and extreme sports, and watches films with subtitles. She wears matching underwear and she's never scared of the partners in her firm, and she doesn't get messed around by stupid men.' She waves an arm around violently, almost knocking over her vodka and coke. Then she drains it in one swallow.

Rachel's friend with the moustache has spotted her, and he's been hovering ever-closer during our conversation. He's now right beside us, practically sitting on our laps. Rachel glances up and notices him for the first time.

'Hi,' she says. 'I'm Roxanne.' She holds out her hand, which he grabs enthusiastically. He doesn't let it go, but holds and strokes it in the creepiest way possible. To my horror, Rachel doesn't fight him off: she just sighs and lies forward on the table, pillowing her head on one arm, while the guy holds on to the other one.

'OK, Roxanne,' I said, getting to my feet and pulling her away from her admirer. 'Time to get you home.'

Rachel doesn't resist, but lets me drag her towards the cloakroom. 'Rachel is over,' I hear her say very slowly and distinctly. 'O.V.R. Over.'

'You're not over,' I reassure her, trying to hand over our cloakroom tickets, grab our jackets and keep an arm around her, all at once. 'You're only just getting started!'

'Thass easy for you to say,' she says. 'You're going to marry David and live in a ginormous mansion. I'm going to end up

162

living in a studio for ever. And in the bathroom of my studio there will only ever be . . . ONE TOOTHBRUSH.'

'Oh, come on,' I say soothingly, trying to put her jacket around her. 'You've had loads of toothbrushes in your time. And you'll have loads more.'

She just shakes her head. As I drag her up the stairs I can hear her muttering: 'One toothbrush' and 'Project Rachel' and 'OVER.'

Oh, God. How on earth am I going to send her home? It's unlikely a cab will take her in this condition. I'd better sober her up first, then take her home with me. There's a bit of a panic when Rachel thinks she doesn't have her jacket, and I have to remind her that it's on her, but finally we reach the top of the stairs and stumble out on to Wardour Street. Rachel seems perked up by the bright lights and loud groups of merrymakers. She turns to me with shining eyes, as if she's just had another major revelation.

'Chips! Less get chips!'

That's actually not a bad plan. Some food might do her good.

'Chips, good idea,' I say. 'Let's see, now, where we can get them. Not here, I don't think – maybe more towards Cambridge Circus . . .' With Rachel still clinging to me, we hobble together across the street like a three-legged race while I wonder how feasible this whole chips expedition is going to be – not to mention how we're going to get home.

'Rachel, you know, it might be hard to find chips,' I suggest. 'I could make us some toast, at home?'

'I want chips,' she says distinctly. 'I bet there's some this way.' And she turns around and starts marching unsteadily up the other direction, towards Oxford Street, where there are definitely not going to be any chips. I pull her back the other way, and she turns obediently, but then the next minute, she changes her mind again, and sits down. On the side of the street.

'Lesh just wait here for a while,' she says, pillowing her head on her arms.

'Oh, no Rachel, we can't sit in the street . . .'

'My feets sore.' She holds out one foot.

Great. How on earth am I going to make her move now? I'm just thinking that I'm going to have to call a minicab to come and get us here, when I see a tall silhouette topped with a brown mop of hair, walking along on the other side of the street.

'God, it's Max.'

I instantly turn around, hoping he doesn't see us. Unfortunately, Rachel immediately starts yelling, 'Max! Hey, Max!'

'Shush! Rachel, stop!' I say, but it's too late: he's heard us, as have most people in the street. He crosses over the road. He looks different tonight, somehow, but I'm too distracted to think how.

'This is my friend Rachel,' I explain, pointing downwards. 'Rachel – this is Max. My new flatmate.'

'Hiya,' says Rachel, still sitting as Max shakes her hand. 'I've heard a lot about you,' she says, and then dissolves into giggles. 'Bloop, bloop, bloop . . .' Now she's miming being in the bath. I look at him helplessly, then back down at her. How the hell did she get so fluthered? Her friend with the moustache must have been slipping her extra drinks, or something.

'Everything all right here?' says a voice. It's a police officer. Two police officers. Or rather, it's one copper and one Community Support person, both in high-vis jackets.

'Yep, everything's fine,' Max says calmly. 'We're going home now.'

'Can you get up, please, miss?' the policewoman asks. 'You can't sit in the road like that.'

'No, thanksh,' says Rachel.

'Rachel, come on!' I'm getting seriously worried: the last thing Rachel needs is to give back chat to a police officer.

'Miss, if you don't get up, we're going to have to pull you up,' says the Community Support person. Rachel just shrugs.

'Come *on*, Rachel,' I hiss. I try to pull her up by her arm, but she shakes me off.

Max crouches down by her side. 'Hey, Rachel,' he says warmly. 'How's it going?'

'Mff,' she says.

'Zoë and I are going to get some chips now. Will you come with us?'

He holds out a hand and, magically, she takes it and gets to her feet. I shoot him a grateful look.

'We'll look after her,' I say to the policewoman. 'I promise. She's never normally like this.'

'Make sure you do,' one of them says, and they wait while we hobble down the street, with Rachel in between us.

'I was meant to be seeing my boyfriend tonight,' Rachel confides to Max, as we limp along. 'But he has a girlfriend.'

'That sucks,' says Max.

Oh, God, Rachel, I think. Please don't start telling Max all about your love life.

'He must be an idiot,' Max adds. Which is sweet of him, considering the state of Rachel this evening.

'Where were you this evening, Max?' I ask, in a bright, conversation-making way, over Rachel's head. 'Were you at a club, or . . .'

'I was at the best gig I've ever been to in my life. But you probably haven't heard of them . . . Man or Astro-man.'

I shake my head. We've reached Charing Cross Road now, where I really hope we can get a taxi if any of them is foolish enough to take us.

'They're sort of surf punk rock and they have this whole thing where they're meant to be descended from space, and they create clones, and the clones are doing gigs. It's hard to explain but they're just . . . awesome.'

I nod distractedly, but I can't really concentrate. I walk to the edge of the road and try and see if there are any cabs approaching. As I do, I try and think: who else do I know who uses the word 'awesome'? Oh, I know. Kira.

'I don't feel very well,' Rachel says. I turn around: she looks deathly pale and has her hand to her mouth. Before I can even react, Max has brought her to the side of the road where – oh dear – she starts getting sick. He even holds her hair. This makes me feel quite guilty, because that's my job. Though I don't have any massive urge to take over from him.

Spotting a newsagent, I run inside and buy some water, tissues and mints and we help Rachel clean up before leaving the scene of the crime and walking 100 yards up the road, where we hail a cab. Or rather, I hail a cab while Max stays a few feet back with Rachel, and we spring her on the cab driver at the last minute.

'I don't want no sick in my car,' the driver says dubiously.

'She's fine,' Max says, helping me bundle Rachel inside. She's so unwieldy that it is actually very helpful having him here with us.

'I'm embarrassed,' Rachel mutters as we drive away.

'Don't be! It's OK!' I say, patting her head.

'But . . . I'm an experienced drinker,' she says, almost to herself. 'How did this happen?'

Rachel slumps back in her seat, eyes closed, and I see Max looking at me over her head. He smiles, and I have to smile back: it is quite funny. I've just realised what's different about him this evening; he's not wearing a baggy T-shirt, but a much more flattering slim-fitted grey shirt. And he's had a haircut. It's an improvement, even if he is still wearing the same pair of jeans and the same basketball shoes – I think he only has one pair of each.

As we swing around a corner, Rachel opens her eyes and turns towards Max, as if she's noticing him for the first time. 'Sorry. Who are you again?'

'I'm Max.'

'Max. Thass nice name.'

'Thanks. My sister Sarah was three when I was born, and she was very into the book, *Where the Wild Things Are*. So she asked my parents if they would call me Max, after the little boy in the book, and they said yes.'

'Oh, how sweet.'

'Yeah, I suppose I'm lucky it wasn't Paddington.'

Rachel's already fallen asleep. She has always been able to do this, even when she's sober: it's astonishing. I've lost count of the number of times I've been mid-conversation with her while we're staying in the same room, and she's just conked out.

'So do you have just the one sister?' I ask Max. 'Where does she live?' I feel bad that I've never asked him about his family before.

'I have two. My older sister Sarah lives in York. She works as an archivist for the city council and she's big into the historical re-enactment scene – you know, where they dress up as people from the English Civil War?'

'Oh.' I had no idea there were such things.

'And Lucy is my younger sister. She's just finished university at Bristol and she's in Thailand right now, doing a diving course. That's her story, anyway.' From his smile, I can tell that she's his favourite sister, and that she's probably getting up to more than diving.

Rachel mutters something, and her head flops on to Max's shoulder.

'Sorry about all this,' I whisper. 'I've honestly never seen her like this, even in college.'

'It's no big deal.'

We ride along in silence, listening to James Blunt on the taxi driver's radio. I really hope Max doesn't tell David about tonight. Obviously David likes a drink, and got up to all sorts of crazy things in his medical student days – I've heard him mention plugging himself into an IV drip to deal with a hangover. But I am glad he didn't run into us this evening. I'm sure he would have been fine with it, but I would have been mortified.

'Zoë.' Max's voice has startled me out of my thoughts. 'Am I getting on your nerves in the flat?'

'Huh? What do you mean?'

'It seems like you've been getting annoyed over something. I can tell I must be doing something wrong, but I'm not sure what.'

Where to begin?

'Well . . .'

'OK, so there is something.'

'Well, for a start, I wish you wouldn't leave your towels on the floor of the bathroom. Just hang them up on the rail so they can dry. And you could rinse out the basin when you've shaved.'

'Oh. Sorry, I didn't realize.'

'And the washing-up. I think it's more pleasant to do it regularly.'

'How regularly?'

What kind of a question is that? 'Like, every time you use something?'

'Oh. But I've seen you leave dishes behind when you go off to work, so—'

'OK, but I still do them when I come home in the evening. I wouldn't leave them longer than a day. And also, you woke me up the other night, when you were having a shower . . .'

'Oh, shit. Sorry. I didn't realise. Is there anything else?'

'Yes. I like keeping the living-room table clear – like, not covered in books and magazines and things. And I prefer white loo paper, not coloured. And maybe we could take turns buying flowers, for the flat?'

'No.'

'What?'

'I will try and be more tidy, but there are limits. I'm not buying flowers, or checking the colour of the loo roll.'

'OK! Fine. Just, try and be tidier, would you?'

Max looks at me thoughtfully. 'Have you ever stopped to think that you might have annoying habits too?' he asks.

'No,' I say defensively. 'I haven't. Like what?'

'Well, whenever I open the door there are always about ten pairs of high heels there, like traps for heffalumps. And you sometimes put back the milk with a spoonful left in the carton, instead of throwing it out and getting a new one. And then there's the loud singing in the shower . . . Anywhere here on the right, please.'

'Hey, don't hold back,' I say, as the taxi pulls up outside our house.

'I don't really mind the singing, though,' Max says, grinning at me. 'In fact, I kind of like it.' He leans forward and pays the driver – eep – £30.

'Let me go halves,' I say, not sure if he's paying me a compliment or not.

'Do you want to wake her up?' he asks, ignoring me and sliding out from under Rachel's head. 'I think you'd better. She might get a fright if she saw me.'

'Rachel.' I poke her gently. 'Rachel, wake up. We're home.'

'Whaass? What? Waah.' She opens her eyes, sees me and groans. 'Zoë. Oh God. I thought it was a dream . . .'

'No, you're fine.' I help her out of the taxi and up the steps, to where Max is waiting by the open door.

'Would you like to put her in my bed?' Max asks, as we go up the stairs. 'Just so you can get a good night's sleep,' he adds quickly. 'I'll sleep on the sofa.'

'Oh – no, it's OK. I'll just bunk in with her.'

Max nods, and starts down the corridor towards his room, leaving me with my arm around a swaying Rachel.

'Max! Wait!'

'Yeah?'

'Um, thanks for helping us out.'

'You're welcome,' he says.

SEVENTEEN

'Room service,' I announce, putting the tray down on my bedside table.

It's 11 a.m., and Rachel has finally stirred. I've brought her coffee and toast, plus a bottle of water and a huge glass of orange juice. I even made her toast the way she likes it, allowing it to cool down completely before applying margarine (madness).

'How's the patient?'

'Like death. I am so, so ill. How could I have got that drunk?' she groans. 'How how how? And, oh God, was I really telling that guy in Bar Italia all about my love life?' She buries her face in the duvet. Suddenly she looks up. 'Zoë. Please tell me we didn't have a run-in with the police?'

'Yes. But it was OK. You got off with a caution.'

'What?' She flings the cover off the bed and sits bolt upright, clasping her fingers to her temples. 'Oh God! A caution! I'm going to lose my job!'

'No, Rachel – sorry. I was joking.' Oops. I didn't know a caution would be so serious.

'And didn't we meet your flatmate?' she asks, frowning. 'What was he doing there?'

'Oh. We just bumped into him, and he sort of . . . helped us get a taxi.'

'You mean he helped you deal with your drunken friend. Oh, God.' She buries her head in her hands. 'Oh my God,' she repeats

170

to herself. 'I'm really sorry, Zoë. I can't believe you came out to rescue me and then I put you through all that.'

'That's OK. What did you think of him though? Do you think he's cute?' I don't know why I'm asking this. I don't think Max will be her type. I just want to know what she thought of him.

'I couldn't even tell you what he looks like.' She reaches for the water with a shaky hand and takes a sip. 'Urghhh. I feel so, so sick. I don't know how I managed to drink so much,' she groans.

I climb on to the bed beside her and flop out. 'I'm not feeling so hot today either.'

'Was I telling Max about Jay?'

'Um . . . you might have mentioned it.'

She groans again. 'I was such a horrible cliché. The drunken, scorned woman.'

'Well, you were right to be annoyed. Jay was an idiot.'

'I know. But the thing is . . . it wasn't a total surprise.'

I sit up and look at her. 'Was it not?'

'No. When you told me about him seeing someone else, I had a hunch that it might be true. That was partly why I reacted so badly. I didn't want to admit it.' She makes a face. 'There were all kinds of things that didn't seem right.'

'What kind of things?'

'For a start, we were never officially boyfriend and girlfriend because he doesn't like to be tied down by "labels".' She makes rabbit ears with her fingers.

'Uh-oh.' Any man who uses the word 'labels', if he doesn't mean Prada or Levis, is bad news.

'And nobody knew at work that we were going out. Which seemed sensible at the time but now I think is highly suspicious. And he closed down his Facebook account – or so he told me – and he would often be busy at weekends.' She rolls her eyes. 'I am *such* an idiot. He was practically waving a big placard saying, "I am two-timing you", and I ignored it.'

I try to think of a bright side. 'Well, if nobody at work knew you were going out, at least that means nobody has to know you've broken up. Are you glad you've found out, though? I mean sooner, rather than later?' I hope she says yes, otherwise I'm going to feel terrible.

'I suppose so. Yes. No, of course I am.' She sighs. 'I know he wasn't right. And I know that it's me, that I'm picking the wrong guys and I need to cop on.'

I'm startled. Is Rachel really picking the wrong men? I suppose she must be.

'But how are you supposed to know who the right ones are? And am I going to keep picking the wrong ones for the rest of my life?' She flops back on her pillow, then turns to me, her mascara-smudged eyes worried. 'What do you think?'

This is one moment where I really wish I could see the future – all of it. But I can't, so I just have to go with my instinct.

'I think that at some point soon, you are going to meet a *wonderful* man who thinks you are the bee's knees.' I poke her duvet-covered leg gently. 'He'll be the number one investor in Project Rachel.'

'Project Rachel? What – oh God.' She buries her head in the duvet again, and I hear a muffled voice saying, 'Project Rachel. Aaargh.' Looking up, she says, 'By the way. How did it go with the whole meet-the-Fitzgeralds thing?'

I explain the entire debacle, from the tea-spilling to Jenny being there – but then I add the good news: that David and I had a proper talk about it, and that things are going really well. I don't mention the boating in Hyde Park; I don't want to rub her nose in my romantic good fortune. 'And in other news, I had my interview last week. For the job of Assistant Buyer.'

'Oh, wow! And I didn't even know! How was it?'

'I think it went well . . . I'll hear in the next week or two, I hope.'

'That's fantastic,' she says. She starts hauling herself slowly out of bed.

'Oh, no, are you leaving already? Do you not want to stay here for a while? I never see you. It's such a nice day – we could go to the park, or go for drinks somewhere outside.'

Rachel looks torn. 'Well – I have a bit of work to do at home, is the only thing,' she says. 'But I suppose I could stay for a bit . . .'

Hm. Maybe, in the same way that I've been giving David space and not guilting him when he has to work, I should do the same for Rachel.

'Don't worry about it,' I tell her. 'If you need to go that's cool.'

She looks grateful and I beam back at her. Maybe I am growing up after all.

EIGHTEEN

Rachel gets dressed while I bring the plates back to the kitchen. I find Max standing at the counter, reading a book and waiting for the kettle to boil. I notice that the kitchen is spotless; he's obviously done all of the washing-up from yesterday. I'm about to compliment him on it when he says, 'How are you feeling today?'

'Not so hot.' I put my plates in the sink and start washing them. 'How are you?' I ask, looking at him over my shoulder. He's wearing a truly awful-looking, ancient navy towelling dressing gown – the kind that, if he were my boyfriend, would be the first thing to go. As he pours the kettle, I catch a glimpse of an unexpectedly broad, brown chest underneath.

'Oh, I'm fine. I've been working pretty hard so I'm giving myself a Spoil Max day.'

'A Spoil Max day? What's that?'

'It's a day when I spend the entire day doing whatever I want. I might take myself to a caff for breakfast, and then go and see a double bill at the Prince Charles, or buy some new CDs . . . today, I think I'm just going to spend the entire morning reading my book in the park, and then I'm going to go for a swim in the lido in Hyde Park, and then in the evening I'm going to Edgware Road with some friends to smoke a sheesha.' He looks out of the window. 'Oh. Maybe not the lido.'

It's pouring with rain. Rachel's come into the room and caught the end of this sentence.

174

'Morning. Sorry about last night,' she says awkwardly.

He replies, 'Not at all.'

They both look back at me, as if asking me to help them out with this encounter.

'That sounds brilliant,' I say enthusiastically. 'Max was just telling me he's going to have a day doing exactly what he wants, which is a Spoil Max day. I should have a Spoil Zoë day.'

'I thought every day was a Spoil Zoë day?' Rachel says. 'Just joking!' she adds as I swat her on the arm.

'I mean, I like the idea of having a designated day,' I continue, ignoring her. 'Of course, you can't do exactly what you want either. Otherwise you could end up spending hundreds of thousands of pounds. So you can do whatever you want, but only . . .'

'Within reason?' suggests Rachel.

'There's a lot more within reason than you'd think, though,' Max says. He pours out his cup of coffee. 'See you both later,' he says, and leaves the room. A second later, he pops his head back inside.

'Zoë, I hope you've noticed I have done all of the washing-up from this morning. And last night.' He indicates the gleaming sink and work-top.

'Thank you, Max,' I say sincerely. 'You're the king of washing-up.'

He clasps his hands above his head like a boxing champion, and bows and leaves the room.

'He's nice,' Rachel says in a lowered voice. 'But I see what you mean. He is eccentric.'

It's lucky I never thought of setting the two of them up. Rachel is far too no-nonsense for him, and he's far too offbeat for her.

Once Rachel's gone, I have a shower of my own, and do a quick waxing job to get it out of the way. Then I make a cup of tea and bring it into the sitting room, where I find Max at the table, still in his horrible dressing-gown, putting photos into an album.

'Do you mind if I watch a DVD?'

'No, no,' he says absently. Now that I look at him again, I see his thing isn't an album. It's a scrapbook, with photos, handwritten captions and what look like clippings from old exercise books. How quaint. I must say my opinion of him has gone up since last night. He's good company in his own way. He's making an effort to be cleaner. He's easygoing and good at dealing with drunks – and he lets me hog the TV. I crouch down in front of the TV and flip through my collection, looking for Season 3 of *Gossip Girl*. The perfect companion for a rainy day.

And then I remember: it's not out until the end of August. So although I was in the middle of it, I can't watch it because it doesn't yet exist. This is a very inconvenient aspect of this whole time travel thing.

'Damn.'

'What?'

'My DVD that I wanted to watch . . . it's not there.' I'm about to concoct a story about lending it to a friend, but stop myself in time, reminding myself that Max doesn't care. It's a relief, because I could really do with one day where I don't have to invent elaborate tales.

I select Season 2 instead – I haven't seen it for a while – and settle back with a sigh of happiness. I'm in my tracksuit bottoms and my favourite, least flattering T-shirt. I've got a mug of tea and a packet of Jaffa Cakes, and it's possible that I'll eat more than one. I still haven't done my fake tan, or my nails, but they can wait.

'Wow,' Max says when I turn it on and get to 'Episode Selection.' '*Gossip Girl*? Really?'

'Yup,' I say. 'Jaffa Cake?' I'm about to press Episode One but then I recall that it begins with a very lengthy bedroom scene between Nate and that older woman, featuring lots of nails digging into backs. Instead I flip to Episode Two, and sit back and watch happily as Blair and Lord Marcus bicycle around the Hamptons. I love the yellow detail on her blouse, and the way it contrasts with her tomato-red skirt.

'*Anyone can canoodle in July and August, but will he be gone by September?*' the *Gossip Girl* voiceover asks. 'No, he won't,' I murmur triumphantly. Or at least I'll be going with him.

'Sorry?' says Max, from the table.

'Nothing.'

A few minutes later, he says, 'Why is he calling that woman Duchess when she's his sister?'

'Because she's a duchess. She's not his sister, she's his step-mother.'

'But he'd hardly call his step-mother Duchess, would he?'

'Nothing in *Gossip Girl* ever makes any sense,' I tell him. 'That's what makes it so great. I really want to see Season 3 but it's not out on DVD yet.' Dammit. I paid good money for that DVD too. I wonder if I'll ever go back to the future and reclaim my old one . . . but the thought is scary and I push it away.

Now Serena and Dan are hopping on the jitney together. I have a feeling there's something explicit with strawberries about to come, but I can't be bothered to change it. It'll broaden Max's horizons. Not that he's even watching; he's glueing something down with great concentration, the tip of his tongue sticking out.

'What are you working on?' I ask curiously.

'Oh. I'm making a kind of memory book for someone. Just a book with some childhood photos and stuff.'

'Oh, really? Photos of who?'

'Me and my sisters, as kids . . . here's someone you'll recognise, too.'

I pause the DVD and go over to see. A tiny Max, all big brown eyes . . . two little girls . . . and a chubby blond boy who looks vaguely familiar.

'Oh, my God. Is that David?' I gaze at the photo. 'He's adorable. I had no idea he was such a chubsicle!'

'Oh. Yeah, he was, I suppose. But that was a long time ago. He's around nine there, I think.'

'Who's the book for?' I ask, when the doorbell rings.

'That's weird.' Unless you're having a party, or expecting a specific guest, the sound of the doorbell is rarely heard in London. 'Just ignore it, it's probably a Jehovah's Witness or something.'

'I'll see who it is,' says Max, going out to the hall to answer the intercom. I flop back on the sofa and reach for another Jaffa Cake. A minute later, he pops his head back in and says, 'It's David.'

'What? Here, now?' I jump off the couch in a panic and look down at myself; pale and tracksuited, hair a mess, with a half-eaten Jaffa Cake in my hand.

'Well, yeah . . . I just buzzed him up.'

'Great! Great. Just tell him – tell him I'm in the shower.' I run to turn off the TV, and shove the *Gossip Girl* DVD case underneath the sofa seat. 'I'll be ten minutes, OK?'

I'm thrilled that it's David, of course, but I was not expecting to see him in this state. I quickly go and change out of my track-suit bottoms into a clinging blue T-shirt from Zara and my Seven For All Mankind jeans. Then I brush my hair and put on very light, natural make-up – just a bit of BB cream, mascara, cream blush and eyebrow gel. I shove a trashy novel under my bed, and quickly fluff up the duvet again and take out a stray coffee cup to bring it to the sink. I don't have time to do fake tan, but it can't be helped; I just hope he won't notice that I've changed colour when I see him next.

When I get back into the sitting room, David and Max seem to be talking about work.

'Make sure you get in there,' David's saying. 'You've got to take those opportunities, or someone else will.' He breaks off as I come inside.

'Here she is,' he says, standing up. I cross the room and go to kiss him on the cheek, because of Max, but he kisses me on the mouth. His hair is damp and he's wearing chinos and a red polo shirt. He looks so great, in fact, that the flat looks extra shabby in contrast. Even his navy trench coat draped over the chair makes it look more bockety than usual. I make a mental note to talk to the landlord about replacing it.

'What were you doing having a shower at this hour?' David asks.

'Oh, you know, just having a lazy morning. Day. What brings you here? How is your little patient?'

'She's fine – no complications.' He looks as if a weight's been taken off his shoulders.

'Oh, that's good. I'm so glad.'

'So I didn't have to go into work and I slept for fourteen hours last night. I'm feeling human again . . . and I thought I'd drop by and see if you wanted to do something.'

Wow. I never would have imagined that David would walk to my house in the rain.

'So what did you get up to last night in the end?' he asks.

'Not much . . . I met Rachel in town for a few drinks.' I give Max a warning look, but he just looks confused.

'Things are a bit busy in work these days – I had to stand Zoë up at the last minute yesterday,' David says to Max. 'You're going to have to look after her for me.'

'I'll do my best,' says Max. He stands up abruptly. 'Actually . . . it's stopped raining, so I think I'm going to head out. I mean, get dressed and head out. Good to see you, David.'

'You too. Let's have that match soon.'

Max glances at me slightly oddly as he leaves. I suppose my lightning change might have seemed a bit strange, but really, who wants their boyfriend to see them looking such a state?

'So,' I say to David, 'do you want to go out and have lunch or something?' Although I know it's silly, I often feel awkward about entertaining David in my place, since his is infinitely nicer.

He lifts his head until we hear the door closing behind Max. 'Well, considering I haven't seen you in a week . . . something definitely sounds good.' He bends to kiss me.

I kiss him back, but as he starts to lead me towards the bedroom, I resist.

'What's wrong?'

'Nothing! Just, you know, I'm a little hung over, and plus . . . I haven't seen you in ages. Can't we just catch up first? Talk a bit? Loads of stuff has happened this week. I've had an interview, and everything.'

David looks surprised, but he instantly recovers his good manners.

'You'll have to tell me all about it. We can go and have lunch – where would you like to go?'

'I don't mind . . . let me just get my bag, OK?' I smile at him and go to find my handbag. The strange thing is that although I'm thrilled David's dropped in like this, there's another part of me that would quite like to just slob out and watch TV. Then I catch myself. In which world would I prefer to watch DVDs and eat biscuits than see David? It must just be my hangover. I brush my hair again, grab my bag and run back out to meet him.

NINETEEN

Monday morning, and I'm in the fitting room, helping Mrs Murdoch, one of our regular customers, decide between two mid-calf Aztec print dresses – one red and one blue. Mrs Murdoch is well known for taking hours to make these decisions, and requiring a lot of compliments and flattery from whoever's on at the time, but I don't mind; we're not busy. That is, I'm inwardly busy wondering when I'll hear about the assistant buyer interview. Last time I heard quite quickly, but that was a rejection. Whereas this time . . .

'Of course the red is very jolly,' she says. 'But the blue is nice, isn't it?'

'I think the blue is lovely on you,' I say. 'It brings out your eyes.'

She steps backwards appraisingly. 'Have you still got it in green?'

Mrs Murdoch is unbelievable; she knows our stock better than we do. 'We do, actually. Let me go and find one for you.'

I'm checking the sizes in the stockroom, from the computer on the till, when Karen comes up to me.

'Message from Julia upstairs,' she says, obviously making an effort to smile. 'Can you come up and see her at twelve-thirty.'

'Oh. My break's not until one . . .'

'That's fine,' she says through gritted teeth. 'I'll take my break then – you can swap with me.'

Now this is an interesting development. She's furious – but she's being polite. Which can only mean – I hurry back to the

181

fitting room with a size 14 for Mrs Murdoch, trying to contain my excitement.

After the usual wait for someone to let me up in the lift, I get to Julia's office to find Julia and Seth waiting for me, plus a little spread of tea and sandwiches.

'Zoë! Take a seat,' Julia says, flipping her impressively long ponytail over her shoulder and typing something into her computer. I admire her sleeveless silk shirt, pistachio skinny jeans and pink wedge sandals, as I sit down. Seth is already seated, holding a cup of tea and saucer, one pinkie perfectly cocked.

'Have a cuppa,' Seth says, pouring me some tea, and pointing at the spread of little Pret sandwiches – *and* brownies. I'm fizzing with excitement. Surely they wouldn't give me brownies if I hadn't got the job? I'm already mentally popping corks with Rachel and Kira, and calling David to give him the good news . . .

'So, bad news first,' Julia says. 'We've decided to go with someone else for the assistant buyer job.'

'What?' I feel as if she's just poured cold tea all over me. 'I mean, oh. I see.' That is pretty effing bad news. I can feel a knot forming in my stomach. Why did they have to haul me up here to tell me that? Are these consolation brownies?

'We decided to go with someone with a little more experience in the nuts and bolts of buying,' Julia says. Am I imagining it, or does she look a little disappointed? I think she does, and I am too. She would have been so cool to work with.

'But the good news,' says Seth, 'is that we've found a very exciting role for you.'

Oh! Wow. This sounds promising.

He puts down his tea-cup and adjusts his tie. 'We're making you Global Head of Trends.'

Now it's my turn to put down my tea-cup, before I spill it for the second time this month. Global? Head? Trends? What?

'Wow! Um, what, what, what does that mean?' I ask faintly.

Julia glances at Seth. 'Maybe I can explain. There are a lot of strategic changes going on right now. We're trying to be a bit more innovative and forward-thinking.'

'And less stuck in the nineties,' Seth says. 'Make that 1890s.'

'So we need someone to keep an eye on trends. Keep their finger on the pulse and give us insights into what customers are going to be wearing, wanting – with a particular eye on womens-wear, of course,' Julia says. 'And speaking of womenswear, I –' she glances at Seth – '*we* want you to be as involved as possible in the actual buying.'

'Keeping it real,' says Seth.

'So we're going to give you a small proportion of the OTB for each season . . .'

'To do with as you wish!' says Seth, throwing his arms dramatically wide.

I nod, trying to hide my panic and thinking: what the hell does OTB mean?

'I'd also like you to see the odd showroom, give a second opinion, come along with us to some shows in the future,' Julia says. I begin to recover as I hear 'showroom', 'opinion' and 'shows'. Those I understand.

'That's – wonderful! I'm honoured.' Stalling for time, I add, 'This is – is this a new position?'

Seth laughs out loud. 'Of course this is a new position. You don't think we needed a Head of Trends to help us restock the same old shirtwaister dresses and hats every year?'

'Um – no?' I look from one to the other, and then go on, 'So – is there, maybe a written list of duties? Of things that fall within my remit?' In other words, what the hell am I supposed to be doing?

'The remit is broad,' Seth says. 'General trends forecasting and mood boards ahead of each season, trends reports to circulate maybe weekly, reports to the board, board meetings—'

'Sorry, just a second. I'm on the board?'

'Only as an associate member,' Julia says soothingly. I nod at her, trying to appear calm.

'It will feed into all sorts of things, including VM,' says Seth, and Julia nods. I nod, thinking: what's VM?

'I suppose the first thing', he continues, 'will be to do a little presentation, some trend predictions for S/S11 – don't you think, Jules?

'Yes, we'd love to hear your thoughts on that,' Julia says. 'You've got a real instinct for this. Your predictions so far have been amazing. Unbelievable, in fact.'

'But –' The word escapes me before I can help it. *But*, I haven't really been predicting anything – I've just been remembering. *But* I can't remember anything about this autumn's fashion shows because I was in such a black hole over David I barely paid any attention. *But* I'm a total fraud and I am not going to be able to do this job.

'But what?' says Julia. They exchange puzzled glances, as if they're beginning to register that I'm not looking as thrilled as I should be. My pulse is hammering in my throat. I have two choices; either I admit that I'm not a real trend predictor, and I'm not qualified for the job, or else I just . . . go with it.

'But nothing! I was just thinking I need to give a week's notice to Karen.'

'So you do. Well, then, you'll start a week from today.'

OK. That gives me a week's breathing space to assimilate it all. It occurs to me that I haven't asked them about a salary. I waver briefly between asking and looking grasping, and not asking and looking clueless, and decide that clueless would be much worse.

'We'd like to start you on sixty thousand pounds,' says Julia. 'With twenty-five days' holiday a year and, of course, a fifty per cent store discount.'

I give her a dignified nod. 'That sounds fine.'

Sixty thousand pounds a year! That's over three times what I was on before! This is unbelievable! OK, it might be terrifying, but I can spot trends: I can do presentations. How hard can it be?

*   *   *

184

I manage to contain myself all the way down in the lift – they give me a spare pass – and towards the till, where I grab my phone before running outside and doing a little dance, right there on Regent's Street. The fear has worn off and I'm ecstatic. This morning I was on the shop floor and now I'm Head of Trends. *Global* Head of Trends! I dial Rachel's number.

'Hi,' she says. 'How are you? How did the interview go?' I'm relieved that she sounds normal, rather than heartbroken over Jay. Though she'd hardly be crying her eyes out in the office – I hope.

'Well, I didn't get the AB job, but you are speaking to the new Global Head of Trends for Marley's Limited.'

I can practically hear her shrieking all the way from her office in St Paul's. 'Whaaat? What does that even mean?'

'It means I'm going to be trend-spotting and reporting on what's hot. And they're paying me . . . well, a lot.'

She shrieks again. 'Reporting on what's *hot*? They're paying you to be Paris Hilton! Oh my God, Zoë. Congratulations! We'll have to celebrate.'

'Yes! But, wait, Rachel – are you OK with the whole, you know, Jay thing?'

She makes a non-committal sound. 'I'm just happy I'm out of it in one piece. Listen, I'll catch you later. Congratulations again.'

After we hang up, I laugh out loud as I remember standing here in the snow, feeling so miserable, the day before Christmas. But that's not going to happen now, because I'll be—

Oh, wait. If I'm taking this new job, what happens when I go to America in less than a month's time? Or to put it another way: if I go to America, won't that mean giving up an amazing new job?

I decide not to worry about it for now. Maybe I'll stay a bit longer and join David at Christmas, once I've built up some experience, and then I can look for another job in the States. Or maybe they would let me work from the States! I am Global, after all. I march back inside to hand in my resignation.

'It's been such a pleasure working with you,' I assure Karen. 'I've learned so much, and I'm so glad we're going to continue to work together.'

She nods, her face painfully contorted with the effort of smiling, even though I can tell she doesn't know how to react, now that her minion has joined the board.

'It's been a pleasure working with you too, Zoë,' she says, adding with a little laugh, 'I always knew you had a lot of potential.'

'Oh, I know you did,' I say enigmatically.

Harriet's had the morning off, but as soon as she gets in, she comes over to find me.

'Zoë! You are not going to believe what happened!'

'What?'

'Someone tried to break in while we were gone!' She shakes her head. 'You were right! They would have got in, but the alarm went off and Mum had put an extra dead bolt on the front door. But how did you know, Zoë? *How* on earth did you know?'

'Well . . . I don't know,' I finish, lamely. 'I just – had a feeling.'

Harriet stares at me for a long minute before saying, 'You must be psychic.'

'Really?' I say weakly. 'You think?'

'Wait! Was that what you were doing that time, on the floor walk with Julia? Making predictions?'

'Well . . .' I feel uneasy about her using the word 'predictions'. 'Sort of. By the way . . .' I tell her about my new job as Global Head of Trends.

'Oh my God! Well, Zoë, no wonder! You are psychic!' I try to shush her but she keeps going. 'You're going to be able to tell them exactly what trends are coming up! What's going to sell and what isn't! They can't go wrong!'

I don't want to tell her that she's wrong about me being psychic, because it's a convenient explanation, but on the other hand I have to put a lid on her at once, before it all gets out of hand.

'Look, Harriet. You won't tell anyone about all this, will you? Swear.'

'Of course not,' she says instantly. 'Cross my heart and hope to die. Anyway,' she adds quickly, 'even if you weren't psychic, Zoë, you'd be brilliant at this job. Absolutely.'

'Thanks,' I say faintly, hoping to God that she's right.

TWENTY

On my first day as Global Head of Trends, I arrive clutching my cappuccino, with a copy of September *Vogue* under my arm. I read it first time around, of course, but I still need it: it's like ammunition. It feels so incredibly strange to walk in past Bruce the security guard, and walk straight through the ground floor towards the lift.

As I go up (using my very own, brand new pass!), it occurs to me that I haven't had a text from David, let alone a good-luck card. But I dismiss the thought as petty and unworthy. He hardly has time to go browsing in Paperchase in between operations, and anyway I only saw him yesterday.

The weather's been grey and cool for the past week and I've spend almost every evening at home, reading everything I can about fashion retail and trying to get my head around what 'trends research' actually means. I've discovered that OTB means 'open to buy', and it's just a word for the amount of budget set aside to stock up on new trends. Max has been away most of this week on some mysterious last-minute trip home, so I haven't seen him much – it's been nice to have the house to myself.

Best of all, David and I just spent the whole of Saturday and Sunday morning together. He was really tired, so we just hung out at his place – although we did make a trip to Hampstead Heath on Saturday evening for an open-air concert. The open-air theme . . . well, continued after the concert. I couldn't completely

188

relax, because I kept hearing noises, but it was so great to see him after a whole week's absence, it was well worth it.

Now it's Monday morning, and I'm here. I don't even know who I'm reporting to, so I go to find Julia, who's wearing J. Brand combats and a cute tank top, and distractedly looking at emails while gulping down coffee.

'Morning! OK, let's get you set up. We have an office for you and everything,' she says over her shoulder, leading me down the gangway between the open-plan desks. A couple of heads look up curiously and I feel self-conscious – what if it's really amateurish to carry *Vogue* around the office? Does it look like I'm trying too hard? On the way, she introduces me to a bunch of people, all of whom seem to be wearing combats and high heels, and whose names I promptly forget, and then shows me into my new office.

'It's not big, but you have a view.'

I have never had my own office before. It has a window over-looking the rooftops of Soho, a swivel chair, a Philippe Starck Ghost chair and a shiny new Mac computer. And it has my name on the door. It says: Zoë Kennedy, Global Head of Trends. As a pinch-me moment, this is right up there with waking up back in July, or my first kiss with David after going back in time.

'We have a buying meeting at eleven – in the meeting room,' she says. 'Can you join us for that? I'm up against it so I'd better dash.'

I walk across the office, thinking: I have a desk. I don't have to stand up for eight hours a day any more! The occasion seems to call for a photo: I snap myself quickly before anyone catches me. Then I turn on my computer. Right. This is it. I have a computer, I have a phone, I have a notepad and a pen. Time to be Head of Trends. A feeling of panic surges over me but I damp it down quickly. I might have faked my way in a bit, but now that I'm here, I can do this job.

I spend the next hour or so surfing trends websites and fashion blogs, and making notes, as well as checking out the Marley's website, which seems stuck in the dark ages. I'm just browsing the websites for Selfridges, Liberty and Harvey Nichols to get some ideas, when someone comes into the office – bearing a huge bunch of pink roses. A dozen? Two dozen? I don't know, because I have never received this many roses before. In fact, I've never been sent roses, ever.

'You've got mail,' says Seth, popping his head out from behind the bunch. 'Look what I found waiting at reception with no one to love it.'

'Oh my gosh!' I dash over and take the bunch, wondering if they might be from my dad. It's unlikely that he would do such a thing, but not impossible. But no. The card says, 'To Zoë – best of luck on your first day. D x.' I'm so touched, and I feel so bad for thinking about the fact that he hadn't texted, that I would text him right now if Seth wasn't still here, clearly keen for a gossip.

'Who's it from?' asks Seth.

'My boyfriend.'

'Aww,' he says, flinging himself into the Ghost chair. 'Tell me, tell me. Who is he, what does he do, how long have you been together?'

At least this is one question I can answer with confidence today.

'His name's David. We've been together –' I still have to calculate – 'just over three months now. He's a heart surgeon.' I know it's shallow, but I still love telling people that, and see them raise their eyebrows in admiration as Seth is doing now.

'Che-ching,' he says approvingly. 'Nice boy, good job,' he adds in a Jewish-mom voice. 'Well, you're not going to meet anyone here, so that's just as well, darling. I just thought I'd drop by and say welcome . . . and leave you a copy of the last trend report from our previous agency.'

He hands me a very professional-looking and alarmingly thick file, with a groovy logo on the cover.

'So you, we, don't work with them any more?'

'No. We're putting all our trust in you.' He beams at me and disappears, before poking his head out from behind the door. 'Are you coming to the buying meeting? I thought I might sit in too.'

Of course; the meeting. It's eleven already. Eyeing the trends report out of the corner of my eye, I grab my notebook and hurry after him, into the meeting room. I have no idea what to expect, so I'm relieved to see it's just a small group: five including me and Seth. Julia introduces us. Clara, the girl with the long dark hair, is a merchandiser – which means she's in charge of the budget – and then there's Amanda, the assistant buyer who got the job I went for. She's dark and neat and wearing a pleated green skirt and a white linen blouse with a Peter Pan collar. Bizarrely, it's almost exactly like my old school uniform, and she also really reminds me of a prefect called Deirdre Hegarty, who once reported me for smoking in the back fields.

She seems surprised that we've joined them and looks enquiringly at Julia.

'Zoë is our new Head of Trends and I wanted her input for this meeting. Zoë, just to fill you in, we're dividing up our budget for next season's bridal wear. So here we have: Wang, Berketex, Temperley . . .' I take a seat and try and look confident, while Julia passes around lookbooks full of photos of wedding dresses.

'But what we really need to know is', says Seth, 'what is Kate going to wear next year? Assuming it's announced soon, that is.'

'I know! If only we knew, wouldn't that make our lives easier. My money's on Temperley,' says Julia.

'Maybe someone up and coming like Sophia Kokosalaki?' suggests Amanda, in an eager, buzzer-pressing way.

'Maybe. Or McQueen?' says Seth. 'It's been a tough year with Lee and everything, but . . .'

'Yes, maybe. What about you? Do you have any ideas, Zoë?' asks Julia.

'Not really,' I admit, without thinking, and then kick myself. Why didn't I just mention Issa? Though, wait – do they even do bridal wear?

'Well, we don't know if there's even going to be a royal engagment, but where do you see trends for bridal next season?'

Everyone stops talking and turns to look at me. I can feel my throat going dry, because I don't see them anywhere. To be perfectly honest, I have no idea about bridal trends. I have to admit I've never even thought about them.

'Um.' I clear my throat. 'I think we're going to see . . .' Julia is frowning; I tell myself desperately, *Just say something, anything!*

'I think we're going to see shorter, more casual dresses. Dresses that people are going to want to wear again. We're in a recession – nobody wants a one-wear purchase.'

Nobody looks too convinced – but I sounded confident (I think). Even though it was a complete shot in the dark. And, now I come to think of it, probably bullshit.

Julia makes a 'maybe' face. 'Well, for next season, we want a good showing of British brands, but it can't all be British. I'm thinking of twenty per cent for Berketex . . .'

I concentrate as hard as I can, but it's as if the conversation is happening in French. By the time I've understood what they're saying, they've moved on to the next thing. I concentrate on writing down phrases I want to look up later: 'category mix', 'at market', 'SSQ', 'like for like'. Noticing Seth looking at me curiously, I hide my notebook so he can't see.

I think I'm beginning to understand, though: Clara wants us to stay with some tried-and-tested formula whereas Julia thinks we should spend more of our budget on a newer designer.

'Last year we did very well with them,' Clara is saying. 'We had an eighty per cent sell-through in all the sizes in the first four weeks. Why not just place the same order?'

'No! That's so last season!' says Seth. I smile to myself: you don't often hear people actually saying that.

'So here are the ten extra from Bellina that we like for next month,' Julia's saying, producing another lookbook. 'I'd like every-one's input, to narrow these down to three.'

Everyone, except Clara, who's punching numbers into her calculator, takes a good look at the dresses, including me. One called Seville catches my eye – it's quite pretty, with a lace detail over the skirt. And there's a knee-length one called Malibu, and then there's one called Moonlight that has a sash. But the others are all almost identical; cream-coloured silk, strapless bodice with a beading detail on the bust, full skirt. I'm looking as close as I can but I honestly can't see any difference. Is this a trick? Or a sort of new-girl joke?

'Well, definitely this one – Moonlight,' says Amanda, pointing to the one with the blue sash. Everyone murmurs agreement, as if that goes without saying.

'What do you think, Zoë?' asks Julia.

I mentally cross my fingers and I point to one in the middle that looks pretty identical to the ones on either side.

'Ooh! Controversial!' says Seth.

'Yes, unusual choice,' says Julia. 'Why that one?'

What? What are they talking about? I'm waiting for someone to say 'Fooled you!' but they're all looking at me expectantly. 'I just think it stands out,' I say weakly.

'I thought you said you were backing shorter lengths,' says Amanda. 'Why didn't you pick the midi one?'

Her smooth, wholesome brow is furrowed, and something tells me she knows a fraud when she sees one.

'Oh, I thought we were covered for that elsewhere,' I say vaguely.

Thankfully, everyone seems to accept this, and I make it through to the end of the meeting without any other mishaps.

'Oh, Zoë,' Julia says. 'Before you go – have you got that address for Keira yet?'

'Um, yes. It's just – back at my desk. I'll email it to you.' Oh, God. I forgot about Keira Knightley, my celebrity friend.

I race back, close the door to my office, and frantically google 'Keira Knightley agent'. After a few phone calls, in a hushed voice so that no one outside overhears, I manage to find a PR agency that will accept deliveries for Keira, and write down the address. Putting down the phone, I almost jump out of my skin when I hear a knock at the door. It's Amanda. For a second I think she's going to stand with her back against the door and say: 'The jig is up.' But she just says, 'Zoë, can you do me a quick report on trends in swimwear? I'm just reviewing our cruise collection.'

'Um, sure. Can you send me . . . some pictures of the cruise collection? Or a list of what you already have?'

She frowns. 'It doesn't really work like that.'

'Of course not,' I say, though I have no idea how it does work. 'But if you could just send me some, um, stuff . . . then I can get started. OK? Thanks!' I stand up and pretty much shoo her out of the door, before returning to the safety of my desk to google 'cruise collection'. I'm fairly sure I know what it means, but I just want to double check.

This is what it must feel like to burgle a house, or to go onstage as an actress without knowing your lines. For the first time, I wonder if maybe I should come clean with Julia and Seth. Maybe tell them that while I do think I have an instinct for fashion, I need more training in the nuts and bolts of what we're discussing? Because I don't understand any of it?

But maybe I don't really have an instinct for fashion. Maybe I just have a good memory and that's it.

To prevent myself unravelling into a panic-stricken mess, I give myself a stern pep-talk. Come on, I think. You can do this, you'll learn. Taking Keira's address, I walk around to Julia's office and tell her that it's best we send stuff to her PR agency.

'Great. Well, I've pulled together some pieces for her – let's send them along, and we can follow them up with a press release.' She shows me two gorgeous dresses, including a full-length, fitted silk dress in a sky-blue and red print on a navy background, with short sleeves and a flounced hem. Plus a beautiful knee-length sheer chiffon burgundy dress with a sort of feather detail on the shoulders. I've already seen these!

'Ah yes, Pilar Norman – these are going to sell really well. In fact, I think they'll sell out in the first week.'

'Really? We don't have very many. Maybe we should back up some more from the vendor, then,' says Julia. 'Do you think Keira will like them?'

'Oh . . . yes. I can really see her in those,' I say, which is true enough.

'Great. So listen – I'm going to be out of the office for a couple of days. How would you like to go along to a showroom for me, and check out a new designer? Peter Sembello. The showroom's in Marylebone.'

'Oh, wow. Peter Sembello? I'd love to!'

'Great. Just ask Amanda if you're not sure about anything.'

I'm relieved that she's trusting me again after my performance at the meeting today. And I'm even more relieved that I have heard of Peter Sembello, and I know he's going to be absolutely huge. Finally, I feel as if I'm back on solid ground.

I return to my office – my office! – wheeling Keira's garments ahead of me on a rail and feeling very Fashion with a capital F. I settle down with renewed confidence to work on Amanda's swimwear trends report. Feeling very glad that no one can see me, I start by googling 'swimwear trends'. It throws up a billion results, and I slowly start sifting through, trying to pick out recurrent themes, saving images and noting their sources. But I'm bewildered by all the contradictory opinions. Blogger A reckons we're seeing a return to retro fifties swimwear; Industry website B is backing body-con. Which is right? Both? Neither? I have no idea.

I decide to abandon my swimwear research for now, and read the previous trends report to see if I'm on the right lines. After just a few pages, my mood plummets again, because it's fantastic. It's incredibly detailed, with tons of data, pages of analysis of online 'chatter' about different brands, and a breakdown of profits from all the department stores in London.

Oh, my good God. There is no way I'm going to be able to produce anything close to this! Ever! This is a disaster! I have a mad impulse to grab my coat, and run right out the door and never come back.

Just then, Seth pops his head around the door. 'All right, darling? I just thought we should get a day in the diary for your first presentation . . .'

'OK. Yes. I'm working on something on swimwear at the moment,' I say, feeling my panic tipping over the edge. 'But I can follow up with a, um, wider report soon I'm sure.'

'All right. How about . . . let's see . . . Tuesday the 31st of August? Ahead of LFW.'

At least this is one acronym I recognise: London Fashion Week. 'Wouldn't it make more sense to present, um, after it so that I can tell people what's been in the shows?' I ask faintly. 'I mean, New York won't even have started by then . . .'

Seth shakes his head. 'By the time it's been in the shows it's already old news, darling, what with iPhones and bloggers and the dailies.'

'Um – OK. Sure.' Today is the 16th of August, which gives me just over two weeks to predict what's going to be in London Fashion Week. Easy. 'And who will I be presenting to? To the board, or . . .?'

'Just to us buying and sales bods I think, for now,' he says.

'Oh, great. I mean, that's fine.' Relief makes me add, 'I've been looking through this trends report from the old agency. It's . . . pretty good.'

'Oh, yes, they are good. But don't worry, darling,' he says. 'You might not have all their metrics and software and manpower and experience, but you have the right instincts and that's what matters. Right?'

'Right!' I agree. 'Right.'

TWENTY-ONE

Unable to take the stress for a second longer, I leave at five-thirty on the dot. When Max comes home, I've changed out of my work clothes into shorts and an ancient grey T-shirt, done my fake tan, and am lying flat on the sofa, watching *Twilight* and half-heartedly eating croutons.

'How was your first day?' he asks.

'Gmmph,' is all I can say. I lift a hand from the sofa and make a so-so motion. 'How was your trip?'

'My trip? Oh – fine. I just went to Wales, to see my folks. That's where they've retired to. Though they might be moving again.'

I'm about to ask him why, but he continues quickly, 'Want anything from the kitchen? Tea? Vodka? Some pills?'

'Tea would be lovely. Could I have the raspberry and elderflower?'

He looks dubious. 'How do I make that?'

'It's in a pink box.'

'Ah. One pink tea, coming up.'

As he leaves, my phone buzzes with a text from David. He's finally replied to the message I sent him this morning thanking him for the flowers. 'Glad you liked them. Hang in there. It's crazy here, but look forward to seeing you Friday xx'. Hm, two xxs. Good.

Max returns with a cup of tea, hands it to me and flings himself next to me on the sofa, with his *Nature* magazine and a bowl of cereal. I've noticed that recently he's been using one bowl all the time, like someone in prison. I sit up.

'You know, you can use the same plates and everything as me. Unless you're keeping kosher or something?'

'It's just habit. In my old place, that's what we did – we just each had our one bowl and plate that we used all the time. To avoid arguments about washing-up.'

'Max! Is that what you've been doing? Is that why everything's so tidy now?'

'Sort of.'

I'm about to tell him to stop – that he doesn't have to worry about washing-up – but then I think, well, whatever works.

We watch *Twilight* in peaceful silence for a while. I'm partly watching the story, partly wondering if I find R-Patz cute, and partly thinking how nice it is to be able to sit around saying nothing with someone.

'So let me get this straight,' he says, after about ten minutes. 'This guy is a billion years old.'

'Well, a couple of hundred, yeah.'

'And he has unlimited wealth and magic powers. And he's still in secondary school?'

'I know . . . it is weird. He could be off curing cancer or something.'

'Or developing safe renewable energy. Or even, I don't know, doing a really big jigsaw puzzle,' says Max. 'What would you do, if you could do anything?'

'What, if I had super powers? That's a great question.' I pause. 'Aside from all the obvious things like curing cancer and world peace and saving the environment? And knowing how to do my job?'

'Aside from those.'

'Well . . . when I was small, I wanted to be a ballet dancer. It's really hard on your body, but I still think it would be wonderful. But now I'd love to open my own shop. Boutique.'

'Yeah? You could do that,' he says, encouragingly.

'I hope so, but it's not as easy as it sounds. You need a lot of capital, obviously, and you need an angle, and to really know the market and have backers and lots of contacts – but that's what I'd like to do, some day.'

'So this new job should help you, shouldn't it? This trends thing.'

'I hope so. But it's scary. I feel so out of my depth; I don't understand anything anyone's saying to me; I'm bluffing all the time . . .'

'But that's a good thing. It means you're learning.'

I hadn't thought of it like that. 'I suppose. I just wish I had studied fashion or at least done a fashion diploma straight after my degree instead of going into management consulting.'

'Why didn't you?'

'I don't know. It was really stupid of me. Everyone seemed to assume I would do something girly like PR so I wanted to prove them wrong. And I thought it would be exciting. And . . . the woman who interviewed me was wearing a really great outfit,' I admit.

'What?'

'Yeah. She was wearing this gorgeous matte brown silk shirt with black leather trousers and a fabulous heavy bead necklace, and some killer heels. And I thought, if I take this job, I'll be able to afford to dress like that. It was so stupid of me. I soon copped on, though.'

'What do you mean?'

'You know. I wised up, and realised there was no glamour involved whatsoever. How about you? If you had superpowers, what would you do?'

'I'd help find a cure for Alzheimer's disease.'

'Oh.' I feel a little shallow at the contrast between our ambitions.

'But failing that, I'll be happy if my experiment comes good. No one person ever is going to find a cure for it, you know. It's going to be a combination of things.'

'I'll cross my fingers for you.' It occurs to me that David's comments about Max being flaky don't really ring true to me any more. He seems very dedicated to his work.

We watch as Kristen Stewart gets in her jeep and drives to school through the deserted forest.

'I always used to think it was so cool whenever I watched American films and TV with kids driving to school,' Max says.

'Me too! I used to think that too! Not that I envy her living there, though. It's so grey and dismal – like the back of beyond.'

'No, it's great. I've been there – not to Forks, but I spent a week camping in Washington State. It was out of this world. So rugged and remote . . . nobody for miles around but a couple of bears.'

It sounds like my idea of hell. 'I don't really do camping.'

'No? You don't like to rough it? That shocks me.'

'Hey, I'm not a total princess – I just don't like camping.' I reach for my buffer and start doing my nails. 'Listen, I've been to Irish college. I know about roughing it.'

'What's Irish college?'

'It's a kind of gulag in the west of Ireland, where you go to learn Irish. You're advised not to bring jeans because it rains so much, and a salad is a slice of ham and a piece of tomato, and you get sent home if you speak English. It's great, though.'

'I take it back. Bear Grylls has nothing on you. So – what would be your dream holiday? Two weeks in Bali? Shopping in New York?'

'Shopping in New York always works,' I admit. 'But what I'd really like to do would be a road trip across America. Start in New York and go all the way to California.'

'Me too. I did lots of road trips in California, but I never went out of state much. There is so much to do there. Wine country, Big Sur, the desert . . .'

'It sounds wonderful.' I wonder if I'll ever do something like that – I hope so. I run my hand down my leg to check if it's dry yet.

'Are you fully baked yet?' Max asks.

'Yes! I'm fine.' I laugh, but I can feel myself reddening a little.

'Sorry. It's just . . . I thought I'd seen it all, growing up with two sisters. But I've never met anyone who has quite as much of an arsenal of beauty gizmos as you.'

'What gizmos?' I protest. 'I've no gizmos.'

'What do you call that? That squeaky thing?'

'This yoke? It's a nail buffer! Have you really never seen one before?'

'No, and I've never heard it called a yoke before.'

'Well, you were obviously born in a barn.'

I throw the buffer at him, and he catches it easily, laughing at me. I'm laughing too. I'm about to swat him in the arm, but I decide not to; it would be a bit too . . . not flirty, obviously, but . . . I'm conscious that I'm wearing quite short shorts, and we're sitting rather close together on the sofa. His warm brown eyes meet mine for a moment before he looks away.

On the screen, Edward has just levitated across the car park and saved Bella from being squashed by the car.

'There you go! He's just done something good with his super-powers. He saved her life.'

'Finally,' says Max. 'Making himself useful.'

I laugh, and look at him as he watches Edward. He's wearing a green T-shirt and his long legs are shucked into a pair of narrow black jeans – obviously a new purchase. Green is a good colour on him; it brings out the hazel of his eyes and the olive colour of his skin. I would love to restyle him – I'd put him in greys and greens, and give him something a bit more fitted, maybe a nice blue chambray shirt, some narrow black cords . . .

I wonder what Max would say if he knew I'd turned back time, and hadn't managed to prevent a single accident, disaster or act of terrorism – except Harriet's burglary, of course. He'd probably think that I was every bit as useless as Edward.

Max's phone rings, and he glances at it before putting it on silent. 'Just my sister,' he says to me. 'I'll call later.' He looks sad.

'Everyone well at home?' I ask casually.

He nods, briefly, and doesn't say any more. What with his reluctance to give me his home number, and now this sudden trip . . . I wonder if his parents might be breaking up or something. I decide to change the subject; I don't want to pry.

'Anyway, getting back to Edward – we don't know what it's like to be two hundred years old,' I point out. 'Maybe he's tried to cure cancer, but it didn't work out, so he's just in school because he doesn't have anything else to do.' I wave my left foot to help it dry. 'Maybe having superpowers would be more complicated than we think.'

Max nods. 'With great powers comes great responsibility,' he says, in a deep movie-trailer voice.

'You said it,' I say, with feeling.

TWENTY-TWO

Somehow I manage to get through the rest of my first week at work, mainly by hiding in my office and working on my presentation, with occasional forays around Soho to soak up the street style. That part of it is certainly fun, but most of the trends I see – wearing ankle boots with summer dresses, or the twisted top-knots everyone seems to have – are not really going to be useful to Marley's. I do notice a lot of high-waisted skirts, but I don't know what that means. Will people be wearing them come next summer, or not? I'm scared to guess.

The highlight is my visit to Peter Sembello's showroom, which doubles as his workshop, off Marylebone High Street. He's really friendly, showing me piles of leather and hardware samples, and talking me through his new collection for next spring/summer, which he says was inspired by walking around Milan, where his father is from. The bags are gorgeous; super-soft leather in beautiful muted pinks and greens and tans, with elegant shapes and simple, striped trims: lots of totes and unisex messenger bags, which Peter predicts will be a huge trend for next year. He also thinks 'It' bags are on the wane and that bags are starting to get smaller, which is a nugget I fall on like a famished squirrel. I come out feeling incredibly inspired and excited, as if I'm finally learning something. (Plus, he gave me a free bag.)

On Friday, I'm at my desk looking at the Sartorialist and wondering if wearing moccasins, no socks and trousers rolled-up qualifies as a trend, when there's a knock at the door. Clara, the merchandiser, comes in.

'I thought we could maybe go over your orders from Peter Sembello,' she says.

'Oh, really? I hadn't realized I was going to be placing any orders. I thought Julia just wanted me to go and check them out.'

Clara frowns. 'No, she told me to discuss the order with you, and she wanted it placed before she came back.'

God. I didn't think that Julia was going to trust me that much with the buying stuff. I'm very glad I have Clara here – she obviously knows the drill.

'Of course,' I say briskly. I've decided that the main thing, whenever I'm not sure about what's happening, is to sound extra breezy and confident. 'So – I've never actually done this before, so maybe you can talk me through what usually happens,' I add, as authoritatively as possible.

'It's up to you really – pick as many styles as you want.'

'OK. Well, let's see.' I take a look at the pictures and try to figure out what seems like a good mix of styles and colours. Clara looks at me intently. I wish she would go away.

I take a pencil and start circling a few styles. Clara gasps, horrified, and hands me a separate piece of paper. Oops.

'You know what – I'm going to take a longer look at these. Can I catch up with you later on?' I say firmly, and usher her out.

With Clara out of the way, I can concentrate properly. It's much harder than it looks, because, obviously, I'm not shopping for myself. I even ask Amanda if she knows how I can look up sales of our bestselling bags for the past three years, which she shows me very reluctantly. Finally, I go back to Clara and together we place the order for twenty bags, which is very satisfying. At least I know I've done something right: I know that Peter Sembello is going to be huge.

I pop out to Benugo for lunch (the joy of being able to buy nice lunches without worrying about the cost!) and when I come back, I'm about to go into the kitchen to make a coffee, when I overhear voices. From the hushed tones, and occasional giggles, I can tell they're talking about someone.

'I mean, it's fine to give her a made-up title and an office to play in, but why does she have to be given responsibility for buying?' It's Amanda. 'She clearly doesn't have the first clue about it. Clara said she just placed those orders in a very haphazard way.'

Haphazard? What a cow! She said they were fine!

'I must say I'm looking forward to her "trends report"' says someone else, with a mean giggle. For a horrible moment I think it's Seth, but it's Louis, the menswear buyer, whom I haven't spoken to much. I stay frozen in place, knowing I should walk away but unable to.

'I wouldn't mind but Julia knows my background is in accessories. Why did she get to buy the Sembello stuff?' Amanda continues, sounding aggrieved. 'What experience does she even have? She's just come from the shop floor.'

Louis chuckles. 'Well, you know the real reason they hired her . . .'

'Why? Who is she sleeping with?' Amanda asks bitterly. Bitch! 'Oh, no, don't tell me – she's a friend of Keira Knightley's. Pull the other one.'

'It's just money. They've been told to cut costs, and she's much cheaper than the agency they were using. Plus, Seth can just use her as his mouthpiece to push things he likes.'

Ouch. I'm about to tiptoe away, when I overhear one last thing.

'I don't think she knows a thing about trends anyway, and certainly not about buying,' Amanda says. 'I give her a few weeks and she'll be out on her ear.'

'Yeah. Have they got any Sweet'N Low here? I'm on a detox.'

I've heard enough. I turn right around and walk outside to clear my head. My cheeks are burning and I have a lump in my throat. I feel humiliated and horrified. Is that what they all think of me? That I'm bluffing, or that I have a made-up job, or that I've slept with someone to get ahead? Or that I'm just here to parrot Seth's opinions?

It's true, says a nasty little voice in my head. You are bluffing. You're not really predicting anything. You're just a sales girl who's had a lucky break.

I stop dead on the street outside Starbucks. OK, fine. Maybe I am bluffing – but that doesn't mean I can't do it. I'm going to fake it until I make it.

I buy a double espresso and march back into the office full of purpose. No more surfing the Internet: I need things that aren't out there already. I start by ringing up all the fashion PRs I can, to introduce myself and ask for press releases, and I ring up a few designer's agents too, to make appointments to see their work ahead of LFW. I ring Sinead Devlin as well, and she gives me some brilliant advice in her laid-back style.

'Every season follows the same rough pattern, you know the way?' she says. 'You'll have your three new trends, and two classic trends. Then within all that, you'll have one retro, one ethnic, and one probably, like, futuristic. Metallics are hot right now – I'd back that as a futuristic trend.'

As I book appointments, and start putting a trend board together, I think: I don't care if I'm treading on Amanda's, or anyone's toes. I am going to give a presentation that will blow their tiny minds.

At 6 p.m., I leave to meet Rachel for a drink. It's another hot, sunny evening, so instead of queuing to get served at a pub, we buy some cold Peroni beers from a corner shop and take them to drink in Golden Square. We're not the only ones who've had the idea; the little square is full of people, including a group that have set up a low high-wire and are practising walking on it.

First we catch up on Rachel's news; she's gradually getting on top of this case at work – I so wish I could tell her she's going to win it, but all I can do is offer pep talks. Jay has asked her twice to go for a drink, and she's said no.

'That's great,' I say, admiringly. 'It must be hard.'

'No, it's really easy actually. I think if we'd stayed together

206

another month – or if I hadn't found out the way I did – it would have been really hard, but I got out just in time.'

I nod eagerly; I'm thrilled to hear it.

'Anyway . . . I've been thinking.' She pauses so long that I have to say 'What?' about twenty times before she goes on.

'Well, Jay is gorgeous and we had amazing chemistry and everything, but he wasn't really that nice to me.' She says this slowly, as if it's a new revelation.

'No, I suppose not,' I say thoughtfully, as if this is just occurring to me for the first time.

'But someone like Oliver . . . and this is going to sound mean . . .'

'Yes?'

'Well, he's just – he's not . . . I mean he has a good job, and everything, but he is freakishly tall. And his ears stick out. And he's always draped in cycling stuff and he's just a bit too – eager.'

I nod, again.

'But maybe that's what I should do. Maybe I should just settle for Oliver. I mean, he's nice . . .' She sounds desolate. 'Maybe that's what everyone does. Maybe that's the secret.'

'I don't think you have to settle. I mean, I haven't settled.'

'No! Well, you're lucky. David is gorgeous and intelligent and successful, and he's nice to you but not too nice. It's perfect.'

'I know,' I say, thinking for the millionth time how lucky I am.

'So how is the new job?'

'A bit like that,' I say, pointing at the high-wire. 'It's exciting but I'm in way over my head, I'm working on a presentation I know nothing about, and I feel like a total fraud.'

'If it's any consolation, I feel like that pretty much every day.'

'Really?'

'Yeah. Just remember, they wouldn't have hired you if you couldn't really do the job. You have a talent and they spotted it, and that's why you're there.'

I wish I could tell her the truth, but I just nod.

'That's what Max says, actually. He's been really great this past week, giving me lots of pep talks.' I laugh as I think of his advice to think, 'What would Christina Aguilera do?'

'What does David say? Have you seen him recently?'

I shake my head. 'Not since last weekend. But we've been texting, and he sent me some lovely flowers for my first day.'

'That's nice . . . still, you must be crawling up the walls.'

'Yes, but I've just decided to treat it like being in a long-distance relationship. I knew August was going to be like this – crazy. Anyway, I'm seeing him tomorrow.'

'Good. What are you going to do for your birthday? Do you still want to do karaoke?'

I shudder, as I contemplate the car crash that was my birthday last time around.

'Not karaoke. Just a small dinner somewhere, not too many people. Maybe just you, me, David, Harriet, Kira, Max . . .' I laugh again. 'Max told me there's a great gig on that evening – some nu-wave folk alt metal or something – but I told him I was fine with dinner.'

'Zoë, are you planning on seeing the doctor any time soon?'

'David? I just told you, I'm seeing him tomorrow. Why?'

'No, I meant any doctor. Because I think you might have a touch of mentionitis.'

'What?'

'You know. Max and I have been hanging out . . . Max's experiment is going well . . . Max thinks I should be like Christina Aguilera . . .'

'That's crazy! I do not have mentionitis. I have a boyfriend. And Max is my flatmate!' At the same time I'm thinking uneasily: have I really been going on about Max? 'He's just a friend. It's just that he's been keeping me company while David's been so busy at work.'

'Aha. Keeping you company, is it? OK stop, stop!' Rachel says, as I swat her. 'I know you would never fancy him. I mean he's nice, but he's not in David's league.'

'Of course he's not!' I say, though for some reason I feel a strange pang of guilt – as if I'm being disloyal to Max. But if I said that, Rachel would take it up completely the wrong way, so I drop it, and we move on to discussing venues for my birthday.

TWENTY-THREE

I get home around nine to find Max with his feet up on the coffee table, eating cereal out of his mug, with a spoon, and playing a video game. He looks even more unshaven than usual, and he's wearing the same T-shirt with the ink-stain that he had on when I first met him. As soon as I see him, I'm relieved to know that Rachel was completely wrong. Even if I wasn't with David, I really don't think I could ever fancy a man who played fantasy video games. And he doesn't fancy me either. How could he, when I take off my nice clothes and make-up the second I get home?

I get into my tracksuit bottoms – or my evening lounge wear as I call them – and go and join Max on the sofa. We used to sit at right angles, each on different seats, but now I feel comfortable enough to flop down beside him in order to avoid the broken seat.

'What'cha playing?' I ask.

'*Zelda*,' he says in a monotone, barely looking up. 'I have to rescue a disembodied princess and return her to her body.'

'There's some post for you, by the way.' I pass him the envelope I picked up downstairs, while I open an envelope from my mum, containing an ad for a sales assistant position at Brown Thomas in Dublin. That's the third Dublin job she's sent me since I moved to London.

Max picks his envelope up quickly, then tosses it aside.

'No need to open that one,' he says, waving his control around like a sword. On the screen a little animated man is fighting a monster.

'No?'

'No – it's a PFO.' He presses viciously, and the monster's head flies off with a satisfying 'thunk'. Seeing my blank face, he adds, 'You know. Please eff off. Thanks for your job application but no thanks.'

'But that will all change when your experiment goes well, won't it?'

He shakes his head. 'Remember how I told you all my data was looking good?'

'Um, yes.'

'Well, lately, not so good. I think I might be on the wrong track after all.'

'Oh.' I haven't seen Max in a few days, so this is the first I've heard of it. He seems to be spending all his time at the lab, though once when I woke up at 4 a.m., I passed by his room and saw a light under his door.

'But you can do another experiment, can't you?'

He gives me a twisted smile. 'In theory, I could do hundreds more experiments. But they're expensive, and my funding is going to run out in six months. Actually, five now.'

'Oh. Right.' I sit down on the sofa opposite him, determined to help him formulate a plan of action. 'So what will you do, when it runs out?'

He pauses the game, puts the remote down and runs his fingers through his hair. 'I don't even want to think about it,' he admits. 'I'm applying everywhere, so if I'm lucky I might get something overseas . . .'

'In the States?'

'Possibly. But I think I'd be lucky. I have been offered something in Switzerland, so that's one option, but it would mean abandoning what I'm doing here. Also, I really don't want to leave the country right now.'

211

I've never seen him looking so morose; he's normally so cheerful. I frown and try and think how to help or advise him.

'So what would be the ideal scenario?'

'The ideal scenario would be that I get a good result from my experiment, and write it up and get it into a really good journal like *Science* or *Nature*. With that under my belt, I'd be almost certain of getting a job.'

I've seen him read these; they're clearly his equivalent of *Women's Wear Daily* or *Vogue*.

'I just wish I had a crystal ball, you know? I wish I knew if this experiment will work, or if the whole thing is a house of cards and I should just jump ship and take the other offer.'

I nod, desperately trying to remember if David said anything about it either way. I wish there was some way I could tell Max what's going to happen, or give him some kind of hope . . .

'I'm sorry,' I say, without thinking. 'I just can't remember.'

'How do you mean, you can't remember?'

'I meant, I just don't know.'

'But why did you say you couldn't remember?' He's frowning, looking at me intently.

'I just do that sometimes. Mix up my phrases. Like, sometimes I'll say "Thanks" when I mean "Goodbye."'

'Right,' Max says, looking at me oddly again.

'Actually . . .'

I close my mouth. I can't believe I was about to tell him that I've travelled back in time. He would think I'd hit my head, and call David and an ambulance in short succession. I'm about to change the subject on some pretext when abruptly the room goes dark, including the TV. I shriek.

'What the hell?' says Max. I can feel him standing up beside me.

'Oh, shit! It's a power cut!'

I had totally forgotten this happening last time; I was at home watching TV when the power went.

'I'll check the fuse box,' says Max.

'It's not the fuse box, it's a power cut. Look, the whole street's out.'

'So it is.' He peers out the window. 'I can call the power company, see if they're on it . . .'

'There's no need. The power will be back by midnight.'

'How do you know that?'

He turns back to me. I can just about see his face but I can't see his expression and I'm worried I've said too much.

'I don't know – it just usually does, when there's a power cut. But meanwhile there are some tea-lights and matches in the kitchen, in the cupboard under the sink. I'll get some –' I start inching in the general direction of the kitchen.

'No, I'll get them,' Max says behind me.

I turn around and bump straight into him. He steadies me with his hands.

'Wait there,' he says, gently untangling himself.

I sit down cautiously, feeling my way in the dark. It's weird that I felt something – almost a little buzz – from the collision and the sensation of his fingers on my bare arms. But it was probably just the shock.

After a few minutes, Max comes back and starts lighting candles, lining them up on the coffee table. When the room is twinkling with a dozen little flames, he stops, and after a brief hesitation he sits down beside me.

'So,' he says. 'Do you know any good ghost stories?'

The awkwardness vanishes as we both laugh. Soon we're talking again, even more than we have on previous evenings – about our families, and our jobs and our friends, and all the little things that it's not worth mentioning except to someone who sees you every day. It feels strangely intimate – especially because we're in semi-darkness. His face does look nice by candlelight, I find myself thinking, before reminding myself that everyone's does.

Max has just finished telling me a funny story about the time his lab did Secret Santa and he ended up buying a scented candle for a very senior and scary male professor by mistake. Now he's gone silent, and he's staring into the flickering flames.

'Zoë . . .'

'Yes?' For some reason his tone makes me apprehensive.

'You know that time we were talking about the Chilean miners who got trapped underground the other week, and you said they'll get out OK?'

'Did I? I don't remember.' I kick myself; I did say that.

'You did; you sounded very sure. And now you're saying that the power will come back on at midnight. Why do you talk about the future in that way?'

I would so love to be able to tell him the truth. Can I? Could I?

Without giving myself time to think about it, I start. Being in the dark makes it feel easier.

'Do you remember the morning I met you at David's? When I seemed all disoriented?'

'I was just thinking about that.'

'Well, the reason I freaked out is that the night before, it was December.'

'Last December?' he asks, sounding confused.

'No, this coming December. December 2010. I went to bed in my own room in December and I woke up in David's in July. I don't know how it's happened, but I've turned back time.'

'That's – sorry, Zoë. That's not possible.'

My heart sinks; I might have known he wouldn't believe me. I try and reply to all his questions – about how I felt when I woke up, and whether I'd taken any drugs or anything, and if I think I might have hit my head.

Finally he says, 'I'm sorry, but I can't accept that something like that would happen. It's not that I don't think you're telling the truth,' he adds quickly. 'I just think there must be some other explanation. You might have some kind of amnesia, or . . .'

'Or I'm crazy,' I say bleakly.

'I didn't say that.' But the word hangs in the air.

'Do you have any proof?' he continues. 'Any world events you could predict, to prove your theory? Any sports results, or accidents or earthquakes . . .'

I rack my brains. And finally, it pops into my head.

214

'I do! I have something! You know those Chilean miners you just mentioned?'

'Sure.'

'Well, they are all alive. They're going to get a note to someone . . . I can't remember how but the note will say something like: "We're all safe, all thirty-three of us, in the shelter."'

Max raises his eyebrows. 'You're sure about this?'

'Positive.'

'OK. We can see if that happens. But meanwhile, I think you should seek some help.'

I stand up. 'Gosh, it must be late. I'm going to go to bed.'

'Zoë, you know I'm not—'

'It's fine. I have an early start. Don't forget to blow out the candles.'

I leave the room quickly, feeling thankful that he can't see my face. I somehow thought that because Max was a scientist, he might be more open to strange new ideas. But it's the opposite, and now he thinks I'm an absolute lunatic. I wish I had never said anything.

TWENTY-FOUR

'So it's my birthday next weekend,' I say casually.

'I know,' David says, helping himself to more coffee. 'I may have been practically on another planet for the past fortnight, but I can still remember important stuff like that.'

It's late on Sunday morning and David and I are sitting outside at Daniela's deli, near his flat. I stayed over with him last night, and it was great. Although the whole outdoors thing is beginning to be a real pain; I'm getting sick of finding bits of leaves in my hair. I think I'm going to have to request that we take it inside next time.

'So what do you want to do for the big day?' he asks, rubbing his eye with his index finger.

Last time we had this conversation I replied without any hesitation, 'Karaoke!'

'Really?' David said, the blood draining from his face.

'You're not a karaoke fan?'

'Ah . . . not a huge fan. But I'll be there.'

The night was a total car crash. Through every song, he smiled and nodded along and pretended to enjoy himself, but it was clearly torture for him: the tuneless caterwauling, the stuffy room, the raucous renditions of endless girly songs like 'It's Raining Men' and 'Girls Just Wanna Have Fun'. There were no other men there; it was basically like a hen night. And then, to make it worse, Kira had one of her usual fallings-out with David – she claimed he

216

kept deleting her songs from the karaoke queue, which was completely untrue (I was).

But the worst – the absolute worst part, that makes me go hot and cold to remember it – was when I sang 'Single Ladies' while attempting to do the dance at the same time. I thought that unlike all the other drunken wailers, I sounded great, and I was giving it loads (fuelled of course with a bottle of white wine). I had made everyone shush while I sang and danced, and I was having great crack – until I caught sight of David wincing. Cringing, even. Shortly afterwards, he got beeped. He claimed that he forgot to switch his beep off, but I suspected he was just leaving because he was so embarrassed by me. When I got home, I was so drunk I passed out completely, and we never spoke of it again.

This time around, I'm not doing karaoke.

'I'm not sure. What would you suggest?'

'How about dinner somewhere local?' We discuss venues for a while, and he says that he's heard good things about a place called Ristorante Pizzeria Notting Hill. Or it could be Pizzeria Ristorante Portobello, he's not sure.

'That sounds great, I'll check it out. How did you hear about it?'

'The anaesthetist was talking about it the other day.' He yawns. 'Who are you going to invite?'

'Just a small group. Rachel and Kira and Harriet from work – oh, and I thought I might invite Oliver. As in, your friend Oliver.'

'Really? Why?' David says. 'I mean, sure, invite him, but I didn't know you knew him all that well.'

'I don't know him all that well, but I like him. And he's your friend, and it would be good for it not to be too girly. And I know that he likes Rachel, or he used to.'

'Yeah, and she shot him down,' David says irritably. He seems to have woken up on the wrong side of the bed. 'But I'll ask him. Oh, wait – are you inviting Jenny?'

This again! Last time, he asked me if Jenny could come to my karaoke birthday, because, quote unquote, 'she loves singing'.

Apparently she was in her college choir, or something equally wholesome. I refused point blank.

'I just want it to be my own friends,' I said. David didn't say anything: he just nodded, but I could tell he thought I was being incredibly childish and rude – which of course, I was.

And I still am. I want to scream, 'No! Of course I'm not going to invite her!' Instead, I take a sip of my coffee and count to three before replying: 'I hadn't thought of it.'

I'm hoping he will take the hint and drop it, but he continues, 'It's just that, if you're inviting Oliver, he'll probably tell her about it, or assume she's coming.'

Aargh, true. I look down at the remains of my toast and scrambled eggs.

'Sure. Ask her along.' I force myself to add, 'That would be nice.'

'I'll text her right now,' he says, and takes out his phone. Then he takes me totally by surprise by saying, 'Thanks for inviting her. It makes life easier for me.'

'No problem,' I say. I'm not really as annoyed as I have been in the past but I'm wondering: is this normal? Why would his life be difficult if he didn't invite her?

David's phone beeps. 'It's Max,' he says.

I swallow. 'Oh? What does he say?' *Your girlfriend's crazy?*

'It's annoying . . . we were meant to be playing doubles – him and some girl in his lab against me and Jenny. But she's sick.'

I immediately wonder who the girl in the lab is – presumably just a friend. David's looking at me hopefully.

'You play, don't you?'

'Well –' It's true that I play tennis, in that I can hit the ball; I'm just really bad at it. But I know David believes that tennis is like riding a bike or swimming or being able to tie your shoelaces. It's just something you do, and it's a bit embarrassing if you can't.

'You can borrow a racket from the club.'

Damn. Last time around, of course, I wasn't roped into this tennis match because David and I weren't having breakfast together. I wish I could make an excuse – but he's been working so hard, and looking forward to this match, and if I don't play, Jenny will never let him hear the end of it.

'Sure!' I say with forced enthusiasm.

TWENTY-FIVE

David is a member of a very swanky little place in Maida Vale with great tennis courts, and a kind of country club atmosphere. As we walk in and the (very pretty blonde) receptionist greets us, I'm struck by the contrast between this place and my cruddy council gym. Everything that David does is just . . . *nicer*.

'Ah, the very man,' says David.

Max is sitting just behind the reception area, looking very out of place in his ancient greying Man or Astro-man T-shirt, blue Bermuda shorts and battered tennis shoes, holding a plastic bag with his other clothes stuffed inside. I've been avoiding him since our time-travel conversation, and I'm finding it hard to meet his eye. Luckily a diversion is caused by David discovering that his Babolat tennis racket has a broken string.

'It's OK,' he says, waving away our concern. 'I always keep a spare.'

Next minute, Jenny shows up, dressed for Wimbledon in matching Nike white miniskirt and sleeveless top, neon-pink headband with swooshes and the same racket as David. Even her trainers are spotless. I feel like a complete animal in my yoga bottoms and purple T-shirt, which was the best I could rustle up at such short notice.

'What are you doing here?' is her opening line to me, after she's kissed David and given Max a half-hearted wave. 'Have you come to be David's WAG?' She snorts with laughter.

'My friend couldn't make it, so Zoë's very kindly stepped in,' says Max.

'Really? Whatevs. I suppose you'd better get changed.'

'I am changed,' I say, through gritted teeth.

'I need to get changed,' says David. 'Just give me a minute. Then we'll beat you both to a pulp.'

'That's big talk,' Max says, throwing a ball up in the air and catching it neatly. 'Big talk for a little man –'

David pretends to hit him on the head with his tennis racket, while Jenny looks me up and down and loudly double-checks the club's dress codes with the girl on reception.

Once David's changed, the next thing is a squabble over teams.

'But we always play together!' Jenny whines predictably, when David suggests that he and I team up against Jenny and Max.

'Zoë hasn't played in a while, so we might be better matched if we split up,' David says diplomatically. He looks particularly gorgeous, all in white with a black wristband; I don't even mind that his swooshes match Jenny's.

Jenny sighs. 'But it would be completely unfair, David – you know all my moves . . .'

Is it my imagination or is she saying that *seductively*? Feeling sick, I look away and catch Max's eye. He gives me a faint wink, but I know he still thinks I'm crazy.

Eventually, Jenny agrees to play with Max. We take our positions – David and I facing the sun – as I pray that I don't make a holy show of myself.

David opens the game with an insanely powerful serve, which crashes over the net at the speed of light. Jenny takes a step forward to smash it straight in my direction complete with Serena Williams-style grunt, whereupon I give a stupid, girly shriek and dodge it. Max starts laughing, but stops as soon as I glare at him.

'Love-fifteen,' Jenny says smugly, looking at David. I hate to admit it, but she looks fantastic on the tennis court: tall and tanned and strong, blonde ponytail flying like Anna Kournikova.

David serves again, and we win the game – just about. Jenny and Max win the next one. Jenny's serve is amazing; she seems to leap into the air and smash the ball at 100 miles an hour.

Of course it would be my turn to serve right after her. As I bounce the ball and try and look competent, horrendous memories of PE at school are coming back to me. I reach up as gracefully as possible, hit the ball confidently – and serve a double fault in quick succession. Jenny claps sarcastically; David says nothing.

To my relief my next ball goes successfully over the net. But my triumph is short-lived: Jenny, barely moving at all, whacks it straight back over, right past David who's standing at the net. David gives me a slightly reproachful look, and goes to stand at the baseline while I do my next serve.

I serve again – another double fault. Oh, God, this is so humiliating. I know I haven't played for a while but I didn't think I'd be this bad.

'Zoë, just try an underarm serve this time, OK?' David says to me, demonstrating what even I know is a remedial move. I know he's trying to be encouraging, but it just makes it worse. 'And then, how about this: you cover the tramlines,' he indicates the lines on the edge of my side of the court, 'and I'll cover the rest of the court.'

'Um . . . OK.'

My next serve, thank God, goes over the net. But the next time the ball comes towards my edge of the court, David races for it, calling 'Mine', and smashes it back towards Jenny, who smashes it back to him, whereupon he smashes it over towards Max, while I dance around in my tramlines trying to look as if I'm doing something.

The game goes downhill from there. I notice that Max seems to be deliberately lobbing me the odd easy ball – but if I go for it, David is on it in a nanosecond, roaring 'MINE!' or even, on one occasion, 'LEAVE IT!' I've also copped on to the reason David was standing at the baseline when I served: it's because I'm really bad, and he knew the ball would go right past him if he stood at the net. Soon it's basically him alone playing against Max and Jenny, who's thrilled whenever she scores a point, slagging David and making little in-jokes.

'That backhand of yours, David,' she calls across at him. 'It does need work . . .'

'Thirty-forty,' says David, wiping his forehead with his sweatband.

I'm surprised to see that Max isn't bad at all. His height gives him an advantage when he serves, and when he has to reach for a ball. Jenny keeps yammering on at him, criticising his serves and plays, but he just ignores her. I make the odd token effort, but I'm scared of getting in David's way, and every time I do have the ball I make a mess of it – half of my serves end up in the net. Though neither of them is as good as David, Max and Jenny are able to take over the game, and before long they're just a few points away from winning. I pray that they do it soon and put me out of my misery.

Max prepares to serve, his sweat-soaked T-shirt revealing more definition in his arms and chest than I would have guessed. I look away quickly as he serves a fault, straight into the net. He runs to retrieve the ball, and as he does, our eyes meet through the net. I'm about to look away when he smiles at me – a strange, excited smile.

Drawing himself up to his full height, he sends the ball whizzing over the net faster than I've ever seen him serve it. David races over to my side to get it, but he just misses it, and I hear him swear under his breath.

'Deuce,' says Max.

'Advantage us,' crows Jenny.

My tennis lingo might not be great but I do know this means that if they win the next point, they win the game. I can't wait: I just want it to be over. A little crowd have gathered to watch us. I feel like the biggest tool ever, lurking in the tramlines hoping the ball doesn't come near me. As David goes to retrieve the ball,

I try to catch his eye but he ignores me. I watch as Max lifts his T-shirt to wipe his face, revealing a glimpse of flat brown stomach and a trail of dark hair.

The next rally is so violent that I retreat right back for safety and watch the three of them smash the ball back and forth, racing all over the court. For a second it looks as if Jenny has it, but David sprints forward to send the ball back; Max is there already and, reaching forward so that he's practically horizontal, just manages to fling the ball back over the net to just inside the white line. David just misses it.

'Game, set and match to us!' Jenny yells.

Whooping aloud with delight, Max high-fives Jenny, and then runs forward to shake David's hand.

'What the hell?' David says. 'That was a mile out!'

'What? No it wasn't! It was a mile in,' says Max.

'The fuck it was. It was out.' I watch in amazement as David flings his racket on the ground, and gestures furiously at the line. 'You can see the mark on the chalk.'

My jaw is on the floor; I can't believe he's being such a baby.

'What do you think?' Max asks me.

David seems to see me for the first time. 'Yeah – Zoë, tell them! It was out!'

I hesitate, embarrassed to contradict David.

'Well?' says David, impatiently.

His tone is so rude, and he's being such a dick, that I say, 'It looked in to me.'

David looks at me incredulously. I'm half expecting another explosion, but he just shakes his head and pulls off his sweatband, wiping his face. 'Fine,' he says. 'Your match.' He shakes Max's and Jenny's hand, looking sulky.

'Hey, come on. You're still two for three since I came back,' Max points out.

David shrugs. He goes to the sidelines, chugs down some water and drapes a towel around his neck, before we all walk out together.

'You want to go for a drink, Dave?' Jenny asks, obviously regretting making him annoyed.

'No. I've got to head home and read up on my operation tomorrow.' We've reached the changing rooms, and he leans down to give me a quick, sweaty kiss on the cheek. 'I'll call you during the week, OK?'

'OK,' I say coolly, still annoyed at him.

'See you later, Max – Jen. Next time you won't be so lucky.' He claps Max on the back slightly too hard and leaves us. Jenny runs after him, saying, 'Dave. Amazeballs game. Beautiful tennis. Beautiful!'

Max immediately turns to me and says, 'Let's go for a drink.'

'What, now? It's only five p.m. And you're all sweaty.' Unlike me – strangely enough I barely raised a glow during that game.

To my astonishment, Max takes me by the arm and starts dragging me, literally, towards the exit. 'No arguing. We're going for a drink. Now.'

As we arrive at the Prince Alfred, people are packed on the pavement outside in the late afternoon sun, drinking beer and Pimms and eking the last bit of summer fun out of the weekend. I grab a spot on the pavement outside while Max goes to the bar. After a few minutes he comes back with a gin and tonic for me – which I'll admit I do need after that game – and a pint of beer and a packet of crisps for himself.

'Thanks.' I take a sip. 'So what's up?'

He raises his pint of lager. 'Here's to the Chilean miners. They're all safe in the shelter, all thirty-three of them. As they said in their note.'

I put my hand over my mouth. 'What? Did that happen already?'

Max ignores me, and continues, 'I've been thinking all day about how you could have known about that. Or about the power coming back on at midnight, or all the other little things you keep mentioning. Ideally, I'd have more data, but as it is, I have to work with two possibilities. You've either got some kind of psychic ability.' He frowns. 'Or else you've travelled back in time.'

I just sip my gin and tonic. I'm not going to try and persuade him; he can come to his own conclusion.

'I don't believe in psychics. But time travel . . . I've been reading up on it and in theory, it's not impossible.'

'Really?' I look up, startled.

'Not in a *Back to the Future* way, but in a very tiny, quantum way. Basically, everything else in the universe travels in lots of different directions, so time shouldn't be any different. Of course nobody's time-travelled yet, that we know of. But theoretically, some day it could be possible, maybe using a black hole and, of course, technology.' He looks at me. 'But you didn't have any technology.'

'I know it sounds crazy . . .'

He shakes his head, before I've even finished saying it. 'No. I believe you,' he says. 'I don't understand it, and I think there must be some explanation – but I do believe that you've had this experience.'

The relief of hearing him say that is incredible.

'But it must be . . . I mean . . . are you having the same conversations all over again?'

'All the time. It's weird.'

'I'll say it is,' he says. 'You're *time travelling*!' He clasps his hands to his head. 'I mean, can you even believe we're having this conversation?' He makes an explosive noise and we both start laughing. I feel euphoric.

'Anyway,' Max says, when we've stopped laughing. 'Have you talked to anyone about this? I mean someone familiar with, um . . .'

'With what? Time travel?' I take a sip of my drink. 'Why, do you think my GP could help?'

'Would you consider coming in to my lab, for a scan?'

I was all set to say yes, but now that it's become an actual thing – and he knows what it's for – I'm worried about what would happen.

'No pressure, but I could win the Nobel prize for this.'

'Max, how can you say "no pressure" and "Nobel prize" in the same sentence?' I laugh. 'Look – I'm not sure. Can I think about it?'

'OK, fine,' he says with a twisted smile. I can tell he's disappointed, so I try to explain further.

'I just don't want to be on page three of *Metro*. Or put into an isolation tent, like ET.'

'Eeee Teeee . . . OK. I wonder if there are any other people who've experienced something like this,' he says. 'Have you tried, um, asking around?'

For some reason this seems the funniest thing yet, and we're both rolling around laughing.

Then I say, 'Anyway. What's new with you?' – which sets him off again.

'Well, my experiment still sucks,' he says. 'But that's not as important as being a time-traveller.' He stands up and holds out a hand. 'Come on. We're going to celebrate.'

'Celebrate what?'

'Zoë, you've just convinced me that you've had a unique experience. As in, undocumented in the whole of human history. Don't you think that calls for a drink or something?'

'Sure, we can have a few drinks here, can't we?'

He shakes his head. 'No. You know how you were saying you keep doing the same things over and over? Well, I'm going to take you somewhere you've never been.'

TWENTY-SIX

Half an hour later, I've put my hair up, piled on the eye make-up, and I'm wearing a short, black dress from Etro, with a halter neck and a low back. I bought it at a sample sale years ago, but I've never really worn it much – partly because the back is such a bitch to do up; it's a very pretty, but fiddly, jewelled clasp.

'Max – would you mind helping me with this?' I ask, coming into the sitting room, one hand holding the straps in place.

He looks up from the TV, and his jaw drops. You don't often see a jaw drop in real life – at least, I don't – but there's no mistaking it. I suppose it's only because he's used to seeing me look so dowdy at home, but I have to admit, it is flattering.

I hold up the straps for him and explain how the clasp works. He takes them in his hands, and does it up carefully. All at once I feel very conscious of how close we are. I can feel his fingertips brush against my skin. For a second I wonder if maybe I'm straying into 'inappropriate' territory. But then I tell myself not to be a prude; I'm fully dressed and we're heading out for a few drinks together. So what?

'Right!' he says in a loud, hearty way, releasing me and almost slapping me on the back. 'Let's go.' I notice he's in his grey going-out shirt, which strikes me as quite sweet.

We get on the tube, me still none the wiser, and emerge at Tottenham Court Road station.

'I'm a little overdressed for Burger King,' I tell him as we come up the stairs, fighting our way through the crowds.

'We're not going to Burger King.'

'*We Will Rock You?*'

'No . . . though I totally could.'

'Please no.' I imagine we're headed for Soho, so I'm confused when he leads me in the opposite way, up Tottenham Court Road, past Burger King, and then into a side alley.

'This is . . . interesting,' I tell him, eyeing all the boarded-up entrances, the dank pavement and the lone Chinese restaurant. My heart sinks as I decide he's probably bringing me to some scuzzy old man's pub. But I'll pretend to like it.

'So you haven't been here before,' Max says cheerfully. 'Good.'

As we follow the curve of the alley, it widens into a small street with a handful of bars facing each other. People are standing outside them, holding bottles of beer and glasses of wine, and I can hear music.

'In here,' Max says, waving me before him into a small doorway, manned by two shifty-looking guys. We step inside and the first thing that hits me is the sound of saxophones playing something with a Latin-style beat. To the right, through some arches, is a live band on a platform, fronted by a girl in a white dress. And people are dancing – from older couples, dancing together very decorously, to gorgeous young Spanish-looking couples, and even kids running around between their legs. It's as if we've stumbled into a wedding or some other family gathering.

'Isn't it great?' Max says, beaming at me.

'It is! It's really cool!' My foot is already tapping and I can feel myself twitching to do some salsa moves as I follow Max to the bar.

'What's it going to be, time traveller?' Max says, sliding on to a stool.

'No, no, this is on me.' We peruse the menus handed to us by a very busy-looking waiter with a moustache. 'I might just have a beer. Actually . . . ooh, margaritas! Do you like margaritas?'

He shakes his head. 'No. I *love* them.'

'Should we get a pitcher?'

'No, that might be a bit much,' Max says. I nod, feeling embarrassed at being a bit excessive, but he adds, 'We might want to move on to sangria. Or beer. Or wine.'

'True, true.' We order our margaritas and when they arrive, clink our glasses and take a sip – or in my case, a long and delicious slurp. I love margaritas; the salt, the bitter sweetness . . . 'This is just the best drink ever, isn't it?'

'Yeah. I hate to say it, but you get better ones in America. It's the same with Mexican food. You just can't get it here.'

'Yeah, well, you're in London now, so deal with it.' I lift my glass to him in a toast. 'Ooh! Shakira!' The band are taking a break, and 'Waka Waka' has just come on. I start dancing to it in my chair.

'You really do know all the moves,' he says, looking at me over his glass.

'I do! We did it in Zumba class, and then I taught myself the routine at home.' I lift a hand up, and then another, doing the moves with one hand while holding my glass with the other.

'I thought you might like this place.'

'I love it!' And I do. It's a bit scuzzy around the edges, and the bar is all pitted with what looks like cigarette burns, but it's so much fun. I finish dancing to the song in my chair, taking alternate sips of my margarita, until it's empty. Max orders two more.

'Hey,' he observes, nodding discreetly towards the far corner of the room. 'They look like they've come to the wrong place, don't they?'

I follow his glance, towards four girls. Two of them look relatively normal: one has a black ballet top with tiny stonewashed Daisy Dukes, while her friend is rocking a mustard-yellow playsuit. The third is wearing a pink batwing T-shirt with acid-washed skintight jeans with *elasticated ankles*, and white croc shoes. Her hair is that grey peroxide that's recently become really fashionable. The fourth girl is basically dressed as a Pierrot.

'What do you reckon? Hipster or Hallowe'en?'

'It can't be Hallowe'en, but it must be fancy dress. I mean, a Pierrot?' I look at her in confusion, wondering if I should add this to my trends presentation. 'Are Pierrots a thing?'

'I don't know. Why don't you ask Graham Oogle?'

'Who?'

'You know – Graham Oogle, the guy who invented Google.'

'Is that why it's called Google? I never knew that,' I marvel. Max is full of random facts.

'Sure. And then you've got Waitrose, named after Warren Aitrose.'

'Really? That's bizarre.'

'And Tesco . . . that's . . . Terry, um . .' His mouth starts to twitch, and he cracks up laughing.

'Oh, you're very smart. Hilarious altogether,' I say, swatting him on the arm. But I'm laughing too.

'Oh. Now this is a great song, do you know it?' Max says. I listen. 'It's called *La Camisa Negra.*'

'I don't know it, but it is a great song. Let's dance!' I hop off my seat, noting as I do that those margaritas have gone to straight to my head. 'Come on!'

'Oh no. I don't dance. It's in my contract. I'm a non-dancing drinking companion.'

'Of course you do!' I grab his hand, but he stays put. 'I'll look after our seats,' he suggests. 'You go ahead.'

'OK, I will.' I normally wouldn't do this, but I am a bit drunk. I start grooving away, losing myself in the music and rhythm. There's something about this kind of music that goes straight to my soul. Maybe I was Spanish in a previous life? Next thing I know, a slightly dodgy-looking guy, with one silver tooth, is all over me. I am happy to dance with him, but not when he starts running a hand up and down my back. As I wriggle away, someone positions himself firmly between us: Max. The other guy looks up at him, then beats a quick retreat.

'Fine,' Max says to me. 'You can try and teach me. Though I warn you, others have tried and failed.'

I smile up at him. 'OK. Put your hand on my shoulder, and then take my hand, like this – no, up higher, and really firmly. Now keep it high, and firm. And then just step back one – and together – two-three – and forward one. That's it.'

After a few false starts, he begins to catch on. 'This is easier than I thought,' he says. 'It's basically just counting, isn't it? How did you learn to dance like this?'

'I took lessons in Dublin. Let's try a twirl.' I lift a hand for him, and he twirls me very neatly before catching hold of me again, looking delighted with himself. I'm breathless and laughing; I haven't had this much fun in ages.

'*La Camisa Negra*' ends and a new song begins. We take a second to adjust to it, but he actually has pretty good rhythm. His shoulder feels strong and steady under my hand; our hips are almost touching. I look up at him and smile, and when he smiles back at me I get that jolt again – like I did during the power cut. I'm starting to feel very uneasy, because I'm feeling things that I'm definitely not meant to be feeling. And his expression as he looks down at me – is that how you look at your friend's girlfriend? I notice how soft and dark his eyes are, and how beautifully shaped his mouth is, before I look away quickly.

'By the way, I forgot to ask you,' I say loudly over the music, clearing my throat. 'Are you free next Saturday – I mean this Saturday? It's my birthday.'

Max nods, then shakes his head. 'What is "birthday" to a time traveller?'

This makes me start laughing again. 'But sure, count me in,' he says, giving me a twirl. 'Is this the same birthday as last time, or what?'

'No. Last time was karaoke. It was a disaster, so this time I'm doing dinner.'

'We'll give you a better time this time.' He bends his head down to say this in my ear, and his head stays close to my neck for maybe a second longer than necessary. It gives me shivers down my spine. Then I feel his hand shift on my waist – as if he's

232

pulling me closer. He *is* pulling me closer. I take a deep breath to try and clear my head, and as I do, Max steps back, gently dropping my arms.

'I think I need a drink of water,' he says. 'Can I get you one?'

I nod quickly, and excuse myself to go to the ladies'. I look at myself in the mirror reproachfully: red cheeks, smudged mascara, dilated pupils.

'It was just the margaritas,' I say aloud. A sultry looking dark girl, coming in behind me, raises her eyebrows as if to say, 'Sure it was.'

Damn, damn, damn. Now I feel embarrassed about going out and facing Max. But nothing happened! It was just a few drinks and a bit of a collision on the dance floor. Before I can overthink it, I march back out to where Max is sitting by the bar. I give him a big, bright smile, flatmate to flatmate, and take the glass of water he gives me, draining it almost in one swallow.

'Maybe we should just go home,' I suggest. 'It's already almost midnight . . .'

'OK, let's do that.' He looks almost relieved.

'That was really fun,' I tell him, as we step out of the bar, into the cool night air. The crowd is still twenty people deep on the pavement, but the roar of their voices gradually recedes as we walk further away. I steal a sideways look at Max, who's deep in thought.

'So, listen,' he says. 'This whole time travel thing.' We both laugh, because it sounds so ridiculous. 'What do *you* think might have caused it?'

I tell him about Christmas, and how miserable I was, and how the old lady told me to make a wish.

'But what did you actually wish for? Was it to turn back time?'

I hesitate. 'Well, no. I wished – I wished that I could have David back. Because we broke up.'

'Oh.' He looks away for a minute, then says, 'So you wanted to get him back?'

'Yeah. I wanted to go back and do things differently.'

233

'And now you have.'

I nod. Silence descends once more, so I start to chatter. 'I love that place, I'll have to come back. You know, I haven't had such a good time in ages. I mean,' I add quickly, 'that's the great thing about London, isn't it? All these little hidden places.'

'But you must miss Dublin sometimes, no?' He looks as if he's making an effort to change the subject too.

I nod. 'I do. I miss my parents, and my friends, and I miss how peaceful it is and I really miss the sea.'

'Really? I'm going tomorrow. To Devon, with some friends, surfing.'

'But tomorrow's Monday.'

'We thought we'd beat the crowds. None of us has to be in the lab tomorrow, so.'

'That sounds like fun.'

He opens his mouth, as if to say something, but then goes quiet again. Then he says abruptly, 'Why don't you come? You've got the day off, haven't you?'

'Yes.' I had booked it randomly with the thought of checking out a sample sale and getting something to wear for my birthday. 'But surfing? I don't surf.'

'No? Well, you can swim, sit on the beach. We're driving down tomorrow, early, and coming back the same day. There's room in the car, there're just three of us going.'

'Well . . . OK, sure!' As soon as I've said this, I wonder if it was wise. But I'm probably being over-cautious. What could be more wholesome or innocent than a day at the beach with your flatmate?

TWENTY-SEVEN

'Zoë! Are you ready? We're leaving in ten.'

I groan and look at my alarm clock: ten to eight. Rolling out of bed, I pull on some underwear and start grabbing together random bits of clothing: denim shorts, flip-flops, tank top, swimsuit. And suntan lotion. I'm sitting at my dressing table, hunting for my waterproof mascara and bronzer, when Max bangs at the door again.

'I'll be there in a sec. I'm just finding my make-up.'

'What are you talking about?' he says, through the door. 'We're going to the beach. You don't need make-up. Come on, we don't want to get stuck in traffic.'

I look at myself briefly in the mirror. I look awful: all puffy and blotchy, with my mascara smudged from last night. I can't remember the last time I left the house without make-up. But I suppose it won't kill me.

I stumble out, remembering to grab my wallet, and find Max sitting on the front steps. He's wearing his usual jeans and T-shirt, and has a beach towel stuffed into his trusty plastic bag. It's a perfect, cloudless morning: blue sky as far as the eye can see.

'So how are you feeling after last night?' he asks, as I sit down and put on my shades.

I make a so-so motion. 'I'm feeling as if that fourth margarita was a bad idea. You?'

'Same.' I'm relieved. Whatever oddness happened last night was obviously just due to a few drinks.

'So remind me, who are we going with again?'

'We're going with my friends Suzanne and Gareth. And Suzanne is bringing along an old wetsuit for you. She has a board too, but the rest of us will hire them. Hey, there they are.' He stands up and waves to a blue Mini that's just pulled up, with a short surfboard on it. A guy and a girl get out. She's wearing sunglasses and a little drawstring dress, and I instantly regret my shorts: why didn't I wear a cute dress?

'Suzanne, Zoë.'

'Hi! Nice to meet you!' Her smile is friendly behind her glasses. She's obviously American, or Asian-American.

'And this is Gareth.' Gareth is short and stocky with mirrored shades perched on his head, three-quarter-length shorts and a Hollister hoodie. He has dark hair, a round, baby face and mischievous blue eyes. I'm surprised; I wouldn't have pictured any of Max's friends owning branded clothing.

'Nice to meet you, Zoë. Can you drive?' is the first thing he asks me, in a beautiful Welsh accent.

'No,' I admit. 'I've failed my test twice.'

'No problem, we'll teach you. There's a nice empty stretch along the A303.'

'Ignore him,' says Max, putting my bag in the boot.

'I was just joking. Obviously we're taking the M4,' says Gareth. 'Suzanne's called shotgun because she gets sick in the back, so you'll have to pile in somehow, big fella,' he says to Max.

'No, it's OK. He can go in the front,' Suzanne says, and she and I get in the back.

She immediately turns to me and starts firing off a series of friendly interrogations in her chirpy voice. 'So you and Max are roommates? Is that how you know each other, or did you know each other previously?'

Max says, 'Zoë is going out with David – you know my friend David Fitzgerald?'

'Oh, aha?' she says. 'He's a surgeon, correct? I remember. You must hardly see each other, right? If he works such long hours?'

'Suzanne!' says Gareth. 'She's barely been in the car five minutes!'

'Sorry,' Suzanne says. 'I have a tendency to ask inappropriate questions.'

'That's OK,' I say, laughing. 'He does work long hours.'

She's pretty strange but I like her. I start asking a few questions of my own, and find out that Suzanne is an engineer and Gareth is a medical writer, and they were both at Imperial with Max. We're now past the Westway, and heading west into the countryside. This is the first time I've been out of London into the countryside in my entire time living here. Soon we're having a lively discussion, sparked by Gareth's suggestion of a detour to Monkey World in Dorset, about whether or not monkeys are creepy.

'How can you find monkeys creepy?' Gareth demands. 'They're so cute.'

'They're too inbetweeny,' I explain. 'Are they animals? Are they people? What are they?'

'They're definitely animals,' Max says.

There's hardly any traffic, and we're whizzing along. After we stop at Chippenham the countryside grows increasingly lush, and green and chocolate-boxy, full of rolling hills and adorable little thatched houses and fields full of grazing cattle. The names are like something out of a children's story – Chipping Sodbury, Peasedown St John. I'm excited to see Glastonbury; the town is hippy central, all the windows full of tie-dye, dreamcatchers and home-made candles.

'Can we put on some music?' Suzanne asks.

'Anything but Max's crap,' says Gareth. 'I don't want any obscure EPs recorded on a xylophone by Eskimos in Nebraska, or whatever it is you've got for us today.'

'I've got Silver Jews and Magnetic Fields,' protests Max. 'They're mainstream.'

'You have the most obscure taste in music of anyone I know,' says Suzanne. 'But you're not all that cool. It's weird.'

'I am cool,' says Max. 'What are you talking about?'

He catches my eye in the rear-view mirror, and smiles. I smile back, thinking: *I'm having a really good time. I'm glad I came.*

Woolacombe Bay is huge, and curved, with sparkling blue breakers framed by towering chalk cliffs rising on either side. There are only a handful of other people here, mostly surfers, and one old man walking his dog. Stepping out of the car, I take my first deep breath of salt sea air. It gives me a rush of sensation: childhood holidays, days spent by the sea, freedom and happiness. Max comes up beside me and stands beside me. We stand together in silence for a minute.

'It's good, isn't it?' he says, and I nod.

We go and hire boards from the little rental place beside the beach. I can barely lift mine, but apparently the longer it is the easier it will be. Then it's time to slather on the Factor 50 and get into our wetsuits. Max warns me that this is going to be the hardest part, and he's right; it's like forcing yourself into a tube of toothpaste.

'Can't I just wear my swimsuit?' I ask, flapping my arms frustratedly.

'No, it would be too cold. Look, it fits you perfectly!' Suzanne says cheerfully, as I finally wriggle it into place, red-faced and panting. 'I'm so glad I kept it. Are we all ready?'

'You two go ahead,' Max says. 'I'm going to give Zoë some tips.'

I turn to him, and have to make an effort not to look really surprised. His wetsuit reveals everything his baggy jeans and T-shirts have been hiding: broad shoulders, a lean, tapered torso, narrow hips and long legs. Wow. How have I never seen this before?

'So the wetsuit fits you,' he says, staring at me and then looking away quickly. 'Great. OK. Tips.' He clears his throat.

'How do I stand on the board?'

He laughs. 'I'm afraid you're not going to be standing today – we're just going to focus on trying to catch a wave.'

He shows me how to lie on the board – not too far forward, not too far back. I can't seem to get it right, so I let him adjust me with his hands, pushing my hips into place. Then he shows me how to attach the board to my ankle with a little leash, so that I don't lose it, and so that it doesn't hit anyone else on the head.

'What if it hits *me* on the head?'

'Good point – try and avoid that. OK, that completes the dry part of the initiation. Let's go catch some waves, dude!' We exchange high-fives and walk down to the sea, where Suzanne and Gareth are already surfing.

The waves are bigger than I'd thought, and for the first time I feel nervous. I can swim fine, but I don't want to be knocked flat by some massive breaker and swept out to sea.

'No need to worry,' Max says, seeing my face. 'I'll keep an eye on you.'

'I'm not nervous,' I lie, as we go into the water together. It's freezing cold.

'You should be.' He flips cold seawater on me, and I shriek and splash him back. It degenerates into a bit of a water fight. Suzanne, hearing us, turns around and waves at us.

We wade in until we're waist high. The tide's sucking under my feet, almost knocking me off-balance, but I'm excited now: seeing the breakers rolling in, I want to catch one and ride it, just the way Gareth is doing now. How hard can it be?

It turns out it's pretty hard. Max goes first to show me; pointing the board towards the sea and then turning as the wave approaches, and paddling harder and harder until he catches the wave at just the right point and zooms in towards the shore on his knees. I try and copy him, but I just can't get the momentum right; either the wave breaks before I catch it, and knocks me sideways, or else it goes right past me, leaving me bobbing pointlessly.

On my fourth attempt, it seems as if I've got the timing right, and I'm paddling frantically to catch the wave in time – but just as I hear Max shout 'Paddle harder! Harder!' I'm knocked right over and tumbled in a freezing, salty washing-machine before I emerge, with the board giving me a vicious knock in the shin for good measure.

'You OK?' he calls over to me. Through the drops of water in my eyelashes, and the dazzling sun, I can just see his lean black silhouette, sitting on his board and bobbing easily in the swell.

'I'm fine,' I call back. 'It was great!' Even though it wasn't right, it was exhilarating.

'You nearly had it there,' he says, wading over to me. 'I tell you what: why don't I grab your board for you and get you onto a wave? Then you can get the feeling of what it's like.'

'Max, I don't want to take up all your time. You should do your own surfing.'

He shakes his head. 'We've got plenty of time. I'm going to leave my board on the shore – wait a second.' He wades out, carrying his board under his arm, and deposits it on the shore, before running back in. 'OK, here we go. Lie on your stomach and hang on with both hands. Not too far forward – perfect. Here's your wave. Just hang on tight!' He pushes hard on the board, wading behind me, and I feel the wave coming in until he's no longer pushing me and the wave's taken over. It's the most incredible feeling; it's as if I'm part of the wave, and all the power of the sea is concentrated in this one action, shooting me like an arrow towards the shore.

'Wooooooaaaaah!' I scream as the sand approaches. My foot starts to flip and then my board has somehow disappeared and I'm crashing under water, hitting the bottom with my feet and arm, but then sitting up, bruised but euphoric.

'I made it!' I scream. 'I caught a wave!'

Twenty feet away, Max is laughing and holding both his thumbs up. I wade back to him, and tell him that I'm going to practise by myself for a while. 'You need your own surf time.'

'OK. Just remember: watch out for the board if you go under. And don't try and catch a wave if someone's on it already.'

I nod, and resume my practising: turning, feeling the swell of the wave, paddling and trying to find that magic moment. It's really hard, and I keep on getting it wrong – but that one moment earlier was tantalising enough for me to want to keep going for it again. I can see why people get addicted.

Near me, Suzanne and Gareth are bobbing on their boards, chatting together and lazily floating, catching waves on their stomachs. I go over to them and we surf together for a while – at least, they surf and give me helpful advice, while I flounder around.

'I don't see Max,' Suzanne says, looking around.

I don't see him either, and I'm seized by pure panic. What if he's gone under?

'Oh, there he is,' says Gareth.

I turn around, and see him, riding a low wave as easily as someone catching a bus. He's standing so upright that he almost seems to be leaning back, one foot in front of the other, arms just barely held out from his sides. I watch as he skims along the crest of the wave, following its breaking line as it moves from sparkling blue and green to white foam. He looks incredible.

'Wow,' I say involuntarily. 'He's amazing.'

'Yeah, he took lessons.'

As clearly as if it's speaking in my ear, I hear Whoopi Goldberg's voice from the film *Ghost*. 'Zoë, you in danger, girl.'

OK, calm down, I tell Whoopi. I'm with David, and Max knows that; we're just friends. The only reason any weird feelings are arising is just because I'm hardly seeing David these days. Max and I are having fun, and he's good at surfing. That's all.

I'm freezing, and I decide to get out for a bit. Leaving my board high up on the beach, I walk over to a little kiosk to buy some hot chocolate.

'Would you like some whipped cream with that?' asks the teenage boy with bleach-blond dreads.

'Yes. And do you have marshmallows? Actually, can I have a hot dog as well?' I ask.

I don't know how surfers stay so slim; I'm absolutely ravenous. After I wolf down my hot dog and hot chocolate, I decide that it's time for a rest.

TWENTY-EIGHT

Twenty minutes later, I'm lying on the beach with my sunglasses, covered in Factor 50, listening to the soothing crash and hiss of the waves on the shore. I'm wearing my oldest swimsuit and no make-up, and I've just noticed a big white streak in my fake tan, but I feel like a million dollars.

I must have dozed off for a minute, because when I open my eyes again, the sun's lower, though it's still lovely and hot. 'Hi there!' says a voice beside me. Suzanne puts out her beach towel, an ancient-looking thing with a picture of the Little Mermaid on it, and drops down beside me in her swimsuit.

'Did you have enough? It's tiring, huh?' she says.

'Really tiring! I had fun, though.'

I hear a familiar voice, and squinting through my sunglasses, I can see Max – half out of his wetsuit and wearing a T-shirt – playing football on the beach with a couple of little boys. It's a truly adorable sight. The two kids, who look around eight or nine, are easily beating him, tackling him effortlessly and scoring goals past him. He looks up, sees me watching him, and waves.

'So, what is the situation with you and Max?' Suzanne asks.

I almost jump out of my skin. 'What situation?'

Her eyes are fixed on him. 'I can tell that he likes you – I mean he really likes you. And it seems that you like him too, but you have a boyfriend, right? Who's a friend of his?'

243

'How do you know he likes me?' I ask, and then correct myself. 'You've got the wrong idea. We're just friends.'

She ignores this. 'I can just tell. I know that it's none of my business, but Max has a tendency to be attracted to difficult women.'

I'm so flabbergasted, I can only reply, 'Oh, really.'

'He had a really bad break-up about a year ago and it was pretty horrible to watch. He takes things to heart, and I don't want him to get hurt. Especially with everything going on with his family,' she adds.

'But what *is* going on with his family?'

Suzanne stares at me. 'You didn't know? His mom has Alzheimer's disease. Early onset. It's really awful. She's only, like, sixty.'

'Oh, my God.' Now it's my turn to stare at him. He's taking a deliberately feeble kick at the goal, letting the little goalie catch it. I feel so terrible that I didn't know. It all makes sense now. Why he wants to stay in the country. His sudden visit home. His scrapbook. Why he wants his experiment to succeed so badly, even. Poor, poor Max.

'Anyway,' says Suzanne, 'you seem really nice, and it would be great if you got together with Max. But not if you have a boyfriend.' She stands up. 'I'm going to head in for a swim,' she says. 'You want to come?'

I shake my head, and she trots down to the waves, passing Max on the way. After saying something to the little boys, he starts walking up slowly towards me, while I try and think what to say to him.

'I thought you didn't like competitive sports.'

'Oh, it's fine if I know I can win.' Flopping down cross-legged beside me, he asks, 'Had enough already?'

'Just hanging ten.'

'What? No. Hanging ten is a really advanced move. It means having ten toes over the board.'

'Oh. I thought it meant taking a break.' We both laugh.

'You might hang ten one day, if you keep it up . . . you did well, for a beginner.'

'No, I was awful! I loved it though. *You're* amazing at it.'

'I've just had loads of lessons.'

We sit in silence for a minute, before I say impulsively, 'Max – Suzanne just told me about your mum . . . I'm so sorry.'

He looks down at his toes in the sand. 'Thanks,' he says, almost inaudibly.

'Is it . . .'

'I don't really want to talk about it.'

'Sorry.'

'Just, not today. Not right now.'

'I understand.' Damn. He's probably trying to forget about it, and then I have to bring it up on him.

He picks up a handful of sand and lets it pour out slowly through his fingers. 'Can I ask you a question? I mean, say something?'

'Of course.' My heart starts to beat a little faster.

'You know, when you said about going back in time to – because of, ah, David.' He clears his throat; it's obviously an effort for him to say the name.

'Yes,' I half whisper.

'Well . . .'

There's a really long pause, and just when I think he's changed his mind about saying anything at all, he continues, 'I just don't think you should have to do something like that, to make a man fall in love with you. That's all.'

If I was surprised when Suzanne gave me her speech, I'm speechless now. What is he saying?

'Ahoy, land-lubbers!' roars a voice behind us. Gareth, now changed back into his clothes, throws himself down beside me, spraying sand everywhere. 'Now, me hearties,' he continues in what I'm guessing is an attempt at a Devon accent. 'I have two words for you. Cream. Tea. In Woolacombe. Clotted cream, jam, lashings of ginger ale. You up for it?'

* * *

245

Soon we're on our way home in the car, stuffed full of scones and jam. Max is in the back beside me this time, because Suzanne was feeling sick, and he's fallen asleep. As Suzanne and Gareth chatter away in the front, I look at him – dark, spiky eyelashes fanned out, face tanned even darker, hair vertical and stiff with salt water.

So he likes me. Back on the beach, I'm pretty sure he was telling me that he has feelings for me. And there's no point in denying it: I'm attracted to him too. I've been telling myself we're just friends, or flatmates, but there's no point kidding myself any more: I fancy the pants off him. If I were single, it would be all I could do not to undo my seatbelt, and reach over to him and . . . well, kissing him would be a start.

But I'm not single. I'm with David, and I love him. He's perfect for me! So how can I have feelings for Max? Not just 'he's cute' feelings, but – bigger ones?

A wave of panic overwhelms me, as I think about what this might mean. Do I have to break up with David? Or say something to Max?

But then I think: I'm overreacting. It's just a crush. I'm a bit hormonal, and I haven't seen David for ages, and now weird feelings for Max are popping up, but they actually don't mean anything. In fact, I've read about this! It's normal. It happens all the time that you might get a random crush on someone inappropriate at work or something, but it doesn't mean there's anything wrong with your relationship. It's healthy, probably.

'You OK in the back?' Gareth asks.

'Fine,' I say, clearing my throat. 'Just tired.'

Hearing our voices, Max wakes up. He looks straight into my eyes, before his smile fades and he turns away.

I feel so horribly guilty. It's fine for me to have a little crush, but Max . . . What if he really likes me? I feel sick to my stomach as I realise how I've been flirting with him, leading him on, dancing with him. I've given him completely the wrong idea. The last thing I would want to do is hurt him. Especially with everything he has going on at home! I'm going to have to pull back and somehow let him know that I'm still very much with David. I have to be honest with him. His statement on the beach was also a question, and it deserves an answer.

Suzanne turns on Magic FM, which is having some kind of nineties hour. We listen to Four Non Blondes, and OMC singing 'How Bizarre', and then the song 'Breakfast at Tiffany's' comes on. I try to block out the words, about two people having nothing in common, because for some reason it makes me feel really sad.

'Have you seen the movie *Breakfast at Tiffany's*, Zoë?' Suzanne asks from the front seat.

'I have, I love it.' I pause and then continue, 'I've always wanted to do that thing of turning up early and standing in front of the window, first thing, and looking in it and having a coffee . . .'

'But why would you have to stand outside? Is it that expensive a restaurant?'

'Tiffany's? No! It's a jewellery store.'

'Oh! I never knew that!' She starts laughing, and I laugh too, though my mind is still on Max. How can I tell him he's got the wrong end of the stick?

After a slow crawl along the motorway, we arrive at the house at five to eight. After saying goodbye to the others, Max and I go up the steps. He puts his key in the lock as I look at the pink-and-orange evening sky.

'I might order some pizza,' he says, as we walk up the hall stairs. 'You want in on that?'

'Um. . . .'

'I have a pizza voucher,' he says, raising his eyebrows. 'And – drum roll – *Point Break* is actually on TV tonight. Sounds like the perfect evening, no?'

It breaks my heart to have to turn him down, but I've got to.

'No, I think I'm going to have a shower and go to bed early. I might just have some cereal or something.'

'Or some croutons? I know they're your snack of choice.' In the half-dark of the hallway, I can see him smile at me. I have to drop a bigger hint.

'Oh, Max, I was going to ask you. You're coming to my birthday on Saturday, aren't you?'

'Of course.'

'Well, great, because there's a friend of mine who I think you might like. I won't make it, like, an obvious set-up, but you can just meet her casually and see.'

'Oh . . . OK.'

Oh, God. When I see the look on his face, I feel as if I've just stabbed him in the back, but I tell myself it's much better to hurt him a little now, than a lot later on.

TWENTY-NINE

After all the dramas of the weekend, I'm quite relieved to get into the office on Tuesday. As I turn on my computer, though, my mind keeps going back to Max. Every time I think of the look on his face, when I told him I was going to set him up with a friend, I feel like a murderer. But I know it's for the best.

My first encounter of the day is with Amanda, giving me some feedback on my swimwear trends report.

'It lacks detail,' she says, fanning herself with it absently. 'You need to tell us what brands we should be watching, what kind of buzz they're generating, sales figures, what our competitors are stocking . . . just basic stuff like that, really. Can you manage that? Or should I ask Julia to give you a hand?'

'No, it's fine. Let me get to it right now.'

Damn. I know she's right about all that extra detail, but I just don't have a bog how to come up with it. And if I don't get it right, I'm positive she's going to say something to Julia, or Seth. I whimper with panic, and get out the previous agency's trends report again, looking for clues as to how they compiled their information.

Shortly afterwards, Julia summons me to her office, saying she has a dress to show me.

I give an involuntary intake of breath, because it's just gorgeous; a silk-chiffon dress in dusty rose pink, with a deep V-neck and back, and a subtle feathery detail on the skirt, which ends just above the knee. It's the kind of dress you could wear out clubbing with an armful of bangles, or dress up with heels and a little jacket and wear to a wedding. I feel a deep ache within my chest; it's almost like being in love.

'I thought we could try sending one more dress to Keira,' she says. 'This one will get her attention, don't you think?'

'I'd say it will.' I'm unable to take my eyes off it. 'It's perfect. Is it Alice and Olivia?'

'No – a new designer called Victoire des Anges. It's a one-off. Did she like the last two we sent her? We haven't heard a thing back, not even from the PR company . . .'

'Yes, I think she did,' I say wildly. I presume she did: I just had them messengered over and didn't hear back. I cross my fingers, hoping to God that nobody checks up on it.

Julia shakes her head. 'I think we're taking a bit of a risk sending things via the PR company. It's not that I don't trust them, but you never know when things will just sit around the office rather than being passed on. Or, more to the point, things can get mislaid . . .'

'I know.' I'm nodding, but my eyes are fixed on the dress. It's as if it's talking to me. And it's saying, *Wear me*. I picture Max seeing me in it at home – but then firmly replace it with a picture of David seeing me in it. At my birthday dinner! It would be perfect!

'So I thought, maybe you should just put it straight into her hands,' Julia says. 'Would you be prepared to do that?'

I tear my eyes away from the dress long enough to look up, and answer her.

'Sure.' I clear my throat. 'Of course I could. I'll make sure she gets it. By the way, did you see the quantities of the Peter Sembello bags that I ordered? Were they OK?'

'Yes, they were perfect.' She hands me the dress and goes back to her computer. 'Sorry, I just have to check something.'

I back out of her office, still staring at the dress. It's so perfect, you wouldn't need much in the way of accessories. Maybe a pair of hoop earrings? Hair up, obviously. Some great shoes . . . I step forward and stroke it gently, feeling the super-fine quality of the material. I pick up the price tag, and almost drop it in shock. I could never afford it, even on my new salary.

Damn. If I send it to the PR agency, some work experience girl will just snaffle it and sell it on eBay. Whereas if I brought it home with me it would be looked after, cherished and loved for the rest of its life.

But if I took that dress, it would be stealing, plain and simple. I turn my back on it, and sit down to focus on my swimwear report again. Body-con. My analysis of this trend is that . . .

Of course, I could just *borrow* it. I could wear it to my birthday, get it dry cleaned, and send it to Keira's PR agency the very next day. And no one would ever know. Before I can stop myself, I've jumped out of my chair, shut my office door, and I'm trying the dress on. I almost can't bear how perfectly it slips on. In fact, Keira would probably have to have it taken in . . . I wriggle over to the slice of mirror beside my door, and gasp. It is *perfect*.

I need to stop myself. I take it off, put it where I can't see it, and focus on trying to improve the swimwear presentation. And work on my own presentation – which I'm giving in, gulp, less than a week's time.

In the afternoon I attend a VM meeting (which I've now, belatedly, learned means visual merchandising). We're discussing Christmas windows, and I'm very relieved to be back on firm ground, both in discussing what we should do with our windows (I firmly back the Four Seasons and the Fairy Tales) and what the competition are likely to be doing.

'I have a feeling that Selfridges will max out on the play theme,' I say, sounding more confident than I have in a while. 'Lots of toys, and a very fun, contemporary look.'

251

'You seem to have a *feeling* about lots of things,' Amanda says innocently. 'Is that how you go about your trends reports?'

'No, but it's true, though,' says the visual merchandiser person, whose name is either Jane or Janet. 'I know someone who's working on it. The theme is play.'

Hah! I think, as Amanda subsides, giving me a look of reluctant respect. Take that. Seth is yawning and flipping through his BlackBerry. I've noticed by now that he has quite a short attention span in meetings; he'll say his bit and then he just tunes out.

After we discuss the windows, we spend some time talking about the new store outfit. This is crucial stuff; sales per square foot are what determines whether we're profitable or not. I'm thrilled to see that Sinead's stuff is getting a prominent place in the store. I can't wait until her scarves become a cult favourite, and we're the store that's making it happen . . .

'So, then, still in accessories,' Jane or Janet says. 'What about the fitting for this new brand – Peter Sembello? Where do you want him to go?'

Everyone seems to be looking at me. 'He's going to be huge, so I think we should give him a very prominent place . . . how about here, to the left, right by the cash register?' I point to the floor plan.

'But that's where we normally put Gucci,' Jane or Janet says.

'Well, maybe Peter's the new Gucci,' says Seth.

'That's true,' says Jane or Janet. 'What do you think, Zoë?'

I pause, to make sure I'm right about this. I have a really clear memory of getting the tube home, and reading in the *Evening Standard* about how Peter Sembello was *the* new bag brand to watch. But even without that inside knowledge, I'm learning to trust my judgement more and I really believe in him.

'Oh, definitely,' I say. 'We have to give him a really nice fitting.'

'OK,' says Jane or Janet, marking on the placement a big PS.

*   *   *

'Hey, girlfriend,' says Seth, trailing me down the corridor. Today he's in a navy jacket, white shirt and black knee-length shorts, with the ever-present moccasins without socks. 'Nice work in there. I love that Sembello stuff. And I love seeing a bit of conviction about a new brand.'

'Thank you! Would you have time to have a quick look at what I've got so far on the trends report? I'd love your input.'

He follows me into the office, where I show him the trend boards and the slides I'm getting ready. I've identified the trends to watch as: printed trousers, coloured denim, colour-blocking, metallic and ladylike.

'Mmmm,' he says.

'What do you think?' I ask, worried.

He sighs. 'It's all very nice, darling. But, not to be bitchy or anything, it's the kind of thing any high street designer could put together. I think you need to think a bit bigger. What are people going to be wanting as well as wearing? What's the mood on the streets going to be? How will people be using their leisure time? That kind of thing. For example, you haven't got anything in there about the internet. Bricks and mortars stores like us aren't going to survive unless we build our online sales.'

Ah. It's all just clicked into place. Seth is always banging on about online. This must be his agenda, and this relates to what Louis, the guy in the kitchen, meant.

'I can definitely put something in about our website.'

'Or lack of website. Yes, I think you definitely should. Don't be tactless . . . but do gather data about what the other stores are doing.'

'OK.' It will be difficult to fit all this in, with just over a week to go, but Seth is smart and I think he's right about this stuff. I think it will really add a strategic edge to my presentation. I could even make some concrete suggestions about our website and all the things I've noticed. I'm beginning to feel really excited: I think this is going to be good.

Just then, my phone beeps with a text from David. Seth is still looking at my slides, so I read it quickly. 'Hey, nearly-birthday girl. Sorry I've been so crap lately. Look forward to making it up to you soon. xxxo D.'

All at once, the weekend with Max seems very far away. I have a huge feeling of relief and certainty: David is definitely the one for me.

'Message from your boyfriend?' asks Seth, obviously seeing the stupid smile on my face. 'Show us a picture.'

I'm laughing, but I also want to show him off, so I find a picture on my phone: my favourite one of David, taken on his terrace. I felt self-conscious taking it, but I also really wanted a picture of him.

Seth whistles. 'Woah. Cut me a slice of that! Sorry, darling, didn't mean to be vulgar. And he's a surgeon? My brother is a surgeon actually. Opthalmic. What does yours do, remind me?'

When I say cardiac, Seth whistles again. I have a sudden unworthy thought: Seth wouldn't react like that to a photo of Max, or to his job. David is more impressive; that's just the way it is.

'Must be hard, though, I bet you hardly see him?'

'It is hard,' I admit. 'I've actually only seen him twice in the past three weeks.' When I say it out loud, it sounds really pathetic, so I add, 'But we're going out this Saturday for my birthday.'

'Ooh! Happy birthday for Saturday, we'll have to give you the bumps. Is that what you're wearing? It's divine.' He points to the dress, still hanging tantalisingly in the corner, and then steps over and examines the label.

'No, that's a freebie for Keira Knightley.'

'Oh yes, your pal! That's so great. Anyway, darling, I'd better get on, I have lots to do and I'm leaving early to go spinning. See you later, and let me know if I can help with the presentation.'

After Seth's gone, I make some notes on what we've discussed, but I can't stop thinking about the dress. I make a snap decision: I'll wear it this weekend, get it cleaned, and then send it on to Keira. With that dilemma solved, I happily turn back to work, determined to make this the best presentation ever.

THIRTY

'Kennedy, party of eight? Come this way.'

Kira and I follow him to a table at the back, exchanging 'Isn't this fancy?' looks. The restaurant seems perfect: casual but elegant, with whitewashed stone walls, an open kitchen with flames leaping up from the stoves, and delicious pizza smells. Everywhere there are huge groups of people sharing trays of pizza standing on little platforms above the tables.

'Good choice,' Kira remarks, as we sit down.

'I hope everyone likes it,' I say. I'm having a sudden attack of hostess nerves. 'Do you think we're OK inside? I tried to book for outside, but they wouldn't let me.'

'It's fine.'

'Good. Whew. Now: if you and I sit here at the end, we can put David beside me, Oliver beside you, then Rachel can sit beside him, Harriet can sit beside David, and then Sinead and Max. Oh, and Jenny. She can go at the end.' I take out some pieces of card.

'What the hell are those?' asks Kira. 'Are you making a speech?'

'Little place cards, to show people where to sit. No?'

'Hello! This isn't the Ambassador's Reception.' She grabs the cards from me, and stuffs them into her bag. 'Stop stressing and have a good time. Let's just sit here in the middle and everyone else can just sit where they want. Excuse me?' The waiter comes over and she gives him her dazzling smile. 'Can we get a bottle of white and one of red? Just the house ones are fine.'

256

She's right: I need to relax the kaks. I don't know why I'm so tense. Partly it's because I'm wearing the Victoire des Anges, and even though it's exquisite, I'm paranoid that I'm going to spill something on it. I cover myself with three napkins, just in case.

'You don't think I'm overdressed, do you?'

'No! Just relax!' She hands me a little wrapped present. It's a Lush soap and handcream, which I remember from last time. 'Where's David, by the way?'

'He's playing tennis this afternoon. But he'll be here soon.'

'Right . . . hey, who's that guy waving at you?'

'Oh. It's Max – my flatmate.' He's threading his way towards us through the tables, dressed in his grey shirt – the one he wore when we went out dancing together. His hair is wet and he's carrying a sports bag, which looks new. I wish he hadn't arrived so early. This is partly why I was so nervous: I haven't seen him properly since our conversation after we went to the beach together.

'But I thought you said he was daggy,' Kira says. 'He's cute!'

'Shush! He'll hear you.'

'Good,' she says, eyes fixed on Max as he approaches.

'Hi there,' Max says. 'Happy birthday, Zoë!'

Kira holds out her hand with a big smile. 'Hi. I'm Kira,' she says.

'Nice to meet you . . . I'm Max.' He hesitates, obviously wondering whether to sit beside her or me.

'Sit here beside me,' Kira says, patting the seat. 'Have you just been to the gym?'

'Sort of. I've just been to Porchester Centre for a swim and a Turkish bath,' he says, stowing his bag under the table. 'It's a really cool old place.'

'I love Turkish baths,' Kira says. 'They are the best, especially if you've got a hangover. Is it a naked one?'

Honestly. Is it a naked one? But Max doesn't seem at all embarrassed.

'Yep. It's single-sex though. Except on Sunday, when they have couples sessions . . . which always makes me think of swinging.'

Kira starts talking about her trip to a Turkish baths in Budapest, where the masseuse asked her if she wanted a 'nudie massage'. She got such bad giggles that she couldn't continue with the massage, and all the masseuses ended up in fits as well. It is a very funny story, and she tells it well. Max certainly seems to enjoy it.

'Happy birthday, Zoë. Sorry I'm late.'

It's Oliver, helmet under one arm and wearing a high-visibility jacket. He waves at the others, gives me a slightly awkward kiss on the cheek and produces a card for me.

'You're not late. It's only ten past eight.' I open his card. It's got a watercolour picture of a bunch of flowers on it, and it says 'Happy Birthday to a Dear Sister'. I start to laugh, and put it in pride of place beside my plate.

'Oh, dear. I didn't see that,' says Oliver. 'Oops. But Zoë, you've become like a sister to me.'

'Thanks, bro.' I pat him on the shoulder, wondering briefly why Max didn't get me a card.

Oliver is still unwinding himself from all his lamps, lights and high-visibility gear. Then he proceeds to hang the jacket on his chair and puts his bicycle lights on the table in front of him. I decide to do something about this before it's too late.

'You know what – let me take some of that stuff.' I quickly produce a cotton bag – I brought along a couple of spares to carry my presents – and start filing all Oliver's stuff away neatly. Rachel will be here any minute and I don't want Oliver to be buried in paraphernalia.

'Why are you stealing my cycling stuff?' he asks, looking bemused.

'Pass me your reflective jacket as well. I'm just tidying it away so it doesn't all get covered in pizza.'

'Oh – sorry. Did it look really messy on the table?'

'A bit. And don't apologise.' I look over at Kira and Max, but

258

they're not listening; they're busy talking about travelling in Eastern Europe.

'Really?' he says, looking amused. 'Do you mean in general, or for my cycling stuff?'

'In general.'

'OK,' he says. He has a nice smile. And he looks so much better when he's not draped in goggles and helmets: he has a nice tan on his forearms, and his dark hair is ruffled. It's also a bit longer – which is an excellent idea as it hides his ears. I have high hopes for him and Rachel tonight.

'By the way,' he asks, 'when are you going to come to our pub quiz again? We really need you.'

'Soon! Soon,' I say, with a bright smile. I'm relieved when Kira proposes a toast.

'Cheers to the birthday girl!' She's poured everyone a glass of wine and everyone raises their glass to me and cries, 'Cheers!' Looking around at all their faces, I decide that so far, this is much better than karaoke. 'Thanks, guys!'

'Where's David?' Oliver asks.

I wish people wouldn't keep asking me that. 'He's on his way.'

'Oh, there he is now,' Oliver says. 'And Jenny.'

It is indeed. Jenny is wearing a denim shirt with the collar flicked up, and pearls. David is wearing a light blue cotton shirt with the sleeves rolled up, and tan chinos. They're both looking very fresh-faced and pink and healthy, both carrying tennis rackets.

'That's weird,' Kira says. She's obviously about to comment on the fact that David's arriving with Jenny instead of with me, but then she stops herself. Which I appreciate.

'Sorry we're late. The couple before us on the court over-ran,' says Jenny.

Wait a second. Did she just say 'The couple before us'?

'Happy birthday, Zoë,' David says, kissing me and handing me a long gift-wrapped object.

'Thanks, David.' I kiss him, and tuck the present away beside my plate, deciding I'll open it later.

'Happy b-day,' Jenny adds, sitting down opposite David. 'Can I get a Diet Coke and two menus as soon as possible,' she tells the waiter before he even gets a chance to open his mouth. 'And can you take this, and be careful with it. It's expensive.' She hands him her tennis racket. 'Dave, do you want to give him yours as well?' she adds, interrupting David who is talking to Max.

'Sure.' David hands his racket over. To my delight, he then ignores her and focuses on me. 'You look absolutely stunning,' he says in a low voice. 'New dress?'

I nod happily.

'Sorry I couldn't meet you for a drink earlier. It's just that we had to play this game or else we would have dropped out of the league.'

'It doesn't matter,' I tell him, realising that it really doesn't.

He clinks his glass with me and looks into my eyes. 'Happy birthday. I'm looking forward to spending this weekend with you.'

I smile at him, feeling even more relieved that we're back on track. Max is still deep in conversation with Kira, which I decide is a good thing.

'Hi, birthday girl, hi everyone! Sorry I'm late.' Rachel has arrived. 'Oh, hi, Jenny,' she adds. 'I wasn't expecting to see you here.'

'Thank you for the present!' I say quickly. Before Jenny cops on that Rachel's repeating her own words at tea back at her, I make a big show of unwrapping the present to cause a distraction. It's the same lovely little vase she got me last time.

'What is she doing here?' Rachel mutters out of the side of her mouth, as she sits down on my other side, away from David and Jenny.

'Wrecking my head.' I deliberately don't look while Rachel and Oliver greet each other in a slightly self-conscious way. But inside I'm hopeful.

Meanwhile, Kira and Max are getting on like a house on fire.

'I miss it so much,' he's says. 'Sometimes I get these cravings . . .'

'I know exactly what you mean,' she says, with feeling. 'It's just not the same here, is it?'

What *are* they talking about?

'You know one place that is pretty good? La Taqueria, on Westbourne Grove. It's right by here. They do a really good breakfast – you should check it out some time.'

Ah. Mexican food. That's a relief. I mean, that's funny.

'Zoë!' It's Harriet. She's just arrived, looking incredibly distressed. 'Happy birthday! I'm so, so, so sorry I'm late – I had to help my sister move house and then there were delays on the Central line, so I got the bus which was such a bad idea – I really should have taken the circle line but it's always so slow. Anyway, happy birthday.' She hands me an enormous package which I know contains a huge *Benefit* gift set, bless her. She's also wearing a frilly, low-cut top which I think is from Nougat – and which I don't own, in any other colour. It really suits her.

'Don't worry! Sit down!' I say, giving her a kiss.

'Hi! Oh no, do I have to sit there?' Harriet's looking at the space at the head of the table, between Rachel and Oliver. There's another one at the opposite end for Sinead – who still hasn't shown up.

'There's plenty of space,' says Rachel.

'No, it's just that I don't want to be at the head of the table – someone important should sit here, not me. Zoë, why don't you sit here? Oh, no, but then you wouldn't be beside David. It's fine,' she says, sitting down. 'I'm just making a fuss.'

Oliver has been looking at her in amusement. 'I'll swap with you,' he says, standing up. 'It's fine, honestly. Give me a chance to play Godfather.' Shaking his head in a manly way at Harriet's protests, he takes his seat. He's now at the head, facing her and Rachel.

'Thank you so much,' Harriet says, looking at him with big eyes full of gratitude.

Max and Kira are still deep in conversation.

'Bells Beach,' she's saying. 'That's all I've got to say. You haven't surfed till you've surfed in Australia.'

'Yeah? What time of year is best?'

261

'Well, it depends. I went there in June last year – it was just out of this world.'

'So how do you know Zoë?' Harriet is asking Oliver. 'Oh, you're a friend of David's. Are you a doctor too?'

'Yup.'

'That's so amazing,' Harriet says. 'I don't know how you do it. You're all so dedicated and intelligent and hard-working.' Oliver laughs, but he looks very flattered. Hm. I hope Harriet doesn't distract him from Rachel.

Text message. It's Sinead. 'Hi, Zoë, looking forward to seeing you for your birthday tomorrow, just checking what time?' I roll my eyes, laughing despite myself.

'Do you know what you're having to eat?' I ask David, but Jenny is already drowning me out with her foghorn voice.

'Hey, Dave, did I tell you my old headmistress wants me to come back and talk about being, like, an inspiration? It's so cringe.'

I roll my eyes and turn back to Harriet and Rachel. 'Are you guys ready to order?'

'Oh! Sorry,' Harriet says instantly. 'I'll look at the menu.'

'It all looks really good,' Oliver says, staring at her pretty dark head bent over her menu, and her generous bosom exposed in her frilly top. Rachel glances quizzically at him, and then at me. Max is telling Kira a funny story, and they're both laughing away. We already seem to have gone through a few bottles of wine. I'm beginning to feel as if I'm sitting in on two great first dates, with me and Rachel as gooseberries – though I have David, of course.

'Guys,' I call over the din of conversation. 'Does anyone know what they're eating yet?'

Once our pizzas have arrived on their little tray platforms, I start to feel better. Mine is delicious; thin and crispy and with barely any cheese but lots of flavour. David is giving me his full attention now, offering me bites of his pizza, pouring me wine and saying nice things. But in between, he also has to listen to Jenny, on his other side, talk about rugby and tennis and medicine, and how tiring it is to be so successful. I find myself wondering: if I married David, would Jenny be his best man?

'Are you all right, birthday girl?' Rachel asks me, digging into her pizza. 'You're very quiet.'

'I'm fine. I was just trying to remember . . . who was it that told us that story about the guy who had a female best man at his wedding?'

'Oh, I know who that is,' says Oliver, listening in. 'David and I both know him, not very well. His sister was his best man, and she wore a white dress for the ceremony.'

'That's the craziest thing I ever heard,' says Rachel. 'Did it match the bride's?'

'No. But it was unfortunate because the sister was quite tall and striking-looking – I think she's a model, in fact – and the bride was . . . a little less so.'

'The poor girl. How awful,' says Harriet.

'That's so creepy and inappropriate,' Rachel says. 'Imagine people looking at the pictures afterwards; they probably think the sister is the bride. Or that he had two brides.'

'Well,' says Oliver diplomatically, 'Yes. It didn't work in that particular instance but I think it's nice when people do things differently, put their own stamp on things.'

Harriet nods in agreement. Rachel says, 'I totally disagree.'

I cringe. I really wish Rachel wouldn't just contradict people like this. Especially men. They do not like it one bit.

'Oh, really?' Oliver says politely. 'Why so?'

'I just don't see the point of having a big white wedding at all, if you're going to have a female best man or have your mother walk you up the aisle or whatever. Either get married traditionally or don't, but I think it's ridiculous when people try and customise the traditional wedding, because that's not what it's all about.'

'Really?' Oliver says, his eyes sparkling. He looks as though he's enjoying this. He turns to Harriet. 'What do you think?'

Poor Harriet looks as if she's been asked to recite the Greek alphabet. 'I . . . like weddings?' she says uncertainly.

'I agree,' Oliver says. 'I like weddings too. People invest a lot of time and money in their weddings, and if they want to have a female best man, or release a flock of doves, or whatever else, why not?'

Rachel, Harriet and I all stare at him. The words 'I like weddings' have created a definite frisson and it's as if we're all imagining ourselves marrying Oliver – even me, for a millisecond.

'But the point of a tradition is that it's familiar, and if you're going to play around with it, it's not a tradition any more,' Rachel says, sounding a bit less sure of herself.

'But does that matter, if everyone concerned enjoys themselves?' Oliver says, reasonably.

Rachel doesn't have an immediate comeback, for once.

'I went to a lovely wedding recently,' Harriet says. 'It was my cousin's and it was in a little village in the Cotswolds, where my uncle and aunt are from. I was one of the bridesmaids.'

'What part of the Cotswolds? I grew up near Witney,' says Oliver.

The two of them start discussing Oxfordshire versus Gloucestershire and swapping notes on all kinds of Bistleys and Barnleys and Burnleys.

'I feel really foreign all of a sudden,' Rachel says to me quietly, giving me the ghost of a wink. But a few minutes later, Oliver turns back to her.

'What are your views on hen parties?' he asks.

Rachel shrugs. 'They're lame?'

Kira looks over. 'I went to one recently where we played the Mr and Mrs game – you know, where they test how well you know your partner? And we did questions for the stag as well. For instance, we would ask David stuff like . . . what would be Zoë's dream job, or dream holiday, did she have a pet growing up, what was her best ever Christmas present . . .'

David puts an arm around me. 'Easy,' he says. 'Dream job is head buyer at a department store . . . holiday is probably shopping in Paris, or the Maldives? Pet, I'm not sure. Christmas present . . .' He turns to me and smiles. 'Brown Thomas voucher?'

I smile, but I can't help catching Max's eye. I know what he's thinking: that some of those answers are wrong. My dream job is owning my own boutique, I didn't have a cat though I really wanted one, and my best ever present was the doll's house I got when I was little. But you always pick up random trivia about your flatmates. It doesn't mean anything.

I also can't help noticing how well he's getting on with all my friends – talking to Harriet about the nightmare of moving house, chatting with Oliver about cycling, making Rachel laugh with a description of his sister's historical re-enactment antics. He's such easy company. But David is very good company too; just in a different way.

We've almost finished eating when my attention is caught by raised voices. Kira seems to be having some kind of argument with David.

'I swear,' she's saying. 'Honest to God. He googled it.'

'That didn't happen,' David says.

'You might be remembering it wrong,' says Jenny in her most patronising tone. Max is looking as if he's trying to keep a straight face.

Kira turns to me. 'I went to the doctor recently,' she says. 'About this pain in my arm I've been having? It's been really chronic, just shooting pains. He didn't even examine me, he just turned around and typed into Google, "pain in arm".'

'Are you serious?' Rachel starts laughing.

'I think you're kidding,' David says, 'or you're mistaken.'

'I'm not lying! He bloody well googled it!' Kira shouts.

'Maybe you should have complained at the time,' Jenny says, 'if you weren't happy.'

'I was in SHOCK!' Kira roars. Everyone at our table is listening, agog, and people at nearby tables are also turning around. David is looking really pissed off, and I'm utterly mortified.

'That reminds me,' Max says. 'I went to see my GP the other day, and they were asking me about how much I drank. Apparently I'm a risky drinker.'

'Really?' I say, grateful for the diversion. 'How much did you say you drink?'

'The questions were all phrased in a rather complicated way. I was trying to explain that I have one to two pints about three to four times a week but I think she might have thought I meant that I have three to four pints, four to six times a week . . . I can't remember now.'

'The fact that you're hazy about simple sums suggests you might have a drinking problem,' Oliver says.

'Those drinking limits are bullshit,' Kira says. 'I mean, fourteen units a week. It's ridiculous. I could drink that in a night.'

'It's a limit, not a target,' says Max.

'There are some pretty great bars around here, speaking of which. Have you been to Mau Mau's?' Kira asks him.

'No, but I've heard of it. Is that the—'

I tune out, and overhear a sweet exchange between Oliver and Harriet.

'So why did you pick orthopaedics?' she's asking him.

'Well, of course, I went into medicine to do good,' he says earnestly. 'And I think orthopaedics is one of the areas where you can do most good and least harm. And it's also easier to combine with having a life, really. A family life.'

How adorable. I glance sideways at Rachel, to see if she's over-heard, but she and David are trying to explain the rules of hurling to Jenny. Max and Kira have just finished discussing the Notting Hill Carnival – I overheard him saying he's always wanted to go, and her saying she's going on Monday – and now they've moved on to films.

'Me too! I *love* Japanese horror films,' she's saying.

Oh, please. I'll give her the Mexican food, and the travelling and the surfing – but I'll bet my left Jimmy Choo that Kira's never even *seen* a Japanese horror film.

Just then, the lights go down, and a troupe of waiters arrive with a birthday cake. Everyone sings 'Happy Birthday' and then claps as I blow out the candles.

'Twenty-one again!' I say. I catch Max's eye. He's the only one here who knows I am having a birthday again – just not twenty-one.

'You seem to still have an unwrapped present there,' David observes.

'Of course! I was saving the best for last.'

I carefully slip my fingers under the tape, trying not to spoil the stiff, beautiful paper, and slide out a long, narrow blue velvet box. For a second I wonder – but he wouldn't, would he? Not in front of everyone?

'Open it,' David says.

I open the box, savouring the click and the feel of the velvet under my fingers. It's a pearl necklace: one creamy strand, with a simple silver clasp. It's beautiful. I don't particularly like pearls, but these are lovely.

'Gosh, thank you, David. It's so pretty.' I turn to him and we kiss, while everyone whoops and cheers. David helps me fasten the necklace on: he's so dextrous it takes about half a second. The pearls look really odd with my favourite gold pendant (shaped like a lightning bolt, purchased in New York) so I take it off.

The card says, 'Happy birthday to the prettiest girl in London. I'm sorry I've been so busy. Hope to make it up to you soon. D x.'

I turn to him, touched, and kiss him again.

'What a great gift,' Kira says magnanimously, obviously regretting baiting David earlier.

'He might have had a bit of help with the pearls,' Jenny says with a wink, settling back in her chair. I narrow my eyes. If she helped him buy my present, I'll . . . I glance at David, but his phone is ringing.

'Sorry, folks,' David says. 'I'm going to have to take this,' and he walks outside, talking on the phone.

'I hope it's just his junior being useless,' Jenny says. 'But if he does have to leave, I can bring his racket along next time we play.'

'Why don't you give it to Zoë?' Rachel asks. 'She's going home with David tonight.'

'But I'll be playing tennis with him,' Jenny says. 'So it makes more sense for me to have it.'

Oh my God. Don't tell me she is actually going to fight me over his tennis racket. She's had quite a lot to drink – her face is flushed and the words are coming out a bit slurred.

'You take it, Jenny, I have a lot of presents to carry,' I say cheerfully. I look over at her where she's sitting by herself at the end of the table, downing her glass in a morose way.

This is a weakness of mine. I can't bear to see anyone standing, or sitting, alone at a party or a dinner. 'Jenny,' I say, making a huge effort to sound friendly, 'come over here and sit beside us.'

She moves over, taking David's vacated seat. While the rest of us are chatting, she just stares into space. I'm just wondering if she's about to pass out, when she turns to me and asks, with drunkenly exaggerated sympathy, 'Are you *OK*, Zoë?'

I could ask her the same thing, but I just say, 'Sure!'

'You must be finding it hard. . . . with David working such long hours these days,' she continues. She's making an extra effort to sound distinct, but her eyes are practically crossing.

'Oh, well,' I say briskly, 'that's the way it goes.' I really hope David comes back soon.

'And what with the news about the fellowship . . .'

'How do you mean?'

'He didn't get that fellowship in Texas that he really wanted. Didn't he tell you?'

Damn. Now either I have to admit that no, he didn't, or else I have to lie.

'Let's not talk about David behind his back,' I say crisply, and turn back to the others.

'I'm not talking about David behind his back,' she says, in a low hiss. 'I'm telling you things you should know, as his girlfriend. But you don't care about him at all, do you?'

I'm unable to speak for a second, I'm so shocked. '*Excuse* me?'

'You don't know anything about David. I've known him since

we were six. You might be the flavour of the month, but you'll never last. I'm the real woman in his life.'

I stare at her, wondering if this is some kind of joke. But the look in her eyes makes me realise she's not just drunk: she's properly, Single White Female, Fatal Attraction psycho.

'Hey,' says David behind us. 'Did I miss anything?' he says, sitting down on the other side of Jenny.

'Jenny was just telling me that she has to leave now,' I say crisply.

She stands up, and gives me a cold smile. 'I hope you have a *great* birthday, Zoë.' She turns around and bends down to kiss David goodbye on the cheek, and as she does, her wrist casually swings backward, knocking her half-full glass of red wine over. I just manage to jump up, but not before a good long splash lands on the side of my dress, staining the pale pink fabric. I let out a huge shriek. 'Salt! Quickly! Please!'

'What's happened?' asks Jenny innocently.

'You know what happened! You knocked that wine over deliberately!' I pour some water over a napkin and start dabbing pointlessly.

She gasps. 'I did *not* do it on purpose! It was a total accident! Anyway – it's just a few tiny drops.'

I'm about to tell her how her few tiny drops are going to cost me several hundred pounds – but then I see David looking at me and I bite my tongue.

Once Jenny's left, I ask for the bill. Rachel brilliantly takes over and figures out what everyone owes, but then there's a fight as I insist on paying even though the others try to over-rule me. Finally, David settles it by paying for me.

'So where next?' Kira says, pouring everyone the dregs of the last bottle. 'Neighbourhood maybe? What about Cherry Jam? Zoë, you like it there.'

I glance at David. 'Whatever you want, Zoë,' he says. 'It's your birthday.'

'Actually, I think we're going to call it a night. Sorry, guys.'

There are general cries of disbelief.

'That's not like you,' says Rachel.

'Oh, come on,' Kira says. 'You're twenty-eight, not eighty-eight. And it's Saturday night!'

I stare down at my dress. 'I just want to get home and get at the Vanish.' David squeezes my hand under the table, and I look at him gratefully.

'OK,' Kira says, 'Well, who else is up for coming out? Rachel? Harriet?' After a casual pause she turns to Max. 'How about you?'

He doesn't even glance at me as he tells her, 'Let's do it.'

'Great,' Kira says. 'Let's go!'

We start getting our stuff together and start trailing out of the restaurant, with all the usual detours and discussion about who's going where. It's still really warm outside. Normally I'd be up for clubbing, but not tonight; what with all the drama and now my ruined dress, I've had enough.

'Zoë, I see a taxi,' David says. 'Are you ready?'

I'm relieved to be able to make a quick getaway. I hug and kiss everyone within reach, and follow David into the taxi.

'Maida Vale, please,' says David.

I look out of the window to see Oliver and Harriet and Rachel walking in front, and Kira and Max trailing behind, talking and laughing. I feel a bit of a pang, but then tell myself not to be so stupid and selfish. If he likes Kira, then I'm very happy for him – for them.

'Where to in Maida Vale?' the driver asks.

'Warwick Avenue, right by the tube station,' says David.

'Actually, can we go to my place?' I ask.

'Of course,' he says, sounding surprised. 'Elgin Avenue.'

Fuelled by most of a bottle of Chianti, I decide to ask something else. 'David, did Jenny help you shop for my necklace?'

'No,' he says, frowning. 'Why?'

I'm about to tell him how she went bunny-boiler on me, and

how she deliberately ruined my dress – and ask him about the fellowship, too – but I don't want to let her ruin any more of my birthday. 'Oh, nothing,' I say.

Once we're inside the flat, I catch sight of a strangely shaped package on the hall table, awkwardly wrapped in silver-and-blue paper. There's also a card with my name on it.

'I'm going to get us both some water,' says David. 'See you in the bedroom.'

I open the card, and laugh when I see the picture: it's an incredibly kitsch concoction of unicorns and fairies by a lake – totally tacky, but I love it. It says:

> To Zoë,
> Happy Birthday! Hope you have a great day and year. And that you have fun second time around, if you know what I mean.
> xoxo gossip girl.*
> *Max

I open up the package. It's the complete Series 3 of *Gossip Girl*.

He must have remembered me mentioning that I wanted it, and ordered it specially. That's so typical of him. I'm so touched (and tired, and drunk) that I have tears in my eyes. Is it wrong that I prefer his thoughtful present to David's expensive one? But then I tell myself not to be stupid. All it means is that he sees me every day and knows my habits. That's what flatmates do.

'Zoë,' David calls from the bedroom. 'You OK?'

'I'm fine. I'm coming,' I yell back, and put away Max's present.

THIRTY-ONE

I know that I should tell Julia about the dress, and offer to replace it, first thing on Tuesday morning, when I get into work. But I'm already nervous enough about my presentation; I decide to wait until after it's safely over. At ten to four, I decide I'd better get a move on and start gathering everything together. As I stand up, my stomach seems to stay in my chair. I take a few deep breaths, trying to calm myself down.

There's a knock on my door. It's Seth. 'Hey, trendster.' He points his index finger at me. 'Are you ready to show us what you've got?'

'I think so.'

'Now, don't be nervous,' Seth says, as we walk down the corridor together, 'but I've been talking you up, telling everyone they mustn't miss this, and we've got some extra people sitting in . . .'

I stop dead. 'Who, exactly?'

'Well, just a few people from the sales floor . . . Aaron from menswear, and your old boss Karen wanted to come along . . . and I think she's bringing along a couple of the sales assistants. But the VIP guest is the MD – John Marley himself.'

Oh, God. The MD! And Karen! My pace has slowed to a totter, and Seth practically has to drag me along. Through the glass wall, I can see the meeting room is full of people – every single person on our floor, as well as several people from the shop floor. I stop again. I can't do this.

'Come on, darling,' says Seth. 'You'll be fine.'

It's too late now; we're already inside the lion's den, AKA the meeting room. The buzz of chatter dies down as we walk in. I look at the sea of faces and have to fight the urge to run. Not that it would do much good; the door is blocked by curious crowds, including a stray model. At the front, sitting on a special chair where most other people are standing, is the tall, grey-haired figure who I know to be Mr Marley. AKA our managing director.

'Good morning, everyone,' I say, but my voice comes out as just a croak. I turn around and sip from my bottle of water, wishing I'd thought to bring in a glass. Then I try again, 'Good morning, everyone.'

That did it. The room is now pin-drop quiet. I notice Karen, standing at the side. Harriet is behind her, and gives me a thumbs-up. I take a deep breath and continue: 'I'm Zoë Kennedy, and I'm here today to talk to you about the trends we can expect to see this coming spring/summer 2011.'

That didn't sound too bad. I turn around and press the projector, and nothing happens. Shit.

'Um – sorry.' I press a different button, but still nothing.

'Just talk amongst yourselves,' says Seth, and darts up to give me a hand.

To my relief, my first slide comes up; Trends Overview SS/11. I look down at my notes and start to read, wishing my hands weren't shaking so much.

'I've identified the following trends as ones to watch this coming London Fashion Week. One of the most popular ones is colour blocking.' I press the slide again, and up pops an image of Kate Middleton wearing a biscuit-coloured suit with nude shoes. There's a ripple of laughter. Damn. 'Sorry, wrong slide.' I press frantically, and finally locate the right one. 'Mixing bright colours head to toe will be a very strong trend for next year's spring/summer, as seen in the following preview from designer Pilar Norman . . .'

Finally, things seem to be going OK: people appear to be paying attention, nobody is laughing and my slides are behaving themselves. Even my dodgy image of the 'metallic trend' – a black jumper with one sequined shoulder, made by Sinead as a sample and photographed by me – seems to go over fine. I occasionally sneak a glance towards Mr Marley, the MD, but he's just watching expressionlessly. Harriet beams at me every time I catch her eye.

'And finally, the ladylike trend.' My voice is stronger now, and I'm almost beginning to enjoy myself. 'Here's Kate Middleton again – in the right place this time.' There's another ripple of laughter, but this time it's friendly laughter. 'Kate is a fashion icon in the making. Her ladylike, covered-up look is very on-trend with the longer hems and sleeves we can expect to see this season. She's already shown herself to be a fan of high street brands such as Reiss and LK Bennett, and as her public profile increases, she will continue to be a loyal champion of British luxury brands and designers, such as Issa and Erdem.'

I turn back to the projector, and with my back to the crowd, puff out my cheeks in a sigh. I think it's going well, but I have no idea; I just hope I make it to the end with no disasters. I click on to my next slide: a picture of the front of Marley's with a breakdown of our profits for the last four quarters.

'So what does all of this mean for us?' I say, rhetorically. 'How do we tap into these new trends and attract new customers, while retaining the loyalty of others who have shopped with us for decades?'

I can tell from people's reactions that this is a pretty good question: I just hope my answer will live up to it. I spend a while discussing the new brands we're introducing and how we are incorporating them into the floor plan, before moving on to online sales. Clicking on another slide, I show the percentages of online sales made by our competitors, versus Marley's.

'So as we see, currently only eight per cent of our sales are online, versus a much higher average among the competition, rising to almost—'

'Ten,' interrupts a voice.

'Sorry?' I look out into the crowd. It's Dominic, one of the merchandisers.

'It's ten per cent of our sales that were online in the last quarter, not eight. As you yourself said in the previous slide.'

Crapola. He's right. I meant to correct that, but I must have overlooked it. I continue quickly, 'Sorry, yes, ten. In any case – increased online sales can only benefit bricks-and-mortar retailers. They provide us with an opportunity to increase profits while reducing costs; to gather information about customers; and to easily track sales of brands and different trends.'

I notice Seth beaming, but I'm still embarrassed about my mistake, plus I've just realised that I forgot to mention the average of online sales among the competition. I'm about to continue into a more detailed bit about luxury brands such as Burberry that are selling directly to the consumer online, when I'm interrupted by a very grand-sounding, and angry-sounding, voice.

'And what happens to all of the "bricks and mortar" stores, when the internet becomes the be-all and end-all? Are we to become simply a showroom?'

Oh, sweet baby Jesus. It's the MD, and he looks a little perturbed: that is, he's leaning forward with a filthy scowl on his face. Sore subject, obviously. I try to think how to smooth things over without contradicting him. 'No – not at all. Online sales, um, as seen in the example of Selfridges, can support the work of a store by building its profile and . . .' I try and think of all the other examples I've noted, but his bulging blue eyes look so furious that my mind just goes blank.

'But people come here to shop because of the experience,' interrupts another voice. Karen. 'If they're going to shop online, what's to stop them just going to Net-a-Porter?' There's a murmur of agreement.

'We – they –' I look desperately over at Seth, hoping he'll defend his pet idea, but he's deep in his BlackBerry.

'It's up to us to choose the ideal mix of brands under one roof, and to use our heritage to cultivate brand loyalty . . . so that people, um, will shop with us.'

Ouch. That was lame. There's some discontented rhubarbing even while I continue with the last (thank God) part of the speech, which is a discussion of store cards and how we can better use them to gather customer metrics.

'And that concludes my presentation.' I wish I could just end it there, but it seems too feeble, so I add reluctantly, 'Are there any questions?'

'Yes, I have a question,' says Dominic. 'You say that our internet sales are low compared to our competitors. But our profits have grown in line as well, over the last three years. Why do we need to get into the online business when it's so risky?'

'Well –' Damn, damn, damn. I didn't actually know that.

'Um – I didn't, I mean, I suppose we always want to grow our profits even further, don't we?' is all I can say. But Seth has finally decided to participate.

'They have grown, but not enough, as well you know, Dominic. Online is the future. It's the only way to reduce costs and compete properly.'

'Reduce jobs, you mean,' someone calls from the back of the room.

I watch in horror as more people start yelling at once. I had no idea this was such a thorny issue. After a minute, Mr Marley himself claps his hands and roars, 'Quiet!' Everyone shuts up.

'We will have one more question, and then I think we should adjourn,' he says.

'I have a final question,' Dominic says. 'This year we're introducing lots of new designers – Peter Sembello, Pilar Norman, Devlin – but we don't have any more physical space in the store. How do you do this without impacting on the space we give to our existing best-selling brands?'

What is this, *Newsnight*? I look helplessly at Julia, who stands up.

'Dominic, there's no question of our existing brands suffering. There's a clear distinction between our hero brands, which will continue to have the best fittings, and the up-and-coming ones, which will be on display together.'

Ooops. I've just remembered telling the visual merchandiser to move Peter Sembello to where Gucci used to be. From the look on her face I can tell that she's thinking the same thing. I'll have to go over to her the second this meeting is over, and tell her that she's got to move them right back.

Just then, a diversion is caused by a work experience girl tapping on the glass window. She puts her head inside the door, and gives a message to Louis, who looks horrified. He hurries over and says something in Julia's ear. She stands up and says, 'Thank you, everyone, for your contributions, I think we should leave it there.' Everyone waits politely for Mr Marley to leave first and then people start to file out, arguing and chattering excitedly.

'Those meetings are normally really boring,' I overhear one person say. 'But that was great!'

I'm glad someone enjoyed it. Julia, Dominic and Louis seem to be in crisis mode; I'm relieved that something's happened to divert attention from how badly I crashed and burned. Seth has already left without even a backwards glance: I suspect he's going to regret using me as his mouthpiece. I start getting my things together and prepare to tiptoe unobtrusively out of the room.

'What's happened?' I hear Amanda ask Louis.

'I'll tell you what happened,' he says, glaring at me. Pausing until he has everyone's full attention, he says, 'We lost Gucci!'

'We what? How?' says Amanda.

'Apparently our Head of Trends,' he spits out the words, 'has decided that Gucci are so over, and that we'd better give their space to Peter bloody Sembello. Whose stuff is a total rip-off of theirs. So Gucci have decided they can do without Marley's in the future. Thanks, Zoë.'

Julia is clasping her hand to her head. 'Is this true, Zoë? Did you really tell Jean to change the floor plan? Why didn't you say anything to me?'

'Or me?' says Amanda. 'You were meant to consult me about that order, and I didn't hear a single thing from you.'

'Do you know how much profit we stand to lose from this?' says Louis. 'Not to mention the PR disaster, if this gets around to other brands. I really hope you haven't pissed off Vuitton.'

'We can't afford to lose Gucci,' says someone I've never seen before.

'You might think Peter Sembello is the next big thing, but I'm really not convinced,' says Amanda.

'No – he really will be, I promise,' I say, faintly.

'Zoë, you need to explain how this happened.' That's Julia – I think – but all the voices are merging into one, until I hear one little voice shouting above them all:

'But you've got to listen to Zoë! She's *psychic*!'

That gets everyone's attention. We all turn around to see Harriet, lingering by the doorway. I feel as if I'm in a dream; everything's happening in slow motion but I can't stop it. Harriet – please don't do this . . .

'She knows everything that's going to happen,' Harriet says, passionately. 'That's how she can predict all these trends. She knew how the summer sale would go – she knew my house was going to be burgled. You have to believe her!' She looks so sincere and well-meaning, but I wish she was a million miles away, or at least, safely back on the shop floor.

Now all the heads turn around to look at me.

'WTF?' says Louis.

'Zoë,' Julia says faintly, 'did you really tell Harriet that you're psychic?'

Everyone's staring at me. And after all the weeks of lies and cover stories and frantically paddling underwater, I just can't do it any more.

'Yes,' I say. 'I did tell Harriet I was psychic. But it's not true. I . . .' The words 'I've come from the future' are hovering on my lips, but I don't want to end up sectioned. Instead, I tell the closest version of the truth that I can. 'I *thought* I was psychic,

278

but I'm not.' I point at the projector behind me. 'It was all just . . . guesses.'

I stop abruptly. Everyone is staring at me in bewilderment. Julia presses both her hands to her face briefly. 'OK. Zoë, go and wait for me in your office, please. Louis, I will speak to Vanessa at Gucci right now and tell her there's been a misunderstanding. Everyone else, please get back to work. I don't want to hear another word about all this, is that understood?'

With shaky legs, I manage to get myself inside my office without meeting anyone's eye – Harriet tries to speak to me but I just wave her away; I can't talk to her right now.

I close the door of my office, collapse at my desk and bury my head in my hands. I am so embarrassed. I keep remembering Harriet saying 'But Zoë is psychic!' and every time I do, I groan out loud. Why did I ever, ever let her think that? Why didn't I just keep my mouth shut?

After a while, Julia knocks and walks in.

'I'm really sorry,' I whisper, barely able to look at her.

'So am I,' she says. 'Zoë, I still don't understand exactly what's been going on. You told Harriet you were psychic?'

I nod miserably.

'But why?'

I shake my head: I can't explain it.

'Maybe you can explain something else,' Julia says.

My heart starts to thump.

'Marianne, the designer from Victoire des Anges, actually met Keira Knightley yesterday, through some fashion contact. She asked her if she liked the dress . . .'

Oh, no. Oh, no no no.

'But Keira never received the dress. And she'd never heard of you, Zoë. She had no idea who you were.'

'I . . .' I stare at Julia, my face getting hotter and hotter.

'Where is the dress?'

'I wore it on Saturday night,' I say in a whisper. 'It got red wine spilled on it. I'll pay for it.'

Julia leans back, pulling on her long ponytail. She doesn't look puzzled or sympathetic any more; she looks really angry. 'I think we need to have a meeting with HR, to figure out where we go from here. For now I'd like you to clear your desk and go home. We'll be in touch.'

She walks out, leaving me staring at my empty desk. I collect a few things from it.

On my way out, I pass by Seth's office. He glances up at me quickly from his computer, and glances down again.

'Darling, that was tricky, wasn't it,' he says evasively. 'Oh well.'

'I'm sorry I messed up,' I say. 'I did try –'

'Yes, I know you did,' he says quickly. 'Never mind. We can talk about it some other time. I just have to make a quick call. Later, yes?' And he practically shoos me out of the office. He's obviously decided he doesn't want to be associated with me any more.

I slink over to the lift, keeping my head down, and pray for it to come quickly. I'm not sure what to do with my special lift pass – maybe I'll just post it back. Somehow I don't think I'll be needing it again.

THIRTY-TWO

Four hours later, Rachel is piling me into a taxi. I see her handing money to the driver.

'Don't do that, Rachel,' I call out, feebly, from the back seat. 'I can pay.' But she's already receding in the rear-view mirror, waving and giving me a thumbs-up. Oh, God. How is it that I've gone back in time, and tried to do everything differently, and Rachel is still putting me in taxis?

'Had a good evening?' the taxi driver asks.

Oh, no. What I can't have, right now, is a chatty cab driver. I just can't deal. I'm not drunk, exactly, though we did share a bottle of wine over dinner. I'm just miserable.

'I'm sorry. I've had a bit of a bad day and I don't feel like talking.'

'Oh, well, I won't bother you then,' he says, in a very offended tone.

We drive on in silence. I'm going to have to overtip him to compensate for my lack of chat.

'This isn't the end of the world, Zoë,' Rachel kept saying over dinner. 'I know it feels like it, but it's really not.'

It's easy for her to say that. Even if they let me stay at Marley's – which doesn't seem at all likely – I can't face going back there. I just disgraced myself in front of the entire company. I can never work anywhere in London in anything to do with fashion; I'm going to have to go home to Dublin with my tail between my

281

legs. My CV is more spotty than a Dalmatian. I'm nearly thirty. Why do I still not have my act together?

The driver is playing Smooth FM – it's 'Back For Good' by Take That, which makes me feel even more melancholic. Before I know it, tears are leaking out of my eyes. I wish I could just curl up and go to sleep and make this all go away, or wake up and find myself in December again. There's only one person in the world I want to talk to right now, who could make it better, and I can't even talk to him any more.

Almost as if I was listening to myself on a tape, I find myself rewinding those words and hearing them again. *There's only one person in the world I want to talk to right now, who could make it better.*

Wait a second. Wait just one second.

Surely that's how you're meant to feel about a boyfriend. But I don't feel that way about David. It didn't even occur to me to call him this afternoon when I got the sack. Whereas Max . . . I think of how much I love talking to him, how wonderful and kind he is, all the times he's helped me when I've had problems at work. I have more fun with him than I do with – well, anyone else. And I think he's gorgeous.

Take That ends and is replaced with – I don't believe it – the twanging chords of that song 'Breakfast at Tiffany's', the one we listened to on the way home from Devon, just before I gave Max the brush-off. The brush-off I now want to take back.

I've been so, so stupid. I don't care if I have nothing in common with Max. I don't care if he's not marriage material or that he's my flatmate, or even that I want to move back to Ireland and he doesn't. My parents will cope. I just want to be with him, if he'll have me.

The taxi has stopped outside our flat. Rachel must have given him my address.

'Goodnight,' he says shortly. Then, seeing my face, he says, 'Cheer up, love, it might not happen.'

'It already has,' I say, as I stumble out of the taxi. 'Twice.'

The flat is empty; Max's door is open and he's not there. A cold fear clutches me; could he be with Kira? But I don't think so. I know they went to the Carnival together – but I think that was just as friends. If anything happened, she would have told me about it.

On complete autopilot, I kick off my shoes and gulp down two Nurofen and a huge glass of water. To hell with cleansing and moisturising, or even wipes. I'm about to put my phone away for the night when I see that I have a text message from Kira. I'm too scared to open it, because I think I know what it's going to say. So I turn my phone off and decide I'll look at it in the morning.

Except, of course, I can't. I have to know the worst now.

'Just had my second date with Max. Wow. Thanks for introducing us. I think this one's a keeper! x K.'

I am so shocked that I actually drop the phone. I sink down to my knees to get it, and then I find that I can't get up again. Their second date. That's that, then. He won't be coming home tonight. I've ruined everything. I've got David back, but I've lost Max, and this is one problem I can't go back to fix.

THIRTY-THREE

'Zoë? Is everything all right?' David asks me.

'What? Sorry. Of course it is!'

We're sitting on his roof terrace, enjoying the September sun. It's Saturday morning and we've just finished a breakfast of fresh fruit, croissants, coffee and juice, which David picked up on his way back from his run this morning.

'I hope you're not worrying about work,' says David. 'You finished your big presentation, didn't you?'

'Oh, yes. Yes, I did.'

Yesterday I got a letter from the head of HR at Marley's, notifying me that I'm now on compulsory paid leave, pending their decision. Whatever that means. I haven't exactly updated David yet on all that stuff. Or my parents.

Anyway, when I'm with David, having dinner in a Marco Pierre White restaurant (as we did last night) or having breakfast on the terrace in his gorgeous flat, it's totally possible not to think about the fact that I've been fired. Or about Max.

He and Kira are definitely an item now. She called me yesterday to give me a full debrief.

'It was really weird,' she said. 'I thought maybe he didn't like me when he wouldn't come home with me on Saturday after your birthday. And then he came to the Carnival with me on Monday, and we spent the whole day together, but nothing – he went home again. But then we met up again the next night – and, oh my God. It was definitely worth waiting for.'

'That's – that's great.'

'But, it's not just the sex,' she said. 'Seriously, Zoë, I really like him. He's just really funny, and laid back and kind and generous . . .'

'I know,' I said, numbly.

'And I know you don't like this kind of detail, but he is seriously hot stuff in bed. You know, he did this one thing I really wasn't expecting—'

'No, you know what? You're right. I don't like that kind of detail.'

'Oh, OK. Let's just say: when I come around to yours, you'll have to wear earplugs! Ha ha ha ha ha ha ha! It was outstanding.'

'Gnuuh, great,' I managed to say. 'Please, can we change the subject?'

'Oh, don't be such a Catholic schoolgirl. It's cool. We're having fun. But I also think . . . well, I think it could be something serious.'

More than anything else in our conversation, that made my heart sink. I've never heard Kira say this before, about anyone.

I've hardly seen Max this week. I met him briefly at breakfast yesterday, but I didn't tell him about my job either.

'So! You and Kira, huh?' I said, sounding like an over-eager uncle.

'Yup,' is all he said. 'Yup. Oh, we're out of milk. I'll go and get some.' He was pulling his jacket on over his pyjamas, and was out the door before I could say anything else. The fact that he wouldn't talk about it makes me think it is serious. After all, Kira really likes him, so there's a good chance that he likes her too.

David finishes his coffee and sits back. 'I have something for you. A belated birthday present.' He hands me an envelope, and I look at him in surprise.

'Open it.'

It's a first class plane ticket to New York. Leaving on the tenth – next Friday – and coming back on the fourteenth.

'I got the fellowship in New York,' he says. 'It starts at the beginning of October.'

'Oh, David. Congratulations!' The plane tickets are helping me with the note of surprise in my voice. I don't understand exactly what he's telling me.

'I'm going to go over there next weekend for a conference, and have a look around. And I would love you to come with me.'

'Oh! Come with you for the weekend, or—'

'I'd like you to come with me for the whole year. But in the meantime, I thought a weekend might be fun.'

'You want me to come with you for the whole year,' I repeat.

'I really do.'

He makes it sound so simple and direct and appealing. It gives me a pang to think that he actually really wants me to be with him – that he needs me.

'David, wow,' I say uncertainly. 'I don't . . . it's so lovely of you to invite me. I'm not sure what to say. I mean – would I be allowed to work over there? What about visas?'

'That can all be sorted out,' David says. 'You could do freelance work, or an internship. Or you could study – do a diploma in fashion or something. You mentioned doing something of the sort before, didn't you?'

'I did, but, you know, it's expensive. Living in New York would be expensive, I mean.' I'm still staring at the tickets in my hand.

'You wouldn't have to worry about that.'

'Um – how do you mean?'

'I mean, you would be living with me. So you wouldn't have to worry about the expense.'

I have no idea what to say to an offer like that – but I can't bring myself to dismiss it. I find myself saying, 'Well, I would love to come with you next weekend.'

'And you'll think about coming permanently?' He asks this quite casually, folding up his paper, but I know that for David, this is pretty much the equivalent of begging on bended knee.

'I'll think about coming with you permanently.'

After breakfast, I speed-walk home, my head spinning. It's only when I'm halfway home that I remember what today's date is. Saturday the fourth; break-up day. And I had completely forgotten. The irony; last time, David broke up with me because he was moving to America. This time, he's asked me to go with him. I did it all according to *The Rules*: acted distant and hard to get, and the result was exactly as they promised.

I don't know what to do. I'm not head over heels in love with him any more – but I was once. Surely I could be again. All relationships have ups and downs, don't they? I find myself thinking of Max, and push the thought right out of my head. I would love to leave London. Fly to America, where nobody will know me, and I can make a fresh start. And then we could move back to Dublin together . . .

I can hear noises from the sitting room. I walk in and there is Max, with Kira. She's wearing his T-shirt and showing off her long brown legs. They're sitting on the sofa drinking tea. Her feet are curled up in his lap. It is the most horrifying sight I've ever seen.

'Zoë! Hi!' Max says, looking surprised.

'Hey, babe!' Kira says. 'Come and join us!'

'Oh, I won't thanks – I'm just – I just came home for a nap. I mean a shower. I'll . . .' I'm backing out the door.

'Have you been anywhere exciting?' Kira asks.

I come back into the room reluctantly. 'Just round at David's.'

'How is he?' asks Max.

I stand by the door, and force myself to reply normally. I tell myself silently: just act like a normal person, talking to her flatmate and his girlfriend about her boyfriend.

'He's fine. He's going to the States.'

'Oh, for the fellowship? Already?' says Max.

'Ah – no, just for a . . . a sort of look-see, I think. I mean a conference.' On an impulse I add, 'He's asked me to go with him.'

Kira sits up. 'For the whole year?'

'He's asked me to go for the year. I'm thinking about it. But meanwhile I'm going over there with him next weekend.'

'Wow, that will be awesome,' she says. Max says nothing.

'Listen, I'd better dash. I'll see you guys later. OK?' I smile at them both, then go straight to my room, close the door firmly and curl up on the bed.

Oh God. That was worse than anything. To see them together like that – I keep having nightmarish flashbacks of seeing her brown feet with their hot-pink toenails, curling in his lap . . . I put my hand to my face and groan aloud. That was hell. I can't ever, ever do that again.

I'm going to have to move out.

Then it occurs to me: if I go to America, I never have to see Max with Kira ever again.

For now, though, I'm trapped in my room. I don't have anywhere to go, and anyway I can't go out in case they see me, or I get a glimpse of them snogging or having sex on the sofa, or something. The irony is: Kira is obviously just his type. She's sporty, outdoorsy, laid-back, casual, no-make-up but hot, into Mexican food and surfing . . . how could I not have predicted this?

Finally, I hear the door close. Thank God. After waiting ten minutes, I put my head around my door cautiously. If they have gone out, maybe I'll watch some *Gossip Girl*. I open the DVD machine, but my disc isn't in it; it's a Japanese horror film called *Dead Water*, one of his favourites. She must really like him to have sat through that.

Well, where did they put my DVD? It drives me crazy when people take out a DVD and don't put it back in its box. I'm still scrabbling around when I hear a noise behind me. It's Max. He's carrying an empty laundry basket in his hand and I can hear the washing-machine start up in the background.

'Oh, hi. Have you seen my *Gossip Girl* DVD?'

He clears his throat. 'The one I gave you?'

'No, not that one. The other one.' I hand him his Japanese horror DVD. 'By the way, just so you know,' I say, hating myself, 'Kira doesn't really like these films. That was a total lie.'

He frowns. 'What's your point?'

'My point is that she wasn't being honest with you.' God, how petty am I being?

Max's reply takes me by surprise.

'Speaking of honesty, have you ever told David the truth? I mean, about the whole time travel thing?'

'No,' I say angrily. 'What's that got to do with anything?'

'So he has no idea what's happened to you.'

'That's none of your business!'

'Don't you think you've been a bit selfish, Zoë?'

'What! Selfish?' I laugh aloud. 'Is this because I wouldn't let you scan my brain?'

'No. I mean you're being selfish because you have an advantage over David. You know things about him that he doesn't know about you. You also seem to have a problem with me going out with your friend, and that's pretty selfish too.'

We're staring at each other, furious.

'Great. Thanks for letting me know how awful and terrible I am.' I walk past him into my bedroom, trembling. It's barely lunchtime on Saturday and already it's the weekend from hell. I feel like I'm going nuts. I pick up the phone and call Rachel. It's one o'clock; she'll be back from the gym by now, and probably doing her chores.

'Hello!' she says, sounding disturbingly chirpy. I can hear the TV in the background.

'How are you?' I ask.

'Fine. I've just been to the gym and I'm at home doing my ironing and watching *Sky News*. How are you?'

I take a deep breath and lower my voice. 'I have feelings for Max and I know I should break up with David, but David wants me to move to America with him, and I'm really, really tempted, because Max is with Kira, and I can't face staying here unemployed and single.'

'What?' There's a shrieking sound and then a scuffle. 'Zoë, I just dropped my phone. What on earth are you talking about?'

'You heard me.'

'How long has this been going on?'

'I don't know. I think it's been building up for a while. You even mentioned it.'

'I know I did but – come on. It's just a crush. David wants you to go to America with him – that's fantastic! That's what you've always wanted, isn't it? How long would it be for?'

I explain about the weekend away and the fellowship.

'Look, Zoë,' she says. 'Max is sweet and everything, but it's *David*. You have something really great together.'

'But that's just it. I don't think we do have something great.'

'How do you mean?'

'I know that it looks perfect from the outside, but I don't think we actually have a real relationship. He doesn't know me, really. I mean – he gave me pearls, and I never wear pearls . . .'

'If you're going to complain about him giving you a pearl necklace, I'm hanging up.'

'OK, that was a bad example. But I don't know what's going on in his head.'

'Nobody ever knows what's going on in a man's head,' Rachel points out.

'And we hardly spend any time together.'

'Then a weekend away would be exactly the right way to fix that. Look, you don't have to decide about the fellowship now. But I say give it a chance for the weekend. And if the whole Max thing is getting to you . . . maybe some time away from him would be good. It would give you and David a chance to figure out what's going on.'

Getting away from Max. Right now, that sounds extremely appealing.

'Maybe. Anyway, how are you? What're you up to tonight?'

'I'm going to Erica's sister's leaving party,' Rachel says. 'It's quite near you actually. Why don't you come?'

'Is that Alice? Where's she going?'

'To LA, with her boyfriend, as far as I know. She's got a job over there, I think.'

'Hm,' I say. I remember Rachel mentioning this leaving party the night I broke up with David. I didn't go, though – I couldn't. But this time, it's different: I have to get out of the house. I agree to meet her at Westbourne Park station at 8 p.m.

THIRTY-FOUR

Rachel shows up at the station uncharacteristically late, and looking a million dollars. She's wearing a peach-coloured top under a little shrunken denim jacket – Rachel in colour! All my dreams coming true! – and a string of pearls.

'Wow! You look great,' I say, hugging her. 'Loving the pearls! Are they real?'

'They are. Freshwater. I was a little jealous when David got you yours . . . But then I thought, I don't need a boyfriend to buy me pearls. So I went to John Lewis and invested in a little gift from me to me.'

We start walking up the hill, towards the Grand Union pub. It's a lovely, sunny evening. People are milling around on the pavement outside the pub, laughing and talking and smoking. I wonder if I'll ever feel carefree again – but then I decide to snap out of it and try and enjoy tonight.

'What did you do last night?' I ask Rachel. She looks as if she stayed in and had a facial, so I'm surprised when she says, 'Oh, just went for drinks with someone.' Which, in Rachel language, means she had a date.

'Who is he?' I ask eagerly.

'Oh . . . nobody special. I don't know if it's anything yet. Just a couple of drinks . . .' her voice trails off, but there's a note of unmistakable excitement in it. She likes this guy. I want to shriek and ask for all the details, but I force myself to be casual.

'Well, that all sounds very intriguing. Will further details be forthcoming any time soon?'

'Maybe,' Rachel says. 'If I end up seeing him again, I'll let you know.'

We've arrived at the pub, which is perched right on the canal. They've apparently booked the room downstairs, so we go down the spiral staircase to find we're among the first to arrive. Erica comes over to say hello. She's quite hugely pregnant, which I hadn't realised.

'Great to see you both,' Erica says, kissing us. 'Thanks for coming.'

She and Rachel talk eagerly about Erica's work. I stand about awkwardly for a second with Erica's husband Raj, before we establish that he's a paediatric surgeon and – small world – knows David.

'I was talking to someone who works with him, recently. One of his former bosses. He said David is the most talented cardio-thoracic registrar he's ever had working with him.'

'Oh, that's great. I must tell him.' While we're talking, I'm able to see myself through Raj's eyes: the girlfriend of the brilliant young surgeon. It makes me feel better.

'Rachel!' A very pretty blonde girl has just appeared. It takes me a few seconds to realise that this is actually Erica's sister, Alice. Last time I saw her, she was clad in a shapeless navy jumper and chewing on her split ends, and I think she'd just been dumped. Her hair is still long but now it has style and shape, and her outfit is very cute: narrow, dark blue trousers, a sleeveless, clingy gold knit top and some very pretty low-heeled snakeskin sandals.

'Do you remember my friend Zoë?' asks Rachel.

'Of course! Thank you so much for coming.'

She even sounds more confident: really poised and happy. I'm still adjusting to the all-new Alice when a very tall guy appears by her side. 'Hi,' he says, giving us a brief but friendly smile. 'I'm Sam.'

This must be the American boyfriend. I do another double-take

293

as Alice introduces us and we all shake hands, because he is hot stuff in a kind of all-American J. Crew way. Then Rachel is claimed by Erica and Raj again. I expect that Alice will abandon me to talk to her other guests, but she and Sam make no move to run off.

'So you're moving to LA!' I say stupidly. 'That's brilliant.'

Alice smiles. 'Yes, next week. It's exciting. I have a job with a literary scout over there and Sam is starting his own talent agency. And we're going to live in Venice Beach!'

Sam puts his arm around her. 'Yup. After two years in London, I'm finally throwing her over the saddle and taking her back West.'

Alice gives him a friendly shove, and I notice something flashing on her ring finger. A mahoosive, as Jenny would say, diamond ring.

'Are you . . .?' I gesture delicately to the ring.

Alice smiles a thousand-watt smile; Sam looks more cool and contained, but he's clearly thrilled with himself as well.

'We're engaged!!' they say together, as if they're the first people who've ever had such a genius idea.

'Wow! Congratulations.' How has her life suddenly become so perfect?

'Sam, mate,' Raj says, appearing beside us. 'Can I borrow you for a sec?'

'Sure. Nice to meet you, Zoë.' And he squeezes Alice's arm briefly before disappearing.

'So what about you? How are things going?' Alice asks.

I am definitely not going to tell Alice, with her perfect life, how messed-up mine is. But then something awful happens. I find myself, well, boasting.

'I'm great! I'm seeing a wonderful guy. He's a surgeon, actually. In fact, we're going to America next weekend together, for a medical conference. In New York. I mean, David's going for the conference and I'm going with him. But I'll probably move there for the year, as well.'

Why am I saying this? I haven't decided if I'm moving or not.

But the miserable truth is, I want Alice to think that I have a great relationship and an exciting transatlantic life, just like her.

'How do you feel about going to the States? Are you nervous?' Rachel asks her, joining us again.

'Very. But Sam's been in London for two years, so it's only fair that I try LA. You don't always know how these things are going to go, do you? Sometimes you just have to hold your nose and jump.'

I look at her thoughtfully. She's right. I don't know what will happen if I go to the States with David – but maybe I should just hold my nose, and jump.

Next thing, more friends of Alice's arrive, and Rachel and I leave her to it and mingle. It's actually a very fun party. Nobody talks about weddings or house prices, or buying a house: instead we talk about random nonsense, including a long conversation about Erica and Raj's neighbours who are Druids. For whole minutes at a time, I manage to forget about Max, and David – until it's time to leave. The others are going on somewhere, but Rachel wants to get the last tube, and I decide to go with her.

'That was a fun party,' Rachel says, as we walk towards the tube. 'Doesn't Alice look amazing?'

'Amazing. It's like she's had a Ricki Lake makeover.' I shake my head.

I expect Rachel to make some cynical crack about how Alice will have to get a little dog and UGG boots for LA, or something, but instead she says, 'Maybe she's just in love.'

I take a sideways look at her.

'You're very starry-eyed tonight. Is this the effect of your date last night?' I'm dying to hear more but I know that chances are slim.

'Maybe.' She grins and giggles – Rachel, giggling? – but refuses to say more.

We say goodbye at the tube station and I walk home, feeling the distraction of the night slipping away and all my problems descending on me again. Max; work; and David. I'll admit that I don't have the passionate, all-consuming feelings for him that I once did, but he's still a wonderful guy and I'm lucky to have him. And he's offering me an escape route.

THIRTY-FIVE

From the plane window, I can see land. The sun is just coming up and I can see the city approaching and even some landmarks: I think I can pick out the Statue of Liberty, and the Empire State Building . . .

'David!' I say, leaning across the aisle and nudging his arm. 'Look – the Empire State Building!'

'Unlikely. We're coming up to Boston,' he says, pointing to the monitor on his screen. 'We've got another hour or so to go.' He smiles and lies back on his seat – that is, his bed. I do the same.

I've never flown first class before and I must say, it's very therapeutic. In fact, if you were looking for a good antidote to having your heart broken, disgracing yourself in front of your whole company and being put on gardening leave, it's pretty much ideal. We have beds where we can actually stretch out, our own personal monitors which are so much better than the crappy ones in cattle class, a luxurious, super-soft powder-blue blanket and lots of little beauty products.

With every mile we've flown, and every film I've watched on my little monitor, London seems further and further away. If Julia or Seth or Karen could see me now, they certainly wouldn't think I was a loser. For a second I drift off into a fantasy in which I conquer the fashion world in New York in some unspecified way. I run into Julia at a fashion show, where I'm in the front row and she's somewhere near the back, but I kindly offer her my seat instead. 'You know,' I tell her, 'leaving Marley's was the best thing ever to happen to me. I never would have—'

'Coffee? Juice?' asks the stewardess, stopping between our beds. She's about to ask David, but I whisper, 'He's asleep', stretching a protective hand over towards him. This is probably the most sleep he's had in weeks if not months. Poor David. He works so hard, and he does need someone to look after him.

'Hey,' he says a little while later, his eyes opening. 'Hello.'

'Were you asleep?'

'Yeah, I think so.' He yawns and rubs his face. 'Weird. I dreamed that they needed a doctor on board, and I tore strips off them because they didn't have a defibrillator. That didn't happen, did it?'

I shake my head, smiling. David's really not the kind of person who tells you his dreams; it seems kind of funny. He looks at me for another second and then squeezes my arm. 'Hey. I'm glad you came with me.'

Because he so rarely says anything like that, when he does it feels as if he's written me a poem or serenaded me on my balcony. Actually, I much prefer low-key declarations like that: I can't stand it when people – men – are all mushy. David would never be mushy; he would never crowd me. I wonder briefly what Max is like in his tender moments – I could see him being romantic, but not mushy – but then I drive the thought away.

'I'm glad I came,' I reply, adding in a low voice, 'And David, thank you for the tickets.' I nearly died when I saw the price on them. What I had thought was the total price for both of us, return, turned out to be the price of just one flight for one of us.

'That's really not a problem,' he says, which I've realised by now is true.

The Surrey is probably the nicest hotel I've ever been in. It's on the Upper East Side (the Upper East Side!) in an elegant town-house that's straight out of *Gossip Girl*, and the interior is all marble floors, modern art, taupe and gold. We have a suite: a bedroom with a huge, white bed with grey and gold cushions, and a separate living room with a low, grey velvet sofa. As I flop down on the bed, I think of the summer I spent here in New York when I was twenty, living in a flea-pit on Avenue E with no air conditioning. This is a little nicer.

'Are any of the other delegates staying here?' I ask as an afterthought. It doesn't exactly strike me as a conference hotel.

'God, no. They're in some Marriott somewhere . . . I thought we deserved somewhere a little nicer.'

That's an understatement. I can't even imagine how much this place is costing. But, as David said earlier, this is the closest he'll probably get to having a holiday all year.

'I'm not really that tired, are you?' I ask, yawning. 'I mean, I am tired but not as tired as I thought I should be, considering it's . . .' I check my watch, and decide not to do the sums.

'I slept on the plane, so I'm OK.' He shrugs. 'Better than most of the time, actually.'

David starts to unpack, and I do the same, hanging up my lovely Helmut Lang dress (sample sale, reduced to 30 per cent) and my new pet trench coat from Isabel Marant (bought with my employee discount, just before I got kicked out). I flip open my map, noticing that we're only a block away from Central Park and the Museum Mile.

'What do you want to do now?' I ask David.

David glances at his watch. 'There's a talk I want to catch that's starting soon.' He pats my arm briefly, and then walks past me into the en-suite bathroom. 'Are you OK to amuse yourself this afternoon?'

'Um . . . sure.' I sit down on the edge of the bed. 'What time do you think you'll be free in the evening?' I ask. But the shower has started and there's no reply. I look at my watch: 1.30 p.m. I'm tired, but I don't want to nap; I'd rather get moving.

After ten minutes, David emerges from the bathroom, wrapped in a luxurious white bathrobe. His hair has got longer recently, simply because he hasn't had time to get it cut, but it suits him, especially all slicked-back and wet.

'I'm not sure what the schedule is,' he says, 'but I'll make sure I'm free by six. I'll book somewhere nice for dinner this evening and we'll go out on the town. Sound good?' He smiles at me, and then goes over to the wardrobe and starts getting dressed. 'I'll send you a text – you've got roaming, haven't you? Or if there are any problems you can leave a message with the desk.'

I nod, and admire the lean muscles under his arms, and his flat stomach, as he slips into his boxers and chinos. I knew that the whole point of the trip was for him to attend this conference, but somehow the luxury flights, and the romantic hotel, had made me think that he might be spending more time with me. We never actually discussed it. But then I look out the window and think: I'm in *New York*. If there's anywhere in the world I would have no problem amusing myself, this is it.

As I step outside, I take a deep breath and exhale with happiness. It's a perfect New York day; the sky is blue, the sun is shining and there's just enough of a tinge of autumn in the air to make the sun refreshing. An elderly couple walk past me, the man leaning on a cane and the woman leading a little white dog on a leash.

'No, no, no, no, no, no, no,' he's saying to her extremely loudly. '*Thursday*. They told us Thursday.'

'They said *Tuesday*,' she replies emphatically. 'Tuesday, Tuesday, Tuesday.' Toosday. It's like something out of a movie. They're New Yorkers! I'm in New York!

I'm also wearing exactly the right clothes: a long-sleeved navy-and-white-striped Petit Bateau T-shirt, skinny jeans and Converse, and my trench coat in case it gets cooler later. I have my Mulberry bag slung over one shoulder, with Sinead's scarf looped through one handle. I pull on my shades, and stride out towards Central Park, drinking in all the little details: the elegant stone buildings with green canopies in front, the uniformed doormen, the American flags, the odd yellow cab streaking past, the X-ING on the pavement. My whole summer in New York, I had no idea what PED-XING meant; I thought it might be some Chinese city that was twinned with New York. I only found out after I left that it was a pedestrian crossing. I imagine telling Max this, and how he would laugh – but then I put the thought right out of my mind.

Within minutes I find myself on Fifth Avenue. Fifth Avenue! Even just looking at the name on a sign gives me chills down my spine. Feeling like quite the New Yorker (I haven't even had to look at a map yet!) I head left, downtown, towards my old workplace of FAO Schwartz. It's unlikely that anyone I worked with would still be there – but they might. And I could try Macy's where I also worked. My old boss Mary, who was from Galway, might be around . . . All my worries about jobs come flooding back into my head, but then I drive them out again. I'm tired of plotting and scheming: I am just going go with the flow. Maybe the Universe will send me a sign.

Seeing a Starbucks, I decide to stop off to buy a Frappucino. One girl, in a cute yellow-and-mustard striped playsuit and raffia wedges, seems to be working on what looks like a fashion blog. I've always hoped to be spotted on the street by a fashion blogger, but to date, this has never happened. She glances at me with very little interest before returning to her page. Oh, well. I see that they do a Salted Caramel Frappucino, which I've never tried before and immediately order.

'Name?' asks the barista.

'Zoë.' Why do they do this? I don't get it. There's no point being my friend; I'm only here for the weekend.

When I get my drink, I notice that she's written 'Zooey.' Wow. That's the first time anyone has ever done that. I stroll outside, sipping my Frappucino, and think: I could totally reinvent myself here. Zooey Kennedy. I could study fashion, and do fashion blogging and maybe some freelance styling . . . I could become, if not an It Girl, maybe an Ish Girl? I decide to hop on a bus downtown, and stroll around the Village, before walking back up and doing a little pilgrimage to the Holy Trinity: Saks, Barneys and Tiffany's.

Greenwich Village has gone even more upmarket since I was

last here – fewer little hippy cafés and thrift stores, and more flagship stores, cute delis and restaurants. Not that I'm complaining. After drooling over the offerings in the Magnolia Bakery, and deciding against it because of dinner this evening, I make a beeline towards Marc Jacobs – first the accessory store, where I buy a load of silver and gold purses and make-up bags that will make great presents for Rachel and Harriet and my mum.

I suppose I should get Kira something too, and I reluctantly choose a keyring. But then I imagine her putting a spare key to my flat on it, and drop it like a hot coal. I'll get her a pumice stone, or a super-strong deodorant from Duane Reade, or something.

With my purchases in hand, I drift over to the flagship Marc Jacobs store across the way. There's a sign in the window that says NOW HIRING. The guy behind the counter looks really kind and understanding; just the right kind of port for my battered vessel. I have a sudden, mad urge to ask him for an application form – but of course, I don't have a visa, so it's pointless.

I go back outside and wander up Bleeker Street for a while, looking at all the beautiful people going past and wondering what the hell I'm going to do with my life. I duck into a café and order a latte to think it over. Should I just go back to London and try and get another job (and flat)? Should I move back to Dublin? Should I move here with David and study fashion? That seems to be the only realistic option. But would it be the right thing?

Beside me are two glowing, tawny blonde women, dressed in biscuit-coloured cashmere and skintight dark blue jeans, one leg of which probably costs as much as my entire outfit. They look like yummy mummies although they're currently unencumbered with kids. They have quite loud, unselfconscious voices, so it's not long before I learn that one of them has given up wheat and feels amazing, and the other is having a terrible time trying to get some money out of her husband to start her up in a scented-candle business.

302

'He doesn't think it's such a good idea, but I told him, suck it up: I just spent the last five years doing your stuff, now it's time for me.'

Wow. She's feisty. I wonder what David would say if I wanted him to be an investor in my scented-candle business. He has essentially offered to support me for a year. But could I let him? Wouldn't I just end up like one of these women – who are currently debating the merits of Botox versus Restylane? And could I really move here with David, when I'm not . . . I'm not . . . As a distraction, I check my phone to see a text from David. He won't be able to be back by six, but he suggests dinner at eight at a place called Daniel on East 65th Street. I decide that it's time to leave the Village and go uptown, and duck quickly into Saks before going home to change.

When I get back to the hotel (after just the briefest visit to Saks, Barneys, Sephora and Bergdorf's) there's a new, friendly receptionist my age.

'Have you heard of a restaurant called Daniel? Is it nice?' I ask. From the energetic way she nods, I can tell it is.

'Should I dress up?' I ask her.

'Definitely. Daniel Boulod also owns Bar Boulod, which is attached to our hotel. It is a wonderful place to eat, but Daniel is probably one of the best restaurants in the city.' She looks around and lowers her voice. 'If you and your boyfriend are staying here, but he takes you to Daniel instead of Bar Boulod, that's a really great sign.'

Great. This means it's time to break out the Helmut Lang.

I look at my watch: six-thirty. I shower quickly, savouring the fluffy hotel towels and the cute free products, and then I slather myself in Chanel Chance body lotion. I don't wash my hair, but just put it up in a high, slightly 1960s bun. I use my new Stila eyeliner from Sephora and give my eyes a flick, use my faithful Bourjois blusher and give my skin a matte finish with my new Chantecaille powder. I don't do anything to my lips; just dot on some Vaseline. As an afterthought, I add a quick dab on my cheekbones to highlight them.

I'm putting away my make-up when I notice David's washbag, sitting beside the sink. I haven't seen his travel bag before, and out of pure nosiness, I peek inside. It's very neat, as I would have imagined: comb, deodorant, moisturiser, condoms, SPF, and some kind of odd prescription drug that I don't recognise.

For a second, I wonder about David's boundless energy; the way he manages to keep going like a superhuman, despite his punishing schedule. And his fit of temper that time we played tennis. And his muscles. What if he's on some kind of steroid? I read the label . . . and see that it's to inhibit male-pattern baldness. Feeling like an idiot, as well as a real nosey-parker, I put it away.

The Helmut Lang is a forest-green jersey maxi dress, sleeveless, with a draped front and a racing back; very simple and easy to wear and pack, very clingy, very sexy. I accessorise with an armful of gold bangles and my new gladiator sandals – very, very cheap today at Saks. It's only 7.10, and I'm meeting David at 8, and the restaurant is no distance. I wonder what to do to kill the time.

I could nap, but I'm not tired, even though it's nearly one a.m. in London. Max is probably asleep, or else he's having one of his insomniac nights prowling the flat or playing computer games. One time I met him at breakfast, hair standing on end and looking absolutely wired.

'Late night, was it?'

'I think I read the whole internet,' he said.

Or maybe he's with Kira.

Lalala: I'm not thinking about Max. I'm just not. I remember that there's a roof top to this hotel, which I haven't seen yet. I decide to go right on up there and have a drink by myself.

Like the hotel, the terrace is something out of *Gossip Girl*: the long bar with the barman polishing glasses, the plump, white sofas and chairs grouped around glass tables, the elegant brown decking and the terracotta planters filled with lush green shrubs.

304

It's quite quiet; there is only a handful of people, sipping complicated cocktails.

But it's the view that's the star: the skyscrapers of New York,
glittering metal or mellow brownstone, ziggurat-shaped or slender
rectangles, spread out as far as the eye can see, broken only by
the greenery of Central Park. The sun is beginning to sink down,
filling the whole sky with an intense golden glow that catches the
edges of the metal buildings and reflects from a thousand
windows. I walk to the edge of the terrace, put my hands on the
railing, and drink it in.

'Would you care for a drink, ma'am?' asks a waiter, materialising
beside me.

'Sure. I'll have . . . a glass of champagne. No, a Cosmopolitan.'

I know Cosmopolitans are a massive cliché but I still love them.
I sink down on the nearest white sofa and arrange my skirt around
my legs, admiring the contrast between the green fabric and my
(fake) tanned legs, and take a sip.

I'm actually a little nervous of seeing David this evening. We'll
be spending more time together this weekend than we ever have
done before, and I don't know what it will be like: maybe we'll
get on each other's nerves, or maybe we'll run out of things to
talk about, or I'll do something gross like leave mascara on the
towel. But as I feel the delicious, ice-cold cocktail slip down, my
worries subside a little. David is crazy about me. And he worries
about things too; look at his anti-baldness tablets.

'Another Cosmopolitan?' the waiter asks, politely whisking away
my (oops) empty glass.

'Um . . .' I look at my watch. Seven-thirty. 'Sure,' I say.

I think that David is going to ask me, this evening, for a definite
answer as to whether I'm prepared to move here with him. As I
sip my second cocktail, trying to pace myself somewhat, I look
out over the glowing skyscrapers and think: *this could be my city.*

Before I know it, it's ten to eight and I've finished my second
drink. I had better leave, right now.

'Can I pay for those two drinks?' I ask the waiter, who says

305

he'll put it on the room. Great. I stand up and slip an unstructured tuxedo-style jacket over my dress, and hurry towards the lift, feeling a slight wobble in my legs. Oops: those Cosmos were stronger than I thought. But they have had the effect of making me very, very relaxed.

THIRTY-SIX

'Wow,' David says, when we meet in front of the restaurant. 'You look fantastic.' He kisses me and adds, 'I would never have guessed you got off a plane this morning.'

'You don't look so bad yourself,' I say. He's wearing a navy suit jacket, chinos and a light blue shirt and looks very handsome and relaxed – not a name badge in sight.

We walk into the restaurant, which is extremely plush and lovely – low lights, tinkling music, white tablecloths and even a discreet string quartet. The hostess takes my jacket and asks if we'd like to go straight to our table or have a drink at the bar first.

'What would you prefer?' David asks me courteously.

'A drink at the bar?' I ask. The hostess directs us to two high stools at the bar – I have to be quite careful when climbing aboard mine, but I manage it without any mishaps.

'Champagne?' he asks me.

'Sure!' I say, sitting up a little straighter so that he won't guess that I've already partaken. When the champagne arrives, we clink our flutes together. It's really impossible to feel at all gloomy while drinking champagne.

'How was the conference?'

'Really worthwhile. I met interesting people, listened to some great talks, watched some brilliant operations . . .'

'What, live?' I ask, recoiling.

'No! What do you think this was, Bodyworlds? They were on

film.' He starts telling me all about a new kind of tiny surgical blade he saw demonstrated, before he stops himself.

'I forget sometimes that I'm talking to a normal person.'

'And did you meet your professor?'

'Yes, I met him this afternoon,' David says. 'He seems great. I mean, he's not Salazar – he's got a different approach – but that's good. I have a good feeling about New York.'

'Sorry, who was Salazar again?'

'He was the guy I really wanted to work with at the Texas Heart Institute at Houston.'

'Oh yes.' I consider asking him why he never told me about all this, and why Jenny heard about it first, but it doesn't really seem to matter any more.

'How about you? Did you shop till you dropped?'

'Well . . . I *may* have done some damage in Sephora.'

'What's Sephora?'

'David! How can you possibly ask such a question? It's the beauty and make-up one-stop-shop. It's like the Texas Heart Institute of beauty.'

'I see,' he says, looking utterly charmed. 'Isn't there one in London?'

I shake my head.

'So that would be one advantage of moving to New York . . . Have you given it any more thought?' he asks casually.

'Yes. But I just don't know what I would do for work.'

'That's fair enough. But just know that you don't have to worry about that. You can take some time off. Do freelance styling. Do a diploma. Whatever you want – I'd help you.'

Wow. He makes it sounds so simple. And maybe it is a little simpler than I thought. The truth is, I'm getting tired of trying to think of solutions and make decisions on my own. David's offer . . . well, it's extremely appealing.

'Though I'm sure Marley's would be sorry to lose you,' he adds.

I give a guilty start, but it was obviously just an off-the-cuff remark. He leans back and stretches, and I see two thin, glamorous and hungry-looking women, who are obviously here on the prowl, check him out, exchanging glances. If they knew he was a heart surgeon, they'd probably slap me off my stool and carry him off back to their cave.

'Are you ready to eat?' David asks.

'Sure.' I appear to have finished my champagne already and I'm definitely now two-levels buzzed. I have to be extra careful to avoid any pratfalls as I slide off my bar stool. A waiter appears from nowhere to lead us to the table. Wow. We've been to some nice places in London, but never this nice. I try to catch David's eye, as if to say, 'This is classy, huh?' But he just smiles at me. Of course, he's more used to this kind of thing than I am.

The service is impeccable. The waiter appears to know the full names and star signs of all the individual cows and chickens who contributed to the menu, and he also seems to have written a thesis on the wines. After a long and enjoyable debate about the merits of each, David chooses the black sea bass with Syrah sauce. I decide to have two starters; zaatar rice flaked-crusted sea scallops, whatever zaatar might be, followed by arugula and lemon ravioli. David chooses a Californian Sauvignon Blanc to go with all this.

'Arugula means rocket,' I explain to David. I somehow picked this factoid up during my J1 summer. 'Not that I ate much rocket. I seem to remember just living on pizza slices and Dunkin' Donuts.'

'It obviously didn't do you any lasting harm,' he observes. 'By the way, I was thinking of going to see some apartments on Sunday. I'd love your opinion on them.'

He takes out his phone and shows me some pictures of apartments. The first one is a loft-style place: small, but very stylish, with an exposed brick wall and huge windows. The other looks cosier, with wooden floors and high ceilings and mouldings. They're both a far cry from my fire-trap on Avenue E.

'Neither is furnished,' he says. 'But that shouldn't be a problem.'

I don't know if it's because David's so relaxed and excited about his fellowship, or being on holiday, or because I'm a little drunk – well, quite drunk – but we're having a really nice time: one of the nicest evenings we've ever spent together, in fact. The food is amazing, and we spend a lot of time describing to each other how great it is. And then, over our second bottle of wine, we end up discussing our friends. I'm interested to learn that Oliver is seeing someone though David doesn't know who. I wonder if it's Harriet. He also says he thinks Kira is quite competitive with me.

'I'm competitive too, so I can see it in other people. Though Max seems pretty smitten with her,' David adds.

'Really,' I say, swallowing my ravioli with an effort.

'By the way, did you know he's in New York right now?' David adds casually.

I almost drop my fork, but luckily manage to cover it up. 'Really? No, I didn't know that.'

'He's over for some work thing. Maybe we could meet up with him tomorrow evening or something.'

I nod mechanically, my mind racing in panic. Max in New York! Why does he have to pop up here? Just when I was managing not to think about him every hour, on the hour. Now David is talking about making plans with Max for tomorrow evening. I reach out my hand and put it over his.

'Why don't we hang out, just the two of us?' I ask, making an effort to sound seductive, not frightened.

To my relief, David nods easily. The conversation moves on to other things – our families, Dublin, what David will miss about London, and both of our J1 summers. David worked in Friendly's Ice Cream parlour in Nantucket, and shared a three-bedroom house with nineteen other guys, one of whom left in the middle of the night with David's rollerblades and four hundred dollars. His mother then decided enough was enough and told him to find himself a short let with a maximum of three other people.

'She said, "I know Irish people live like pigs when they go abroad, but you won't be one of them."' He laughs, and I'm laughing so much I have to wipe away a tear. I didn't think his mum was capable of being so feisty; it's the kind of thing my own mum would say.

'It is nice talking to someone who knows what a J1 summer is,' says David, smiling at me. I nod back. Whatever our differences, we're from the same place, and it means a lot. My thoughts of Max have died down a little – thank God. I take another sip of wine to help the process along.

'Would you care for some dessert?' asks the waiter.

I'm not really feeling like dessert, but David is having one and insists that I get one too.

'You can just have a taste,' he says.

David orders the passion-fruit vanilla vacherin, and I order a milk-chocolate dacquoise with salted caramel ice cream – this seems to be, literally, the flavour of the month.

'It's not like you to have dessert,' I tease him.

'Well, maybe this is a special occasion. Though it's far from vanilla vacherins I was raised,' he quips, and we both laugh.

I take a minute to look around the beautiful room, the elegant people, our half-empty glasses of outstanding wine. I still have to pinch myself sometimes. Whatever about all my doubts and disasters, I went back to do everything differently with David, and it worked. I'm here.

'The chocolate dacquoise . . . and the vacherin?' the waiter says, interrupting my thoughts.

Oooh. It's far from dacquoise I was raised too – or vacherin – but they look outrageously good. If all the food in New York is this delicious, I'll have to take up something really brutal, like spinning or Bikram yoga.

'The dacquoise comes with a side dish. Enjoy,' the waiter says, and disappears.

What side dish? I look down at my delicious chocolate dessert – tiny and rich, with a little mound of golden salted caramel ice cream. And to the left, I see a plate with a small aqua-blue velvet box.

I look up. David is watching me intently. He's not the only one: the people at the table beside us have spotted the box and are exchanging smiles.

'Zoë,' David says, taking my hand. I look at him, dazed. I literally can't speak.

'You know I love you.' He swallows, and my heart skips a beat. David has never said that before. 'I want you to come to America with me, as my fiancée – or even better, as my wife.' Seeing that I can't move a muscle, he reaches gently past me and opens up the box to reveal a massive diamond solitaire ring, brilliant cut, on a platinum band. I instantly recognise it as the classic Tiffany setting. It's such a cliché, but I gasp: it's absolutely breathtaking.

'Will you marry me?' he asks me in a low voice.

'I don't know what to say,' I stammer. It's such an idiotic response but it's the best I can do. I wish I had a clearer head. I wish I hadn't had those two Cosmos, plus champagne, plus most of a bottle of wine . . .

'Say yes?' he asks, half smiling, half appealing. A few conversations around us have stilled, and I know that people are watching me, waiting. The diamond is catching the light, hypnotising me with its rays.

'Yes,' I whisper.

David smiles triumphantly and leans forward to kiss me over the table. I kiss him back, not quite believing what's just happened. There's a sprinkling of applause from some of the tables, and the quartet starts playing 'Here Comes the Bride'. I grip the edge of the table with my right hand, as David picks up my left hand and gently slides the ring on to my ring finger, where it sparkles in the candlelight. I'm euphoric, drunk, confused, terrified, jet-lagged, and engaged.

THIRTY-SEVEN

I wake to the sound of my own throbbing head. I give a low groan, and reach out towards the nightstand, hoping that I'll miraculously encounter a glass of water, but there's nothing. I groan again, rub my eyes, and feel something scratch against my face.

Oh. It's my engagement ring.

It's not that I don't remember what happened last night. I remember exactly. I was having dinner with David, and we had a few glasses of champagne, and now we're engaged. I feel like I'm on a moving escalator that's travelling at warp speed, taking me somewhere I never expected. *But it's fine*, I repeat to myself. *It's great!*

There's a note on the pillow beside me. 'Gone for a walk. Back soon – D x.'

I go and pour myself a glass of water from the mini-bar and drain it down, before going to the bathroom. My eye-make-up is all smudged, and not in a sexy way: my backcombed hair has become a bird's nest. God, I really hope David didn't see me like this.

I sit down on the toilet seat and gaze at the engagement ring, turning my hand to see it change in the light. It's so huge, and magnificent-looking, it sort of reassures me. I was having all sorts of doubts, which is normal, and the mention of . . . someone being in New York freaked me out, but David's proposal was a sign. It was so romantic, too; it'll make a great story. And the ring is just *astonishing*. I can't stop looking at it.

'Zoë! Are you in there?' It's David! I lock the bathroom door and start combing my hair, wincing as my brush catches in the back-combed mass.

'Just a second . . .'

'Breakfast is here,' he calls out.

Pulling off the ring, I jump into the shower and wash my hair. Then I cleanse away my panda eyes, pat on a bit of tinted moisturiser and some Benetint blusher, and brush my teeth and tongue before slipping on my fluffy hotel robe, hoping I look cute and demure in it rather than housewife-ish. I carefully put the ring back on, relieved that it hasn't got lost in the last ten minutes, and step outside.

David's looking smart in a navy cashmere V-neck sweater over a white T-shirt and jeans, pouring coffee from a silver jug into two cups. There's an array of pastries and fruit in a little basket, plus a silver container full of doughnuts and waffles.

'Good morning.' He looks up and smiles. 'Did you sleep well? I just went out to get the paper.' He indicates the *New York Times*, lying on a side table. 'Which made me think, we'll have to figure out a wording for our announcement.'

I pour myself and him some coffee. 'Um, what announcement?'

'In the *Irish Times*,' he says, sitting down and breaking open a croissant. 'No?'

'Oh, sure!' I suppress my feeling of panic. 'But can we tell people in real life first? I have to call my parents.' I look around wildly, as if a reporter might be hiding behind a sofa.

'Of course,' says David, reassuringly. 'Although they already know.'

'What? How?'

'I called your father to ask for his permission.'

'Oh! I see. Wow. What – what did he say?'

'He said he'd have to ask your mother.' Nervous as I am, I can't help smiling: that's such a typically Dad reaction. 'But she seemed pretty happy.' He smiles, and for a fleeting second I wonder: does he look smug? But then I reproach myself.

'We can call them now, though. It's lunchtime in Dublin.'

As we listen to the ring tone, I keep thinking how surreal this is; I'm still not totally sure if I'm awake or not. Things get even weirder when Mum answers the phone and bursts into tears.

'I'm sorry, I don't know why I'm crying at all,' she says, sounding embarrassed. 'But we're so happy for you, pet. It's wonderful, wonderful news. Here's your father.'

Dad is briefer, but also sounds very pleased. Mum soon grabs the phone back and asks about the ring.

'What's it like? Is it beautiful?'

'Oh . . . It's gorgeous. Huge.'

'Just two carats,' says David modestly, in the background.

'Would you like me to call Father O'Sullivan and see what he says about Blackrock Church? Next summer would be nice, wouldn't it? We could have the reception in the yacht club, where your cousin got married . . .'

I'm in a daze: I've barely just got engaged and she's already ringing the parish priest. I say yes because I can't think how not to. They ask all about how David popped the question and then they ask to speak to him, and are really sweet, welcoming him to the family and hoping we'll be very happy. Mum starts talking about when we can come over and visit, but Dad reminds her that this is a transatlantic call, and eventually we hang up, promising to talk again soon.

'Now let's call my parents,' says David, checking his watch.

'Do you think they'll be pleased?'

'Sure.' David smiles at me as he dials, but I'm very nervous. 'Hello. Yes, it's me . . . Is Dad there? I have some news for you both. Zoë and I are engaged!' There's a pause. 'No, not Chloe, Zoë. You met her at the Connaught . . . yes, that time.' There's a longer pause; David's smile becomes a bit more set and rigid, as he gives some brief details. 'Last night. In a restaurant. Um, we're not sure. As soon as possible, I suppose. Yes, fine. OK.'

'Well?' I ask faintly, once he's hung up.

'They're pleased,' he says briskly. 'They say to tell you congratulations. Mum wanted us to get off the phone quickly so she could ring Lough Rynn Castle, and check out availability.'

'Oh God. Really?'

He nods. 'They get booked out years in advance.'

'But – would you not prefer to get married in Dublin?'

He shrugs. 'I suppose we could do the Shelbourne – if it's big enough. But we're going to have to have at least two hundred people, maybe three hundred.'

I decide I have to speak up.

'All of those places sound great, but – I don't know, I've always liked the idea of getting married on the beach.'

David stares at me. 'On the beach? People don't get married on beaches.' Seeing my stricken expression, he leans over and kisses me. 'We could certainly honeymoon on the beach. Maybe Mustique? Or the Maldives?'

This is all happening way too fast. I hate the idea of a gigantic wedding; I've always wanted just close friends and immediate family. And I'm already stressed at the idea of our mothers coming to loggerheads over the location. But then I tell myself not to be so ungrateful. Wedding at Lough Rynn Castle – or the Royal St. George Yacht Club, depending on which of our mums prevails – and honeymoon in the Maldives: who on earth would not want that?

I get dressed quickly – a belted vintage wool dress that seems suitably fiancée-like, and flat boots – and David and I leave the hotel to celebrate with a romantic day in Manhattan. I wonder uneasily for a minute if we might have an unwelcome encounter, but then I push the thought out of my head. There are six million people in Manhattan – maybe more? We're not going to bump into— anyone we know.

'So,' he says as we walk outside, 'I thought we could start with a carriage ride around Central Park, and then go for lunch at the Boathouse and maybe head to Tiffany's later.'

'That sounds wonderful . . . but why Tiffany's?'

'Well.' He smiles down at me. 'You might need a bracelet to go with that ring?'

'David, that's crazy – I don't need anything else . . .' But it reassures me to think that he's willing to do all this for me.

It's a beautiful autumn day, and our entire morning is like something out of a dream – first our carriage ride, which seems cheesy before we get on the carriage, but then is a lot of fun. Our driver somehow guesses we've just got engaged – or maybe he can tell from the way I keep staring at my ring – and gives us an extra lap of the park before dropping us off at the Boat House, where we sit looking out on the little lake, eating the most delicious quiche and drinking white wine.

'I was thinking of proposing here,' David says, 'but I couldn't wait.'

Every time he says something romantic like this, it reassures me, but at the same time, it makes it feel harder to – well, put a stop to things. Not that I want to, I tell myself quickly. This is wonderful; I'm really lucky. My parents are over the moon: surely that's a sign that I'm doing the right thing? Then something occurs to me.

'How did you get my parents' number, David?'

'Max had it. Of course I could have just called directory enquiries in Dublin, but I thought there are probably a fair few Kennedys in Blackrock . . .'

'So does Max know you were going to propose?'

'Yeah, I told him,' David says cheerfully.

I don't say anything, but I can't help thinking about Max now. I have to wonder what he thought when David told him we were getting engaged. Did he feel any flicker of regret? Well, probably not. He's with Kira now, and I just have to put him out of my head.

Next we go for a drink at the Oak Room at the Plaza – David orders champagne though I'd much rather have a stiff gin and tonic. But as we start wandering down Fifth Avenue in the general direction of Tiffany's, I'm feeling increasingly uncomfortable.

'David, we really don't need to get anything else,' I say. 'You've already given me this beautiful ring . . .'

'I insist. An engagement present. Just something small.'

I keep on looking at myself sideways in shop windows, wondering if I look any different with the ring on my finger – which I still can't stop staring at. But I'm also slightly paranoid about being mugged. From my stint on the jewellery counter at Marley's, I'm pretty sure this ring might have cost in the region of five figures. Which is kind of obscene really . . . but then I tell myself not to be so unromantic and ungrateful.

We're just coming up to Tiffany's when David's phone starts ringing.

'That's my prof – I have to talk to him and it might take a while. Can I meet you at Tiffany's in ten minutes or so? Under the clock?'

'Of course.'

I make my way to the elegant, pinky-beige sandstone building on the corner of Fifty-Seventh and Fifth, and I go and join the crowd gazing into the Tiffany's window. It's a really clever display of yellow diamonds: necklaces, bracelets, cocktail rings, engagement rings, all cunningly arrayed on little models of New York street scenes – a ring hanging from a lamp-post; a necklace suspended around the gate of Central Park, a bracelet draped over the arch at Greenwich.

I think of how I stared into the window of Marley's back in December – that is, this coming December – and wished to have David back. If I made a wish now, standing here, what would it be?

Next minute, I gasp aloud, because Max is right behind me, reflected in the window. He's wearing a red scarf, and he's smiling at me. What's he doing here? I whirl around quickly – but he's vanished. I'm scanning the horizon desperately, but he's not there;

318

there isn't even anyone who looks like him. I obviously imagined it. A feeling of desolation overwhelms me.

'Zoë?' says a voice behind me.

I turn around, and the hope dies when I see that it's David. 'Sorry about that,' he says. 'He just wanted to ask me a couple of questions. Will we go in?'

As I look at the glittering door of Tiffany's, everything becomes clear to me. I don't want anything in there except what I just glimpsed in the reflection of the window. And if I go in there and let David buy me more expensive stuff, I won't be able to live with myself any more, because I don't love him. I think I'm in love with Max.

I clear my throat. 'No, I – I'm really tired, David. Sorry. Can we just go back to the hotel?'

'Of course,' says David, ever the gentleman. 'Anyway,' he continues as we turn away and start battling our way through the crowds, 'there is a Tiffany's in London.'

On my way home, David talks about the merits of various different castles and stately homes for our reception, his choice of best man (Oliver), and how to fit our wedding and honeymoon in with his fellowship – he reckons sooner would be better, in order to get me a visa. He also has lots of ideas regarding the venue for our engagement party, which we'll have to have quickly before we leave London – in fact, he thinks it would be fun to throw a leaving party and make a surprise engagement announcement at it.

I would never have thought he'd be so into engagements; he's an actual groomzilla. It makes me feel even more guilty, because I'm preparing the best way to break things off as soon as we're back in the privacy of our room.

But as soon as we enter our hotel lobby, all my prepared speeches die away, because sitting there, looking totally out of place – and *not* wearing a red scarf – is Max. He's scribbling a note on a piece of paper that he's leaning on his knee.

'Hey!' David says, striding forward. 'Look who it is!'

Max stands up, stuffing his note into his pocket as he shakes David's hand. I jam my left hand quickly into my coat pocket and give him an awkward wave. My heart is pounding and my knees are shaking; I don't know where to look or how to act.

'Hi,' he says abruptly. 'I was uptown and I just thought I'd drop by and say hello.'

'Well, this is great timing,' says David. 'We have some news.'

'Oh?' says Max, his smile fading slightly.

'We're engaged!'

Max smiles and nods and says all the right things, but his eyes aren't smiling and his shoulders seem to sink.

'Congratulations – both of you,' he says, nodding mechanically. 'That's great news.'

'Show Max the ring, Zoë,' says David. I draw my hand out reluctantly from my pocket and extend my hand.

'Beautiful,' he says, clearing his throat and looking even more desolate. I'm in anguish, wishing I could tell him the truth – that I'm about to break up with David. But I can't do that to David.

But if Max is upset . . . that *must* mean that he still has feelings for me. How do I tell him what's really happening before it's too late?

'Why don't we get together for drinks tonight?' David says. 'We've got dinner plans but we could meet before. Where are you staying?'

'Um – mid-town. No, I . . . now that I think about it, I've actually got something on tonight. You two should celebrate alone. I just wanted to say hi.' He starts backing away.

David looks surprised, but says, 'How about tomorrow? We'll call you.'

'No – my phone doesn't have roaming. But I'll see you guys back in London.'

'Well, if you're sure. Bye.' David shakes his hand again, and then turns back to press the lift button.

I'm desperate to say something to Max – or just mouth the

word, 'Wait' – but he turns away, and the next second, David's calling me. I go into the lift, and as the doors close I get a glimpse of Max's stricken expression. As David and I go up in the lift, I can feel Max slipping away from me with every floor.

THIRTY-EIGHT

Back in our hotel room, David starts talking again, this time about our plans for tomorrow. 'I'm going to spend the morning at the conference, but then I thought we could go and see some apartments in the afternoon. And then, this evening . . . we've got a dinner invitation from my prof. He lives up on Riverside. It sounds like a really cool apartment, with a view of the Hudson –'

I've honestly never known him so chatty; he's away with the fairies. 'That sounds – wait a second, David, wait. I've to tell you something.'

'Sure.' He looks up, surprised.

'I think . . .' Oh God, this is horrible. 'I think we should slow down.'

'Slow down?' repeats David.

I force the words out. 'I mean – I don't – I'm sorry. But I can't marry you.' There; I've said it.

He frowns, and is quiet for a long while. Then he says, 'Where is all this coming from?'

'I just – I'm sorry, but I've been having doubts and I know I shouldn't have said yes, but it's all happened so quickly. But I . . . it's not you, you're wonderful, it's me. I just don't think we're suited.'

David's reply astonishes me. He says, 'I think you're just having cold feet.'

Now it's my turn to stare at him, as he continues. 'Sure, it's

322

perfectly normal. I know it's all happened very quickly. And the move to the States, and everything. But this is . . .' He shakes his head, and says, 'Look. Why don't we just go out tonight, have dinner, and then we can talk about it properly?'

I might have known he'd throw a dinner at it. Taking a deep breath, I decide to try a different tack. 'David, why do you want to marry me?'

'Why do I want to marry you?' he repeats, looking confused. 'Well, because you're gorgeous, and sweet and charming. Why wouldn't I want to marry you?'

He doesn't get it. But I feel I owe it to him to try and explain.

'But I'm other things as well, you know. I get stressed and annoyed and tired and cranky, and I don't always look perfect. I get jealous of Jenny. And I find your hours really difficult to deal with . . . I'm not . . . I'm not as perfect as you think I am.'

For a second I wonder if maybe he's going to say that I don't have to be perfect, that he loves me just the way I am. But he focuses on something else.

'You find my hours difficult to deal with? But you've been so understanding about my hours – you've never complained when I had to work, you've always been really cheerful . . . I thought you were OK with it all.'

Oh God, this is so awful. I should have just told him I don't love him; it would have been kinder.

'Is there someone else?' I look up quickly, but there's no suspicion on his face. He doesn't know enough about my life to guess even for a second that I might have feelings for anyone else – let alone Max. Feeling cowardly, I shake my head.

'I think I should leave,' I say in a low voice. 'I'll find another place to stay tonight and I'll change my flight. I'm so sorry, David.'

David looks out the window in silence. I can see he's thinking, assessing the situation, and I'm reminded of something he said on one of our early dates, about years of training going into split-second decisions: whether to cut or not, when to try and resuscitate

323

a patient and when to let them go. When he looks back at me, I can see he's made his mind up.

'Well, if that's the way you feel, then I suppose there's no more to be said.'

He opens the wardrobe and pulls out his leather messenger bag, and grabs the room key. Then he turns to me.

'Do you need any help finding a place to stay and getting yourself home?' he asks in a formal tone, not meeting my eye.

'No, thank you,' I whisper.

'Then I'm going to take a walk while you sort yourself out. Goodbye, Zoë.'

'Goodbye, David.'

I feel awful but incredibly relieved. I stand up, thinking maybe we should exchange a kiss on the cheek, even if it's not exactly hug time. But after patting his pockets, he goes to the door – and he's gone.

As soon as the door closes, I sit down heavily, my knees shaking, trembling with adrenaline. I can't believe this has all happened so quickly. I had a longer conversation with Orange when I decided to leave them for O2. In fact, Orange fought much harder for me to stay.

I still can't get my head around the fact that I was engaged to David, let alone that we've now broken up. It's so sad. I feel as if we've communicated more in that last conversation than we did during our entire relationship. But no amount of communication could have solved the problems we had. I could have been happy with David for the rest of my life – provided I went along with everything he said, and never showed him who I really was.

With a sigh of relief and regret, I pull the ring off my finger, pick up the phone and dial reception, telling them I need to leave something in a safe, for David Fitzgerald in room 223.

I pack up my things, and after a brief conversation with the same nice girl on reception, I make my way to the subway and catch a train to a budget hotel in mid-town. The cheapest – or least expensive – option is to leave the day after tomorrow, so I decide to give myself a day's recovery in New York before flying to London. I briefly consider flying back home to my parents, but I'm not ready to break the news to them yet about David. And anyway, I need to see Max as quickly as possible. He's still in New York: I want to find him and explain things, before he goes straight back to Kira. I don't even know if he does have feelings for me – but I have to find out.

Unfortunately, finding Max is harder than it seems. I ring his phone but there's no dial tone, and I remember he doesn't have roaming. So I go to email him, and realize something really stupid: we've never exchanged emails and I don't have his email address. I turn to Facebook as a last resort, but I know that he rarely looks at Facebook – and anyway, I don't want to do this via fecking Facebook.

It's so frustrating, but I think I'm going to have to wait until I get back to London, where I will sort out the giant mare's nest I've made of my life. But before I do that I'll have a day to regroup in New York. I decide to begin it by going to the place that makes everything better, and doing something I've always wanted to do.

THIRTY-NINE

It's eight-fifteen a.m. I'm standing in front of the window at Tiffany's with a coffee and a bagel – I couldn't find anywhere that sold croissants. I'm not wearing a ball gown and pearls, obviously, but I'm feeling a little bit Audrey-like nonetheless, wrapped up in my trench coat, jeans and ballet flats.

'Excuse me?' says a polite voice. 'Can you take picture please?'

It's a diminutive Japanese girl in full Audrey Hepburn regalia, complete with three-strand pearl necklace, long black gloves and sunglasses perched on her head. She has a croissant in her hand; I wonder where she managed to find it.

'Oh, wow, of course. You look wonderful,' I tell her, looking through the lens, and pressing the button.

I hand her camera back and she thanks me, looking delighted with herself. In contrast, I'm feeling blue. I look at my watch – eight-thirty – and finally admit to myself why I'm here. I was hoping Max would remember that I'd always wanted to come here first thing. I'm sure I remember telling him, when we were in the car on the way back from Devon. And I pictured him turning up here to find me as a romantic surprise.

But he didn't. And why on earth would he, when he thinks I'm engaged to David? He's probably still with Kira – she might even be here with him. I must have just imagined seeing him here yesterday, and there's no way he's going to magically show up here this morning. I start walking in the direction of

Saks, deciding to try and lose myself in a morning of retail therapy.

Of course, as soon as I'm inside Saks, I remember that I've spent way too much money and am currently broke and unemployed. So instead I get a free makeover at Sephora and head down to Century 21 for a quick browse. Then on impulse I find myself walking over towards the bay to look at the Statue of Liberty.

The whole time I'm going into a deeper spiral of doom. I've hurt and humiliated David; I'm going to have to break the news to my parents, who will be confused and disappointed. And Max – but I can't bear to think about Max. I buy a hot dog and decide to get an outside opinion, before I go any crazier in my own head. I call Rachel, and drop a few bombshells in quick succession; David's proposal, my acceptance, and my change of heart.

'I didn't know I missed so many episodes,' she says, sounding bewildered.

'I know you probably think I'm crazy, breaking up with David . . .'

'No, I don't think you're crazy,' she says seriously. 'It's funny, but I was thinking, after your birthday dinner, that you weren't really being yourself. You were sort of being public Zoë, even with David. Especially with David. You just seemed much more relaxed around Max. You should go for it with him.'

'I think it's too late. He seems happy with Kira, and even when he finds out David and I broke up . . . I don't see him wanting to be second choice, you know?' I decide to change the subject before I become even more depressed. 'What about you? Any more mystery dates?'

'Mystery dates? Oh. You mean with Oliver.'

'Whaaaat? Rachel! Tell me everything.'

It seems that on the night of my birthday, Harriet went home and Rachel and Oliver, and Kira and Max, went to the Notting Hill Arts Club. She and Oliver had a few more drinks and got into a massive argument about politics – and then out of nowhere, they were kissing.

'The chemistry was incredible,' she says. 'And we've seen each other three times since then, and I really like him and yes, Zoë, you told me so.'

'I'm thrilled. And not just because I told you so.' I sigh, feeling happy that at least, among all my debacles, one little bit of match-making went right.

After we've chatted some more I hang up the phone. It's getting to be dusk now, and I'm not sure what to do with my last evening alone in New York. I decide to go to the Angelica cinema and just see whatever's showing.

I hop on a bus going uptown, and stare out at the packed streets, with people flowing in every direction. I wonder if by any strange chance I might see Max – he's staying in mid-town. But then I think how horrible it would be to find that he and and Kira are here on a romantic trip. I could have completely imagined him looking upset yesterday.

The bus is flying along; we're passing the Flatiron building when I realize that I've forgotten where the Angelica is, exactly.

'The Angelica?' says the woman beside me, when I ask her. 'Oh, no. The Angelica is all the way downtown, in SoHo. You've missed it completely. You need to get out right now and catch the bus back. What time is the show?'

I hurry off the bus and cross the road to try and locate the bus going the other way. But it's all seeming like a bit of a mission and my feet are getting really cold and tired in my little ballet flats. I find myself dodging through people in a queue and realize it's for the Empire State Building. On impulse, I decide to go up; it'll hopefully give me a sense of perspective. Either that, or I can throw myself off it.

The Empire State building is, of course, full of couples, most of whom seem to have just got engaged. I shuffle past them, and lean out on the edge of the terrace to look over the city, its lights twinkling in the dusk, with the huge dark rectangle of Central Park in the middle. I wrap my trench coat more tightly around myself, shivering. It's really cold now; I'm glad I have my gloves. As I look out at all the twinkling lights of the Manhattan skyline, I'm surprised to find myself feeling a real glimmer of hope. Marley's might not have worked out – OK, that's an understatement – but there are other jobs.

I wander around the terrace for a while to get my money's worth, drinking in the sights and also idly people-watching. I realise that maybe I've been a bit stupid thinking that a department store is the only way to get buying experience. What I really want is hands-on experience in a small boutique. And then . . .

Then it hits me. The whole reason I want to open my own boutique is because I love giving fashion advice and styling people. And there's nothing stopping me from doing that! I think of how Rachel's always talking about the women in her office who don't have time to shop, or don't know what suits them. I could do some personal styling for them – take them shopping, or visit them at home to do a wardrobe makeover. I could do it for free to begin with, and then start charging a percentage or a flat fee. And eventually, once I've built up some word of mouth, I could do a private sale every few months to individuals – it could even be a social thing, with wine and snacks, maybe even in Rachel's apartment if she'd let me. It would be perfect! I'm pacing faster and faster, and almost knocking down sightseers. I decide to head home and write down some ideas.

I'm walking towards the exit when my eye is caught by a figure looking out at the skyline. It's dark, and he's about fifteen metres away, but I immediately know that it's Max. Just like I know that the girl beside him is Kira. I recognise her full-length puffa coat.

I make a dive for the exit, threading my way through the crowd, desperate to get out of there before they see me. I can't believe I fooled myself that they weren't together. If I have to confront them both here, now, I really will throw myself off the edge.

An attendant is blocking my way. 'Excuse me, miss,' he says. 'No running on the terrace.'

'I'm not running,' I whisper desperately. 'I just have to get out of here.'

He puts his head on one side curiously. 'Is that so? How come?'

I finally manage to shake him off, but just as I'm nearly off the terrace, a voice behind me says, 'Zoë?'

Even before I turn around, I know it's him.

He's wrapped up in a navy pea coat, with a woolly hat on his head.

'Hi,' I mutter. I look around cautiously for Kira, but I don't see her.

He puts his head on one side. 'Hi to you too,' he says neutrally. 'Fancy meeting you here.'

'And you.' I shrug, and give him a brief smile. 'Look, I'd better get going. I don't want to interrupt anything.' I turn away and start walking, but before I've gone two steps, he's seized me by the shoulders.

'Interrupt anything?' he says hoarsely. 'I've been waiting here all day for you.'

'What?' I say, bewildered. 'But what about Kira?'

'What about her? Zoë, we're not together. And I know you're with David, and I don't want to ruin that for you, but . . .'

His voice trails off as I pull my glove off, to show him my bare left hand, and start babbling.

'No, I'm not – we're not engaged any more. Or together. But are you sure you're not here with Kira? I could have sworn I saw her – or someone with her coat—'

Suddenly I'm not talking any more; I'm being kissed, and gathered into his arms. His lips are cold, but it's hands down the warmest, most passionate kiss I've ever felt. I can feel his heart beating, and his hand in my hair, as I melt into him and kiss him back. Then he releases me and looks at me with a look of total happiness.

'Finally,' he says.

*   *   *

330

We wander around the viewing terrace, barely looking at the view. I spot the woman whom I thought was Kira; the coat is the same, but the lady inside is at least fifty, and her hair is white instead of white-blond. I don't think Kira would be too flattered by the comparison, so I don't point it out to Max – who's telling me that he's not here for work at all.

'I came to New York to apologise for everything I said to you.'

'It's OK. I'm sorry too.'

'No, it's not. When David told me he was going to propose to you – honestly, I kind of lost it. I decided I had to tell you how I felt, so that at least you knew. But then when I saw it was too late, I decided to leave you alone and let you be happy.'

'But then . . .'

'But then I wasn't sure if you really *were* happy, so I decided to wait around and find out.'

It's the most romantic thing I've ever heard of. I can't get over it – any of it.

'But what are you doing here? I mean up here?' I gesture around the building.

'I didn't know where you were staying and I didn't want to call you in case you were still with David. However, I've been reading about game theory lately, and – why are you smiling?'

I shake my head; I'm smiling because I'm so happy to be hearing his theories and factoids again. 'Go on.'

'There's a theory that says if two people want to find each other in Manhattan, but don't have any way of getting in touch, the likeliest place they'll meet is on top of the Empire State Building. Or Times Square, but I didn't think you would like Times Square.'

'You're right, I hate it! But this . . .' I step back and take in the sight of him, and the lights of Manhattan behind him. 'This is a miracle. Oh my God! We're on Fifth Avenue! It's a miracle on Fifth Avenue!'

Max shakes his head. 'It's not a miracle – just game theory.' But from his smile, I can tell he thinks it's every bit as miraculous as

I do. 'Do you want to go inside? You look cold.' I nod, and we turn to go. I don't even realise that his arm is around me until we have to separate to go through a doorway – it feels so natural.

'Hey,' I say, as we head towards the exit. 'You weren't at Tiffany's yesterday, were you? Wearing a red scarf?'

'No. I do have a red scarf but not with me . . . and I don't even know where Tiffany's is. Is it a department store?'

'No, a jewellery store. I could have sworn we had a conversation about it.' There's a huge queue for the lift. I'm about to join it, but Max sweeps me to one side, pushes me up against the wall and kisses me again – an even more passionate kiss that leaves me literally breathless. He looks a bit dazed as well.

'Sorry, we had a conversation about . . . what?' he asks, pressing buttons at random for the next lift – we seem to have missed the first one. Maybe two.

'Doesn't matter,' I say, gazing at him.

Max's budget hotel is definitely not as glam as the Surrey. The room is tiny, there's a sink in lieu of an en suite, and the colour scheme is sort of eighties, and not in a good way (orange bedspread and synthetic blue carpet). The noise of traffic is really loud outside. But I don't care. We're in our own little world: tangled in each others' limbs, fully clothed (well, mostly) and kissing the way I've never kissed anyone before, ever.

'Max – I'm not going to sleep with you,' I mumble between kisses. I think I need to say this, because what with him pinning me down, our bodies pressed together, his hands travelling up and down my body and my shirt mostly unbuttoned (by me) it seems to be moving swiftly up the agenda.

'Oh. OK . . . of course.' He pauses, and then adds reluctantly, 'Ever?'

'No! Not never – just not on a first date . . . What's so funny?'

'Sorry, Zoë, it's just . . . this is hardly our first date. But I totally understand. You're right.' He rolls off me, and squeezes my hand before taking a deep breath and exhaling.

332

'But we can still, you know . . . kiss and stuff,' I mutter, feeling about sixteen.

'That sounds good,' he says, smiling at me. I gaze back at him, taking it all in. The little room with the siren blaring outside. His adorably tousled hair on the orange pillow, his gorgeous features, his dilated pupils. The hollow in his throat where his pulse is beating, the crumpled T-shirt that's ridden up, revealing the trail of hair on his stomach; the discreet bulge in his jeans . . .

He clears his throat. 'Why don't we go out and get a drink, or a bite to eat?' he says, obviously trying to sound casual and normal. He starts to sit up.

'No.'

'What do you mean, no?'

I pull him back down. 'I've changed my mind.'

'Oh, have you now?'

We both start to laugh, and then I roll over and pin him down.

'Are you sure?'

I nod, and start unbuttoning his denim shirt. After all, I think, as I kiss my way slowly down his chest and listen to him groan softly, this isn't our first date. Then I stop thinking, because I'm busy pulling off his terrible clothes, and exploring every inch of his gorgeous body, strong arms, flat stomach, smooth skin. And then we can't wait any longer. There's a brief awkward moment while he roots around for a condom and I try not to think about when he got it or why – but then I forget all about it, because it's just me and him. It feels brand new and exciting, but it also feels completely right and familiar. And then before I know where I am, we're having mind-blowing, bite-the-pillow amazing sex, which I didn't really believe existed – until now.

I'm so happy I can't stop smiling. We're curled up together: me snuggled into the crook of his arm and chest, his chin on top of my head, my leg flung over his. We've barely detached ourselves from each other for about three hours, except to order room service.

We've spent almost as much time talking as anything else: about

333

me being fired, which he obviously didn't know about – and how he ended things with Kira, and how our feelings changed over the past few weeks. I tell him again that I'm sorry I put him, and David, through all that.

'Well, I don't come out of it too well either,' says Max. 'But the strange thing is, I don't feel half as guilty as I should. I think he'll get over it.'

'I think so too. And maybe, now, he will end up with Jenny.'

'I wonder,' says Max. He looks as if he's deliberately not saying something. I poke him.

'I don't know. You know how that day, at the tennis club, he talked about how he always carries a spare? I think that's her.'

'God. I think you're completely right.' I hadn't thought of it like that before, but I think Max's assessment is spot-on.

'But what about Kira? Is she OK? Actually no, don't tell me. It's none of my business.'

'Would it make you feel better to know that she got pretty sick of me? She thought I was a bit square and too wrapped up in my experiments.'

That makes me feel a fraction better, though I still don't think she's going to be too happy. But then again, our friendship has always had its ups and downs. If she's sore at me about Max, it's a price I'm willing to pay.

I'm about to ask Max about how his mum is, but I decide to wait; he can bring it up when he's ready. We lie in silence for a while, before he says, 'So what are you going to do about work?'

'Well, first I'll have to to wait and see Marley's say, when they contact me . . .'

'Why don't you contact them? Make an appointment, tell your boss – your ex-boss – that you were under stress but that you'd really like the chance to start again.'

'I could. But actually I've had an idea, to set up on my own. I'd have to get another job and do it on the side, but I think I could manage it.' And I tell him about my idea: personal styling and at-home shopping for busy career women.

334

'That sounds fantastic. I think this is all going to be great,' says Max.

I smile at him. For the first time, I'm starting to think it will be. There's so much I still need to do – break the news to my parents; break the other news to Kira; find a job; but now that I have him on my side I know that I can do it.

But as I run my fingertip over his gorgeous mouth, something else starts preying on my mind.

'What are you worrying about now?' Max asks me.

I laugh. 'Is it that obvious? Well . . . just about the whole going back in time thing.'

'What about it?'

'What if I wake up some morning, and I'm back where I started? I mean, back in December? I didn't even know you then.'

He nods.

'Or what if I'm hallucinating you right now? I mean for all I know this entire thing is some sort of lucid dream. What if you go to the bathroom, or something, and you never come back? Or I melt into a pile of ectoplasm?'

'If you do, can I write about it for *Nature*?'

I thump him again, and he hugs me. Then he rolls over on to his back, and sighs.

'Look, I know what you mean. It is scary. And I don't think there are any guarantees. But that's the same for all relationships, isn't it? We never know what's going to happen. All I can say is, I intend to stick around for as long as possible.' He kisses me, then holds me at arm's length to look into my eyes. 'Will you do the same?'

'I promise.' We smile at each other.

'Good. Now let's sleep on it.'

FORTY

The next morning, I cautiously test for my hangover the way that you probe the site of a missing tooth after a trip to the dentist. Holy God, it's vicious. My head is killing me, and I'm completely parched. I'm also stuck to my pillow – I obviously didn't get around to taking off my make-up. I can't believe we got a rickshaw, what were we thinking? At least my Christmas shopping made it home; I see I dumped my bags in the corner of the room.

Yawning, I drag myself out of bed, put on my dressing gown and Totes toasties, and crawl to the kitchen where I pour out a glass of water, swallow two Nurofen and put on some coffee and toast. It's so cold I do a little dance, shifting from one foot to the other, as I wait for my coffee, and stare at Deborah's chart on the fridge. I note that it's my turn to clean the fridge this week – in fact, there's a red circle, meaning it's overdue.

Deborah walks into the kitchen, fully dressed right down to her sensible kitten-heeled shoes. She has these things that clip on to them and make them into snow shoes, but she hasn't put them on yet: they will be waiting in their usual place in the hall. She looks at me and says, 'Ooh! You're going to be late for work, you know.'

'Mmm,' I say, imagining sticking a fork into her head.

She reaches into the fridge and pulls out her little lunch box with Friday's sandwich – chicken and lettuce. Imagine being that organised. I can barely get dressed most mornings. The clock on the cooker says 8.37. She's right, I'd better get going – though happily, I don't have to be there until ten this morning.

I finish my breakfast and hop in the shower, using my Philosophy shower gel that I got in the work Secret Santa (I bet it was from Harriet). As I stand under the steaming water and lather up, I breathe in the uplifting orangey scent and realise, despite my hangover, I'm feeling weirdly OK compared to last night – compared to the last few months, in fact. I actually feel *happy*.

I stop dead, as my dream from last night comes back to me. I dreamed I was back with David. I can't remember exactly what happened but I definitely remember that it was all going really well and I didn't make any mistakes . . .

But I wasn't happy. I was with David, but I wasn't happy.

Now there's an interesting thought.

I dart back into my room and pull out some clothes, getting dressed as quickly as possible to avoid frostbite. Black polo neck, black pencil skirt and black opaque tights, sensible but pretty flats. I spray half a can of Batiste into my hair and scrape it up into a bun. I layer on lots of foundation, Benefit Dandelion powder, and loads of mascara – but I still look dreadful. Oh well. I grab my bag, coat and scarf, pull on my snow boots, and stumble out the door.

It's a winter wonderland. The sky is blue and the snow is still lying crisp and white all over the gardens and on the rooftops. People are inching along carefully, all bundled up like snowmen. It's cold enough to see my breath, but it's lovely and crisp. Bits of my dream keep coming back to me as I walk, and so do memories of what it was like with David sometimes. I mean he was perfect and everything, but . . . in all fairness he wasn't always a barrel of laughs. Weird thought but true.

I head over to Starbucks opposite Maida Vale station to get my coffee, but it's shut due to staff shortages according to the sign on the door. Normally this would grind my gears, but this morning I'm all about the Zen: I'll just go to the one near work.

Sitting on the tube, I notice an ad for evening diplomas in various courses – including fashion buying. I take down the details there and then, and decide that in the new year, I am going to enrol in a course, and ask for another meeting with Julia to see if I could even do overtime, work experience, job shadowing, anything. If buying doesn't work out, I'll find another way of owning my own boutique – but it will happen.

Then it hits me. The whole reason I want my own boutique is because I love giving fashion advice and styling people. I'm pretty sure there's a job going as a personal stylist at Marley's. I could apply for that.

I don't think I'm still drunk, but I'm definitely on a high. I feel the way you do sometimes after a yoga class, when you look the same outside, but inside everything's been sorted out. For example, Jenny. I can't believe I was worrying about her last night. David's relationship with her really was completely weird! I was totally within my rights to object.

'Ha!' I say, realising too late that I've said it out loud. The carriage is half-empty, though, and nobody seems to notice.

It's funny. I thought there was only one way to be happy, and that it meant being with David. But now I think: maybe there are lots of different ways to be happy.

I'm really early somehow, so I decide to get out at Regent's Park and walk down. The walk is so amazingly pretty that I have to stop a few times to take photos. As I take my third photo, my phone starts ringing. It's Rachel.

'Wassup?'

'God, you sound chirpy!'

'I feel chirpy. I'm near Regent's Park, and it's so beautiful. I'll have to show you my photos. What's up?'

'Nothing, just, you were so sad last night, I was worried about you.'

'Thanks, but – I've woken up with a bit of a new perspective. I think it's all going to be fine. And, there's something I want to ask you.'

I quickly explain my personal-shopping idea, and Rachel says she thinks it sounds great. 'Someone here was just saying she needed something new for a ball, but she doesn't know where to start.'

'Great! Let me know if she'd like me to take her shopping.'

'I will,' Rachel says. 'Wow, Zoë. Next year is your year. I can feel it. Here, you'll never guess who just friended me on Facebook.'

'Who?'

'Oliver! Isn't that a coincidence? I might drop him a line,' she adds, ultra-casually.

'Might you now. Well, fair play to Oliver.' I'm secretly thrilled, but I match my casual tone to hers.

'By the way,' says Rachel, 'you might want to brace yourself when you check Facebook.'

'Why?'

'Just check David's page and call me back, OK?'

I don't really want to check David's page. But it's going to bug me now until I do. I log on to Facebook on my phone, and the first thing I see is a picture of him beside a pretty dark-haired girl. He has his arm around her, and they're obviously a couple. That is pretty bad. But then I look closer and see that, between their heads, popping up like a meerkat, is Jenny.

It actually makes me laugh, which does a lot to take the sting out of the discovery. Well, good luck to them both – all three of them.

As a result of all my snapping and phone calls, I'm not so early any more, but I still have time for a quick detour into Starbucks. I catch sight of myself in the door's reflection as I shuffle in, and wince: my skin looks decidedly green under my make-up, my nose is red and I have massive circles under my eyes. Oh well. It's sort of seasonal colours.

Inside they're playing Ella Fitzgerald and it smells of coffee and gingerbread. I'm about to order a skinny latte but then I pause. Maybe I should try a gingerbread spice latte? It smells lovely . . . or I could get a piece of gingerbread, and have it with my skinny latte? No, I should just get the gingerbread latte. Except then maybe I'll want a normal latte as well . . .

'Excuse me. Are you waiting?' a voice asks behind me. I turn around and see a rather foxy-looking man. He's tall, with reddish-brown hair standing on end, and sleepy brown eyes. He's wrapped up in a red scarf and a black overcoat, with a magazine tucked under his arm.

'Hey,' he says. 'Zoë, right?'

I frown. Can't place him.

'I'm Max,' he says. 'We met that time with David? In that pub near Paddington?'

'Oh! Of course.' I do remember now. It was early on with David; I don't think I paid much attention to anyone else who was there at the time.

'Do you work near here?'

'Yes I do, in Marley's. How about you?'

'I work at a lab in UCL – I'm just around here for a meeting.'

'Any coffees?' the guy behind the counter asks. Max turns to me. 'Zoë?'

'Sorry, I just can't decide between the gingerbread latte and my usual skinny latte.'

'Why don't you have both? One gingerbread latte, one skinny latte and a cappucino, please,' he says to the guy behind the counter. 'My treat. You're sure you don't want any extra treats?' he asks me, over his shoulder. 'Cupcake? Chocolate coin?' I shake my head, laughing. His manner is irresistibly friendly and makes me feel as if I've known him for ages.

'Thanks, that's really kind of you,' I add belatedly as we wait for our coffee.

'Well, it is Christmas. Also, I'm celebrating. I just got an article accepted . . . in here.' He taps the magazine under his arm, grinning broadly. He looks absolutely delighted with himself, and though I don't understand why it's such a big deal, I find myself smiling too.

'Congratulations! What magazine is it? *Nature*? I'm more of a *Vogue* girl myself.'

Oh, my God. I'm actually flirting. I haven't flirted in months!

'Cappucino, skinny latte, and gingerbread latte,' the man says, putting our coffees down.

Max hands me my two drinks in a cardboard holder, and holds the door open for me as we leave the coffee shop. We seem to be going the same direction, and fall into conversation as we walk through the snow, me taking alternate sips from my drinks – which are both delicious. I find myself telling him about all the weird and wonderful customers we get at Marley's, and we find out that we're both spending Christmas in London – his family have come to visit him here.

'After this meeting, I'm on holiday,' he says. 'And I'm going to celebrate by spending the entire day doing whatever I want – starting with a pub lunch with some friends. Then I might see *It's A Wonderful Life* at the BFI . . . or whatever I want to do.'

'That's such a great idea!' I say enthusiastically. 'A whole day doing whatever you want. Like a Spoil Max day.'

He stares and smiles down at me. 'Well – yeah. That's exactly what I call it. A day when I can do whatever I want. Within reason, of course.'

'There's a lot more within reason than you'd think, though,' I suggest. Now, where have I heard that before?

Max smiles at me again. 'I totally agree. Well, this is me,' he says, pointing to a side street. 'Bye, Zoë. Happy Christmas.'

'You too. And thanks for the coffees. Both of them.' I wave, and we go our separate ways.

Gosh, Max. He's very, very cute. I wonder why I never saw it before? I feel a little disappointed that he didn't take my number, but I tell myself not to be so silly. Hopefully I'll bump into him again some time.

I'm nearly at the front entrance of Marley's, and I've just paused to take a look at the Fairy Tale display when I notice someone coming up behind me, reflected in the windowpane. I spot the red scarf first, and then I see it's Max.

'Look, just in case we don't bump into each other again, can I take your number?'

341

'Sure! Here you go . . .' I find a ridiculous grin breaking out over my face as we exchange numbers.

'Great,' says Max. 'I'll give you a call in the New Year . . . or even before? I mean, if you're here for Christmas, and I'm here for Christmas . . .'

'That sounds good,' I say, smiling.

'OK. I'll call you.' As I watch him walk off in the snow, I can't stop beaming. I don't know exactly what's going to happen, but something tells me this Christmas is going to be one to remember.

ACKNOWLEDGEMENTS

Thanks to everyone who helped me while writing this book, especially the busy people who made time to speak to me about their jobs. Thank you to Carrie Frost, Jessica Nesbitt and Ciara Foley for talking to me about fashion buying, and to Sandy of Coco & Sebastian for insights into fashion designing. Thanks to Dr Alex Liddle and to Dr Syed Rehman for answering questions about the life of a surgeon and to Dr Anne Hsu for doing the same for neuroscience. I am never writing a book with so many careers in it again. Thank you to everyone at Headline especially the lovely Sherise Hobbs and Lucy Foley, and to my brilliant agent, Rowan Lawton, a beacon of sanity in crazy-author-land. And thanks to Alex, who cheered me on, and checked the spelling of Man or Astro-Man.